### Praise for *The Last Hunt*

Named a Best Book of the Year
by *Deadly Pleasures Mystery Magazine*

"*The Last Hunt* serves up mystery and intrigue in South Africa . . . An explosive, suspenseful, and unexpected ending that will have readers applauding." —*Florida Times-Union*

"Two disparate plotlines merge to form an explosive conclusion in this political thriller . . . Despite their human flaws, Griessel and Cupido have integrity, which they display as they encounter massive corruption in the current South African political administration, corruption that proves to be at the centers of both plotlines. The latest Benny Griessel novel is a compelling page-turner and a searing portrait of the author's native country." —*Booklist* (starred review)

"A double-barreled tale that's sprawling, shape-shifting, and, in the end, deeply satisfying." —*Kirkus Reviews*

### Praise for Deon Meyer

"Deon Meyer is one of the unsung masters." —Michael Connelly

"The undisputed champion of South African crime. Meyer grabs you by the throat and never lets you go." —Wilbur Smith, bestselling author of *Courtney's War*

"Meyer . . . vividly depicts the story of South Africa in his novels, from the hope and turmoil of the fall of apartheid to the corrupt and desperate aspects of present-day Cape Town . . . Meyer's novels have an insistent forward motion, and the ones featuring Captain Griessel in particular have a pleasing relentlessness." —*Los Angeles Review of Books*, on *Cobra*

"A serious writer who richly deserves the international reputation he has built." —*Washington Post*, on *Cobra*

"Deon Meyer's name on the cover is a guarantee of crime writing at its best." —Tess Gerritsen, *New York Times* bestselling author of *Playing with Fire*, on *Icarus*

# The Last Hunt

## Deon Meyer

*Translated from Afrikaans*
*by K. L. Seegers*

Grove Press
*New York*

First published in Great Britain in 2019 by Hodder & Stoughton
An Hachette UK company

Originally published in Afrikaans in 2019 as *Prooi* by Human & Rousseau

*Published simultaneously in Canada*
*Printed in the United States of America*

First Grove Atlantic hardcover editon: April 2020
First Grove Atlantic paperback editon: April 2021

Library of Congress Cataloging-in-Publication data is available for this title.

ISBN 978-0-8021-5693-8
eISBN 978-0-8021-5694-5

Grove Press
an imprint of Grove Atlantic
154 West 14th Street
New York, NY 10011

Distributed by Publishers Group West

groveatlantic.com

21 22 23 24   10 9 8 7 6 5 4 3 2 1

*For Marianne, with love*

Now it is pleasant to hunt something that you want very much over a long period of time, being outwitted, out-manoeuvred, and failing at the end of each day, but having the hunt and knowing every time you are out that, sooner or later, your luck will change and that you will get the chance that you are seeking.

Ernest Hemingway, *Green Hills of Africa*

State capture, noun: The efforts of a small number of people aiming to benefit from the illicit provision of private gains to public officials in order to profit from the workings of a government.

*Mail & Guardian,* 14 September 2018

# PART I

# I

Daniel Darret's peculiar relationship with Madame Lecompte began in violence. And so it would end.

He lay sleepless in the heat and humidity of August, his bedroom window wide open. But the place Camille Pelletan was like an oven, stuffy and oppressive. At half past midnight demons from his past hunted him awake. He pulled on shorts, T-shirt and his black Nikes, and took the three flights of stairs down. In the square the cat was perched on the roof of his neighbours' grubby old Renault. The look they exchanged was of co-conspirators: *we, the restless creatures of the night.*

That blasted cat. Wackett. Irrationally named by the neighbours' three-year-old, back then.

He took his regular walking route past La Flèche Saint-Michel. The basilica square, the market such a hive of activity by day, was deserted now. Across the railway track and the dual-carriage highway, to the edge of the water – he was in need of the cool breeze near the river. Then north, briskly along the left-bank promenade. The old city of Bordeaux brooded in deep night silence to his left, a slumbering animal.

At Colbert Park a solitary teenager rolled up and down, up and down, skateboarding; for a few minutes wheels on concrete walls and wooden platforms were the only sound. He wondered what kept the child awake at this time of night.

He crossed the Garonne via the new bridge, the engineering marvel, pont Jacques Chaban-Delmas, and on the right bank turned south. He could feel the breeze from the dark river cooling his face, just for a little while. His thoughts were on the day's work ahead, his modest responsibilities while Monsieur and Madame Lefèvre spent their summer vacation in Arcachon. At first he was unaware of the tall woman in the shadows of the Park of the Angels, Le Parc aux Angéliques.

Only once she uttered a sound did his focus shift. It was then that he registered the fear in her voice as he saw her and the ghosts flitting among the trees. Immediately, instinctively, he swung in her direction.

There were five of them after her, hunting her. They were agile and lean and strong, one carrying a baseball bat. He heard them jeering, their excited cries like the baying of a pack of wild dogs. Two were close to catching her. They were so intent on her that they were oblivious to Daniel. One yelled, '*Girafe!*' Daniel understood: the tall woman's gait was awkward, like a giraffe's. He heard the others crowing. The leading man gave a sudden spurt of speed and bent low, his hand smacking her ankle so that she collapsed silently, clumsily, onto the grass. The man grabbed her by the hair.

'No!' shouted Daniel. It was a reflex, involuntary, and in that instant he could see the immediate future, the consequence of what was about to happen. He knew it involved huge risk to himself. Now, here. And afterwards.

They looked round, saw him. One pulled a knife, the blade flashing in a pool of light from the streetlamps of the quai des Queyries. The wielder of the baseball bat had broad shoulders and muscular arms, tattooed with coiling black snakes. The weapons showed this was not a chance encounter. He remembered the media uproar and police frustration over the riverbank muggers who had been ambushing late-night, drunken party-goers recently.

They formed a crescent. Young men, barely in their twenties, full of confidence. He knew, at that age, the fierce, irrational drive of ego and peer pressure, and that they were going to attack him in unison now. He felt the burden of his age, the muscle memory his body had lost, about to be pitted against the imminent violence.

One bellowed a war cry. A primitive sound spurring them to action.

He felt the rush of adrenalin. He hit the one with the snake arms first, the biggest. His timing was poor, the blow without power or momentum. The knife-wielder stabbed at him, lightning-fast – he was too slow pulling back and the blade raked across his ribcage. A fist hit his throat, another his cheekbone, hard blows. He shuddered, staggered.

He was going to die there tonight.

Snake Arms raised the baseball bat, the others moving back to make room for the blow. Daniel stepped forward, desperate, hit him with a fist against the temple, hard and solid. The blow made a sick, hollow sound, like a watermelon hitting the ground. Snake Arms collapsed. Another picked up the bat. Daniel spun on the ball of his foot, reaching for the knife-wielder with his right hand – too slow: the blade sliced his palm, deep. He grabbed again, grasping the man's wrist with his left hand, pulled him closer violently, smashing his right palm full on the nose, the momentum upward and forward. Knifeman staggered back onto the ground and sat, keening in pain. Daniel felt warmth, blood streaming from his palm and seeping down his side from the rib wound.

Two men jumped onto his back. He rushed backwards and violently smashed one into a tree trunk with his full weight behind it. He heard the man's ribs crack, felt his arms loosen around his neck, but the other man hit him from behind, fist against his ear, another blow to his neck. The fifth man, bearded face twisted in hatred and rage, rushed at him with the baseball bat.

Daniel turned, trying to use the one on his back as a shield. It didn't work. The bat hit him on the thick flesh of his right shoulder, bounced off and smacked painfully into his ear. Now blood streamed down his neck as well. Something came loose inside him, rage that stripped away the rust and resistance of years, the restraints and barriers so long and carefully kept in place. He gripped the bat tightly, twisted it out of the man's hands, seeing the eyes of his attacker turn wild and scared at the speed and power of the move. Daniel hit his head with the bat and the man dropped to the ground. He banged the butt of the bat rearward, hitting the throat of the one on his back – the strangling arm around his neck released. He swivelled, the man shielding himself with a forearm. He swung the bat, breaking radius and ulna, a sharp, high shriek released into the night.

Footsteps behind him, and just in time he saw Knifeman, his face bloodied, eyes staring, the blade coming up from below. Daniel jumped backwards and struck out, one strong movement: the tip of the bat struck the knife hand, the weapon flew high and dropped into the grass. He stepped forward and jammed the bat into the man's belly, spun around – but there was nobody left with any fight.

He had to get away. There would be consequences – some of the muggers were seriously injured.

He walked across to the woman. She was sitting on the ground, gazing at him. He realised she was older than he'd thought. Her face was strange in shape and expression, her unusual features now frozen with fear and fascination. 'Come on,' he said, offering his right hand to help her up, then saw blood dripping freely from it. He switched the baseball bat, gave her his left hand. He didn't know if she would take it – he was a big black man with blood on his hands, head and clothes, in the night in the dark of the park.

She took the hand, and he pulled her to her feet. She stood, dazed. 'We must get away,' he said, with urgency.

She nodded. He took her arm and led her through the shadows to the lights of the rue de Sem. He looked back. The men weren't following them. He tossed the baseball bat, high and hard, deep into the middle of the broad river.

At the pont de Pierre he told her, 'Just keep walking,' and pushed her gently, his hand behind her back. She nodded, continued to walk. He wanted to vault over the railing and take the steps down, so that he could rinse the blood off his face before he went home. But he saw her stop and turn back towards him.

'*Merci*,' she said softly.

# 2

*August, Benny Griessel, Bellville*

The professional life of a policeman or -woman revolves around the three-flap file that folds shut to just two centimetres wider and longer than an A4 page. The legendary docket. Not an aesthetically pleasing document, it is made of cheap, thin cardboard of a light-brown shade, often disparagingly compared to a smelly by-product of babies. The badge of the South African Police Service is printed on the front, at the top, and just below that, in the biggest, boldest letters in the entire document, *CASE DOCKET • SAAKDOSSIER*, the official complete title. Nevertheless, detectives, state prosecutors and judges invariably refer to it simply as the 'docket', regardless of which of the country's eleven official languages they speak at home.

It has three flaps and six pages, each filled from edge to edge in black with words, sentences and abbreviations (in English and Afrikaans, a last remnant of civil-service bilingualism), as well as blocks and dotted lines that may seem intimidating and chaotic to the inexperienced or uneducated eye. But to those who use it daily, the docket is a masterpiece of efficiency. Over decades it has evolved and developed into a criminal case's perfect guide and travelling companion – from that first visit to the crime scene, to the final guilty verdict. The six cardboard pages themselves contain crucial information, but they also serve as a surprisingly durable wrapper for the documents (often scores, sometimes hundreds) that a case accumulates in its lifetime. The docket is a warehouse and encyclopaedia, a bibliography, case Bible and thriller novel, all in one.

As long as you know how to read it, and provided it has been created and maintained by a diligent, knowledgeable police officer.

Just before eight, at the close of Tuesday-morning parade, Colonel Mbali Kaleni handed Captain Benny Griessel a docket. He and his colleague, Captain Vaughn Cupido, knew two important things about it at first glance:

1. It wasn't their own docket being returned after Colonel Kaleni had reviewed it with her painstaking thoroughness: the first block at the top left corner indicated Beaufort West as the station of origin and the name of the first investigator was Sergeant A. Verwey.
2. It was a hot potato. They had glanced immediately at the middle of the front page, below *Crime Code*. On this file were the numbers that made every detective in South Africa's heart beat a little faster: *31984*. The justice system's administrative code for murder.

'I want you and Captain Cupido to focus on this case exclusively,' said Colonel Kaleni, with emphasis on the last word. She was the commanding officer of the Serious and Violent Crimes Unit, in the Directorate for Priority Crimes Investigations – better known as the Hawks. Her first name meant 'flower' in her mother tongue, Zulu.

Griessel and Cupido knew in that instant that, for the foreseeable future, their professional lives would revolve around this particular docket. And they were not especially pleased. Plus it was an inherited case, which meant it came with deficiencies and various kinds of baggage, including inter-departmental politics and professional jealousy.

Moreover, the investigation was at least eight days old, according to the case number (written in the topmost middle block of the docket's front page). And the *Date and time of offence/incident* (second large block on the docket's front page, left) was nearly three weeks ago. The first seventy-two hours, the critical make-or-break period for any murder case, was long past.

It invoked a groan from Cupido, who said: 'Why do we always get the cold-case dregs, Colonel? The runts of the litter?'

'Because you are the best of the best, Captain,' said Kaleni. She was so unhurried, methodical and obedient to regulations that she frequently drove the more free-spirited Cupido crazy. But she knew how to get the best out of her people. 'And that is what the case needs. Because international tourism is involved, there seem to be jurisdictional grey areas, and local law enforcement has not been impressive.

The provincial commissioner asked us to step in, and he specifically requested you and Benny. He says if anybody can solve this, you can.'

'Damn straight, Colonel,' said Cupido, blithely oblivious to her skilful manipulation.

'Furthermore, the victim is a former member of the Service,' said Kaleni. 'It's the Johnson Johnson docket.'

She waited for the penny to drop, but the two detectives, like most members of the Violent Crimes team, had been working night and day over the past month to solve the murders of city nightclub bouncers. They just stared at her.

'The guy who disappeared from the fancy train,' she said, as if they ought at least to know about that. 'There have been stories in the media.'

'Johnson Johnson? That's his name? For real?' Cupido asked.

'Yes.'

Griessel shook his head. 'Sorry, Colonel. We haven't heard about it.'

'Okay. It's all in the docket,' she said.

But it wasn't all in the docket. They unpacked the contents in Griessel's office across the expanse of his government-issue desk and began studying them.

Like all SAPS dossiers, the content was divided into three sections: Part A, B and C.

Part A contained the interviews, reports, statements and the photo album. In the Johnson docket this information was sparse. There was a page of scrawled notes about a telephone interview with a Mrs Robyn Johnson, the preliminary report of a forensic investigator from the SAPS in George, and a few poor-quality photographs of a man in a white shirt and black suit lying beside a railway line. The pictures showed a body already decomposing. A serious head wound marred his features. The boots of SAPS members surrounding the corpse were also visible.

'*Jissis*,' said Griessel, pointing them out. It indicated poor control of the crime scene and endless difficulties for the state prosecutor, should the case go to court.

'*Ja*. Country bumpkins. What do you expect?' Cupido said rhetorically.

Correspondence with other SAPS departments or external institutions, like banks or employers, was stored in the docket's Part B. It contained only a single copy of an Article 205 subpoena that the detective in Beaufort West had used to acquire information on a mobile phone from Vodacom.

Part C was the investigation journal on the SAPS5 form. That, too, had been skimped on. The final entry recorded moving the body to the state mortuary in Salt River only two days ago. No post-mortem had yet been done. The body had not even been officially identified as that of Johnson Johnson.

Griessel sighed.

Cupido stood up and cleaned the whiteboard on the wall. 'Benna, let's try and make some sense of this thing,' he said.

Griessel worked through each docket entry from the start, while Cupido created a timeline with cursory details on the board. They were still busy at lunchtime. They sent out for takeaways from Voortrekker Road. Griessel ordered a Jalapeño Mayo burger with chips from Steers, his current favourite. He could eat what he liked because he was riding at least 140 kilometres per week on his mountain bike up and down the slopes of Kloof Nek. He was seven kilograms lighter than he had been a year ago.

The contents of Cupido's stylish wardrobe were becoming uncomfortably tight. He wanted to conquer the heart of his new love, gorgeous Desiree Coetzee from Stellenbosch, who loved cooking and eating out. But his spare tyre bothered him. Considerably. So he was following, in secret, the same diet he had freely mocked Colonel Mbali Kaleni over when she began practising it – the famous Banting lifestyle espoused by Professor Tim Noakes. Embarrassed by his formerly outspoken criticism, he had confessed this only to Griessel.

Cupido ordered two fish fillets from Catch of the Day, no chips, and a Coke Zero. They ate and worked until, by three o'clock, they had a rough grasp of how the case fitted together.

Johnson Johnson (34), according to a file entry, was a 'private protection consultant'. Seventeen days previously, on Saturday, 5 August, he had boarded a luxury Rovos Rail train in the Cape with his client, for whom he was acting as bodyguard, a Dutch tourist, Mrs Thilini Scherpenzeel. The train was en route to Pretoria.

'Thilini Scherpenzeel,' Cupido rolled the words in his mouth. 'That's *some* name, pappie, all elegance. I bet you she's a looker.'

Johnson had last been seen on that Saturday: after he had enjoyed dinner with Mrs Scherpenzeel on the train, he had escorted her to the door of her compartment. A spokesperson for Rovos later confirmed that Johnson was not on the train when it arrived in Pretoria on Monday. His client and the train staff had assumed he had left the train voluntarily on Saturday night, as his suitcase was also missing. It was only found on Monday when the train reached its destination in Pretoria, pushed deep under his folding bunk.

That Monday afternoon Johnson's ex-wife Robyn realised he was missing. Late that night she reported it at the police station in Brackenfell, the northern suburb of Cape Town where she and Johnson lived apart.

No attempts to trace Johnson had yielded fruit.

One week later, on Monday, 14 August, the body of a man was found beside the main railway line near Three Sisters in the Karoo. The apparent cause of death was massive skull fracture. A SAPS forensic investigator from George found blood, tissue, bone splinters and hair on the steel pole of an electrification pylon, at a height that indicated the deceased had hit it when he jumped from the train, or was thrown. There was a broken cell phone in his inner jacket pocket. It was his body that appeared in the photographs in the docket.

On Wednesday, 16 August, the investigating detective from Beaufort West, Sergeant Aubrey Verwey, established via the IMEI number of the broken phone that the deceased was most probably the missing Johnson Johnson.

That was more or less the sum total of the information at their disposal.

Cupido put down the blue marker and took a step back. 'Jurisdictional nightmare,' he said. 'Brackenfell, Pretoria, Three Sisters, Beaufort West, and nobody knows where this dude died. We'll have to start from Ground Zero.' Ground Zero was a spot in the Karoo beside a railway line beyond the tiny hamlet of Three Sisters. Cupido phoned Beaufort West, talked to Sergeant Aubrey Verwey and made an appointment to drive through the following day to inspect the scene where Johnson Johnson's body had been found.

Griessel began to collect the scattered photos and documents, slipping them back into the yellow-brown folder. 'Let's go and talk to the ex,' he said.

'And we have to see Thilini Scherpenzeel as well,' said Cupido, hopefully, 'sooner or later.'

'Aren't you the man courting a certain Desiree Coetzee of Stellenbosch?' Griessel asked.

'I am that man,' said Cupido. 'My interest in Mrs Scherpenzeel is purely professional.'

'Of course,' said Griessel.

It was just past three in the afternoon. They walked out, down the half-lit corridor, some of the fluorescent lights flickering, others dead.

# 3

He was unsettled for days after the fight at the river, and grateful that his employers were away on vacation. His face was bruised and swollen, his hand bandaged.

The sense of risk gnawed at him. He lived in the multicultural Saint Michel neighbourhood; there was a mosque just a block away from his apartment. It was common knowledge that the French DGSI, the Direction Générale de la Sécurité Intérieure, was active there. His lifestyle and connections would have reassured them long ago that he was harmless, but his photo would be on a database somewhere. The police in the city were efficient, too, with an extensive system of CCTV cameras at their disposal. It would be possible to connect him to the fight and track him down. Even if he pleaded self-defence, even if there was a witness to confirm it, it was the attention, the close scrutiny, he wanted to avoid. That was something he couldn't afford.

He was disturbed that five young amateurs could do him so much damage, disturbed at how age had weakened and slowed him.

And now he had to start looking over his shoulder again, had to keep close watch on place Camille Pelletan below his apartment window again, keep his ears tuned when he heard a siren, tense at the sight of a uniform. That was a life he never wanted back.

The newspapers covered the story, of the five who were involved in a 'bloody gang war' across the river. Two were sought for other crimes.

There was no knock on the door, no policeman eyeing him dubiously.

It all blew over. The swelling on his face subsided.

But nothing was quite as it had been before.

And then Madame Lecompte spotted him.

# 4

They stopped in the parking lot of the Fairbridge Mall in Brackenfell, and made for the big pet shop at the back near the railway line. They walked side by side, Benny Griessel and Vaughn Cupido. Griessel, with his tousled hair, always overdue a cut, the dark almond eyes that had been described as Slavic: he had been on the wagon for more than two hundred and forty days now, but his long battle with the booze had left deep tracks on his face, making him seem a decade older than his forty-six years. Next to him, a flamboyant Vaughn Cupido, a head taller, aged thirty-nine, sporting an elegant winter coat, had been saying for months: 'The big four-oh, *pappie*, it's coming for me. And you know what they say, when forty hits, you have to hit back . . .' He hadn't yet revealed how he would retaliate.

The pet shop looked like a mini farmyard and farmhouse. The big sign read *Robyn's Ark*. They had to enter through the gate and cross the garden, with its chickens, rabbits and ducks, before they reached the shop entrance. The interior reeked of bird droppings, dog food and cat urine. A cacophony of parrots, canaries, finches and puppies filled the air. One entire wall was lined with fish tanks, which contained the only silent life form there.

A woman approached, thirty-something and full-figured, her make-up and hair a bit overdone, earrings large, nails long, painted dark crimson. 'I'm Robyn,' she said. 'You're from the SAPS, right?'

'The Hawks,' said Cupido.

'I know policemen. I was married to one for a long time,' she said. 'It's about time they got the Hawks involved.'

They introduced themselves, asked if they could talk to her about Johnson Johnson.

'Of course, but everyone called him JJ. Come through, we'll talk in my office.'

'We're very sorry for your loss,' said Cupido. 'It must have been really hard.'

She stood at the door, waited for them to enter. 'Yes, it's hard. Especially for the children. But it's been three weeks and I'm coping better. I actually knew, when JJ didn't pitch up that night . . . I actually knew. So I've had time to grieve . . .' She closed the door behind them.

They sat around her desk. She lit a slim cigarette. The detectives took out their notebooks and pens.

The walls were decorated with posters of animals – dogs, cats, ducks – with comic expressions and funny captions. The colourful files on the shelf behind the desk lent a cheerful air to the room. A framed photograph of two girls, perky ponytails pulled back from their pretty faces, stood on the desk. It felt strange to Griessel to be talking about death.

'Excuse us, ma'am, but we want to start right at the beginning,' said Cupido. 'Cast a fresh eye on the whole investigation.'

'We're going to ask questions that you will already have answered,' said Griessel.

'It's okay, shoot,' she said, and drew deeply on her cigarette.

'Mr Johnson was in the Police Service a long time,' said Griessel.

She nodded and tapped the ash off with a long fingernail. 'From age eighteen, two years before we got married. He was Flying Squad at the station in Hermanus, then made detective in Bellville, spent five years at the VIP Protection Unit in Pretoria before he turned free-lance. Private protection consultant.'

'What precisely did that work involve?' Griessel asked.

'JJ . . . His ambition was to be the go-to guy at all the five-star hotels for briefing the tourists on staying safe in South Africa, and he'd be available if they wanted to hire him as a bodyguard. But it's not easy to get in with the grand hotels. JJ said they're a closed system – they don't like money flowing to the outside. So, here and there he got briefing opportunities with the smaller tour operators, and sometimes he rode shotgun for them – that's what he called it. He would ride along in the bus with them, just to give them peace of mind. It was in the last few months that the bodyguard jobs started coming in. But not officially, through the hotels,' she said.

'His name was Johnson Johnson, genuine? Just like that?' asked Cupido, who had a thing about names.

'Yes. His mom christened him that. All her life she said the double feature gave him gravitas and dignity. Bless her soul. But everyone called him JJ.'

'How long did he freelance?' asked Griessel.

'Nearly two years.'

'Solo?'

'Yes. He even had an offer from Body Armour, the protection agency in Cape Town, but JJ said, why would he give twenty per cent of his income to someone else? He wanted to try on his own. The first ten, twelve months were tough for him, but he never stopped marketing himself and networking. He handed out his business card everywhere. And I do mean everywhere. Stuff started trickling in, and from about January things were improving. He never missed a single payment in child support, I'll have you know. Those two girls,' she pointed at the photograph on the desk, 'were everything to him.'

'When were you divorced?'

'When he was in Pretoria, three years ago. I stayed here. You know, the shop, I had no choice – I'm the sole proprietor ... But a long-distance marriage just didn't work for us. JJ ... Let me just say, like most men, he wasn't good at being alone at night. But we managed to conduct the whole divorce thing in an adult and civilised manner because of the kids. JJ rented a flat down the road, so they often stayed overnight at his place. And we were the best of friends ...'

'His home address was here in Springbok Park, Olympus Street,' Griessel said.

'That's right.'

'And you can provide us with the keys?'

She opened a drawer, took out a set and put it on the desk. 'Please don't leave a mess. I have to vacate the place before the end of the month.'

'Of course,' said Griessel.

'Ma'am, we'd like to know the sequence of events, please, from when he left here on the train,' Cupido said.

'You last saw him on Saturday, the fifth of August?' Griessel asked.

'You can give us as much detail as you can remember,' Cupido added.

'I understand,' she said, and drew on the cigarette again as if it gave her the strength to go on.

Robyn Johnson said her former husband had dropped off his daughters at the pet shop just after nine. They had spent the night with him at his flat, as they did most Fridays. They were four and six years old, and they immediately began to whine that they wanted to go with their father because 'Daddy's going on a fancy train, Mommy. Why can't we go too?'

'So I asked him, "What's the story with the train?" He said some Dutch aunty had hired him. His business-card distribution was paying off again. The maître d' at the Cape Grace Hotel had recommended him. And the aunty was going to Pretoria on the Rovos Rail. It's ultra-luxurious, and he'd get his own cabin and everything. Plus she was paying him good money for his services.'

'He didn't say anything else about the client? Why she needed protection?'

'Nothing more. He was serious about the confidentiality of the client relationship. I respected that, so I didn't press him.'

'He was cool? No worries?' asked Cupido.

'That day?'

'That day, that ball park.'

'JJ was always cool. He used to say worry never sorted anything, just burned up energy you could use to solve the problems.'

'Okay,' said Cupido, 'and then?'

'Then he said to me, "Jewel" – he called me "Jewel" because my name, Robyn, means "ruby" – "I'm flying back one o'clock Monday. I'll be in Cape Town at three. I'll come pick up the kids at four." Now, there's a few things about JJ you have to understand. Number one, he's never late. Not when it comes to those two girls. Never, ever. Number two, if something unforeseen happens that could delay him, he always calls. Always. Number three, every night he calls his girls. Depending on his schedule, somewhere between six and eight, but every night he phones, unless he tells me, "Jewel, I'm busy tonight, send the girls my love." That man had his faults, but he was a wonderful father. He lived for those two girls.'

'Point taken,' said Cupido.

Griessel nodded and scribbled in his notebook.

'Right. So, he phoned that Saturday night, and I heard him tell the girls they were at Matjiesfontein, the train had stopped there, and he told them how fancy the train was, how they had high tea, I ask you, and he sent them some photos on WhatsApp.'

'What time did he phone?' Griessel asked.

'Just after six.'

Griessel made a note.

'Do you still have the photos?' asked Cupido.

'Yes. My phone is in there.'

'We can look at them later, thank you. Are there any photos of the Dutch aunty?'

'He would never do that. He was too discreet. Only photos of his compartment, all that lovely wood panelling, and the cake they had for high tea – JJ had a sweet tooth . . . And of the historic buildings at Matjiesfontein, and the outside of the train.'

'Okay.'

'Please continue,' said Griessel.

'So. That Sunday evening, he didn't call. I began to worry just a little bit – what was going on? – because he always called. Always. But you say to yourself, He's working, maybe it just wasn't convenient. And you wonder, you just can't help it, how old the Dutch aunty is, and what she looks like, because JJ is JJ, if you know what I mean . . . Anyway, I let it go. Until the Monday. All day I heard nothing, which was fine, but when three o'clock came and he didn't appear, and then four o'clock and still nothing, I phoned him, because, as I said, he was never late when it came to picking up the girls. But his phone went straight to voicemail, and I thought, Okay, maybe he's still on the plane, maybe it was delayed, and I left him a voice message and said, 'Call me, JJ. You're making me worry.' By six o'clock I knew there was trouble. That was when I called Rovos. Those people were very nice, you can imagine, they can't just hand out details about their passengers, but they went out of their way to help, and I think they could hear how upset I was. They did say there was one passenger who got off the train sometime on Saturday night or Sunday morning, they couldn't give me details, but I should maybe go ahead and report it. So I went to the police station here – there's a warrant officer who worked with JJ in Bellville, Neville Bandjies, they would even still *braai* together sometimes, and we made out the missing-person report. But I already knew, that night, something very bad had happened because Johnson Johnson loved his two little girls too much not to call them.'

# 5

It was pure chance. Daniel Darret was standing at his front door, key in hand, in the same instant that the woman came round the corner.

Place Camille Pelletan is small, really just a widening of the rue Marengo where it crosses the rue Saint-François – like the bowl of a tobacco pipe at the end of the stem. It wasn't much busier than some of the other streets in that part of the Saint Michel neighbourhood. There were always people on the way to the basilica or the Capucins market. More on Saturdays.

His new alertness made no difference: the timing was pure bad luck, the woman rounding the corner just as he was poised at his door. He turned around when he heard her heels on the cobblestones. And she looked at him. An instant of recognition. And then, just when she seemed about to smile shyly, Daniel looked away, unlocked the door, slipped in and quickly shut it behind him.

He leaned against the door, swearing. The cat, Wackett, replied to him halfway up the stairs.

# 6

A week and a half later, when the call came through from Sergeant Aubrey Verwey of Beaufort West, the shock was not as great as you'd expect, Robyn Johnson said. 'In a way it was a relief, you know? I mean, you can stop wondering if it's true or not. But you're also angry. Who did this? And why? I mean, JJ was just such a nice guy . . . And *how*? How did JJ end up like that beside the railway tracks? So much anger. And hate. For the faceless people who did this. These animals, these bastards . . . He was a good person, he had his flaws – don't we all? – but inside he was a good man.'

She shook her head fiercely, as if to rid herself of the negative emotions. 'You must catch them,' she said quietly. 'Please, you have to catch them.' She stubbed out her cigarette with a trembling hand, her eyes welling with tears.

'We are the Hawks,' said Cupido. 'That's what we do.'

Griessel gave her a moment, and then he asked: 'Ma'am, how was Mr Johnson's . . . health?'

'His health? It was tip-top. Why do you ask?'

'His mood. Was he wound up?'

'I told you JJ wasn't the type to worry.'

'Ma'am, we understand that kind of question isn't pleasant for you,' said Cupido, 'but we have to look at this from every possible angle. So, fact is, there really was no chance that Mr Johnson fell off that train by accident. Two things could have happened. Either he jumped or he was pushed. If my colleague asks about your ex's health, what we really want to know is if maybe he suffered from depression. It's another way of asking the awkward question, did he jump?'

'Okay. Sorry. I understand now. No. Never. Not JJ. He . . . There were times when I thought he was too happy-go-lucky. If you'd seen him with his two girls . . .'

'Ma'am, the other possibility,' said Griessel, 'the big question we usually ask in an investigation like this, is whether anyone might wish him harm.'

She considered that, then shook her head. 'JJ was nice. That was his problem. He was just so damn *nice*.'

'But he was a policeman. A detective. Did he ever mention anyone threatening him, someone he'd arrested?'

She thought for a moment, then shook her head again. 'He hasn't been a policeman for two years.'

'We understand that, but still, did he ever say anything?'

'Not that I know of.'

'No gang affiliations?' asked Cupido.

'JJ comes from Ashton. There are no gangs there.'

There *were* gangs in Ashton, but they could tell she wanted the interview over with now.

'Okay. He didn't, in the lean times, borrow money somewhere?' asked Cupido.

'You mean from a loan shark?'

'That's right.'

'No. He knew he could come to me. As a matter of fact, he *did* borrow money from me, at the beginning of the year. But he paid it all back by June. And he was busy these last four months or so. He was making good money.'

'How did he manage his admin? Did he have someone to send out his accounts? Do the books?'

'He managed all that himself.'

'What was his system?' Cupido asked.

'What do you mean, his system?'

'Did he keep files on his clients and his payments?' Cupido pointed at the shelf of multicoloured ledgers behind her.

'No. He did that on his laptop.'

'Where is the laptop now?'

'I . . . It's usually in his flat, locked in the sideboard. Or else he took it along in his case. I didn't think to look.'

'Don't worry, we will,' said Cupido.

Griessel put his pen and notebook into his jacket pocket. They stood up. 'Mrs Johnson, what do you think happened on that train?' Griessel asked.

'If you had to speculate,' said Cupido.

She looked up at the ceiling. She tapped her long nails on the desk. Slowly she stood up. From inside the shop, with apparently deliberate timing, a parrot said, out loud and crystal clear: 'Fuck you, Fanus.'

The tension in the room dissolved.

'That bird,' she said. 'How am I ever going to sell it with a mouth like that?'

They smiled.

'You have to understand, I loved JJ with all my heart,' Robyn Johnson said.

'Noted.'

'First I thought it had to be a robbery – I mean, in this country everyone's stealing now. From the president all the way down. I wanted it to be something like that. Random. Bad luck.'

They waited silently.

'But then I thought, on that train full of grand, rich people, why would they rob JJ? And then you've got to come to the point and admit that he did have a roving eye.'

They nodded in understanding.

'My best guess is that JJ was messing with another man's wife on the train. A man who wouldn't stand for it.'

In the parking lot Cupido checked his watch and said they were leaving at six in the morning for Beaufort West. Tonight he was having dinner with Desiree, and she didn't want to be too late as it was a weekday night, school term, and she was very strict with her son, Donovan.

So, they drove back to the Hawks' offices in Market Street, Bellville, and made arrangements for the next morning's trip. 'Your turn to bring music for the road, Benna,' Cupido said, over his shoulder, his coat flapping behind him as he strode down the corridor, on his way to Stellenbosch.

Griessel made notes on the docket's Part C and said his goodbyes through open office doors as he headed out to his car. When he

reached into his jacket pocket for his keys, he found the bunch for
Johnson Johnson's flat and decided it was as good a time as any to take
a look. The woman in his life, Alexa Barnard, was in Johannesburg for
meetings with her record company's musicians. He wasn't in the
mood to sit alone at home watching meaningless TV.

He drove to Brackenfell.

Johnson's flat was in a townhouse complex just a block away from the
Sorgvry Police apartments, where Colonel Mbali Kaleni had lived
until a couple of years ago.

Griessel parked in the bay for number five, picked up his murder
case and walked to the front door that bore the same number. He
opened the case, removed forensic gloves and the small Canon
Powershot camera, unlocked the security gate and door, picked up the
case again and went inside. The door closed behind him. He stood still
just inside the threshold.

He would never grow accustomed to searching the home of a
murder victim. There was a dreadful silence, as if the space knew the
owner would not be returning, the uneasy feeling nonetheless that you
were invading privacy, the constant tension that you would overlook
something vital, or damage a piece of evidence because you didn't
know what you were looking for.

He began with the sitting-dining-kitchen area, an open-plan design
with a sofa, two chairs, a coffee-table with a stack of DVD boxes of
children's films. A TV and Blu-ray player on a stand. No paintings, no
dining table, just a long, low sideboard against the wall, and the breakfast nook with three bar stools at the kitchen counter. He took photos
of everything before he began the search.

He located the right key on the bunch he was holding to unlock the
double doors of the sideboard. On the left, plates and glasses, coffee
mugs and a few dishes. Plus alcohol. A quarter-bottle of Klipdrift
brandy, half a bottle of Three Ships whisky, a few small bottles of sparkling wine and two full-sized bottles of red, still sealed. For a second
his demons stared into his eyes. On the right, a tangle of cables and
chargers, an old ADSL modem, the box of an LG phone and ripped
envelopes containing municipal and cell-phone accounts, receipts and
a memory stick. No laptop. Griessel locked the sideboard again.

He deposited the memory stick in a plastic evidence bag, went to search through the kitchen cupboards and the fridge, then the two bedrooms. One was for the children. There was nothing of consequence in the cupboards or bedside drawers.

In Johnson's room the bed was made, the built-in cupboards reasonably tidy. An attractive old chest of drawers faced the bed. The top drawer held personal documents – including an ID, a driver's licence that had expired the previous year, the divorce decree. Photos of the children. And a photo of the family when it was still whole. They were seated on a couch – not the one in the front sitting area. Johnson was in the middle, surrounded by Robyn and the children.

He was a lean man. Fit. Handsome. With a smile full of confidence, and an expression that said: 'Look at the beautiful things life has given me.'

As he systematically searched and recorded his findings on the Canon, Griessel thought about photos. Some of them lied. The picture of the Johnson family was about three years old. It might once have been displayed on Robyn's desk. Or on JJ's wall where he lived in Pretoria. It spoke of harmony and happiness, foretold a fairy tale.

And now look at them.

He was pretty sure he didn't have any photos like that. When he and Anna, his ex-wife, were that age, he was working night and day at the old Murder and Robbery squad. Working and boozing. His life was a haze of violent crime and liquor. He had snapped the few photos in existence with a point-and-click when they'd holidayed in April. Ten days of sobriety by the sea at Langebaan or Hermanus, his mind back on his job, his heart on brandy. Only Anna, his daughter Carla and his son Fritz in the pictures. The kids were lively, happy. The look in Anna's eyes – was he imagining it with hindsight? – a little hesitant, afraid of the monster in her husband, the post-traumatic stress disorder that no one properly understood back then.

Those photographs had predicted their future much more accurately. Because he was missing from them.

Carla was twenty-two now. She had begun work as a public-relations officer on a wine estate. She'd studied drama, but hadn't found work in the entertainment industry. Fritz was nineteen and in his second year at AFDA, the Cape film school that Griessel could not afford. And Anna was married to a lawyer. When he and Anna saw each other occasionally, she always seemed relieved to be shot of him – and a bit embarrassed by his unfashionable clothes, his apologetic manner. And why wouldn't she be? He was still only a policeman, a recovering alcoholic, barely eight months dry, and his greatest wish was to ask the other recovering alcoholic in his life to marry him. He had already bought the ring for Alexa. It was locked in his top drawer at work.

He kept telling himself he hadn't asked her yet because he wanted to make the engagement special. An occasion she could recount with pride and delight. But, truth be told, he was scared.

Benny Griessel sighed. He finished up, locked the house and left.

He had found nothing.

# 7

Daniel's life had been deliberately uncomplicated before Madame Lecompte and the violence in the night.

He worked as an assistant to the furniture restorer Henry Lefèvre. The old man with thick, silvery-white hair and moustache was a genius wood-wizard who could mend priceless seventeenth- and eighteenth-century pieces so perfectly that the best antique-furniture experts in Europe could not spot the repairs. But Lefèvre had Asperger's syndrome. His mind was in the socially problematic range of the autism spectrum. He made no eye contact and had no sense of empathy with the feelings and intentions of others. That made him very hard to work with. Colleagues quickly felt that he was insulting, humiliating or ignoring them, even though that was not his intention. 'He doesn't have a filter, and he thinks everyone else is like that,' his wife, Madame Sandrine Lefèvre, told Daniel when she interviewed him. 'The assistants last only a week or two, Monsieur Darret, even though we pay more than double the usual salary. If you're easily offended, you'd better say so. And rather look for another job.'

She ran a neighbouring antiques shop in the Chartons district – *Madame Lefèvre. Antiquités, Brocante* – that sold her husband's handiwork, among other things. She was a very clever woman.

Daniel told her then that he thought he could handle the Asperger's. And she hired him – mainly because he was big and strong, and accepted the salary without negotiation. Madame was desperate, just like he was.

It took him months to come to terms with the old man's strange behaviour. Eventually a bond developed between them, unspoken, amorphous and strange. It existed in the silences of the workshop, in the rhythm of their working together, and in the rare, fleeting flickers in Lefèvre's eyes that spoke a softer, more accommodating language. And he fell in love with the Lefèvre process, the art of making broken things whole again.

Daniel rose at six every weekday, drank strong coffee, ate his oatmeal, fed the cat, cleaned the one-bedroom flat, washed and shaved, and walked to La Boulangerie on the rue des Faures at seven o'clock. He greeted the bakers by name, and they him. He would buy two croissants and two *chocolatines*. The latter he would eat as he walked to work, while they were still warm from the oven. The croissants went into his small rucksack, to be eaten at ten with his tea.

He was always the first at work. He would unlock the workshop and breathe in the scent of furniture polish and varnish, glue, wood shavings and sawdust, the stacks of planks and the strange, mysterious musk of the old, worn-out pieces. Every morning the aromatic blend varied slightly, determined by what *le génie* had last chiselled or sawn, sanded or polished.

This was his regular daily routine when the Lefèvres were there: he would sweep and dust, pack and hang tools exactly as Lefèvre liked them; he would restack planks and furniture, check stock, replenish where needed and make a list of orders. At nine Madame would arrive, and they would consult about the tasks of the day. He marked the repaired items and carried them to the service entrance where the delivery truck would collect them just before ten. Then he ate his croissants with tea, and when the *génie* arrived, he worked with Lefèvre as he directed until Madame brought lunch to the back. They ate separately, each on his own wooden crate on opposite sides of the workshop. And he stole with his eyes everything that Henry Lefèvre did with the wood and furniture.

Sometime after three, Madame would quietly beckon him away and he would shift things around in the shop for her, do small deliveries or help transport pieces with the panel van. Sometimes he would work on his own project, when the schedule allowed. After five he would go home, without saying goodbye to Monsieur, for by then the cabinet maker was already deeply immersed in his own world.

It was a long day's work, physically challenging, as he was on his feet practically all the time, and had to lift and carry heavy items, usually alone. Exactly as he liked it. It kept him fit and tired him out, so that he barely had energy at night to yearn, or mourn, or remember.

In the evening after work he watched television. Soccer. Old films. News. Or read about events in his home country on his second-hand tablet.

Saturdays, he cleaned the flat from top to bottom. He went to the market for his weekly purchases of cheese and ham, slices of terrine or pâté, *saucisson* and fruit, Wackett's fish, and for a glass of wine and a chat with Mamadou Ali, who worked for the florist and was generally known as Ali du Mali – Ali from Mali. He had no other real friends; people didn't know much about him.

On Sundays he would clean his motorbike in the small garage he rented in the rue Permentade, then go for a ride on the BMW, alone. To Saint-Émilion for lunch. Or Arcachon, or Bayonne, now and then as far as San Sebastián across the Spanish border, or the twisting roads and landscape delights of the Périgord. He returned before sundown, put the motorbike away, and went home. Monday he would be back at work.

That was his life, more or less, before the woman and the violence in the night.

More than a week after she'd seen him at his front door, on the Tuesday afternoon, she was standing there waiting for him. The giraffe lady. Beside the big flowerpot at the entrance to his old three-storey apartment building.

# 8

*August, Benny Griessel, Three Sisters*

'Right here,' said Detective Sergeant Aubrey Verwey, pointing to a dry gully in a patch of Karoo bushes beside the railway track. 'They found him right there. With his brains hanging out, and he'd been there eight days already. You can imagine. Not a pretty sight.'

'You mean the guy who works for the railway?' Cupido asked, his irritability showing. He had been in a mood since early that morning when they drove out of Bellville at six.

On the way to Beaufort West – where they were headed to pick up Verwey – Griessel told Cupido about his search of Johnson's townhouse. But he could see his colleague's attention was elsewhere. Initially he thought it was because of the earliness of the hour.

Now they were standing beside the tracks in the expanse of the Great Karoo, nine kilometres past the Three Sisters filling station. They had to walk for twenty minutes down the dusty service road from the chained gate beside the N1, as the man from Transnet hadn't arrive with the key to unlock the padlocked gate. Despite the blue skies the August wind was bitterly cold. Neither Cupido nor Griessel had brought warm clothing. 'It's a semi-desert, for crying out loud. You'd expect a bit of heat,' said Cupido, indignantly, to Griessel as they emerged from the car.

'Yes, the Transnet section manager,' said Verwey. He was young. His haircut was trendy, a complex array of indents, layers and waves.

'The same one who was supposed to bring us the key?' Griessel asked.

'That's correct.' As though he was under cross-examination in court.

Cupido shook his head slowly and sighed audibly. 'Okay, let's take it from the top.'

'Captain?'

'Tell us the whole story, Sergeant, how all this unfolded for the SAPS in Beaufort West.'

'It's all there in the docket.'

'I know it's in the docket, but the docket is not exactly a masterpiece of detail and eloquence, to put it mildly.'

'My docket is professional,' said Verwey, stung. 'Strictly by the book.'

Griessel intervened before Cupido could react. The dossier wasn't a shining light of efficiency, but he could see this was not the time to bring it up. 'You know how it is,' he said to Verwey. 'A docket is a summary. We want the bigger picture.'

Verwey must have suspected he was just being humoured. He squared his shoulders slightly, shooting Cupido an indignant glare. 'My docket is professional.'

Griessel nodded. Cupido mercifully refrained from speaking.

Verwey stared across the plains. 'The Transnet *guy* . . . Chungu, that's his name. He found him here.'

Griessel nodded again, encouraging.

'Chungu inspects the train tracks between Beaufort and Hutchinson – that's his territory. He was driving past here, and he smelt something, something rotten, and he said that's not such an uncommon thing. Sometimes the trains hit a kudu or something, even a donkey from time to time. So, he looked out and saw nothing, because Johnson was lying half in the *sloot*. So Chungu stopped where the smell was worst, got out of his railway bakkie and stood just about there, and then he saw Johnson lying here. He saw the white shirt first. And then the flies and maggots and the whole *smittereens*, and the smell was so bad he couldn't take it. He drove his bakkie away, and then he phoned the Beaufort West station.'

'*Smittereens*?' Cupido asked.

'That's correct. Totally broken up. Johnson Johnson's head. Completely smashed.'

'I see,' said Cupido. 'This Chungu, does he follow a routine for his inspections?'

'What do you mean?'

'He found the body on a Monday, right?'

'Right.'

'So, does he check this bit of track every Monday?'

'Oh. Okay, I see what you mean.'

'Well?'

'I'll have to ask him.'

'So he called the Beaufort West station and they sent the two constables,' Griessel coaxed.

'That is standard practice,' said Sergeant Verwey.

'For two constables to come and throw up on the crime scene?' Cupido asked. 'To let the entire troop of the Karoo's Blue Bums trample over everything?'

'The crime scene was on the train. They just threw Johnson off here,' said Verwey. 'That's not rocky science.'

'Rocky science?' asked Cupido.

'That's correct. Rocky science. It means it's not too complicated.'

'I can see clearly now,' said Cupido, and Griessel was sure that something serious was bothering his colleague. Under normal circumstances there would have been a hint of amusement in his voice by now. He would have shot Griessel a sidelong glance and they would have suppressed a chuckle that later, driving home, they would share. But today wasn't normal circumstances. Something had angered Cupido, last night perhaps, or very early this morning, a brooding, growing rage, contained like steam in a pot. Griessel knew Cupido: it wouldn't help to ask before Cupido was ready to talk. And it might burst out before he did ask. He just wanted to prevent that happening right here and now.

'And then?' Griessel spurred him on.

Detective Sergeant Aubrey Verwey of Beaufort West SAPS was oblivious to the undercurrent. He drew himself upright for his moment in the limelight, and he talked. About the two uniforms who finally got their nausea under control enough to inspect the corpse closely. And then, judging by the quality of the black suit and white shirt, they'd concluded that it wasn't 'just a local joker'.

'Local joker,' Cupido repeated sternly.

'That's correct,' said Verwey. 'So they radioed in for a detective.'

The station commander of Beaufort West had sent Aubrey Verwey. When he arrived at the scene there were two police vehicles from the tiny SAPS station in Hutchinson, and two from Victoria West. The bush telegraph of the law in the Karoo was very effective. They didn't suspect that it was Johnson Johnson's body, as none of them had seen the reports in the news the previous week.

Verwey emphasised that he had reprimanded the curious officers for trampling over the crime scene, told the men from Victoria West that he felt *fokkol* for their arguments that this location was just across the Northern Cape boundary and therefore fell within their jurisdiction. Detective Sergeant Aubrey Verwey had been called out, and therefore it was Detective Sergeant Aubrey Verwey's case. And, as he had done with the two Hawks, he had emphasised the word 'detective'. ·

Verwey had tied a handkerchief over his nose, but it hadn't helped. He'd put on his latex gloves, stretched the yellow crime tape and ordered everyone to stay behind the line. He'd taken photos with his Samsung cell phone because the Beaufort West police photographer's entire camera bag had been stolen five months ago. From the police station. It hadn't yet been replaced, so the cell phone was the best he could do. He also searched the pockets of the victim, and found his cell phone, in pieces. The device must have been smashed when Johnson Johnson struck the pylon beside the track, or perhaps had hit a stone on the ground on falling out of the train. 'Beyond reasonable doubt. Totally beyond reasonable doubt.'

And that was all that was to be found in the pockets of Johnson Johnson. The cell phone. An LG G5.

'So I tagged it and I bagged it,' said Verwey.

'Then I found the blood and brains on the 'lectric pylon, just over there. You can still see it. The CSI man from George only found his way up here the next day, and I told him, 'You must analyse that.' Then I phoned my Station Commander and he reported it higher up, and the police spokesperson in the Cape told the media that a John Doe was found beside the railway . . . A John Doe is what you call an *ou* that's dead but isn't yet IDed.'

'We live and learn,' said Cupido, casting his eyes up to the *'lectric pylon*.

Griessel took a few deep breaths.

'And then some reporter from *Die Burger* called me and she asked, "Isn't that Johnson Johnson?" That was the first time I even heard of the *ou*. But I told her, no comment, 'cause the victim wasn't IDed. Only when I processed the sim card from the LG phone was it beyond reasonable doubt that it was Johnson Johnson. Completely beyond reasonable doubt.'

They drove back to Beaufort West. Cupido at the wheel, Aubrey Verwey in the back seat. Verwey talked a lot, mostly about the cases he had solved with his ingenious detective work: *crystal meth* dealers, house burglaries, stock theft and two local domestic murders.

They suspected he had an agenda. When they drove into Beaufort West, he said: 'Okay, what must I do to become a Hawk?'

Cupido made a strangled sound, like a dog being kicked, but quiet enough that only Griessel heard it.

Griessel said: 'Just keep on doing what you're doing.'

'But you guys will put a word in for me, right?'

'We'll try.' As close to the truth as he could say.

They dropped him off at the police station in Bird Street. 'Hold on a minute. Vodacom's call list has come in. I'll get it quick,' said Verwey, and ran into the building.

Cupido dropped his head and banged it a few times on the steering wheel.

Griessel smirked.

Verwey was back with the envelope. 'These are Johnson Johnson's cell-phone records. It came after I sent you the docket.'

They said goodbye, and as they drove off, Verwey shouted: 'Put a word in for me!' He stood on the pavement waving until they disappeared around the corner.

Griessel felt a bit sorry for him. To be stuck in this place . . .

They filled up at an Engen station. Griessel went to buy meat pies and cold drinks. Then they took the N1 back to Cape Town in silence.

Just a kilometre on from the entrance to the Great Karoo National Park, Cupido abruptly pulled off the road without warning, heading into the dusty lay-by, with its spindly saplings and concrete tables and chairs. He stopped the car and got out, leaving the door wide open as he paced a short distance away. The spot was deserted, no other cars or people in sight. He stood still, turned around.

'*Jissis*, Benna,' he said. Rage and despair, all in one.

# 9

Here it comes, Griessel knew, and it was a good thing.

'That,' said Vaughn Cupido, pointing in the direction of Beaufort West, 'that is the future of the SAPS.'

The full impact of his statement seemed to overwhelm him, because he shuddered. 'That is the future of the Hawks. That is the future of this land. That "rocky science". That "*smittereens*". I ask you. *Smitte*-fucking-*reens*.'

He came back to the Ford. 'For fuck' sake, Benna, they can't even speak properly. How can they write? No wonder that docket looks like a dog's bum. How they gonna conduct a murder investigation? "The crime scene was on the train" so all the Blue Bums could throw up where they liked. No, *o jirre*, Benna, here comes anarchy. We're in deep shit.' He waved his hands in despair. 'Did you see his hair? There was more time invested in that haircut than in this case. And then he tries to tell us what a John Doe is. *Jissis* . . .' Cupido stared out over the wide plains.

'What happened, Vaughn?' Griessel knew Verwey was just the trigger. Something else had cocked his colleague's gun. It must have been serious, because for Vaughn Cupido to brood for 444 kilometres was virtually unequalled.

Cupido took a deep breath. Another impotent wave of the hands. Then he stood in the car's doorway. 'Last night, when I was at Desiree's . . .' he began. A deep, drawn-out sigh. '. . . her son was there, Donovan. And he's got this new friend, Brantley. What sort of name is Brantley, Benna? Brantley. I ask you. What were they thinking? No wonder the kid turned out to be this facetious little wise-ass. Anyway, Brantley is very quick with the lip, an' he asks me, "Uncle, is Uncle in the Hawks?" And I say, "*Yebo*, yes, I am a captain in the Hawks, *pappie*." And he tunes me, "My daddy says you're captured." And I say, "What do you mean, captured?" And he says, "You know, those businessmen from India who became rich and then became crooks and then captured the president . . . My daddy says the Hawks are captured too. Everyone is captured now. Those Indians own you, you're getting rich from envelopes under the table, and the people are getting poor from all the capture." *Jissis*, Benna, you know how I feel about the Hawks. They are my life. My pride. But that's nothing. Brantley was messing with me in front of Donovan. For months I've been trying to win that boy's trust, trying to connect with the kid, 'cause I'm serious about Desiree, and I know the road to a real relationship runs through her kid . . . Now Brantley's throwing this capture idea around and I see Donovan looking at me like he *knew* this guy wasn't going to turn out well.'

'Ay,' said Griessel.

'So I sit there and think, I could say, "No, we're not captured, us Cape Hawks, our Serious and Violent Crimes Unit, we're still clean, even though the shit has hit the fan in Durban, and nobody knows what the hell is going on in Jo'burg," but us, Benna, we work our asses off. We used to be one hundred and forty-two brave souls, five years back, and now we're barely thirty, but fuck knows, we're clean and we work. Night and day. And I sat there thinking, I can't even take Donovan to work with me to show him we're clean because the Department of Public Works is too damn useless to come fix our toilets and lifts, our lights and tiles. So what do I do, Benna? What must I do? And then we come here and Detective Sergeant Aubrey Verwey is this arrogant little moron, the future of the SAPS, with his "Okay, what must I do to become a Hawk?" All that ambition, but they don't want to do the work for it. And then I thought, Everything's going to hell, and I want to beat someone until they listen, Benna. Please fix the dykes. Somebody must fix the dykes 'cause I feel like that boy with all his fingers in the holes in the dyke, but it's springing another leak and another, and I haven't got any more fingers left. I'm going to lose Donovan and I'm going to lose Desiree, and I'm going to lose my pride. And then? What do I have left, then, Benna?' Cupido walked back towards the veld. He stood beside the wire fence, hands on hips, staring out at nothing.

He came back at last, got into the car.

'I can tell you you still have me. But the Department of Personal Works has also neglected me a bit. My lift's stopped working long ago,' said Griessel.

'Hah!' There was just a dash of humour in Cupido's retort, but it brought a measure of relief.

'The one thing this country has taught me, Vaughn,' said Griessel, 'things never get as bad as you think they will. And things are never as good as you want them to be. There was a time when I nearly gave up hope. When it looked like everything . . . The wheel turns. Things will come right, Vaughn. Sometime or other. Not so right that we'll be dancing in the street. But they will get better.'

That was the best he could do for now.

Cupido turned the key. The Everest's engine took. 'I hope you're right.' Twenty kilometres further on, he said: 'Give me that meat pie. Where's the music you brought along?'

Griessel passed him his pie and a cold drink, took out the old David Kramer album, *Jis Jis Jis*, and pushed the CD into the player. Before Leeu-Gamka they were both singing along. Near Laingsburg, Cupido laughed, for the first time that day, at the lyrics of 'Tjoepstil'. Just outside the town he said: 'That was a good one, Benna. Department of Personal Works.' And he chuckled quietly.

Beyond Touws River Griessel phoned Rovos Rail's Cape Town office to ask for Mrs Thilini Scherpenzeel's telephone number.

They put him through to Mrs Brenda Strydom, the railway company's head of communications. She said they had read in the press that the case was in the hands of the Hawks now. If there was anything they could do . . .

'We'd like to talk to you tomorrow.'

'Of course. But please understand that not all our rail personnel will be here tomorrow.'

'I understand,' said Griessel.

'We have compiled a list of contact details of everyone who was on the trip on the fifth to the seventh of August. You may contact them anytime. We will also fly the hospitality manager of that train to Cape Town if you want to talk to him in person. He has been placed on standby.'

'Thank you very much. We can't say yet if that will be necessary. But I'd like to interview Mrs Scherpenzeel as soon as possible.'

'She has already agreed to allow us to make her contact details available to you. Here is her number . . .'

'Hold on,' he said, as he clamped the phone under his neck and took out a notebook and pen.

When she read it out to him, he said, 'That's an overseas number.'

'Yes. She went back to the Netherlands a while ago. We did notify the detective.'

'Sergeant Verwey?'

'No, it was . . . Just a moment . . . Here it is, a Warrant Officer Bandjies.'

'From Brackenfell.' The man who had helped Robyn Johnson when she'd reported Johnson Johnson as missing.

'That's right. He contacted us after the disappearance. We notified him that Mrs Scherpenzeel had gone home. He said it wasn't a problem.'

That was before Johnson Johnson's body had been found, so Griessel couldn't fault Bandjies' decision. 'Thank you,' he said.

'Mrs Scherpenzeel did request that you call in the morning between nine and twelve. She usually rests in the afternoon.'

That made him wonder how old she was. He asked.

'Ninety-one,' said Strydom.

Cupido was listening to the conversation while he drove. 'How old, Benna? Twenty-nine, right?' he whispered.

'I see,' said Griessel to Strydom.

'And so active still,' she said. 'Wide awake and on the go. Incredible woman. You know she's the widow of Joop Scherpenzeel?'

'Who?'

'Joop Scherpenzeel, the billionaire. The man who started the Sonnenborgh brewery. In Utrecht.'

'No, I didn't know.'

'An exceptional woman,' said Brenda Strydom. 'Truly an exceptional woman.'

As he ended the call, Cupido was asking again how old Scherpenzeel was.

Griessel told him.

'It's just not my day, Benna. It's just not my day.'

'But she's still very active, Vaughn. Wide awake and on the go. Widow of a billionaire too.'

'You're just a regular ray of sunshine, aren't you, Benna?'

# 10

He didn't recognise her immediately. Initially he was aware only of the strangeness of her appearance there: she was elegant and dressed with care, bright red lipstick under a jaunty sun hat. But she stood awkwardly, arms folded, as if she knew how obvious it was that she didn't belong in the coarser texture of the Saint Michel neighbourhood.

Then he realised it was the giraffe lady. Instinctively he looked left and right, because it didn't make sense for her to be alone – if she was here, she must have brought trouble with her, as she had before.

There was no one else, only Wackett on the threshold, and his first thought was: What does she want?

'I'm sorry,' she said. He realised she could see the frown on his face, his discontented body language.

She walked towards him self-consciously, with that odd long, loping stride of hers, and held something out to him. Paper, an envelope. A letter. 'I am no threat to you,' she said, her voice rich and full, as you would expect from a tall woman, one who was almost as tall as he was.

She waited for him to take it from her outstretched hand. He hesitated. He didn't want her here, hadn't wanted to see her ever again. She was a risk: she knew something about him that he wanted to keep hidden.

'Please,' she said.

If she was a pretty woman, sensual, or sly and self-confident, he might have turned and walked away. But precisely because she was so maladroit – clumsy and ill at ease, *ordinaire*, tall and gangly – his heart opened to her, an impulse of generosity, and he took the envelope.

All she said was '*Merci*', then turned and walked away, her heels click-clacking over the cobbles that in ages past had been ballast for British ships, he the one left standing awkwardly now, with a feeling of guilt for treating her as Lefèvre would. As he looked up he saw Wackett stalking away from the doorway, a look of reproach on her face.

He waited till he was back in his little kitchen before opening the letter. The paper was expensive. Her handwriting was beautiful, artistic curves and curlicues, like something from the Middle Ages. There was an address. Rue Montesquieu. He knew the street. It was in the so-called Golden Triangle, an area of expensive shops and the swish apartments of the rich.

A day, date and time was noted on the page: Thursday evening, seven o'clock. A faint trace of perfume with it.

He swore, first in French and then in the language of his birth. He would have to go.

At the very bottom she had signed off: *Élodie Lecompte*. An elegant name.

He tucked the letter back into the envelope, and tossed it angrily into the green pottery bowl on the mantelpiece of his unused fireplace.

The eighteenth-century edifice was built of sparkling-clean restored limestone, stately and beautiful. There were only three bells beside the large door facing the street. Which meant that her apartment occupied an entire floor.

He rang the top bell. It was sixteen minutes past seven; he wanted to make clear that he was there under protest, through sheer force of circumstance, in no mood for trouble, not intimidated by her wealth or her apparent status. His deliberately casual outfit said it too: white T-shirt, laundered jeans, black Nikes.

The door growled open electronically. He climbed the wide limestone stairs, three floors. He lifted a hand to knock on the attractive wooden door, but it opened immediately. She was barefoot, in long black trousers and white blouse, looking self-conscious again. He greeted her, and she greeted him, then waved him in and closed the door behind them.

'Thank you for coming,' she said, and led the way through the entrance hall where a large portrait hung, a playful vision of a tall, elegant woman, her headscarf reddish brown, her gown festooned with fairies and butterflies.

He gazed at it.

'Sniege,' she said.

'Pardon?'

'Sniege Navickaite. The artist. She's from Bordeaux.'

'Oh,' he said. He felt a sense of compassion because the painting was, in a way, another version of Élodie Lecompte, tongue-in-cheek, a prettier, leaner interpretation, with self-confidence and style. He wondered if she had been aware of that when she bought it. A kind of self-parody.

The ceiling was high, the sitting room spacious, walls covered with art. He didn't know much about art, but he recognised a variety of styles from different eras. He did know antique, expensive, quality furniture very well and he could see much of that here. Deep, rich hues in the soft late-afternoon light shining through the large, high window.

She invited him to sit, barely looking at him as she asked him if he would like something to drink. Wine, perhaps? Red? White?

'Red wine, please.'

She nodded as though that choice bore her approval. She walked to a beautiful drinks cabinet where bottles and glasses were ready on the shelf. He chose a chair opposite her, in gilded oak and cotton; he thought it might be the work of Jean-Baptiste-Claude Sené from the late 1700s. He wondered if Lefèvre had ever worked on it – it looked in perfect condition. Then he wondered what she wanted, this peculiar woman who could afford a Sené. Did she want to thank him, reward him? Or was it a need for something more sensual, the experience of the big black man? These were the only logical conclusions he had reached since she had delivered the letter to him.

She drew the cork and poured; he stood up to take the glass.

'What is your name?' she asked, and sat down opposite him.

'Daniel.'

'Daniel, I have Spanish ham and cantaloupe. And a baguette and cheese. It's so hot, I didn't think . . . I'm not a cook.' She was grave and formal. Shy. 'If you wish to eat,' she said. 'I . . . If you don't want to be here, you can leave. You won't hear from me again. You have nothing to fear.'

'Why would I have something to fear?'

'The way . . . That night . . . You were in such a rush . . . I think you are . . . Excuse me, but I think you are an illegal immigrant. Or perhaps the police . . . I . . . It doesn't matter to me. I don't want to blackmail you.'

'I have all my documents. A passport.' One interpretation of the truth.

She nodded apologetically.

'My record is clean.'

'*Bien sûr.*'

He looked at her. She sat on the edge of the chair, tensely leaning forward, waiting in expectation for his answer. 'Is that what you want from me?' he asked. 'To eat with you?'

'No.'

She sipped from her glass. He tasted his. It was good wine.

He waited.

She stood up. It was a process, like a complex toy unfolding. She walked to one of the big doors. 'Come and see.'

He hesitated, but there was still an innocence about her, childlike.

He put down the glass, stood up and followed her. She walked into the next room and stopped, watching him.

The late-afternoon light shone through big windows. In the middle of the room an easel and a big canvas, white and bare. On the walls were paintings of people. Photo-realistic.

'I want to paint you,' she said. Under her breath, as if afraid of his answer.

He took another look at the people on the walls. White and black and brown, men and women, here and there a child. In modern, regular clothes. Good-looking people. Some seated on chairs or standing beside one. Others stood alone.

'This is *your* work?' he asked.

'Yes.'

'It's amazing.' He searched for the right word. '*Magique. Sublime.*'

'Thank you.' She waited for an answer.

'How long does this take? How long would I have to come . . . and sit?'

'Oh, no, if I can just take a few photos before it's dark. Then you can come and look every now and then, if you want to.'

Relief. '*D'accord,*' he said.

# I I

When they were beyond De Doorns, Griessel started going through the information that Vodacom had provided in connection with Johnson Johnson's cell-phone number – the usual records of calls made in the last three months before his death, one list sorted according to date, the other according to phone number.

'Spot anything?' Cupido asked, as they crawled up a hill, stuck behind a heavy truck.

Griessel took out his notebook and double-checked Robyn Johnson's number before he replied. 'His ex . . . The calls she mentioned, when he phoned the children that Saturday night on the train, the fifth of August . . .'

'Yes?'

'They're all here. But he called somebody else, later that night. Twenty-one oh seven . . .'

'Whose number?'

'I don't know.' Griessel took out his phone, tapped in the number and called.

It rang twice, a man's voice answered: 'Yes?'

'Hello,' said Griessel, 'who's speaking?'

'Who do you want to speak to?' Irritated.

'My name is Benny Griessel. I'm a captain in the South African Police Force, investigating the death of Mr Johnson Johnson—'

The call was cut off. Griessel examined his phone's screen. 'The signal's disappeared,' he said, and waved at the towering mountains on either side of the road.

'Who was it?'

'Don't know yet. A man. I'll call again soon.' He kept an eye on the little signal bars on his phone.

'So, Benna, when are you going to pop the question?'

Cupido knew that Griessel wanted to propose to Alexa Barnard. They had often discussed his struggle over the choice of place, the timing and the speech.

'I thought Sunday.'

'This Sunday?'

'Yes.' He felt a hollow in the pit of his stomach, and it wasn't just because of the meat pie.

'Brave, Benna. Brave. And where, if I may be so bold?'

'Okay. I thought, Alexa loves good food . . .'

'Check.'

'And she loves atmosphere . . .'

'Check.'

'And she loves beautiful places . . .'

'Check.'

'So I looked at the best restaurants, the top-ten list . . .'

'Cool.'

'And I thought the Overture restaurant. It's number six on the list, and close to Stellenbosch. I looked up the website. The view is spectacular, it looks romantic . . .'

'I was wondering when you were gonna mention "romantic".'

'And I can just about afford it.'

'Check. But you know it's on a wine farm, hey? With both of you being alkies, I'm just saying.'

Griessel sighed. '*Ja*, I saw that. The thing is, it makes no difference where I take her. There will always be alcohol nearby.'

'Except, just say, sunset on the beach at Cape Point. Little picnic basket, blanket on the sand, sea breeze in her hair . . . Chicks love that kind of thing. That's what I scheme, when the day comes for me to propose to Desiree – if she and her boy still want a captured Hawk by then.'

'I thought about a beach. Camps Bay, Clifton . . . But you know how the Cape weather is – that sea breeze will blow you and your blanket all the way to Robben Island. And I imagine dropping the ring and it disappearing into the sand. Fuck knows, I don't have money for another. I've got fourteen months before I've paid off this one.'

'Good point.'

'Do you think Overture could work?' Griessel asked.

'Sounds great. Do you want me to check with Desiree? She knows all the larny spots in Stellenbosch.'

'Please.'

They emerged from the pass and the Breede River valley opened in front of them. Griessel checked his phone again. The signal was back.

He called.

'The subscriber you have dialled is not available at present. Please try again later.'

He tried another seven times before they got back to Bellville. The number stayed busy.

They were back in the office by seven. They updated the dossier.

Cupido phoned Stellenbosch, and reported to Griessel: 'Desiree schemes the Overture is pure class, you can go ahead. And she says: "Good choice."'

'Thanks, Vaughn.'

'Are you going to tell her tonight? About the Overture?'

He hesitated, then said: 'Yes.'

He and Cupido heard the tone of his voice. Cupido put a hand on his shoulder. 'Good luck, Benna.' He said goodbye and left.

Griessel stayed behind alone. He unlocked the drawer where he kept the ring, right at the back, in the pretty black box. He took it out. Opened it. There it was, sparkling and beautiful.

*Jissis.*

He put it away again carefully. Locked the drawer. He looked up the number of the Overture restaurant. Found it. Stared at it.

It was a big step.

They had been together for nearly five years – he didn't always know what that word meant. They had been living together for the last three years, in her house in Tamboerskloof. He'd met her when he was investigating the murder of her husband. She was a suspect, a wreck. She was a faded star, the once-famous singer Xandra, the darling of the nation way back when. They often played her old hit song 'Soetwater' on the radio:

*'n Glasie vol sonlig,*
*'n soet kelkie klein.*
*Skink Soetwater.*
*'n Mondjie vol liefde*
*'n slukkie vol pyn.*
*Drink Soetwater.*

*A small glass of sunlight,*
*A goblet of rain*
*A small sip of worship,*
*A mouthful of pain*
*Drink sweet water.*

Her sensual voice and that sultry stage persona, a future full of promise, all drunk away due to stage fright, self-doubt and a husband who kept fooling around with other women. Until there was nothing left of her career or herself. But then her husband was shot, and she inherited the record company and was forced to make a new start. Griessel fell in love with her because she was down-to-earth and honest, broken and brave, because of her naïveté and generosity, her compassion, her sense of humour and ability to laugh at herself. He loved her because of her simplicity, and the straightforward way she loved him. Just like that. And she admired and respected him. Him. Benny Griessel, former alky, at forty-six still just a captain in the police force, all because of his drinking. But she raised him up, made a fuss about him, her 'master detective', her 'King Hawk', her hero.

He played a bit of bass guitar in a four-man band called Roes (meaning 'rust'), and they sometimes performed at dances and weddings. She would come and sing with them and say, 'You're such a talented man, Benny,' when he knew damn well he was just another mediocre musician.

He couldn't deny that he also loved her for the sweet sensuality that still survived beneath the scars of her life.

But, fuck it, it was a big step to take.

Because he had made a terrible mess of his first marriage. And because his sponsor at Alcoholics Anonymous, Doc Barkhuizen, had told him two alcoholics together was a recipe for trouble. Because Alexa was very rich, and he didn't even have the twenty thousand rand that the ring had cost him. He'd had to take out a bank loan for it, cash-strapped because of his police salary, a son at film school and all those years of throwing away money on booze and paying too much maintenance to his ex.

He sat looking at the number of the Overture restaurant. It was a very big step.

He had so little to offer her. But at least he could give her an unforgettable will-you-marry-me evening, a night with a beautiful story to retell. An evening worthy of her.

He took a deep breath.

He made the call.

They lived together in her house at 47 Brownlow Street, on the slopes of Signal Hill. The pretty Victorian double-storey had an upstairs balcony with a great view over the city.

Griessel parked in the garage, walked in through the kitchen door. Alexa was standing at the stove wearing her apron with *You stir me!* across the front. He'd come up with the words, and had the apron made for her. It had been his Valentine's Day gift to her last year. She was fond of it. Cooking was not one of her talents. She was an exceptional businesswoman. And when she sang, as she occasionally did, she could still bring the crowd to their feet. Her piano-playing was still good. But she had zero aptitude for cooking, despite declaring it a 'passion'. Her attention was easily distracted when the phone rang or a text message came through so she would lose track of the ingredients she had already added to the pot. And her sense of taste was pretty dodgy. She would close her eyes and taste a dish, smacking her lips and declaring it 'perfect'. But once she'd dished up and begun to eat she would frown and say: 'Something's not right now. Can you taste it too?'

And he would lie, saying: 'No, no, it's delicious.' Well, if that was the greatest sacrifice required of him in this relationship, he was happy to make it.

Now he was faced with another necessary lie. A lie about Sunday week, as the restaurant was fully booked for this coming weekend. He'd have to get her to Overture without revealing his true plans.

It was cold outside, but the kitchen was cosy. Her face lit up when she saw him. 'Benny,' she said, with genuine joy, 'you must be exhausted.'

He kissed her, held her tight. 'Not too much.'

'How was the Karoo?'

'Vaughn says the Sweet Buggerall is growing pretty well, but I like the . . . space.'

She laughed. 'I'm making tomato bredie.'

He sniffed the rich stew. 'It smells good.' Vaguely true at least.

'Wait till you taste it! We can eat whenever you're ready.'

'Let me just wash.' He stood in the doorway, turned round. He had to ask her. Now.

She looked back at him, her eyes so soft.

He turned and went to the room to shower, a quick four-minute one as the Cape had serious water restrictions, the worst drought in memory. There was talk of Day Zero, when the dams would be empty. Water Armageddon.

But that wasn't what worried him. It was his dinner date with Alexa. It was a very big step.

# 12

Six days after the meal and photo shoot with Élodie Lecompte he went back, driven by curiosity. Curious about 'his' painting, and about her. At seven p.m. he rang her doorbell with a hint of unease. Was it vanity that had brought him here? Or was he just searching for himself?

He heard the window open on the third floor. He looked up. She was checking who was there. She leaned out and raised her hand. Smiled. The window shut. She buzzed him in.

Upstairs at her door he found her more informally dressed this time, jeans and an olive-green T-shirt. Barefoot again. 'I'm glad you came,' she said, and offered him wine.

He said no, thank you, he just wanted a quick look at the painting. Disappointment showed in her eyes, but she nodded. '*Bien sûr.*' Of course. He started wondering about her again, who she was, what story lay behind her. The aura of loneliness surrounding her. On that first evening she had revealed very little, just busied herself with the camera and the photos.

He followed her into the studio.

The painting of him was on the easel, huge, two metres high. The outline of his body was drawn, his face already complete. It felt odd seeing it, how she had captured him. There was life in it. His life. And his longing. He was amazed at her skill.

'*Ça vous plaît?*' she asked. Do you like it?

'*Oui,*' he said softly.

'*Vraiment?*' Really?

How could she doubt it? '*C'est . . . formidable.*'

She smiled in a way that he hadn't seen before, true joy. 'Then you must drink a glass with me. Champagne.'

How could he refuse?

They sat down in the salon. 'When did you start painting?' he asked her.

'After my husband died,' she said. 'I painted him over and over until I had him back.'

'What did he do?'

'He was a professor of paleontology. He was a wonderful man. I miss him every day.'

She stood up suddenly. 'One moment, please.' Quickly she left the room, her bare feet stepping silently. She was back with a framed photo, held it out to him.

He wasn't a handsome man, her late husband. Tall and painfully thin, with heavy-rimmed spectacles and a moustache that couldn't completely hide a partially restored hare lip. But there was something gentle and compassionate in his smile.

He wondered for a moment, then asked: 'Did you take this photo?'

'Yes,' she said.

'He loved you very much,' said Daniel Darret.

An intense look in her eyes. 'And I loved him.'


The art of making and restoring furniture had captivated Daniel since the day he'd begun working with Lefèvre. The loving attention, the careful work, systematic process of transforming the worn and broken into magnificent and valuable. He gradually began to develop the desire to be able to do it too. He had watched Lefèvre, inconspicuously and patiently, through every phase.

Nearly two years ago he'd begun buying his own set of tools at the Saint Michel flea market, hand-picked, to measure and saw, plane and chisel, hammer and sand. He brought the pieces one by one to his corner of the workshop. Said not a word.

Two months ago when he'd brought in the oak planks and put them down in his corner, Lefèvre had looked up. The old man stood, ran his fingers along the grain, bent and sniffed it. Picked up each plank and measured it with an eye. Put it down again. Said nothing. His way of granting his approval.

Daniel started making the table slowly. He worked on it when he had an idle half-hour. Sometimes he stayed after hours. Occasionally he would come in over a weekend. He took his time, aware that he had much to learn, ready to pay his dues.

Now and then Lefèvre looked over at him at his task. Expressionless.

It was a *table de ferme*, a farmhouse table. He had chosen this design deliberately – patterned on a beautiful example that Madame had sold in the front shop – because it was so simple. Just over two metres long, eighty-eight centimetres wide, seventy-five centimetres high, a top, four tapering legs, a frieze on all four sides. And two basic drawers at the front.

A few days before the August holiday, he arrived at work in the morning to find that Lefèvre had dismantled his right-hand drawer. He knew why. The joints were not good handiwork. He just nodded to *le génie* when the old man entered, and later Daniel refashioned the drawer.

He had almost finished now. He was busy with the final sanding, in some discomfort as the bandage on his hand was troublesome. But he liked the work, the rhythm, the smell, the mechanical repetition. He thought he would make six chairs for it, his next project. He had enough wood.

By four o'clock the heat of the August afternoon drove him to finish. He swept up the fine wood dust, cleaned the tools and diligently packed everything away, as if Lefèvre were looking over his shoulder. He locked up and left.

The rue Notre Dame was quiet. Only at the Monument aux Girondins was there any activity, tourists taking photographs, two children seeking relief in the water of the fountain. It took him between twenty and thirty minutes to walk home. His route was never precisely the same, but always zigzagged past his favourite spots. He knew the history of most of the buildings, squares and streets. Nearly every day he very deliberately walked past the Grand Théâtre, breathing in the atmosphere of the square.

Today he walked down the pedestrian street of the rue Sainte-Catherine: as most of the people of Bordeaux were at the sea, it wasn't the usual crowd.

Five hundred metres before the cours Victor-Hugo he saw Lonnie May. Later he would wonder whether it was his heightened state of awareness since Élodie Lecompte and the violence in the night that made him notice Lonnie. But now he thought he was imagining it. Over a decade had passed since he had last seen him. Perhaps it was just someone who reminded him of Lonnie. The familiar figure was twenty metres ahead, searching, constantly checking his phone. Daniel followed him, keeping his distance. It couldn't be. Memories flooded back and he shook his head. Ay, that old life. But the suspicion grew that it really was Lonnie. The alert way of walking, the stocky figure, shape of the head, shiny pate.

And something that bothered him vaguely.

He stared at the man, realising that it was Lonnie, but older. Lord, we're all getting old. He wanted to speed up, call out to his old comrade.

He didn't do it, an uneasy feeling, undefined. Something was wrong. Then he realised what it was.

There was someone else, practically alongside Daniel, whose attention was fixed on Lonnie. Daniel knew the signs, almost-forgotten training that he remembered now. The man was following Lonnie.

# 13

The man tailing Lonnie was tall and lean, dressed in blue jeans, blue shirt and a grey jacket. Dark hair, cut short. And he was damn good. Daniel walked into Giovanni Gelateria, to increase the distance between them. Lonnie May? Here? Old, alone, in August, in Bordeaux?

Daniel scanned the range of ice-cream flavours and macaroons, pretending to be making up his mind. He felt a tingling, thoughts buzzing as he sought to draw conclusions, make connections. What did Lonnie's appearance have to do with the Élodie Lecompte incident? Had the mills of justice ground so finely and so far back as to draw in his past – and Lonnie's? Who was Grey Jacket? French National Police?

But here, now? It was no coincidence. Just three blocks away from his apartment.

Lonnie was fiddling with his phone, as you would when using Google Maps to pinpoint a place. Daniel's address?

Daniel mumbled, '*Pardon*,' to the man behind the counter, turned around and walked out. He looked to the right. Grey Jacket was loitering in front of Burger King. Lonnie must be standing at the big crossing of the cours Victor-Hugo. Careful: Grey Jacket was no amateur. Daniel knew the techniques of tailing: you scanned the whole area. It had been hammered into them. The man would be alert to everything. Perhaps not even alone. Daniel could not remain standing there.

He made up his mind, walked purposefully towards Grey Jacket, then turned quickly left into rue de Guienne, and immediately right again. He would be able to approach Lonnie and his follower from a new and unexpected angle in the main thoroughfare. He would also keep an eye open for any other people following Lonnie.

He was just in time to spot Grey Jacket in the *cours* on the pavement next to the newsagent. The man turned his head left, right, searching.

Daniel walked towards him. He would buy a newspaper. Lonnie had disappeared.

The tail didn't look at Daniel: he took four steps to the left, turned around. He attempted to cross the *cours*, but the traffic light was red for pedestrians and there was a stream of cars. The hunter had lost his prey. It was obvious.

Lonnie May. As cunning as ever. He must have realised he was being followed.

All that Daniel could do was make a long detour home. He didn't want to attract Grey Jacket's attention by following him. It took him nearly twenty minutes. He approached his home from the direction of the basilica so that he had a wider view of the little square in front of his building. He didn't see anyone. He unlocked the door, went inside and ran upstairs, dripping with sweat from the heat and agitation. He stripped off his clothes, pulled on a pair of shorts, opened the shutters in front of the window and fetched a kitchen chair. He sat just far enough back in the bedroom to be able to watch the square below without being seen easily.

More than an hour and a half later, Lonnie May walked down rue Marengo. He was in a hurry, the bald head swivelling left and right as the old man kept scanning his surroundings.

Lonnie, Lonnie, how grey is the little hair you have left. But your steps are still sprightly. The trickle of Daniel's memories rose to a flood.

Lonnie spotted the address he was looking for. No hesitation, he approached the door.

Daniel waited for the doorbell to ring. It didn't.

Lonnie was walking away.

# 14

Daniel remained seated for another half-minute before he understood what had happened. He leaped up, exited the room and ran down the stairs. A brown envelope lay on the threshold, pushed through the letterbox.

*For Daniel Darret.* In black ink.

He picked it up, but he had already guessed: Lonnie knew his new name. That implied a thousand things. Lonnie had traced him, which must have been a difficult, possibly long, process, as Daniel had erased his tracks thoroughly. It meant that Lonnie must have realised he risked revealing Daniel's new identity. So, ever-loyal, he must have believed the end justified the means. He wasn't here for a chat about old times.

Lonnie was in trouble.

He hurried up to his flat, found a knife in the drawer, slit the envelope open carefully.

*Umzingeli*
*Saint Andrew. Under the organ. 10.15.*
*Lonnie*

It was the first word, the name by which he was addressed, that gave him the shivers, and opened wide the sluice gates of memory.

# 15

In the morning he met Cupido across the road from Cape Town station, in front of Rovos Rail's reception hall.

'So, partner,' Cupido asked, first thing, 'all systems go?'

Griessel knew what he meant. 'I made the reservation. Sunday after next.'

'And?'

'I'll ask her tonight.'

'Okay.' With sympathy: Cupido, too, wrestled with what he called his confirmed-bachelor commitment issues. They crossed the street in silence.

Mrs Brenda Strydom, head of communications for the railway company, was in her fifties, attractive and tastefully groomed. She was holding a file. She invited them to sit in one corner of the big Rovos departure lounge, a beautiful room with an old-fashioned atmosphere. A lone waiter stood discreetly in a corner. She asked them what they would like to drink, placed the order, and came to sit opposite them. She slid the file across the coffee-table. 'Thank you for coming,' she said.

'It's our job,' said Cupido with a hint of sarcasm. He was suspicious by nature and aggressive where big money and luxury were involved.

Griessel was familiar with this response. It was part of their team dynamic – they had learned over the years how to make it work to their advantage. When Cupido was obstinate, Griessel would play a gentler, more approachable role.

Strydom didn't miss a beat. 'I know. But the death of Mr Johnson is a very serious matter to us, as I'm sure you'll understand. We run the most luxurious train in the world. Most of our clients are from overseas.

Our reputation as a safe mode of travel means everything to us so it's of critical importance that this case is solved speedily and effectively. I'm here to assist you in any way you may deem necessary.'

'Thank you, ma'am,' said Griessel.

'Call me Brenda. I brought you—'

'Is it genuinely the most luxurious train in the world?' Cupido interrupted her.

Strydom nodded, as if it wasn't the first time someone had asked that question. 'Yes, it is.'

'Okay?' Still sceptical.

She counted off the reasons on her fingers. 'To start with, we have a private twenty-three-hectare railway station in Pretoria, including a museum and a workshop where we restore the carriages ourselves. There are even a few antelope roaming around. It's unique. Our sleeping compartments are the biggest of any train on earth. Each has its own bathroom, which is twenty-five per cent larger than any rival's. The royal suites each have a bath and a shower. There are eleven tons of train for each passenger, which is also twenty-five per cent more than any other train. All our guests eat at the same time – we don't have multiple sittings. I could continue . . .'

'That's okay,' said Cupido. Then, with a measure of pride, 'Cool. Who'd have thunk it? In our little corner of the dark continent . . .'

She smiled and pointed at the file. 'I prepared all the possibly relevant information for you. There is the complete rail section register, which is kept by the driver. It tells you what time the train arrived at every stop, when, and how long it stopped for, et cetera. There are the contact details of all our staff who worked with the train – here, on the train itself and at our station in Pretoria. They all know about the investigation and will give you their full cooperation. As per regulation, we use drivers from Transnet. Their details are also in the file, but I don't have control over their cooperation.'

'Thank you,' said Griessel.

'I've also included a list of all our passengers and their booking forms. The forms have their contact and passport details. Most of them also filled in details of their travel arrangements after the train trip. Many are overseas tourists and might have left the country already.'

'How many passengers were there?'

'On this specific train, sixty-five. Only seven were South African citizens.'

Griessel and Cupido exchanged a glance. They knew it was going to be a long and difficult process to contact each one and collect information.

Strydom saw the look. 'Every carriage has a host or hostess who takes care of the people in that carriage. They meet their passengers here in the lounge before the train departs. They take care of the luggage and see to the needs of our guests. Mrs Scherpenzeel occupied a royal suite. Her hostess was Cathy Bing. Mr Johnson stayed in a pullman suite. His hostess was Sam . . . Samantha Albertyn. They will have most of the information about Mrs Scherpenzeel and Mr Johnson. I have marked them clearly on the lists.'

'That will help a great deal,' said Griessel.

'The pleasure is ours,' she said. 'But please talk to Sam first. She has a few pieces of interesting information.'

'Oh?'

Strydom hesitated. 'I don't want to speak on her behalf, because I might get the details wrong. She is expecting a call from you . . . There is one other matter you might find interesting. Mrs Scherpenzeel booked her place on the train back in January. On the third of August she contacted us again with a request for us to accommodate a companion as well.'

'Johnson?'

'That's right. She was very lucky, as we'd had a cancellation, a man and his wife from Australia, whose daughter had given birth three weeks early. We could make their compartment available to Mr Johnson.'

They made notes.

'Okay,' said Cupido. 'Let's start at the very beginning. From when people make a booking.'

Brenda Strydom explained to them that Rovos's reservations came to them from various quarters – from international and local travel agencies and from individuals who booked directly via the internet or the telephone. It was a simple process: you booked, you paid, you travelled on the train. There was a single reservation form to complete, where passengers provided their name, address, contact details and passport number. That form was included in the file in front of them.

On the day the train departed, they were received in the lounge and accompanied to the train. That specific train had stopped at Matjiesfontein for a short tour with a local guide, and again at Kimberley on the Sunday morning. The guests went on a tour of the Big Hole, the iconic, gaping wound thousands of diamond diggers left after the mining frenzy of the late nineteenth century. They were transported by minibuses from the station and back again.

Usually the train halted on each of the two nights near or at Beaufort West and Klerksdorp to offer the passengers a pleasant night's rest and keep to the schedule. The timings and duration of the stops depended on delays on the railway. And there were always delays.

'The big question,' said Cupido, 'is how hard it is to get onto the train if you're not a passenger.'

Strydom was ready for that. 'Captain, nothing is impossible. But it would be very, very difficult. There is excellent security here at the station, at Matjiesfontein and in Kimberley. But if you were very lucky and managed to get onto the train, there is nowhere to hide.'

'Unless you have a contact on the train.'

'That wouldn't help much, as the compartments are cleaned while the passengers eat. Little gifts are left on the pillows. You really have nowhere to hide.'

'But how would your staff know if someone didn't belong on the train?'

'They meet their guests here in the lounge. They are greeted in person.'

'I see.'

'Your staff . . . How much do you know about their background?' Griessel asked.

'Before they're employed by us?'

'Yes.'

'We have an employment agency that does very good work with background checks.'

'Do you check for criminal records?'

'As far as I know. Why do you ask?'

'Johnson was in the police,' said Griessel. 'We'll also have to look at arrests he made. Maybe someone on the train recognised him, someone who didn't want to be recognised.'

She thought about that for a moment. 'It's very unlikely.'

'How easy is it to open the windows?' asked Cupido.

'From outside, impossible. From inside, very easy. All the windows can open. It's part of the experience. A unique experience.'

'So, it's easy to climb in?'

She paused, then: 'No. The windows are high. You'd need a ladder or something . . . The train is arriving on Saturday morning again from Pretoria. Why don't you come and see for yourselves?'

'Brenda,' said Cupido, 'he was thrown out on the left side of the track. Would that be from a cabin or a corridor?'

'The left side would be from a compartment.'

They walked back to their cars.

'You don't throw an *ou* off a train unless you're very angry with him about something,' said Cupido. 'And you can't be that angry with an *ou* if you don't know him.'

'The pictures of Johnson in his flat . . . He was fit. Strong. You don't just have to be very angry, you have to be very strong too,' said Griessel.

'Or there would have to be more than one of you.'

'It was someone who was already on the train, Vaughn.'

'How do you scheme that?'

'Let's say it was someone who was angry with him. That person would have to know he'd be on the train, where it stopped, how to gain entry. And then get to Johnson and overpower him. That's a lot of knowledge, lots of planning. Scherpenzeel was looking for a place for Johnson on the train only two days before departure.'

'I read you, Benna.'

They stood staring at the station.

'Footwork,' said Griessel.

'Amen,' said Cupido.

'See you at the office. I have to visit the shrink first,' said Griessel.

'When is it going to dawn on that aunty you're batshit crazy beyond redemption?'

# 16

*August, Daniel Darret, Bordeaux*

He hardly slept a wink. It wasn't the heat that kept him awake but the memories. He tossed and turned in bed, reluctant to go out in the night and walk his usual insomniac route. The police might still be on the lookout for him, despite the press reports.

At a quarter to five the sun rose, and he couldn't stay in bed any longer. He washed and dressed. Dark clothing, to be unobtrusive in the hustle and bustle of the street. The training of another lifetime gradually returning.

He inadvertently found himself crossing the pont de Pierre. Midway on the bridge he stopped and made sure nobody was following him. Then he walked up avenue Thiers. He battled the ghosts in his mind, tried to focus on Lonnie May. What did he want? Why was he here? And he didn't like any of the possible answers that came up.

Lonnie had chosen the cathedral of Saint-André. Good choice for someone unfamiliar with the city. There were better locales. He could think of a few. Mollat's bookshop, for example, always busy. Or the huge Village Notre Dame, Madame Lefèvre's biggest rival antiques shop. Quiet corners, easy to keep an eye on the entrances.

What did Lonnie want?

Why was Lonnie being followed?

Twenty minutes later he stopped. He looked at the ugly modern edifice of the unemployment office. He realised he hadn't picked this direction by chance. It was here in La Bastide that he had first exposed his new identity to official eyes, tested it. It was here that his new life had begun when they'd told him about the job vacancy at the Lefèvres.

Did he really want to meet Lonnie?

He didn't want to sacrifice this life.

Lonnie would say: 'Tiny, this place is your balm.'

'Tiny' had been his nickname, back in the day.

Lonnie would tell him: 'Tiny, this country and this city are an anaesthetic. But some time you'll have to face up to yourself, your history and your existence. You need to find healing, tame your demons.' Lonnie was always the voice of reason, the responsible mentor, the conscience. Honest Lonnie. Loyal Lonnie.

He didn't want to tame anything. He wanted to finish his farm-house table, then the chairs, one by one, and keep learning how to work with furniture. One day, perhaps in four or six or ten years from now, when Henry Lefèvre was too old to work, he would like to follow in his footsteps, until he himself was too old, and then he wanted to teach someone else, draw his pension and die here. Embalmed, anaes-thetised. Memory-free.

He stood there for half an hour watching the trams go back and forth, back and forth, slim, modern shapes like bullet trains. Then he turned and walked back to his apartment to try to eat some breakfast before the meeting with Lonnie.

Nearly a thousand years ago a pope had declared this church holy, the Saint-André Cathedral, which the locals referred to simply as Bordeaux Cathedral. Daniel had been in it before, but it was too big for his liking. When he felt the urge sometimes to sit and ask for strength, the strength to forget, he chose the simplicity and gentle dilapidation of the Saint-Michel basilica, or the intimacy of the Église Sainte-Croix.

He knew why Lonnie had picked Saint-André. The magnificent, massive interior space made it easier to spot people, even in a crowd. The crush was never too bad. Only one entrance and exit to watch, on the big place Pey Berland, where you could spot a tail with greater ease. The square had four potential escape routes and one of the busiest tram stations in the city.

Daniel chose the rue du Maréchal Joffre because it was quieter. He made certain that nobody was following him. He took his time, so that he wasn't too early; the cathedral opened at ten.

He went inside with a few tourists, cameras draped around their necks. He pretended to be overwhelmed by the pomp of the interior, so that they could move on, so that he could see if they took any interest in him. At 10.12 he turned around, walked out again quickly, just to be absolutely sure.

Nobody reacted.

He went back inside, turned right, walked down between the hundreds of chairs arranged in tidy rows to the hollow below the spectacular organ. He couldn't see Lonnie anywhere. Up the ten steps to the space beneath the organ balcony, he sensed Lonnie was there, to the right in the hidden corner, with his pot belly, thick eyebrows, glasses and bald head. He walked up to his old comrade and they embraced, and Daniel Darret, once Thobela Mpayipheli, wept silently. The first person from his old life – Lonnie May, dear Lonnie May. The longing for the land of his birth and all his lost loved ones overwhelmed him.

Lonnie, so much shorter, his head reaching only up to Daniel's chest, his spectacles pushed askew in the press of the embrace, said: 'An agnostic and the Xhosa son of a Protestant preacher furtively embracing in a dark corner of a Roman Catholic church. You can't make this stuff up, Tiny.'

They laughed through their tears.

They positioned themselves so that Lonnie could look out over the church interior. 'Two of the buggers have been on my tail all the way from London. That lean and hungry look – thought I was too old to spot them. Must be running all over Bordeaux now, trying to find me,' he said, in his familiar staccato style, and he laughed his Lonnie laugh, low and secretive. But there was a tension in him.

'Who are they?' Daniel stood in the corner, leaning with his back to the wall.

'Russians, I think.'

'Russians?'

'It's a long story.'

'I'm sure.'

Lonnie was gazing at him. 'You're looking great.'

'Not getting any younger.'

'Don't talk to me about age . . . Jesus, Tiny, it was a job finding you.'

'You seem to have managed pretty well.'

Voices grew louder, tourists approaching. 'I . . . We need a better place to talk. This isn't going to work for very long.'

Daniel had suspected as much. He had already thought of a good place. 'Au Bistrot. It's a restaurant on the place des Capucins, across from the market. There's a cellar, only one stairway, one entrance. I know the owner, François.'

'Good food?'

'The best.'

'Twelve thirty?'

'Yes.'

'It's good to see you.'

'I'll reserve judgement until I know why you're here.' He could see from Lonnie's face that the news he brought was not good. But Lonnie just nodded, and left.

Daniel Darret waited ten minutes before he followed.

# 17

Lonnie had a bag with him, a small rucksack that he put down beside the table. They spoke Afrikaans, in the cellar of the Au Bistrot, because Lonnie said they couldn't be too careful. Even if they were alone down there.

Daniel said: 'The waitress is Dutch.'

'Then we'll be quiet when she comes down.' Lonnie leaned across the table and his voice was quiet, urgent and tense. 'Thobela, I know my sudden appearance has upset you. I won't keep you in suspense.'

He steeled himself. 'Tell me, Lonnie.'

'We can't afford our president any more. The damage he's doing is too great.'

Daniel didn't need to ask which president. He read daily about the bad news from his birthplace. 'What has that to do with me?'

'We want you to . . .' Lonnie's home language was English, and he searched for the right phrase in Afrikaans, failed. He glanced at the stairs. 'You have to take him out, Tiny.'

The brutality of it, the confirmation of who he was, literally rocked him. He shook his head slowly to try to hide the shock. 'No,' he said.

'I know, Tiny, but—'

'No, Lonnie. You must find someone else.'

'There isn't anyone else.'

'No.'

Lonnie sighed. 'I knew you would react this way. I'll let it sink in a while. I'll give you my full sales pitch. You don't have a choice.' He picked up the menu. 'You'll have to translate this for me. I haven't a clue what it says.'

# PART II

# 18

Alexa called Thursdays their healing days. Griessel didn't like that term. It was too . . . *girly* was probably the kindest description he had for it. Too New Age, too affected, too soft, too oh-shame-I'm-broken. And he thought it unrealistic: he didn't consider himself *capable* of complete healing. Not with his past, not in this job.

The reality was much more as Cupido would tell him, 'Go sort out your shit,' usually qualified with the gentler 'I need you, Benna. The Service needs you.'

It seemed easy for Cupido to cope with the stress of being a detective. When it came to his personal life or political views it was a different story, but even then, his coping mechanisms were much more effective than Griessel's former boozing. To blow off the worst of the steam, Cupido would explode, scream and shout. And then be extra silly, cracking jokes about everything, a way of sticking out his tongue at the world – 'Don't let the buggers get you down.' Griessel guessed that was the result of Vaughn Cupido growing up on the mean streets of Mitchells Plain, a jaunty line of attack to counteract the deprivation and hardship.

For Griessel Thursday was simply his see-the-shrink day, and Alcoholics Anonymous evening. He attended the meetings with Alexa, when they could make it. Their healing days, these past eight months, since he had quit drinking again.

It did help, there was no denying it – the psychologist had made a big difference. And the AA nights reminded him of his powerlessness against alcohol, of the way he had to fight his fight day by day. That he wasn't alone.

The shrink was a pretty woman, Griessel's age, late forties. In her office there was a big brown teddy bear that stared at him with glass eyes. Accusing. He hated it. He wished she would take it away, but he'd never found the courage to say so. Nonetheless she was the single greatest reason he had been able open the cabinet in Johnson Johnson's empty flat, look at all the bottles of booze coolly, calmly, close it and move on. It was decades since his craving for alcohol had been so mild.

The psychologist mostly handled SAPS people. She'd taught him that he had a fear of harm from others. She said it was common among policemen and soldiers, in combination with post-traumatic stress disorder. And Gliessen had hitched a sail on all four vanes of the fear windmill – survivor's guilt, divorce guilt, over-inflated sense of responsibility and self-hatred. It all boiled down to this: in his line of work he was exposed to every wicked thing people did to each other and the deep knowledge that he couldn't protect his loved ones from it. This fear and his overblown sense of responsibility had driven him to drink.

He worked with her to analyse all the traumatic events in his professional life – all the death and murder, the gruesome crime scenes, the cold-blooded acts – until he understood that he was not responsible for the damage caused, that there was nothing he could have done to prevent it. Even though he was a policeman, who was supposed to do just that.

She also encouraged him to discuss his work and circumstances with his loved ones.

Just as he had done last night with Alexa, after his quick shower. He'd told her about Johnson Johnson, about the grainy cell-phone photos of the body beside the railway track, and how that had made him feel. And Alexa had made sympathetic noises, dished up the tomato bredie and said: 'Come on, enjoy the food, you'll need your strength.'

And the stew – praise God – wasn't too bad after all.

He parked in front of the house in Stellenridge. The psychologist's office was attached to it, with a separate entrance. Keeping the damaged apart from the whole. He realised he was a few minutes early. Once more he tried the last number Johnson Johnson had phoned before he died. There was still no answer, no voicemail.

He took a deep breath and went in at the little gate. He wondered if he should ask the shrink why he was so scared to ask Alexa to marry him.

★   ★   ★

He stared at the teddy bear, and the teddy bear stared at him. He explained to the psychologist about the Johnson Johnson case and told her he'd made good use of the techniques she'd taught him when he was looking at the photographs. He mentioned the liquor in the cabinet, and his small victory.

She praised him, but cautiously: she was a smart woman who knew that flattery made him uncomfortable. She called it Griessel's 'self-hatred question'.

They went on to talk about his children. About his good relationship with his daughter, Carla, and his poor relationship with his son, Fritz, who still wouldn't believe that, this time, his father had truly stopped drinking.

He didn't talk to her about Alexa and popping the Big Question.

Then he drove back to Bellville. As always, he felt empty, tired and just a tiny bit better.

At the office he went straight to the Hawks' Information Management Centre, commonly known as the IMC. It was the support unit at the DPCI, utilising a broad range of technology in solving crimes. He gave the cell-phone number to the commander of the centre, Captain Philip van Wyk, and asked for his team to identify the owner. He handed in the memory stick he had found in Johnson's flat for analysis. Then he collected Cupido and they went to Colonel Mbali Kaleni's office.

'How did it go, Benna?' Cupido wanted to know.

'She said it's not me, it's the weird guys I have to work with.'

'Shrinks,' said Cupido. 'They're the craziest *mofos* of them all.'

They told Colonel Kaleni that it would be a long and complicated investigation, and explained to her the problem of the sixty-five passengers, nearly thirty rail employees and an analysis of Johnson Johnson's arrest records. They were hoping she would allocate more members of the Serious and Violent Crimes Unit to the docket. They asked her if she could use her influence on the pathologists to speed up the Johnson post-mortem.

'I'll see what I can do. Captain Cloete is in here every five minutes.' She was referring to Captain John Cloete, media liaison for the Hawks, pronouncing his name 'Cluetee'. 'The press are driving him nuts. A reporter from *Rapport* has put in a formal request for an interview with you two. I told him it's not possible.'

Murder on the world's most luxurious train, Griessel thought. Of course the media circus would be in full swing.

'We can make time for an interview, Colonel,' said Cupido.

'*Hayi*,' she said, in her mother tongue, shaking her head, and waving them back to work.

They walked down the passage. When they were far enough away, Cupido mimicked Kaleni's Zulu-English accent: 'Maybe I should call Captain Cluetee myself.'

'You're mocking a woman who is now a lot slimmer than you,' said Griessel.

Cupido looked wounded. 'The knife is in, Benna. Don't forget to give it a twist.'

Griessel just grinned.

'I'm serious, Benna. A *lekker* article in *Rapport* saying the man on the case is the legendary Captain Vaughn Cupido of the Hawks would go a long way to show that Donovan boy I'm not so bad.'

'I think he already knows that.'

'You scheme?'

'It's like Eddie Mack sings, Vaughn, "Everybody loves a fat man."'

'Who?'

'Eddie Mack, the blues singer.' Griessel's favourite music, the classic blues.

'Never heard of him. But fuck you and fuck Eddie Mack, I'm not that fat. Let's phone that aunty who was Johnson Johnson's hostess.'

'. . . and, oh, how a fat man can love.' Benny Griessel sang the rest of the Mack chorus.

At his office Cupido said: 'Benna, every time you come back from that shrink, you seem to be a little lighter.'

And Griessel knew it was true.

In Cupido's office they phoned Samantha Albertyn, Johnson Johnson's hostess on the Rovos train. They made the call with the speakerphone on. They could tell from her voice that she was nervous. In the background they could hear the click-clack sound of a train on the track. 'I don't know how long the signal will last – we're just past Mafikeng.'

'Mafikeng?' asked Cupido. 'Why Mafikeng?'

'This is our Victoria Falls train.'

'Okay,' said Cupido. 'Cool. We'll call you back if the signal drops. Can we talk about Johnson Johnson?'

'It's so tragic,' she said. 'It's . . . All our guests are so nice. It's never happened. It's just tragic . . .'

'It is, Sam, and we want to catch the man who did it.'

'Was it a man?' Her voice carried respect for their skill.

'We don't know yet, Sam. It's just my way of talking.'

'Oh.' Disappointed. 'Okay. I've only got the one thing that I'm sure of.'

'Yes?'

'His bed. He . . . When our guests go to dine, we refresh the compartments. Around seven. I made his bed . . . Mr Johnson was staying in a pullman suite. That means there's a sofa we fold out in the evening to make a double bed.'

'Okay,' said Cupido.

'Let me explain . . . We have a specific way of making up the bed, because the back is against the wall, a way of folding the sheets and the bedspread tidily.'

'Check,' said Cupido.

'The next morning, when they eat breakfast, we service the compartment again. I saw that the bed was made. But not the way we do it. It's . . . I don't want to . . . It's just what I think . . .'

'It's okay, Sam,' said Cupido. 'Just give it your best shot.'

'It looked like he . . . or someone tried to make up the bed like it was. But I could see that it wasn't *our* way.'

'Okay.'

'I could also see . . . I think . . . I don't think he slept in the bed. The pillows . . . A person can tell from the pillows . . .'

## 19

'That's great, Sam. That's very important,' Cupido said to Samantha Albertyn. 'That was the first night, hey? The Saturday night?'

'That's right.'

Griessel spoke for the first time, identified himself, then asked: 'You met him that morning in the lounge at Cape Town station?'

'That's right.'

'Did you see him on the train again?'

'Yes. I did his compartment briefing with him. We show them how everything works.'

'Was that the last time?'

'No. I saw him in the corridor, and at high tea, and when they were on the way to dinner. You tend to bump into people on the train – it's not that big. And everyone uses the same corridor.'

'We know it's hard to remember everything, but could you see if his behaviour, his mood, had changed? Or if he perhaps . . . if something had upset him?'

A momentary silence, so that only the sounds of the train could be heard. 'No. He was just very nice, every time I saw him. That's why it's so tragic.'

'Sam, Mrs Strydom said you had a few interesting things to share. Was it just the bunk?' Cupido asked.

'The bunk? Oh, you mean the bed.'

'Yes.'

'That's the only thing I'm sure of.'

'Is there something you're not so sure of?' Griessel asked.

'I don't know if I should mention it. What if I'm wrong?'

'We'll keep that in mind, but you must tell us everything,' said Cupido.

'Please,' said Griessel.

She was silent for so long that they thought they had lost the connection. Then they heard her take a deep breath. 'When I was unfolding the bed ... I thought there was a laptop on the ... The pullman, there's a little table, where you can sit on the sofa and work. When you open the bed, you have to unclip the table and pack it away in the cupboard ... and there was a laptop because I remember thinking I'd better not knock it off. Once I bumped a guest's iPad off the table and the screen cracked.'

'That's good, Sam. His wife said he had a little laptop, and we couldn't find it in his house.'

'Oh! Okay. So I wasn't imagining it.'

'What about the laptop, Sam?' Griessel asked.

'I found his case, on the Monday. It was pushed deep under the bed, and it wasn't closed. I – I opened it ... We still thought he'd got off somewhere.'

'Yes?'

'And the laptop was gone.'

They talked to her until the signal disappeared, but they didn't learn much more.

Griessel immediately phoned Brenda Strydom. 'We'd like to know what happened to Mr Johnson's luggage.'

'You have it,' she said.

'We do?'

'Yes. You came to collect it,' she said. 'The police in Pretoria.'

'Do you know which station? Or which policeman?'

'I'll find out right now. They would have signed for it.'

He thanked her and rang off. He told Cupido what she'd said.

'Probably the village idiot from Beaufort West had it collected. Awkward Aubrey.'

Griessel laughed. Cupido and names.

There was a knock on the office door frame. Philip van Wyk of IMC walked in with a completed enquiry form. 'The telephone number, Benny,' he said, handing the form to him. 'It belongs to Sergeant Kagiso Dimba of the VIP Protection Unit.'

'Our Protection Unit?'

'Yip. SAPS, Pretoria.'

'That's the last *outjie* Johnson phoned?' Cupido asked. 'The one whose phone is now dead as a dodo?'

'That's him,' said Griessel.

'This case is a mess,' said Cupido.

'And that memory stick,' said Van Wyk. 'There were three porn videos on it.'

'Homemade?' Cupido asked.

'No. Professional stuff, probably downloaded from the internet.'

Before he phoned, Cupido checked what time it was in the Netherlands.

A man answered. '*Goedemorgen.*' The phone was on speaker.

'*Goedemorgen*,' said Cupido, in his best Dutch accent. 'May I please speak to Mrs Thilini Scherpenzeel?'

'*Het spijt me. Mevrouw Scherpenzeel is niet beschikbaar.*'

'This is Captain Vaughn Cupido of the South African Police Service in Cape Town. When will she be available?'

'*Slechts een moment, alsjeblieft, Kapitein.*'

The sound of the receiver being put down as he went off to call her.

'*Slechts een moment, alsjeblieft, Kapitein*,' Cupido echoed, in a drawling whisper. 'It's like Afrikaans for drunk people. In your drinking days you would easily have talked Dutch, Benna.'

Griessel laughed.

About thirty seconds later, politely: '*Bedankt voor het houden, Kapitein. Ik verbind je door.*'

Another pause as the call was forwarded.

'*Kapitein*,' said Cupido. 'Nice ring to it. Kapitein Vaughn Cupido. Van der Valke.'

'"Van der Valke" sounds more like drunken German,' said Griessel.

'You ordinary people have no appreciation for us linguists.'

'Yes?' A strong woman's voice over the small speaker.

'Mrs Scherpenzeel?'

'Yes.'

'*Goedemorgen.* This is Kapitein Vaughn Cupido. Van der Valke in Cape Town. How is the weather in Holland this morning?'

Silence.

Then: 'I find it best to speak English with Afrikaans people, because of the risk of misunderstanding, especially when a call is as important as this one. I also find it highly irritating when people refer to the Netherlands as Holland. There is no Holland. There are two provinces, North Holland and South Holland. I am in neither. I am in the city of Utrecht, which is in the province of Utrecht. Now, shall we talk about the very, very tragic death of Mr Johnson Johnson?' All in the Queen's English.

'Yes, ma'am,' said Cupido, meekly.

'Good. If you furnish me with an email address, I will send you my prepared statement. It has been notarised and approved by my lawyer, and it should contain all the information you need. However, if it is in any way inadequate, I will be happy to take your call at your leisure.'

'Between nine and twelve?' Cupido asked.

'No. I will take your call any time after nine in the a.m. and before nine in the p.m. This is very personal and very important to me.'

In the silence after that call Griessel's phone rang. He recognised the number. He answered: 'Prof?'

'How are you, Nikita?' asked Professor Phil Pagel, chief state pathologist. He'd been calling Griessel 'Nikita' for the past fifteen years, since their first introduction when he'd taken one look at Griessel's face and said: 'That must be how a young Krushchev looked.' Griessel had had to look up who Krushchev was.

'Well, and you, Prof?'

'When your Colonel Mbali Kaleni calls and tells us to get a move on, we realise there have been better days, Nikita. But I can't complain. And you'll be glad to know we'll collectively move on immediately with the unfortunate Mr Johnson Johnson. There is just one tiny problem. As you know, I may not legally put my dissection knife into Mr Johnson before the body has been officially identified. Can you assist?'

'Of course, Prof.'

'Nikita, just a word of warning. The cadaver is in an advanced state. Please keep that in mind in choosing whom to send to identify him.'

# 20

No detective liked visiting the state mortuary in Durham Street, Salt River. To begin with, it was ugly, in that unimaginative government-architecture style (if you could call it style): low brown-brick-and-red-roof buildings behind a dilapidated fence of concrete poles. It had a Spartan and depressing interior, the narrow corridors, cold, bare, tiled floors, the reek of formalin and phenol, disinfection and putrefaction. To stand by while a pathologist performed the post-mortem dissection was always a disturbing experience, regardless of how many times one had experienced it before. But it was at its discomfiting, upsetting worst when a body required identification, with the heart-rending emotions and raw grief of the next of kin.

For that reason Vaughn Cupido took out a five-rand coin from his black leather wallet and asked Griessel to choose.

'Heads,' said Griessel. He knew he'd lose. He always lost when Cupido flipped the coin, even when he himself provided the money.

Cupido launched it with skill, caught it, smacked it on the back of his left hand. 'Sorry, Benna. Tails.'

'Let me see.' Because his colleague hated the identifications even more than he did.

'O ye of little faith,' said Cupido, and showed the coin to Griessel. Tails.

'*Fok.*'

'What can I say? The universe loves me.'

After a pause, Griessel said: 'I'm going to phone Robyn and hear if she has any objection to me asking the warrant officer from Brackenfell to identify the body.' He knew what lasting harm it could do to the woman to see her ex-husband in that condition. And he wanted to spare himself the trauma of her grief.

'Good thinking,' said Cupido. 'I'll wait for the email from the *kwaai* aunty from Holland.'

'The Netherlands, Vaughn, the Netherlands.'

*17 Soestdijker Road*
*Den Dolder*
*Utrecht 3734*
*Netherlands*

**To Whom It May Concern**

I am Mrs Thilini Scherpenzeel, a Dutch citizen permanently residing at
the above address. I am 91 years of age, of sound mind and body. I confirm
that the contents of this statement are true to the best of my knowledge and
belief and that I make this report voluntarily, knowing that, if it is tendered
in evidence, I would be liable to prosecution if I have wilfully stated
anything which I know to be false or that I do not believe to be true.

I have no conflict of interest of any kind in this matter.

Herewith, my statement: I undertook a holiday to South Africa from
19 July (the date of my flight from Schiphol to Johannesburg) to 8 August
(the date of my return flight from Johannesburg to Schiphol).

During that time, I spent seven (7) days in the Royal Malewane safari
lodge in the Greater Kruger National Park (20 July to 27 July), and
nine (9) days in Cape Town as a guest of the Cape Grace Hotel (28 July
to 5 August).

From 5 to 7 August, I travelled with the Rovos Rail train from Cape
Town to Pretoria. I found South Africa to be a beautiful, friendly, hospitable country, and I am deeply saddened by the events that transpired
during my visit. I wish to extend my most heartfelt condolences to the
family and friends of Mr Johnson Johnson, and would like to request the
investigating officer to forward me the telephone number or email address
of his family. I would like to offer my sympathy personally.

During my stay in Cape Town, I had daily contact with the daytime
concierge of the hotel, a lovely man by the charming name of Vinnie
Adonis. I do apologise for not knowing his full and proper name. Mr
Adonis was very helpful in organising the various day trips I undertook
during my stay, inter alia to Cape Point, Stellenbosch, Franschhoek and
up Table Mountain. He constantly urged me to be careful while exploring
the city and peninsula, as men often do when confronted by a woman of
my age, I presume. He also mentioned, on several occasions, the services
of a personal security expert he could recommend.

I would like to hereby clearly state that Mr Adonis never overstepped *or intruded in any way, and was always at his most courteous and profes-sional in all his dealings with me.*

*However, being a well-travelled and world-wise nonagenarian, I surmised that this personal security expert was a friend of Mr Adonis, and that Mr Adonis was extending a helping hand in procuring employ-ment for his friend.*

*I am the widow of a well-known businessman and entrepreneur, the late Joop Scherpenzeel, who founded the SonnenBorgh Brewery in the Netherlands. Therefore, I am acutely aware of the necessity for private and personal enterprise. Furthermore, I am of the opinion that job crea-tion is the cornerstone of a sound and prosperous economy. Thus, my sole reason for contemplating the employment of this private security expert was to make a small contribution to the wonderful people and the strug-gling economy of this marvellous country, as I had the means and opportunity. I did not require any personal protection or security. I am perfectly able to take care of myself.*

*I met Mr Johnson Johnson in the lounge of the Cape Grace Hotel on the morning of 3 August, at my request. I enquired as to his background, his current profession, and his hopes and dreams. He impressed me as a thoroughly courteous, kind and ambitious individual. He showed me photographs of his beautiful daughters. During the meeting I took the decision to ask him to accompany me on the Rovos Rail journey to Pretoria in his professional capacity. It is a decision I have deeply regretted since hearing of the tragic fate of this family man, since I feel some responsibility for placing him on the train, in harm's way, and triggering whatever circumstances transpired to engineer his very dreadful demise.*

*Nonetheless, I contacted Rovos Rail, and was fortunate enough to procure a booking for Mr Johnson. I proceeded to call Mr Johnson, assisted by Mr Adonis, reserved his services, and met him in the Rovos Rail departure lounge on the morning of 5 August.*

*Soon after departure, Mr Johnson joined me on the viewing deck in the very last carriage of the train. He indicated various landmarks as we travelled out of the city, showed me the proximity of his home as we passed through the suburbs, and lamented the sad state of public train transport in the Peninsula.*

*He then escorted me to the lounge after I complained of the wind chill, and we spent most of the afternoon there, enjoying high tea and the magnificent views of the Breede River and Hex River valleys, meeting other passengers, and engaging in conversation with them. It was, to say the least, most agreeable.*

*In the late afternoon – I did not make any pertinent effort to check the exact time – the train stopped at the delightful historic village of Matjiesfontein, where Mr Johnson accompanied me on the guided tour. In the hotel pub, a man was playing the piano, and Mr Johnson impressed me with a fine singing voice as he indulged in Afrikaans traditional folk songs.*

*He then accompanied me back to the train, and we both retired to our compartments to freshen up for dinner.*

*At around seven thirty, Mr Johnson collected me from my compartment, and we proceeded to the dining car for what turned out to be a five-star meal. We were invited to share a table for four with a charming couple from Taunton in the United Kingdom, whom we had met at high tea. I am a former pupil of Queen's College in Somerset, so had much to catch up on and discuss with them. Regretfully, Mr Johnson must have felt a little excluded by this conversation. Although he was quiet, he seemed at ease and relaxed.*

*This brings me to the one thing of note that happened, during the latter part of dinner. I can only recount it as I remember it, but I must admit to being distracted by the most interesting conversation at the table. Thus, the following is based on an impression, rather than certainty: Mr Johnson seemed to recognise someone in the dining car. I distinctly remember him raising his hand as if to greet that person, but it was an uncertain gesture, as if he wasn't exactly sure that he knew him or her. As we were sitting next to each other, we shared the same view. I recall following his gaze, but as several people were leaving dinner at the same time, I cannot identify the specific person his gesture was aimed at, man or woman.*

*The moment passed, and I never enquired as to whom he apparently recognised, for which I am now very sorry.*

*We retired to our respective compartments soon after, at about ten minutes to nine, as I wanted to call home from my compartment at nine o'clock. Mr Johnson escorted me to my door, in gentlemanly fashion, and wished me a pleasant night's sleep.*

*That was the last time I saw him.*

## 21

'Okay.' Vaughn Cupido addressed his empty office aloud when he'd read the Scherpenzeel statement. 'Okay.' If Johnson Johnson had recognised someone on the train perhaps they could focus only on the South African passengers, for now.

'Not a good sign when a man starts talking to himself,' said a voice from the doorway. Captain Frank Fillander, the greying veteran of the Serious and Violent Crimes Unit, entered the room. Behind him were more members of the team, Captain Vusumuzi 'Vusi' Ndabeni and Captain Mooiwillem Liebenberg.

'I can't have an intelligent conversation with anyone else in this place, Uncle Frank.'

'Fear not, the cavalry is here,' Fillander said, and settled himself comfortably into a chair facing Cupido.

'The colonel sent us,' said Liebenberg. 'She said you and Benny are too useless to handle this docket on your own.'

'That's not entirely true,' said Ndabeni, always anxious that his colleague's humour might be hurtful. 'We're here to help.'

'New suit, Vusi,' said Cupido. 'Very stylish.'

'Thank you, Vaughn.' Small, slight Ndabeni had the best dress sense in the unit, despite Cupido's valiant efforts.

'So, are we going to indulge in chit-chat or are we going to solve the Great Train Robbery?' said Fillander.

'Murder on the Rovos Express,' said Vusi. 'Classic.'

Johnson Johnson's former colleague, Warrant Officer Neville Bandjies of the Brackenfell SAPS, stood beside Griessel in the Salt River mortuary's identification room. The room was small and bare, with a bench against the wall and a faded blue curtain over the viewing window. Plus a bucket beside the bench.

Bandjies was plump; the blue uniform stretched tightly across his midriff. 'I'm ready,' he said, taking a deep breath and straightening his shoulders. At least it wasn't his first time identifying a body, he'd told Benny.

Griessel rapped on the window. The pathology assistant drew back the curtain. The body was stretched out on a trolley, covered with a green sheet, only the head and neck visible.

'*Jirre,*' said Bandjies.

Griessel understood. The damage was gruesome.

Bandjies crumpled, grabbed the bucket and threw up into it. After a while he looked up. 'Sorry, Captain. But to think, it could be your pal . . .'

'You don't need to be sorry. This is a bad one.'

'It looks like him,' said Bandjies, and straightened up. His breathing was rapid.

'You're not sure?'

Bandjies reluctantly approached the window, made a noise in the back of his throat and called to the assistant: 'Can you uncover his arm? The right arm?'

The assistant moved the sheet.

'Turn the arm a bit.'

The assistant complied.

Griessel saw the tattoo. One word, black ink, fancy lettering: *Robyn*.

'It's JJ,' said Bandjies. And threw up again.


Cupido told them everything he knew about the docket. He split up the tasks among the detectives. He asked Frank Fillander and Willem 'Mooiwillem' Liebenberg – the man the Hawks called their 'weapon of mass seduction' because he was dangerously attractive to women – to contact the foreign passengers. 'There were sixty-five passengers on the train. Johnson's Dutch employer has been covered already. Benna and I will do the seven locals. That leaves you with fifty-seven. Email or phone, as you see fit. We want to know if they saw Johnson, or knew him. We want to know if they noticed anything, ordinary or extraordinary. Basically, your good old fishing expedition.'

Then he asked Vusi Ndabeni to ask Sergeant Aubrey Verwey of Beaufort West where Johnson's damaged cell phone currently was, so that they could ask IMC to try to get it going in order to analyse it. A photo, WhatsApp messages maybe. Anything.

Then he began to look at the South African passengers.

Professor Phil Pagel let Griessel know they should be finished with the preliminary post-mortem after three, and it was better that he didn't attend as it would be 'an uncomfortable one'. Pagel knew of Griessel's post-traumatic stress disorder as he'd asked the professor's advice when the shrink had first diagnosed it. That was why Pagel wanted to spare him exposure to the mangled corpse.

Griessel didn't want to wait at the mortuary. He left via the Durham Street gate and walked down to Albert Street. He liked this area of Salt River and Woodstock: it reminded him of the hustle and bustle of Parow in his youth – the energy, the melting pot of cultures, the variety of old and new businesses packed shoulder to shoulder. Here, he thought, a little bit of the old Cape lived on, but not for long. Woodstock was changing rapidly, the houses being bought up and restored by young people who worked in the city but were not prepared to face the daily nightmare traffic jams to and from the suburbs.

Everything changed. Always. It never stopped.

He realised it was close to noon. He walked into the Old Biscuit Mill. All the eating spots looked expensive. He took a seat at Redemption Burgers and ordered the Straight Ace and a Coke Zero. He took out his notebook and looked over his notes. He must phone Pretoria, but he couldn't focus his mind on it. The question of proposing to Alexa haunted him. Why hadn't he told her last night about the Overture dinner?

He didn't know *how* to ask her to marry him. *That* was his problem.

If he invited her and they drove there, arrived at the place and ate their top-ten-in-the-country food and drank their top-ten-in-the-country mineral water and talked . . . When should he ask her – at the beginning, the middle, or the end of the dinner?

And how? It had to be romantic. It had to be a story she would take pleasure in telling, the story that would follow them as a couple for ever. The story she would tell to her friends, or in the next interview with *You* magazine.

How should he present the ring?

There was one way you always saw in the movies – where you put the ring in her glass of champagne. But they were both alcoholics. He couldn't have the ring brought to her like that. And, besides, he'd heard of a woman who'd downed the champagne – ring and all. And the couple had had to wait two days, aware of the most unromantic journey the ring was taking, before they could get properly engaged. Whatever with that, you didn't put a ring in a glass of mineral water, no matter how top-ten-in-the-country the liquid was.

He would simply keep the ring in his jacket pocket. After the starters he would take it out of his pocket, open the little box and let the diamond glitter in the lights. Not that there would be much glittering: the diamond wasn't that big. He would put it on the table in front of her, then ask her. Or should he ask her first, then take out the ring? What if she didn't want to order a starter?

Maybe Vaughn knew about these things. But, still, so many potential pitfalls. First and foremost, he must not forget to take the ring with him. And he had to put some thought into his little speech. He couldn't just say, 'Alexa, here's a ring, marry me.'

He wasn't big on speeches.

This was a big step. And complicated.

He ate with gusto: the burger was delicious. He paid and left, and when he was outside, he looked up the number for the VIP Protection Unit in Pretoria. He called, asked to speak to Sergeant Kagiso Dimba, who'd received the last call from Johnson Johnson.

A constable told him Dimba was on duty, unavailable, and she would leave him a message.

Griessel walked back to the mortuary and sat down in the waiting room.

Eventually an assistant came to call him and took him to the theatre where Phil Pagel was doing unmentionable things to Johnson's skull with a small electric saw, the sound of it as high and irritating as a giant insect.

Pagel was the most intelligent man that Griessel knew. Outside the theatre he dressed flamboyantly, was tanned and fit for his sixty-plus years, with a long, aristocratic face. But now Pagel was wearing his white pathologist's garb, large plastic protective goggles on his face, gloves, everything speckled with dark blood and tissue from the saw, as he bent over the stainless-steel table where Johnson Johnson lay.

It was the smell that always bothered Griessel the most.

Pagel put down the tool and sudden silence fell. 'Nikita, you're looking well.'

'Morning, Prof. Thank you, Prof.'

'Lost weight?'

'A bit, Prof. I'm cycling.'

'Excellent. And I hear the water wagon is still running on all cylinders,' Pagel said, picking up a pair of forceps and fiddling at the back of Johnson's head.

'I'm holding up, Prof, holding up.' The law-enforcement community was small. Word got around.

'Impressive, Nikita. Respect.'

And then, with a last, theatrical tug of the forceps and a sharp, wet sound, Pagel pulled something out of the skull, held it up to the light and examined it. 'Here is your cause of death, Nikita.'

It was shiny metal, in the form of a snapped-off blade, about six centimetres long. 'Okapi,' Pagel read the inscription. 'Made in South Africa.'

Griessel came closer. He deliberately didn't look at the cadaver, focused on the blade instead. 'Saturday Night Special,' he said. The Okapi's street name.

'Indeed,' said Pagel. 'Pushed in just under the occipital bone. Piercing the cerebellum till just under the brain stem. Instant death. Nikita, I would be most surprised if there was any significant bleeding at the scene. The angle of the stabbing action is from behind and below. Quite some momentum – it's not easy to get a blade in here, especially not your Okapi. It's made for cutting, not stabbing. If only I had a rand for every Okapi blade that broke off . . . You don't get it out easily. The considerable frontal skull damage is in all probability post-mortem.'

'He hit a steel pylon when they threw him out of the train, Prof.'

'He was already dead, Nikita.'

'Defensive wounds, Prof?'

'Not that I could see, but I will take a closer look. Our problem is that the body has been exposed to the Karoo. Birds, insects and, I suspect, a jackal or two. I'll spare you the details, save them for the official report.' Pagel put the Okapi blade in a plastic evidence bag, handed it to Griessel.

He looked at it and sighed.

'Not what you expected?'

'This is trouble, Prof.' The Okapi was the concealed weapon of preference for the township gangs and organised crime on the Cape Flats. Untraceable, anonymous and very common. It brought a new dimension into the case, one that didn't fit at all.

# 22

While the professor continued his examination, Griessel filled in the chain of evidence forms for the Okapi so that Phil Pagel could sign them off. On the spur of the moment, and because the pathologist was a wise man with whom he had already shared so many personal matters, he said: 'Prof, I need your advice.'

'Of course, Nikita.'

'Prof, let's say you wanted to ask the woman in your life to marry you . . .'

'Hypothetically, of course,' said Pagel, and smiled.

'Yes, Prof. And let's say you take her out to a grand restaurant, one Sunday night. At what stage of the evening do you propose to her? The thing is, there's a chance she might say no. There's always that chance, and if you ask too soon, the whole evening is ruined, and if you ask her too late, it might not be as romantic as . . .'

Pagel nodded while his hands worked over the mangled head. 'Interesting theoretical dilemma, Nikita. Very interesting.' He looked up at Griessel. 'Here's my theory, for what it's worth. And you must understand I only ever did it once in my life. Therefore I must base it on a broader philosophical principle. Ask her during the minuet.'

'Prof?'

'A dinner, like so many things in life, Nikita, is like a symphony. You don't want to do anything major in the allegro. It's too early. The second movement, the adagio, is too serious. The last part, the rondo, is too late. Therefore, ask her during the minuet. It's light, it's enjoyable, it's happy.'

'Prof, I have no idea what that means.'

Pagel sighed. 'Forgive me, Nikita, I get carried away sometimes. Let me try to put it in more practical terms. I would say the right time to propose is just after the main course.'

★ ★ ★

Griessel drove to Plattekloof, to the SAPS Forensic Science Laboratory. There was a smattering of rain. It only ever rained like that in the Cape nowadays. A smattering. He could remember the winters when he was at school, cold fronts moving across the Peninsula for two weeks at a time, constant rain and gale-force winds until you were sick of the grey, wet and cold. Not now.

Everything was changing.

He was also. Slowly but surely.

He ought to be in the minuet of life, but he was still fucking around in the adagio.

His phone rang while he was in Plattekloof Road. He could see that it was Mbali Kaleni. He pulled off the road, because she was extremely strict about cell phones and driving. She would always ask first: 'Are you using hands-free?'

'Colonel?'

'Benny, I just had a call from the CO of the VIP Protection Unit in Pretoria,' she said. 'The general implied that you are harassing one of his team. I said I didn't believe that could be true.'

He explained to her what had transpired.

She clicked her tongue in annoyance, as she often did. 'Those people think they're gods because they race around over the speed limit with their ministers in blue-light convoys. Leave it with me.' She rang off.

Strange, he thought. Most peculiar. It was a murder investigation. The victim was a former member of the VIP Protection Unit. You would expect a bit of sympathy and assistance. Not this.

But this was a different world. He'd heard that that unit was a kingdom in its own right, these days. He would have to wait and see what Kaleni could manage.

Vaughn Cupido's cell phone rang just before three: it was Brenda Strydom from Rovos. 'Captain, I'm terribly sorry,' she said, 'but the policeman who signed for Mr Johnson's luggage, his signature is indecipherable. I apologise sincerely. Our staff in Pretoria said the man was in uniform, he had stars or some such on his shoulders, and showed her an identification card. I have a scan of the form here, and we think it is Sikhakha or Siknakna or Sukhaha or Sikhakhane, but we can't say with any certainty.'

'Spell those names, please.'

She did. Cupido made notes, then said: 'No problem, ma'am. Do you have a date for the collection?'

'Wednesday, the sixteenth of August. It was around four o'clock.'

'Okay. Cool bananas. Thank you, ma'am.'

He looked up the number and called Pretoria Central police station. He asked to talk to the commander and asked the colonel if he had any information about the people who had collected Johnson Johnson's luggage at Rovos.

'Who?'

Cupido explained.

'Never heard of the man, Captain.'

'Do you have an officer by the name of Sikhakha, or Siknakna, or Sukhaha, or Sikhakhane. Or something like that?'

The colonel thought it over. 'None of the above.'

Cupido thanked him, and reluctantly phoned Sergeant Aubrey Verwey of Beaufort West.

'Detective Sergeant Verwey.'

'Aubrey, this is Vaughn Cupido of the Hawks. I just want to find out who you arranged with to collect Johnson Johnson's luggage at the train station in Pretoria.'

The silence that ensued gave Cupido his answer.

Verwey said: 'I didn't know about his luggage.'

'Thank you,' said Cupido, and terminated the conversation. Useless *maaifoedie*, he thought. What an idiot.

Next he checked his notes and looked at the whiteboard on the wall. He saw that the luggage had been picked up mere hours after the news had gone the rounds that Johnson Johnson's body had been found beside the track beyond Three Sisters.

The South African Police Service's Forensic Science Laboratory in the Cape was in Silvertree Lane, Plattekloof. It was a large, impressive building, in the shape of a giant C, four storeys high. Four chunky arms extended from it, housing respectively the departments of Ballistics, DNA Analysis, Scientific Analysis, Document Analysis and Chemistry.

Griessel went in search of two particular members of the PCSI, the elite Provincial Crime Scene Investigation, with which the Hawks usually worked.

They saw him coming, Arnold, the short, fat one, and Jimmy, the tall, thin one. Together they were known as Thick and Thin, in the clichéd quip that they loved to recite themselves: 'The PCSI stands by you through Thick and Thin.' They thought they were hilarious. The Hawks tolerated them mostly because Thick and Thin were very good at their job.

'Hey, Benny,' said Jimmy.

'You're so skinny now, you'll have to drink some coffee to cast a shadow,' fat Arnold said.

'Yes, you'll need some fattening up again, like a Christmas turkey, eh. More of a hungry Hawk than a hunky one, these days.'

Jimmy gurgled with laughter at his own wit, sounding a bit like a turkey himself.

'*Ja, ja, ja,*' said Griessel, used to Thick and Thin's peculiar brand of humour.

'Talking of birds, what kind of bird can carry the most weight?' Jimmy asked.

'I don't know.'

'The crane.'

'Good one, good one,' said Arnold. 'Benny, what bird can kick your Hawk's ass any day?'

'I don't know.'

'Steven Seagull.'

Jimmy cackled.

'Who?'

Arnold was clearly disappointed that his joke had fallen flat: 'You don't know who Steven Seagal is?'

'No.'

'That's the trouble with the Hawks. No culture. None.'

'That's why they talk about culture *vultures*,' said Jimmy.

They chuckled again. Griessel grinned. 'Are you guys finished now?'

'We hear you're planning to get married, Benny,' said Arnold.

Word got around and, boy, with these two it got round much faster. He didn't respond.

'Here's a good one. Did you hear the one about the masochist and the sadist who got married?'

'No.'

'This girl was a sadist. She meets a guy in a bar. He's a masochist. They get chatting, and find out about each other. They fall in love, and think they'll make the perfect couple. I mean, what better? But they decide there's no hanky-panky before the wedding. They're saving themselves for a hectic honeymoon, okay?'

'Okay,' said Griessel. What else could he do?

'So, that first night, the guy comes out of the bathroom naked, and the girl's sitting on a chair in her sexy undies, and he says: "Hurt me, baby, hurt me." And she just smiles and says: "I won't, I won't."'

Jimmy and Arnold screamed with laughter as if it was the first time they'd heard the joke. Griessel laughed with them.

Finally, wiping his eyes, Arnold asked him: 'So, what can we do you for?'

Griessel handed them the bag containing the Okapi blade. He explained its origin, and asked them to test it for everything, but especially for the fingerprints he hoped to find.

They made the usual noises about how difficult it was to investigate a surface that had been subjected to that kind of situation.

'What about all your new equipment?' he asked. They had bragged all over the shop when the new electrochromic and fluorescence technology had been installed. On metal surfaces it could trace and photograph fingerprints that were invisible to the naked eye.

'We don't want to make any promises,' said Arnold.

'We only do miracles on Fridays,' said Jimmy.

'If it rains,' said Arnold.

'And it doesn't do that much any more . . .'

Griessel knew how they worked. They lowered expectations so that they could crow even more if they made a breakthrough. He had them sign the necessary documentation so that the evidence chain of custody transfer paperwork was up to date, and then he left before they could get started on any more jokes.

# 23

He found Cupido in his office at his computer. Griessel sat down in front of his colleague. 'Johnson Johnson was stabbed in the back of the neck with an Okapi before he was thrown off the train. That was the cause of death.'

'Saturday Night Special?' Cupido was incredulous.

'That's it.'

'Shit, Benna.'

'My sentiment exactly.'

Cupido looked up. 'This is a weird case, *pappie*. Very weird. To start with, a SAPS member picked up Johnson's luggage at Rovos in Pretoria only hours after the system heard he was dead. And now that member is missing in action. As if he never existed.'

'I also had a—'

'But wait, there's more. The Flower sent in the cavalry. Uncle Frankie, Vusi and Mooiwillem. They're trying to contact all the foreigners, so I started with the local passengers. And here's the thing. First up I run them through the database to see if they have criminal records. And, lo and behold, five of them are clean. The other two, wait for it, are ghosts, *pappie*. False identities. Phantoms, missing in action, as if they never existed.'

'How do you know?'

Cupido reached for the folder that Brenda Strydom had given them, took two registration forms out of it. 'Okay, check this out. We have a Mr Terrence Faku and a Mr Oliver Green. Each one in his own pullman compartment. Both from Cape Town, Faku in Kensington, Green in Newlands. Aged seventy-two and seventy-one respectively, home language Xhosa and English respectively, right?'

Griessel looked at both forms. 'Right,' he said.

'Okay,' said Cupido. 'Now, here's our problem, Benna. Neither of those passport numbers exists. They look right, because they've got

the right number of digits. But the system says "not found". There are
no such numbers. So, I schemed, the system's the system, never
perfect, let me check the addresses. No such addresses. Those streets
don't exist, Benna. Ghosts, missing in action, never existed. Two old
fogeys, seventy plus. Faku and Green. Fake. Now why, Benna, would
you use a fake ID and a fake address for a Rovos train trip? Why?'

Griessel just shook his head. Then he said: 'The sergeant at the VIP
Protection Unit, the one who phoned Johnson last, he still hasn't called
back, but his commander called Kaleni and warned us not to harass
him.'

'Harass him?'

'That's what he said.'

'*Jissis,*' said Vaughn Cupido.


They were discussing the anomaly of an Okapi knife on a Rovos train
when Colonel Mbali Kaleni walked in and said in disgust: 'I came to
tell you that I spoke to Sergeant Kagiso Dimba's commanding officer
at the VIP Protection Unit. And this time he promised to have the man
call you. They are a bunch of self-important idiots.'

'Thank you, Colonel,' said Griessel. His cell phone rang, and he
recognised the number. He answered.

'This is Dimba from the VIP Unit in Pretoria. Why are you looking
for me?' He sounded irritated and disrespectful.

Griessel was annoyed. 'Because you were the last person Sergeant
Johnson Johnson called. And he was murdered, and I am investigating
the case. Do you think that's a good enough reason to be looking for
you?' He heard Kaleni click her tongue in anger.

For a moment Dimba was quiet. Then: 'Yes.'

'And the duration of the call was one minute and twenty-three
seconds.'

'I don't know.'

'Why did he call you?'

'We worked together, back in the day. He called to say hi.'

'For only one minute and twenty-three seconds?'

'Are you saying I'm lying?' Dimba shot back aggressively.

'I'm not saying, I'm asking. He just called to say hi for eighty-three
seconds?'

'I was busy. I could not talk to him.'

'What were you doing?'

'I said I was busy.'

'I heard that you were busy. What were you busy with?'

A sigh. 'I was with people. We were talking. There was noise. I said I will call him back.'

'Did you?'

'Yes. But he did not answer.'

'Could you tell me exactly what he said?'

Another sigh, longer, deeper, more irritated. 'He said hello, and how are you. He said he missed the unit, and he asked about our other friends.'

'That's it?'

'Yes. I said, "I can't really talk, I'll call you back."'

'He didn't mention that he was on a train?'

'No.'

'He didn't mention that he saw anyone familiar on the train?'

'I told you what he said.'

'How often did he call you?'

'That night?'

'No, in general. Did he call once a week? Once a month?'

Another hesitation. 'Maybe once a month.' And then quickly added: 'Maybe less.'

'To say hi?'

'Yes.'

'Did you call him? From time to time?'

'Not really.'

'Thank you, Sergeant Dimba. That's all for now.'

Dimba discontinued the call without another word.

Griessel looked at Cupido, then at Kaleni. 'That was strange,' he said. 'He's lying. Through his teeth.'

'Colonel,' Vaughn Cupido said, 'this docket is weirder than a warthog on a merry-go-round, I'm telling you.'

Headquarters of the Hawks was a large building in Market Street, Bellville. It was originally designed and built for the South African Revenue Service, but the planning was poor: SARS quickly outgrew it and found a new, larger, home two blocks north, in Teddington Street. Consequently, the Directorate for Priority Crimes Investigation moved in. The DPCI could never entirely fill the building. And in the last few years the numbers of personnel had gradually dwindled, leaving the building with its wide corridors and multiple offices to develop a ghostly atmosphere, helped on by the pitiful inability of the Department of Public Works to keep it maintained.

After five, when the other units of the Hawks began leaving for home, it could be eerily quiet. That was why Colonel Mbali Kaleni's voice carried with ease down the passage and echoed when she called Fillander and company to a meeting.

Fillander, Liebenberg and Ndabeni's footsteps reverberated on the tiled floor, and they crowded into Cupido's office. Griessel and Kaleni sat opposite Cupido.

'Tell them what we know, please,' said Kaleni.

In turn, Griessel and Cupido brought them up to date with the latest developments.

'There are two important matters here,' said Kaleni. 'The first is, why did Johnson Johnson call a former colleague at the VIP Protection Unit? Of all the people in the world, at that moment, just after nine on a Saturday night, from a train. And why would Dimba lie? And why did he protest about being harassed when we were calling about a murder investigation?'

'Because they're a bunch of . . .' Cupido stopped himself because Kaleni did not tolerate bad language ' . . . idiots.'

'Yes,' she said. 'But they've always been a different type of idiot. This is new.'

There was no arguing with that.

'And then,' she continued, 'there's the matter of the Okapi. We know it's a township gang weapon. How does that tie in with Johnson? Or Dimba and the VIP Protection Unit?'

'He recognised someone that night, Colonel,' said Griessel. 'Someone Dimba also knew. Maybe a waiter or a cook or something. We'll have to take a close look at all the train personnel. Rovos might have missed a criminal record somewhere.'

'Maybe Johnson and Dimba were dealing a little, some coke or dagga on the side, for the VIP politicians they were protecting. Maybe they were being supplied by a township gang. Lots of them up there in Gauteng,' said Cupido.

'We'll have to get Johnson's bank records, going back,' said Fillander.

'We'll have to get Dimba's cell-phone records,' said Ndabeni.

'We'll have to try to identify the two old fogeys,' said Cupido.

'That's the strangest thing in all of this. Two old men. It just don't fit,' said Kaleni.

'Maybe they were just getting away from their wives,' said Fillander. 'Maybe they're not connected at all.'

'They're connected,' said Cupido. 'I feel it in my bones.'

'But they're ghosts,' said Kaleni.

'Photos,' said Liebenberg, and everyone looked at him.

'What do you do when you're a tourist on the most luxurious train in the world?' he asked. 'You want to show all your friends you were there so you take photos. We have to call all those passengers and ask them to send us their photos. The ghosts must be on one of them, even if only in the background.'

'That is a brilliant idea,' said Kaleni.

'Of course, only those showing other passengers,' said Liebenberg. 'Just to narrow it down a little.'

'*Ja*. He isn't just a pretty face,' said Fillander.

# 24

Footwork.

In the old days, before the whole world began leaving digital footprints with cell phones, GPS and the internet, that term meant a detective was on foot when investigating a crime. House to house. Up the street and down the street. Searching for witnesses and clues and evasive bits of the docket jigsaw puzzle. It was always pure drudgery, frustrating, exhausting and time-consuming, but that was what you had to do when searching for needles in haystacks.

The members of the Hawks' Serious and Violent Crimes Unit still spoke of footwork, even though it was not as literal these days.

From just after seven in the evening, Griessel and Cupido sat at their computers in an attempt to connect ID numbers to criminal records. Footwork of the fingers, arduous and mechanical. Each individual's details had to be typed in separately. Then they had to wait for the system to respond, and then they fed in the next one. The speed of the system depended on DPCI's line speed and the demand on the central servers. And the accuracy of the investigators' typing, a factor that gradually deteriorated as the night wore on.

They divided the details of the train employees between them. It was a quarter past eleven when they finished. There wasn't a single positive result. Rovos employees were as clean as a baby's conscience.

Arduous footwork that had produced nothing.

They drove home, discouraged and weary.

In the city centre, Griessel stopped at the traffic lights at the junction of Strand Street and Buitengracht. A thought occurred to him and he turned left, towards Cape Town station. He parked in front of the Rovos reception hall. He got out of his car, walked to the parking area behind the station, then towards Adderley Street, looking for the city's CCTV cameras.

There might be footage of the two seventy-year-olds arriving at the station. At least the Metro Police, ineffective as they were, kept the data for ninety days. That was, if all the cameras were working.

He lingered beside the broad main street. It was close to midnight. He remembered his days as a young constable at Caledon Square station, on night duty, walking these deserted streets in the early hours, driving around in an old Datsun police van. How often had he breathed in the atmosphere of this area, the breeze off the harbour redolent of sea and fish, the mountain like a sturdy sentinel behind? And the silence, as if Cape Town took a breather at night to recuperate before the madness of another day.

Knowing that in some way he was jointly responsible for the state of order.

Lord, his life had been so uncomplicated and easy in those days.

He lit a cigarette and stood looking at the imposing traffic roundabout where the fountain once spouted its plumes, back before the Great Drought. Now it was dry and silent. No traffic to speak of. Only a minibus taxi every few minutes, ferrying nightshift workers home.

He couldn't see any cameras.

He sighed. Alexa would be asleep already. He should go home.

Alexa was still awake. She was sitting in the kitchen with her MacBook, busy with spreadsheet numbers and a mug of hot Horlicks. She clucked over him, exclaiming how exhausted he must be. Would he like a hot drink, or food? She'd made soup, and bought fresh bread from Knead Bakery in Kloof Street. He said, no, thank you, they'd had something at the office.

He wavered, wanting to ask her now. His heart beat faster. He had to get it right, had to lie convincingly, control his body language. Don't sit down with her: that would be too formal, too here-comes-something-big. She mustn't suspect.

He said: 'This train docket is wearing us out.'

'Ay,' she said, and touched his hand. 'I can imagine.'

'But we should be finished next week. And then ... Vaughn mentioned a restaurant outside Stellenbosch that you would love. So I wondered ...'

'Benny! That would be marvellous.'

'He even phoned them. They've got space, next Sunday night.' He kept his tone light and casual, then stopped breathing. Would she suspect, spot the snake in the grass? Usually she was the one who planned and made reservations. 'Just to get out a bit,' he added for effect.

Alexa looked at him. There was an instant when he thought, *She knows*, but then her face brightened. 'Oh, that Vaughn,' she said, 'he's such a darling.'

'He is . . .'

He sat down, half disappointed that Cupido was getting the credit, half relieved to get away with the fib. And mildly amused at what his colleague would have to say about the 'darling' label.

'Thank you, my master detective,' Alexa said, 'for thinking of something nice in between all your work. Come on, tell me about your day.' She closed the laptop.

He lay with her in his arms. She always fell asleep so easily. He listened to her breathing, astonished at her ability to put the day behind her so smoothly.

It was because their worlds were so incredibly different. Hers was filled with music and numbers, his with murder and mayhem.

And on the edge of sleep he knew why he was so scared to ask her to marry him.

At five in the morning he went for a ride on his bicycle, the old black-and-white Giant he'd bought at Mohammed 'Love Lips' Faizal's pawnshop in Goodwood.

It was dark and chilly. In the winter he wore tracksuit pants and a long-sleeved T-shirt, a faded windbreaker and cycling gloves. He didn't like the tight, pretentious, expensive gear that sports shops kept trying to sell him. He was soon perspiring, riding up the steep gradient of Kloof Nek. Then he turned left, towards Table Mountain cable-car station, and followed the contour road all around the flank of the mountain to the lookout point where he could see the lights of Parow and Bellville, and the Rhodes Monument below.

All the way he was thinking about his revelation last night. He knew what the source of his fear was: he was terrified Alexa would say no.

He knew she loved him immensely, but what if she was even more afraid than he was? She'd been so damaged by her first marriage. Would she take the chance on a second, with the – slight but undeniable – risk that it could happen again? Maybe the informal arrangement they had now was more acceptable to her. *If it ain't broke, don't fix it,* as Cupido would say.

She knew only too well the dangers of a marriage between two alcoholics. And there was the financial gulf between them. Alexa's wealth wasn't the sort that could supply a Lamborghini in the garage or a mansion in Hermanus, but in comparison with the pauper policeman he was, she was extremely well off. And a good businesswoman to boot. At some stage she must have weighed up the pros and cons of marriage, how it would affect her assets. How could he let her know that he didn't want her money, not even a tiny share of it? He couldn't just pluck out the ring and say: 'Alexa, marry me, but don't worry, we can draw up a pre-nup contract because I'm not after your money.'

He knew she wouldn't just say no. She would look at the ring, and then at him, and then her face would slowly melt, tears would roll down her cheeks, she would take his hand and say with consuming tenderness: 'Ay, Benny, I'm so sorry, but I can't . . .' He could see it. She wouldn't embarrass him.

That was something to be thankful for.

But, still, would he take it like a man if she said no?

While he was still struggling just to pay for the ring?

And what would he do then, on the other side of a 'no'?


He drove to work with his focus on the docket, and with slight unease, a niggle in the back of his mind, knowing that somehow they had overlooked something. He ran through everything from the beginning again, so absorbed that he didn't experience the usual frustration over the delays caused by the freeway construction works and the traffic jamming the N1 beyond Panorama.

Was it something about Robyn Johnson, the ex-wife of the victim, that bothered him?

No, despite the crime statistics that indicated they ought to view her as a suspect.

The lying Sergeant Dimba?

That wasn't what was evading him. He knew Dimba was lying. They would find out why.

The stolen laptop? The missing baggage? The Okapi blade?

He gave up when he parked in the DPCI basement. He knew it would leap out and bite him when he wasn't expecting it. He just had to keep on probing.

## 25

The corridor became a gallery. The IMC printed out all the photos that the train passengers had sent, in black-and-white to keep costs down. Captain Frank Fillander taped them to the wall, on the left-hand side as you walked from Mbali Kaleni's office. First there was a row at eye level, but as the day advanced more photos kept arriving, and the entire wall between the detectives' offices became a chronicle of the journey from Cape Town to Johannesburg, people looking relaxed and smiling, chatting, eating, drinking and looking out over the spectacular scenery of mountains, valleys and plains.

Fillander, Mooiwillem Liebenberg and Vusi Ndabeni tried to iden-tify each passenger on the photos by writing the names in thick black ink beside the faces. It was a slow, torturous process, as they had to make sure who had sent the email and study the accompanying descriptions carefully – not always easy as the information was some-times unclear. The faces were still unfamiliar to them, the photos taken from different angles, and the clothing changing depending on the day the photograph had been taken. The passengers were predomi-nantly white and sixty-plus. 'And,' said Vaughn Cupido, when the trio came to complain about their task, 'seventy is the new sixty, so don't go looking for two geriatrics. They might be pretty sprightly. Just keep going. Keep going.'

Griessel and Cupido were doing footwork of their own. After morning parade they drove to the court to obtain article 205 subpoenas for Johnson's bank account, and the cell-phone records of Sergeant Kagiso Dimba and Robyn Johnson.

'So, have you invited her to the fancy dinner, Benna?' Cupido wanted to know.

'I have,' said Griessel.

'And?'

'She's coming. And she doesn't suspect a thing. I don't think.'

'I'm proud of you, partner.'

One question still weighed heavily on his heart. 'What am I going to do if she says no?'

For once Cupido was lost for words.

'There's always the possibility, Vaughn.'

'*Jissis*, Benna, don't even think it. Don't jinx it from the start.'

'I have to think about it.'

'Of course she'll say yes. That woman loves you big-time. I saw it with my own eyes.'

'I know . . .'

'So don't come talk shit to me.'

'Okay.' Griessel considered for a while. Then: 'I also don't know how to propose. I mean, how do you say it?'

'That's more like it. I can help you with that one. You know I've got the gift of the gab.'

At half past ten they handed over the signed subpoenas to IMC, and on the way out, overhearing one of Captain Philip van Wyk's staff say something about the Johnson bank statements, Griessel knew what had been bothering him the whole morning. 'Follow the money,' he told Cupido.

'What do you mean?'

'The two phantoms. Faku and Green. They must have paid for the train trip.'

'Check.' Cupido's face lit up. 'How did we miss that one? We're off our game, Benna.'

Probably because my head is full of wedding bells, thought Griessel, and Cupido, of course, was fretting about Desiree's boy. But he didn't say any of it. He phoned Brenda Strydom at Rovos to get the payment details of the two mystery passengers. She asked for ten minutes to find them. She called back to tell him that Faku and Green had paid cash into the Rovos account, and gave him the details. Griessel hid his disappointment, and asked for the contact details of Faku and Green's hostess on the train.

'They paid cash,' he told Cupido.

'When?'

'The nineteenth of May. To a teller at First National branch in Table View.'

'Damn.'

Disappointment, as all bank branches had CCTV cameras that stored images of clients when they went in and out, and completed transactions with the tellers. But the images were usually only kept for thirty or forty days, sometimes, at certain bank groups, up to sixty days, but 19 May was too far in the past.

They sat down to telephone the phantoms' rail hostess, but Joanie Delport's number rang and rang before switching to voicemail. They left a message, then wandered out despondently into the corridor to watch Fillander adding to his photo gallery.

The day's only breakthrough was just after three when Philip van Wyk came to fetch Cupido and Griessel. He led them to IMC's big office where the analysis of VIP Protection Unit's Sergeant Kagiso Dimba's cell-phone records was projected onto a big screen.

'The first thing we looked at was that night of August the fifth, the night of the murder,' said Van Wyk. 'The call from Johnson Johnson to Dimba was at twenty-one oh seven. Duration eighty-three seconds. Consequently, the call ended twenty-one oh eight, plus change. As you can see there, Dimba called Johnson back almost immediately, at twenty-one oh nine. And then another six times, the calls between thirty and forty-five seconds apart. Johnson didn't answer any of them.'

'Interesting,' Griessel said.

'Why?' asked Cupido.

'Dimba told us he called back. He knew we would find it on his phone records, but he tried very hard to create the impression that he was in no hurry to call back.'

'But he was.'

'That's not all,' Van Wyk said. 'Dimba made a seventh call. Right after his last attempt to call Johnson back. At twenty-one fifteen, to this number.' Van Wyk used a laser pointer on the screen. 'It belongs to the head of the VIP Protection Unit, Colonel Lucas Gwala. That call was nine minutes and sixteen seconds long.'

'*Aitsa,*' said Cupido.

'We also checked the location of Dimba's phone that night. When Johnson called him, he was connected to cell-phone tower 357801 in Sunnyside, Pretoria. That's near the Sunnyside police station, but it doesn't mean he was at the station. He was on the move after that. At twenty-one twenty-one, tower 355301 in Park Street picked him up, and at twenty-one twenty-nine he connected to tower 354941 at the Union Buildings.'

'That's where the VIP Protection Unit is based,' said Cupido.

'He was stationary there for almost an hour and a half, at the Union Buildings,' Van Wyk said.

'Okay,' said Griessel, making notes. 'So, Dimba talked to Johnson, and then immediately phoned back six times. When he didn't get an answer, he phoned his boss, then drove to his unit at the Union Buildings in a hell of a rush, where he remained for over an hour.'

'That's correct.'

'I smell a rat,' said Cupido.

'The stench is worse than you think,' said Van Wyk. 'There are a few more interesting things that the database shows us. Number one, we have six months of phone records for Johnson and Dimba. In that time they haven't called each other once. I think we can assume they were not best friends.'

'Johnson didn't just phone to say hi,' said Griessel.

'Damn straight,' said Cupido.

'The other fly in the ointment,' said Captain Philip van Wyk, 'is that the detective from Beaufort West was not the first to request Johnson's phone records.'

'Really?'

'We use the same few people at Vodacom to exercise a 205 subpoena. You know how it is, you get to know them and you talk, build relationships . . . When my sergeant spoke to them this morning, the guy said it was the first time he'd had a case being investigated from three different places at the same time. It had to be a very important matter. So Sarge asked, "What do you mean, three places?" And the *ou* said Pretoria, Beaufort West and us. And Sarge asked who the investigator was from Pretoria, as we didn't know about him. Here's the interesting thing. On Sunday, the sixth of August, Colonel Lucas Gwala, commander of the VIP Protection Unit, obtained a 205 for Johnson's records. Even before the body had been found in the Karoo. Before anyone knew that Johnson had been murdered. One day after he'd been thrown off the train.'

'Hit me with your laser stick,' said Vaughn Cupido.

'That's the same *ou* who called Mbali and told her we mustn't harass Dimba,' Griessel said.

'How does that rat smell now?' asked Philip van Wyk.

'I perceive the pungent perfume of shenanigans,' said Cupido. 'Shitty shenanigans.'

It was then that Joanie Delport called back.

# 26

There was undisguised disbelief and a touch of indignation in Joanie Delport's voice during the whole phone interview. She wasn't the least bit intimidated by the detectives, a little disdainful, even, her tone making plain she thought they weren't the sharpest pencils in the box.

'The two old chaps?' she queried. 'The two old *oupas*? Really?'

'That's right,' said Benny Griessel. 'Terrence Faku and Oliver Green. We want—'

'But they were just two old men. Real old *oupas*. Lovable, harmless grandpas. Why would they . . . ? No, it can't be.'

Griessel didn't want to give her too much information, as they knew how easily everything ended up on social media. 'Miss, we're not saying they were the ones. We're looking at everyone on the train.'

'Oh. Okay. But . . . you don't need to worry about them.'

He asked her to start at the beginning, when she'd met them. Her self-confidence wavered for a second. 'There are so many passengers, two trains a week. I can't remember everything.'

'I understand. Just tell us what you do recall.'

She said she remembered their arrival in the departure hall at Cape Town station, because they came a bit late, and were a little embarrassed about it. They turned up in the doorway at the end of the group welcome, each pulling a little suitcase behind him. There was just enough time to say hello before they had to head for the train. She emphasised the positive about the two men, acting as their advocate for the defence. They were 'darlings'; they apologised for being late because of the heavy traffic. 'You get all sorts of people on the train. Nice ones and not so nice, and some are *too* nice. We call the ones like the two *oupas* "Goldilocks guests" – not too hot, not too cold, just right.'

Terrence Faku called her 'my dear'; Oliver Green asked if he could call her 'Joanie'.

She'd shown them to their compartments, each in his own pullman, adjacent to one another.

'Did they ask to be next to each other?'

'You'll have to find out from Bookings.'

Griessel asked if she'd had much contact with them on the train.

'Not really. They kept to themselves. I saw them in the morning and the evening. Two or three times they were sitting in the white man's compartment chatting and having a drink. They talked a lot.'

'The white *oupa* is Green.'

'Obviously.'

'What did they talk about?'

'I'm no eavesdropper, Captain,' she answered curtly. And then, more gently: 'I just . . . I remember coming into Mr Green's compartment while they were chatting. But I don't listen to the guests' conversations.'

'Did you see them in the lounge?' Cupido asked. 'Or the viewing car?'

She thought about that. 'I can't remember, I can't remember precisely . . . We aren't there the whole time, you understand, we've got work to do. I know I did see them in the dining room.'

'Would you recognise them from a photo?'

'Of course!'

'When are you due back in Cape Town?'

'I'm en route back on the train now. It arrives early tomorrow morning.'

Griessel realised it was Friday. The week had flown. 'Can we bring a laptop with photos? Tomorrow morning?' he asked.

'Sure.'

'Joanie,' Cupido said, 'our problem is we can't get hold of the grandpas. We just want to find out if they might have seen something. We've phoned, looked for their addresses, but they're nowhere to be found. It's kind of strange, and we want to make sure they're okay.'

'I see,' she said.

'So, did they tell you anything about where they live or what they do? Anything that can help us find them?'

She was quiet for a long time. 'They said they were pensioners. From the Cape, I think . . .'

'That's it?'

'It was . . . I don't know exactly how it happened, but maybe I asked . . . Most of our passengers are from overseas. So if there are South Africans, you do ask a bit, what they do, where they're from. I remember I had this picture in my mind of the two old chaps chatting on the veranda of the old-age home in Cape Town, two old friends.'

'Did they say they lived in an old-age home?' Griessel asked.

'I really don't . . . The thing is, I try to build a picture in my mind of each guest, who they are, and where they're from so that I can chat to them a little . . . So, I ask a few questions, though you can't get too personal – lots of these people are very private. The picture I had, they were in a retirement home, but I can't swear that's what they said.'

'Anything else in that picture?' Cupido asked.

'Let me think about it. I'll tell you tomorrow.'


The Directorate for Priority Crimes Investigations in the Cape was a creature with many tentacles. The various units included CATS (Crimes Against The State), the Organised Crime Unit, Statutory Crimes, who also dealt with white-collar crimes, Philip van Wyk's IMC, and Mbali Kaleni's Serious and Violent Crimes Unit.

The overarching head was Brigadier Musad Manie, the 'head honcho of the Cape Town Hawks', as Cupido sometimes referred to him with a measure of pride. Musad, the Hawks investigators had discovered from a Muslim friend, meant 'loosed camel' in Arabic. Members of the South African Police Service liked giving their fellows nicknames. Senior officers in particular. That was how, in the DPCI, he had come to be known as 'the Camel'. To the *hase* (rabbits or hares, as policemen generally called the general public, since people who needed the police usually looked like frightened hares in the headlights), it would seem strange because Musad Manie was nothing like a camel. He was a strong man, broad in the chest and shoulders, with a face of granite lines, and a determined chin. Straight from Hollywood Central Casting.

If the Camel intercepted you in the corridor outside the IMC rooms and asked you to pop in, you turned briskly and went with him, while rapidly running through your mind for any recent transgression, the probability being high that you were about to be dragged over the coals. For something serious.

That was exactly what Griessel and Cupido did at 16.17 that Friday afternoon. The Camel invited them to his office. They followed Manie immediately, exchanging a single anxious glance of solidarity.

Colonel Mbali Kaleni was already seated at the round conference table in the brigadier's office. She seemed more concerned than angry. Manie asked the two detectives to join her. He sat down, made a tent of his large hands, thrust out his formidable chin. For Kaleni's sake he spoke English. In his mellifluous tone he said: 'Gentlemen, I had a call from the national commissioner.'

They were silent. They knew he was referring to the national commissioner of the SAPS, not the national head of the Hawks. They knew this meant a great deal more trouble.

'It was an interesting call, to say the least.' Manie's tone was pleasant and devoid of irony, as if describing some unique experience. 'The commissioner told me he had spoken to the national director of Public Prosecutions, and he then talked to our honourable minister of police, before giving me the call. And both these esteemed gentlemen asked him to convey to me their full support in the matter. Now, Lieutenant Colonel Kaleni has briefed me on the details of the case concerning the late Johnson Johnson and I am, to say the least, a little puzzled. But let me not speculate. This is what the commissioner told me. It seems that Johnson called a Sergeant Kagiso Dimba on the night of the fifth of August – Dimba being a former colleague of Johnson at the VIP Protection Unit. And during that call Johnson told Dimba that he was going to commit suicide.'

Cupido made a sound as if he were choking. Manie held up a hand for order.

'And he also gave Sergeant Dimba the reason for his planned suicide. He said he was going to kill himself because he just couldn't contemplate a future without his beloved wife.' Still no hint of sarcasm. 'Dimba was, of course, deeply upset, and tried to talk Johnson out of it. But Johnson just said goodbye, and even though Dimba called back several times, Johnson did not answer. So, Dimba called his commanding officer, Colonel Lucas Gwala, to ask what he should do. The good colonel told Dimba to come and see him, which he did. They realised there was nothing they could do, because Johnson never divulged information during his call to Dimba as to his whereabouts. Nothing, except to get an article 205 subpoena, and try to find out where Johnson was. Which they did the next day. Our national commissioner also told me that Sergeant Dimba has been racked with guilt, because he did not provide Benny here with full and complete details about the call. But, says the commissioner, it was because he wanted to protect a former colleague and dear friend's reputation, and the good name of the VIP Protection Unit.'

Mbali Kaleni said, '*Hayi*,' and clicked her tongue.

The Camel raised a huge hand. 'Sergeant Dimba and Colonel Gwala now wish to extend their deepest apologies to me, to Lieutenant Colonel Kaleni, and to Benny. They realise their loyalty was somewhat misplaced, but they hope we will understand that it was all done in the spirit of protecting the Great Police Brotherhood.'

'They don't know about the Okapi blade in the back of Johnson's head,' said Benny Griessel.

'Obviously,' said Kaleni.

'And so, the commissioner asked me, in the light of this information, that we do not persevere with an investigation that was evidently a suicide, and lay the matter to rest.'

## 27

'Is that what you want us to do, Brigadier?' Cupido asked.

'That is all, colleagues. Thank you very much,' said Musad Manie.

'Thank you, sir,' said Kaleni, and stood up.

The detectives followed her example, said goodbye to Manie and followed Kaleni out of the door.

In the corridor Cupido said: 'But, Colonel, this is crazy. The man was stabbed. He was murdered.'

Kaleni kept on walking, her heels click-clacking down the passage.

'Colonel, please,' said Cupido, desperation breaking through into his voice.

She halted. The short Zulu woman looked up at him. 'Captain, did your mother ever read Dr Seuss to you?' she asked.

'Colonel?'

'Dr Seuss. Did your mother ever read his books to you?'

'No, I . . . uh . . .' said Vaughn Cupido. 'We were a very healthy family.'

'Dr Seuss wrote children's books, Captain.'

'Oh, right.'

'You know what my favourite quote from Dr Seuss is?'

'No, Colonel.'

'"The more that you read, the more things you will know. The more that you learn, the more places you'll go." My mother made me recite it over and over again.'

'It's a good one,' said Griessel, who also had never heard of Dr Seuss, but he knew she was giving them a hidden message and he was trying to understand it.

'So, we will walk to the library. To learn and to go places,' Mbali Kaleni said.

They followed her, dumbstruck, out of the Hawks building, turned left and first right into Carl van Aswegen Street, to the Bellville Library Centre.

Just over two years ago Colonel Kaleni had been very large. Vaughn Cupido had taken exception to the euphemism. 'The Flower is fat,' he had said. 'It doesn't help to throw around politically correct terminology like "rotund" or "plus size" or "overweight". She's fat. Very fat. Finish and *klaar*.' In those days his relationship with her was strained, the result of a personality clash and his envy at her promotion.

In the meantime, Kaleni – to everyone's surprise – had lost a great deal of weight by following the Banting lifestyle, and in the crucible of fighting serious and violent crime the relationship between her and Vaughn had advanced to a ceasefire, and eventually to wary mutual respect.

As she walked to the library ahead of them, Cupido thought how strange it was: she was just a slim shadow of her former self, but she retained the gait of a fat woman. The old waddle that said, 'I'm fat and I don't tolerate any nonsense,' was still there, especially when she was on the warpath. As now.

She led them to a quiet corner of the library and waved them to seats at the table.

They sat down. She sat too.

Kaleni looked around before leaning forward conspiratorially and whispering: 'You know I love this country.'

'Yes, Colonel,' they said quietly.

'You know I am an honest person.' Her expression was most solemn.

'Yes, Colonel,' said Griessel.

'Painfully honest,' said Cupido. 'Sometimes.'

She ignored his remark. 'You know I like to do things by the book. Even when it's difficult.'

'Yes, Colonel,' they both replied.

'Now, I must tell you I can no longer be honest and do things by the book,' she said.

They waited for her to explain. She stared out of the library window, turned her face back to them and took a deep breath. 'I don't have to tell you about the state-capture mess.'

Griessel looked at Cupido, who said: 'No, Colonel. We know.'

'We are in very deep trouble. The whole Crime Intelligence Division of the SAPS is corrupt and captured. There's no doubt that the national director of Public Prosecutions is a corrupt and captured man. And that our minister of police is a corrupt and captured man, and so is the president of the nation. Captured and corrupted by three Indian criminals who masquerade as businessmen. I'm not sure about the national commissioner of police, but he takes his orders from the corrupt minister, so he has no credibility any more.'

'But we are not captured, Colonel,' said Cupido, with passion.

'That's right, Captain. We're not captured. And that's exactly why I cannot now be honest and do things by the book at the same time. Because the book says to follow the commissioner's orders. And we're not going to do that. These are the darkest days in our nation's history since apartheid. These are desperate times. My mother and father were activists in the struggle. There were times when I was very worried about the risks they were taking, the things they were planning and doing. They always used to say: "Desperate times call for desperate measures." So now I'm saying that. I believe the VIP Protection Unit in Pretoria is corrupt and captured. They're trying to hide something, and I think that something is very serious. And I think that something can be very detrimental to those three Indian criminals and their state capture. I think Johnson Johnson heard or saw something on that train that's making all the corrupt people very nervous, and that's why the minister and the director of Public Prosecutions put so much pressure on the commissioner. That's why they concocted this nonsense about a suicide. And why the commissioner called Brigadier Manie. But the brigadier didn't order us to stop the investigation. Like Dr Seuss said, the more you read, the more things you will know. I read between the lines of the brigadier's instructions. And between the lines he indicated to us that we should continue with the investigation. And that we should be very, very careful. And that's exactly what we're going to be doing. Very carefully, very low-key and very crafty.'

'What do you mean?' Cupido wanted to know.

'You remember the Cobra?' she asked them.

They nodded. They remembered the case well – a few years ago a British scientist was abducted near Franschhoek and the Hawks had

had to clean up the nest of hired assassins. Griessel was shot and barely escaped death. In the process they had to sidestep South Africa's National Intelligence Agency too.

'It'll be like that again. Under the radar. Except we'll have to be even more careful. This time we don't know who we can trust. Even in our own midst.'

'Are you saying there are Cape Town Hawks who are . . . captured?' Cupido seemed to have difficulty linking all those words in the same sentence.

'I'm saying we can only trust each other.'

'Jesus,' said Cupido. 'The kid was right.'

'*Hayi*,' said Kaleni. 'Don't use the Lord's name in vain. What kid are you talking about?'

Cupido explained about his girlfriend's son.

Kaleni shook her head. 'This is not what we struggled for,' she said. 'Even the children know . . .'

As the late-afternoon readers began to fill the library, she had to lean closer across the table to make her whispered words audible. She said they were not going to use any of the SAPS systems during their investigation. The corrupt and hijacked had eyes everywhere. They would monitor the systems so they would not mention the Johnson docket again in morning parades. And talk to no one about the case.

'But what about Uncle Frankie and Vusi and Willem?' Griessel wanted to know.

'You'll have to make them read between the lines,' Kaleni said. 'And I'll have to allocate other dockets to them as well.'

'We can trust them, right?' said Cupido.

'Of course.'

Cupido sighed in relief.

'This case is going nowhere, Colonel,' said Griessel. 'We've got nothing. Only the knowledge that Dimba is lying and that the VIP Protection Unit is trying to mislead us. Apart from that, we have zero.'

'Zilch,' said Cupido.

'Have you exhausted all avenues of enquiry?'

'No, Colonel.'

She gave them the familiar Kaleni look, intense and serious.

They closed off the Johnson Johnson docket in the SAPS national computer system, listing the cause of death as suicide. Griessel made copies of everything in the physical file before delivering the original to Kaleni for her signature.

In the corridor, Cupido began taking down the photos that he and Fillander had put up with so much effort. He stored them in his office.

They went to tell Fillander, Ndabeni and Liebenberg that the docket had been closed. They also whispered into each man's ear to gather in half an hour's time, a quarter past six that Friday afternoon, at Johnson Johnson's flat in Olympus Street, Springbok Park.

Fillander phoned his wife to tell her he would be late – again.

They set off, to put up the photographs in the victim's flat, in the open-plan living area, and the passage, in both bedrooms and in the one and a half bathrooms. They worked till close on midnight to complete all the information about the people on the photos and make cross-references.

They found no trace of Faku or Green.

# 28

Benny Griessel was dreaming. He was sitting opposite Alexa Barnard in an expensive restaurant, scrabbling through his pockets, but the ring was gone. Then he realised it was on the table, beside the candle. The candle was burning with a deep red flame, casting an unnaturally rosy glow on Alexa's face.

'Do you want to ask me something, Benny?' She seemed impatient.

He picked up the little jewel box with the ring in it. His fingers trembled and he fumbled opening it. The diamond looked minuscule. He felt so ashamed, wished the earth would swallow him. His voice was shrill, nervous and pleading: 'Alexa, marry me. Please.'

He stared at her intently. He watched her face slowly melt and the tears begin to roll down her cheeks. She reached for his hand, took it with great tenderness. 'Ay, Benny, I'm so sorry, but I can't . . .'

He awoke, shivering with fear.

Saturday morning.

The Rovos train was beautiful. In the twilight of a platform at Cape Town station, its elegant gunmetal grey and silvery white was in stark contrast to Transnet's grubby, dilapidated carriages and the graffiti-smeared Metro Rail rolling stock. It was like a visitor with the style and elegance of a bygone era, holding out the promise of exotic destinations.

Joanie Delport met them on the platform. She handed them a document in an elegant Rovos cover. 'This is a photocopy of the train's log,' she said. 'Mrs Strydom said she's sorry not to get it to you sooner, but it's only available in hard copy.'

'The log?' Cupido asked.

'Yes. The hospitality manager of the train keeps it. He writes down when the train stops or departs. What time and where.'

They thanked her.

She invited Griessel and Cupido to step on board.

In the long corridor of the carriage the ochre of the wood glowed in the light of stylish lamps. There were beautiful original paintings on the panels, and the carpet under their feet was thick and luxurious.

Even Cupido was quiet.

She showed them the compartments. They looked at the names of rivers above each one, at the large windows, the beds and sofas, the ingeniously designed bathrooms. Staff busied themselves vacuuming and dusting, bringing clean linen, making beds. She led them through the dining room, with snow-white tablecloths, crystal and silverware, and at last to the lounge at the very end, where they could sit on deep couches to show her the hundreds of photos of the passengers on the laptop.

Initially she said no to each photo, not spotting Terrence Faku or Oliver Green in any of them. Later she just shook her head. Photo after photo, without success, while Griessel and Cupido's hopes faded and their hopes plummeted.

But when photo 286 appeared on the screen, she suddenly said: 'Wait, go back one.'

Cupido tapped the computer. The previous photo reappeared. It had been taken in the dining room during lunch as light was pouring through the windows, a Karoo landscape outside.

Delport leaned close to the screen. She stared for a long time, then lifted a finger and said: 'There. That's . . . I think that's Green.'

The photo had been taken with a cell phone. The windows were bright, the people in the dining room poorly lit. And the man she pointed out was four tables away from the camera, only the back of his head and small part of his profile visible. His head was turned twenty degrees to the right, as if he was planning to look at the view. His right arm was partly raised and he had something in his hand. A piece of cutlery, perhaps. And opposite him, just a glimpse of his companion, the upper part of a grey-haired man's hairline. A black man, perhaps.

They didn't sigh. They didn't moan. Griessel just asked: 'Are you sure?'

'I . . . Almost certain . . . Yes, yes, it has to be him.'

Cupido marked the photo, then went on to the next.

It turned out to be the only one where she could point out either of the two phantom men.

Joanie Delport offered them coffee, but they declined politely, and asked if they could go to where Mrs Scherpenzeel slept, then to Faku, Green and Johnson's compartments.

First she had to determine exactly where Mrs Scherpenzeel had stayed, then led them from the restaurant carriage to her royal suite. A few minutes later they walked towards the locomotive, to Green's compartment, and two carriages on to where Johnson would have slept. She slid the door open and they stood in the pullman suite where Johnson had been stabbed in the back of the head with an Okapi blade.

Griessel inspected the sliding lock of the door to the corridor. Small, neat and effective.

'Some of the passengers forget to lock the door from inside at night,' she said, 'because there's no key to turn.'

Griessel told her that, as he understood it, Johnson's sofa would have been converted into a bed by the time he returned from the dining room.

She nodded.

He tried to picture it: the sofa folded out into a double bed, the small table moved out of the way. A narrow strip of floor between the door and the window, where Johnson would stand and talk to Dimba on his cell phone. His back to the door?

Cupido waited patiently, because he knew what his partner was doing. It was Griessel's gift to imagine himself into that moment. But Vaughn knew this was a skill for which Griessel had paid a price.

Griessel slid the door open and shut. It was relatively quiet. When the train was on the move, there would be the noise of wind and wheels on the track. The clickety-clack over the rail joints. Johnson would have been focused on the phone call, listening to Dimba. His voice might have been loud and heated. He didn't hear the door open. The wound was deep and straight, a fast, powerful, stabbing action, from directly behind.

Griessel looked at the wooden blinds hanging above the windows. 'Are the blinds closed at night?' he asked Delport.

'Yes, but a lot of the guests open them again if we're moving.'

'How often are the windows and blinds cleaned?'

'After every trip.'

Too late to get fingerprints.

He walked to the window. It shifted easily, opened wide. Two people to lift the body and swing it out. Johnson had weighed ninety kilograms approximately. It would have taken some effort. Driven by the adrenalin of fear, urgency and murderous intent. Two men of seventy-something who were still fit and lively.

Difficult. But possible.

'Thank you,' he said, and turned around.

Outside, at the car, Cupido said he would give the photo to Lithpel Davids. Perhaps he could do something with it.

Sergeant Reginald 'Lithpel' Davids worked with Philip van Wyk at IMC. Everyone considered him a technological miracle worker.

Griessel said that Lithpel was still trying to get Johnson's phone to work.

'We haven't got a thing, Benna,' said Cupido.

'There are more photos on the way.'

'If we haven't got lucky *yet*, what are the chances?'

'I know.' He shared the feeling that they weren't going to make the breakthrough with this one.

'We can talk to the ex again. She might have learned something about corrupt politicians from JJ's stint at the VIP Protection Unit. Maybe she knows the Green guy on the photo.'

'Maybe he said something to WO Neville Bandjies, his old friend from Brackenfell station.'

'But who can we trust?'

'I don't know. Robyn . . . The VIP Protection Unit cost her her marriage. I think we can trust her.'

'Maybe you're right. See you at the office.'

From the Hawks' offices they drove together to Robyn's Ark in Brackenfell, the traffic around them dense and slow.

Cupido took out his phone while Griessel was driving and found what he was looking for: 'Okay, Benna, so last night I was doing some research. I found this website, Wedding Bells dot com. Everything you ever wanted to know about getting hitched but were too bashful to ask. And there's an article about how to pop the question. This dude reckons, "The secret to asking for your beloved's hand in marriage is to keep it simple. The moment can be tense and overwhelming for both of you, and women have a sixth sense about these things anyway. So, a James Joyce stream-of-consciousness speech just won't do."'

'James who?'

'Joyce. I cannot lie to you, I had to google him. He's an Irish novelist who wrote this hectic novel. A landmark, they call it. *Ulysses*. About an *ou* in Dublin, the whole book is just what this *ou* thinks. The whole time. Think, think, think. Crock of shit, it sounds like to me. Anyway, the general idea is, keep it simple. And then . . .'

'What does "keep it simple" mean? Do you just ask straight out?'

'No, brother, it means don't embroider. Don't make a long speech, don't go fetch the baboon from behind the mountain, don't beat about the bush.'

'But *what* do you say?'

'Well, that's what I'm trying to help you with. I gave it extensive thought, and I suppose you tune her – wait for it, this is good stuff. You tune her, "Alexa, you are the love of my life. I want to spend the rest of my life with you. I would be deeply honoured if you would accept my hand in marriage." That's all you say.'

Griessel was quiet for ages, then said: 'It's not bad, Vaughn . . .'

'Not bad? Of course it's not bad. It's perfect.'

'Thank you,' Benny Griessel said. And he meant it.

But he remembered his dream and shivered.

# 29

The pet shop was a hive of activity. Outside in the garden children were playing with the rabbits and feeding chickens, ducks and geese; inside, customers were shopping for puppies, bird cages, fish tanks and pet food.

They looked for Robyn, who spotted them first. 'Out! Out of my shop,' she said, as she approached them.

'I'm sorry?' said Vaughn Cupido.

'Out. And make it snappy.' Her voice was calm, as if she didn't want to disturb the customers.

'What's the matter now?'

She came right up to them. 'Suicide? You've got to be kidding me. You're useless. Get out of my shop. Now!'

'Where did you hear *that*?' Griessel asked.

'In the newspapers. That's where I have to hear it, because you're too useless to come tell me yourself. Now get out.' She pointed at the door.

They turned round and left, stopped outside.

'*Fok*,' said Cupido.

Griessel called the Hawks liaison officer.

'Benny?' John Cloete answered.

'When did we tell the press that the Johnson Johnson case was suicide, John?'

'It wasn't us. I hear it came from Pretoria. The commissioner's office.'

'Yesterday?'

'Yes. Last night. Too late for TV, but early enough for the morning papers.'

'Thanks, John.' He rang off and passed the message on to Cupido.

'They're in a hurry, Benna, the commissioner's office. Like there's pressure.'

'Yes.'

'What do we do now? Are we going to talk to Neville Bandjies?'

'I don't know, Vaughn. I just have a feeling about him . . .'

'That he's corrupt?'

'No. That he'll put his career first if they give him difficult choices.'

'Right.'

'We'll have to wait till the shop is quiet and try Robyn again. Do you feel like feeding the chickens?'

'Story of my life. I'm a swooping Hawk, but now I get to feed the chickens.'

They waited outside in the weak winter sun and chilly wind. Every now and then they saw Robyn Johnson glaring at them, but she didn't come out to chase them away.

They talked about the Johnson docket. They went through everything they knew, evaluating the information, building theories, breaking them down again.

At eleven minutes past eleven, short, fat Arnold from PCSI phoned Griessel. 'Suicide? You reckon it's *suicide*? I'm riding along on a fancy train, and I pick up an Okapi and stab myself in the back of the head, break off the blade, then throw myself out the window. Because I'm Superman and I'm just tired of living. Brilliant detective work, Benny. You don't need *us* any more. You don't need the SAPS. You can write comic books and make bags of money. Are you sure Johnson didn't eat kryptonite? Just do us a favour, don't waste our time. We have other cases open, piles and piles of them. We've got a backlog of weeks. Months. But when you asked, we dropped everything. And now it's suicide. This honeymoon is over. Just so you know.'

'Are you finished?'

'Yes. With the Hawks I am completely finished.'

'Did you find something on the blade?'

'You won't believe it, but we found Batman's fingerprints. We can say with absolute certainty that he really is Bruce Wayne. So the big question is: why did Batman take off his Batgloves? If you can work that out, you'll know instantly who committed suicide. Oh, wait, it was Johnson. Superman Johnson. Case closed.'

'Did you find something, Arnold?'

'Coriander.'

'Coriander?'

'That's right, coriander. Johnson Johnson cut himself some biltong before he stabbed himself in the back of the neck. The Last Supper. Biltong. Patriotic to the end.'

'Are you serious?'

'What's going on, Benny? What the fuck is going on?'

'The national commissioner's office told the press that it was suicide. And instructed us that the case is closed.'

Arnold was silent for a long time, until he said: 'I see.' And then: 'What do we do with the blade? And the report?'

'Send it to Mbali. Are you serious about the coriander?'

'Yes. Coriander and red wine vinegar. Microscopic residue. Enough to suggest the knife was used to carve biltong.'

'No fingerprints?'

'Nothing we could work with.'

'Thank you, Arnold.'

'What's happening to us, Benny?' It was a rhetorical question.

Arnold rang off before Griessel could reply that he didn't have a clue either.


He phoned Joanie Delport. She said she couldn't really talk because she had guests in the reception hall.

'Did you ever see Faku or Green eating biltong?' He heard voices in the background, people laughing and chatting.

She said: 'I'll call you back.'

After seventeen minutes of watching children feeding and petting animals, and customers coming and going, the call came.

'Faku. I didn't see him eating biltong, but on the table in his compartment, there was . . . You know when you carve biltong, the fine bits it leaves, and those little shells from the spices?'

'The coriander?'

'Yes. Every evening I wiped the table clean, because he would carve biltong there.'


After twelve it quietened down. Robyn Johnson came out and sternly said they should go through to her office. She let them wait there for her for another quarter of an hour. Then she entered, closed the door and burst into tears. 'JJ didn't commit suicide,' she said, through her sobs.

'Robyn . . .' Cupido consoled her.

'What do I tell the girls? What do I tell them? Daddy didn't want you any more and he killed himself? It's impossible. You're useless – that's not what happened.'

'We know,' said Cupido.

She sprang to her feet. 'You know?' she screamed. 'You know my children's daddy didn't kill himself, but you told the papers that? What sort of people are you? What sort of cruel, heartless animals are you? Don't you think about the children? Don't you think about the families and friends and the legacy of a good man? Those two girls of mine, this is going to haunt them for the rest of their lives. People whispering behind their hands, their daddy killed himself. Did you think of that?'

Cupido kept holding his hand in the air to calm her down, but she ignored it.

At last she sat down. Her shoulders shook. Tears on the desk.

'We're so sorry . . .' Griessel tried.

'Shut the fuck up,' she said.

'It wasn't us who told that to the papers,' Cupido said.

'Are you not the SAPS?'

'It was Pretoria. They're trying to hide something. We're under orders to drop the case.'

She looked up, her eyes bloodshot. 'My God,' she said.

They told her they were going on with the investigation, but she mustn't tell a soul. No matter how difficult it was. She wrestled with the thought, the injustice of it, the damage, but eventually, after they had explained in broad strokes what they knew, she nodded.

'That nest of vipers,' she said. 'That VIP Protection Unit. JJ told me that's what it really was, a vipers' nest. Politicians carrying on. Young girls. Prostitutes and groupies. Booze. Lots of booze. The high life. And the bodyguards have to arrange it all, and the bodyguards have to cover it up. And the bodyguards take the spoils, the leftovers. That's their compensation. JJ was discreet, but over time he let things slip.

Never any details. Never named names. They were all too loyal, the whole lot of them. But I'm telling you here today, that unit, that's what ruined my marriage.'

'Did he mention corruption? To do with the Indians? State capture?' Griessel asked.

She wiped away her tears. 'One time . . . After he'd left the unit, six months ago now, state capture was all over the news all the time, those emails that were leaked. I went to pick up the girls one night at his flat, and they were already asleep, and he said: "Come sit." He opened a bottle of wine, and we talked like the old times. And then he came out with these things. Not a lot, he was being quite vague. I could hear he was torn between disgust and loyalty. Funny business. Shady stuff. Midnight meetings, bags of cash the Indians brought them. Then the Johnnie Walker Blue Label would start flowing, and money would be packed out on the tables, like drug-dealers. He said he would never forget it – they had such sly smiles, those Indian magnates. Like "We own you, you dumb natives." Then they would pour a drink for the bodyguards too, pretend to be their biggest buddies, arm around them. But always those sly smiles . . .'

'That's all?'

'That's all he said to me. But I could sense there was more.'

'Who was he guarding in those days? When the Blue Label was flowing?'

'Dumisa. The minister of state security.'

# 30

They walked into Sergeant Reginald 'Lithpel' Davids's cubicle behind the IMC locale. He was wearing designer ripped jeans, a T-shirt and sandals. The T-shirt bore the words: *The universe is made up of protons, neutrons, electrons and morons.* There had been an attempt to give him the new nickname of 'Lollipop' due to his tall, skinny figure and massive Afro hairstyle, but the old one had stuck – for years he had had a bad lisp before it had been surgically corrected.

'Don't your feet get cold in those sandals, Lithpel?' Cupido asked.

Davids didn't look up from the computer screen. 'If I could hang around outside on a Saturday morning, like a normal person, they would be cold. But now I have to sit here trying to enhance pics of geriatrics for two *cappies* chasing a dead-as-a-doornail docket. So, no, my feet are fine, but my heart is cold. Towards you.'

'You know you're just a sergeant, don't you?'

'So everybody keeps reminding me. Temporary situation, though.'

'Can we have a look?' Cupido pointed at the screen.

'Be my guest.'

They walked around the desk and stood behind him.

The face of the man who might be Oliver Green was somewhat clearer, better lit, but the photo was very grainy. Griessel was disappointed. 'Is that the best you can do?' he asked.

Lithpel shook his head in disgust. 'Now let me get this straight. You send me a badly exposed pic taken with a five-year-old iPhone Six Plus. A mighty eight megapixels, praise the Lord. And then some other idiot compresses it too. And you ask me, *cappie*, if that is the best we can do?'

Griessel realised he had stepped on sensitive toes. 'Sorry, I know you're doing your best, Lithpel. I was just asking . . .'

'*Cappie*, what you see here is nothing short of a miracle, thanks to me and the best off-the-shelf software the SAPS can afford. Unless you want to send it to the FBI or spend a gazillion bucks on a private lab, that's the best it's ever going to be.'

'What if we can get you the original uncompressed photo?' asked Cupido.

'You're going to get a little less noise, but not all that much. I can give you a version that's cropped less, where the man is a bit smaller. It will be less grainy.'

'Give us a couple of options. Anything.'

'Okay.' He manipulated the mouse. 'Printing the first one now.'

'Johnson's cell phone?'

'I've got it up and running. No good news. A few SMSes, a few WhatsApps, mostly to the ex, and a few tourism contacts. He was on Instagram and Facebook, but he didn't post much. He was more of a lurker. And he liked puzzle games, *nogal*. There's no smoking gun there.' He showed the phone that was lying on the workbench between his equipment. 'Feel free to fiddle. Oh, and my *cappie* said that that Johnson dude's bank statements are on his desk. They came in late.'

They studied Johnson Johnson's bank statements. They told a heroic story of a man struggling to keep his head above water, and eventually just managing it. There were no remarkable deposits, no odd transactions. Just a former policeman who had to scrape by, with a gradual improvement in the last months of his life, as his ex-wife had suggested.

They drove back to the pet shop to show Robyn the three photos that Davids had printed out.

She shook her head. She didn't know Oliver Green. She asked: 'Was it him who killed JJ?'

They said they didn't know.

'Am I imagining it or is he a bit on the old side?'

They just looked at her.

'That's all you've got? That old man?' she asked in disgust.

They had nothing to say in their defence.

While they were with her, Griessel's phone rang. It was Professor Phil Pagel. Griessel let it go over to voicemail.

He only listened to the message once they were walking to the car. 'Nikita, I saw the newspaper. I assume you have your reasons.'

Shame burned through him. It was just like it was back in the apartheid days, the lies and deceit.

They phoned ahead, drove to Oakglen, in Bellville, where Colonel Mbali Kaleni lived. From the front door of her little townhouse they could smell baking. Kaleni opened the door. She was wearing a white apron. 'You're just in time for fresh zucchini bread. No carbs,' she said, and Cupido swore she gave him a meaningful look.

They sat in the breakfast nook. She asked if they wanted coffee. They said, yes, please. She put the kettle on, fetched a block of mature Cheddar from the fridge and began to grate it.

Griessel opened the docket and took out the three photos that Lithpel Davids had provided. He put them on the counter, so that she could see. 'This is the only photo we have of one of the suspects.'

She looked at it while she grated. 'Perhaps there's just enough for someone to recognise him, if we had the freedom to call on the media's help.'

'We want to give you our theory,' Griessel said, taking out his notebook. 'A lot of it is just speculation, but it's the best we have.'

'Go ahead.' She put the grater into the sink, began to make the coffee.

'Our two suspects, Mr Terrence Faku and Mr Oliver Green, booked the Rovos train between Cape Town and Pretoria, using those false identities,' said Griessel, 'three months in advance. They booked adjacent compartments. They must have had their reasons for using false names and passport numbers, and for wanting to be close to each other, but we have no idea what those reasons were. What we do know is that the fake IDs were not created to perpetrate this crime. When they booked their trip, Johnson Johnson didn't even know he was going to be on it. We think this is significant. I'll get back to that in a moment.'

'Okay,' said Kaleni. She put the mugs of coffee on the counter, beside the artificial sweetener. 'Help yourself.' Then she went to the fridge and took out some jam. 'Sugar-free jam,' she said, and looked at Cupido again.

He wondered if she'd heard somewhere that he was also on the Banting diet now. Who would have told her? You just couldn't trust anyone.

Kaleni took the zucchini bread out of the oven. It smelt delicious. She put it on a cooling rack. 'Sorry, Benny, please proceed.'

'So, on the fifth of August the two phantoms board the train, and mostly keep to themselves. There are no photos showing them in the lounge or the viewing car. Only one, in the dining car. If we add that to the fake IDs, we can say that maybe they didn't want to be seen, and seen together, too much. They wanted to fly under the radar. But they did eat together. So, they mustn't have been *too* worried about the risk. Which is a bit strange. Why then go to the trouble of using false IDs?'

'Well, maybe because it was easy,' said Cupido. 'Rovos doesn't ask people to present their passports before they board.'

'So,' Benny Griessel said, 'we've drawn up a timeline for the night of the fifth of August.'

'Everybody is having dinner, from seven o'clock onwards,' said Cupido.

'Johnson is sitting with Mrs Scherpenzeel, and we assume Faku and Green are sitting together,' said Griessel.

'Then, somewhere close to nine,' Cupido went on, 'people start getting up and leaving, and Johnson recognises one of the two phantoms. Maybe for the first time. But he doesn't get up, he doesn't say anything.'

'At ten to nine, Mrs Scherpenzeel tells Johnson she wants to call home. They get up and he escorts her back to her compartment,' said Griessel. 'And at eight minutes and twenty-three seconds past nine, we believe Johnson was killed. Those are our two markers.'

'Benny and I walked through the train this morning,' said Cupido. 'We think leaving the dining car, walking an old lady to her door and saying goodnight might have taken five minutes, max.'

'So, Johnson says goodnight to Mrs Scherpenzeel, and now he's walking to his own compartment, towards the front of the train,' said Griessel. 'This will take him past the doors of Faku and Green.'

'Johnson made the call to Kagiso Dimba at seven minutes past nine.'

'So we have twelve minutes in which something happened that connected Faku, Green and Johnson,' Kaleni mused.

'A connection,' said Cupido, 'that had two consequences.'

'The first was something that made Johnson call Dimba, a man he had not spoken to in many months, a man he used to work with,' said Griessel.

'The second was that Green and Faku needed to kill Johnson Johnson,' said Cupido.

'We think they had to do it together, because Johnson was young and fit,' said Griessel.

'Our team contacted just about all the passengers on that train. Nobody heard anything like an argument or a scuffle. So, Johnson walked past the compartments of Faku and Green, and maybe stopped by to say a few words. Or he saw something. Or the two phantoms recognised him as a danger or some such.'

'It took us just over four minutes to walk from Mrs Scherpenzeel's compartment past Faku's to where Johnson would have slept. But with other passengers in the passage, let's stretch that to more than five minutes,' said Griessel.

'And,' said Cupido, 'let's say we add another minute for Johnson to finally enter his own compartment, take out his phone, find the number and make the call, we still have about four minutes unaccounted for.'

'Maybe Johnson just stood in the passage, looking out of the window,' said Griessel

'Or in his compartment, opening the window. Or taking a leak. But he didn't take off his jacket. Or lock his door. Which makes us think maybe he called the moment he entered his compartment.'

'So, he's talking to Dimba,' said Griessel. 'The sliding door is very quiet, and he's on the phone, and the train is making a noise on the tracks, so he doesn't hear them . . .'

'They must have followed him, or how else would they have known where his compartment was? Something must have happened, something to make them follow him. Something more than just saying a few words . . .'

'And they come in, and stab him with brute force in the back of the head.'

'Brute force. So something must have made them very angry,' said Cupido, 'to use an Okapi biltong knife in such a way. Or very desperate.'

'We have this one little piece of evidence,' said Griessel, 'that ties

Faku to the Okapi. Forensics found traces of coriander and red wine vinegar on the blade, and Faku's hostess confirmed that he carved biltong in his compartment.'

'If you take the fake IDs, their behaviour and the biltong, it's likely they were the perpetrators.'

# 31

'Now, here's another interesting thing,' Griessel said, as he paged through his notebook. 'We got hold of the train's log book. It records when the train stopped, where it stopped, and for how long. At the time the murder was committed, the train was moving, about seventy kilometres south of Beaufort West. But then, at nine thirty-four, it stopped at Beaufort West station, until five minutes past four the next morning . . .'

'So these two guys, the two phantoms, knew they had a dead body in a compartment and they were scheming how to get rid of it for six hours,' said Cupido.

'Because they knew an investigation would tie them to Johnson. Somehow. Or at least their false IDs would make them suspect. But the fact that they sat with that body for six hours and *then* decided to dump it out the window, along with the cell phone, and maybe take his laptop . . . It does say something.'

Kaleni had been listening attentively. Then she nodded, took out three plates and set places for them on the counter.

'Johnson's ex-wife says he did mention a few things about the Indian businessmen who are now suspected of corruption and state-capture activities,' said Cupido. 'That he witnessed some late-night shenanigans with politicians. Johnson was bodyguard to the minister of state security at the time, Mr Dumisa.'

Kaleni clicked her tongue. 'He's a Zulu, that one. He should be ashamed of himself.' She put a tea-towel over the loaf, picked up a bread knife and began to slice it carefully and skilfully.

'We know that the VIP Protection Unit tried very hard to find out where Johnson was. That tells us the call to Dimba was interrupted, probably by the murder,' said Griessel. 'Because I'm sure if he had the time, Johnson would have told Dimba exactly where he was. And if he had done so, someone would have been waiting at the Rovos station in

Pretoria when the train arrived. They – and we think it was the VIP Protection Unit – went to fetch Johnson's luggage at the station only after he was reported missing and IDed. They were in a big hurry to do that, so they must have been worried about something that would incriminate a politician. Or the unit. Or something like that. Maybe Johnson's laptop, which disappeared from the train. Perhaps there were photos on it . . .'

'. . . of the corruption shenanigans,' said Cupido. 'Photos or other evidence.'

'Okay,' said Kaleni. She put slices of fresh baked bread on a plate and pushed it towards them.

'Johnson recognised either Faku or Green—' Griessel said.

'Or both of them,' said Cupido.

'—because he knew them from his days at the VIP Protection Unit. How do we know this? Because he called Dimba. Of all people. Which could mean that Faku and Green worked for the state, or maybe they worked for one of these anti-corruption organisations.'

'And we were thinking,' said Cupido, 'the reason he called could have been because he saw the two old guys together. Maybe it was the combination of them that rang alarm bells.'

'Strange bedfellows,' said Kaleni.

'Yes,' said Griessel. 'Maybe he recognised just one of them in the dining car, then saw them together and made some sort of connection. As I said earlier, the two phantoms didn't know that Johnson would be on the train because they made their booking months before Johnson knew he was going to be Mrs Scherpenzeel's bodyguard. It must have been coincidence, one way or another. Bad luck . . .'

'Come, eat,' she said, and sat down opposite them.

They thanked her.

'Why did they have to kill him?' said Griessel. 'That's the big question. It doesn't make sense. They used false IDs, but they arrived at the station together, they dined together. They must have known someone might recognise them.'

'Maybe,' said Cupido, 'they thought there would only be foreigners on the train. But that's a little stupid, and I don't think they're stupid. If we look at the way they made the payment for the trip, the passport numbers . . . I don't think they're stupid.'

'Something happened when Johnson went back to his compartment,' said Griessel.

'And only three people know what that was,' Cupido added.

'If we can't question Dimba, we've got nothing,' said Griessel.

'If we can't use this photo to identify Green, we've got nothing,' said Cupido.

'There are just too many maybes,' said Griessel.

'We really have nothing,' Cupido admitted.

'Yes,' said Colonel Mbali Kaleni. 'That's true. But the bones must be thrown in three different places.'

They stared at her.

'It's an old Zulu proverb. "The bones must be thrown in three different places before you can accept the message." It means you have to look at a question many times before you can come to a conclusion.'

'We're not allowed to look anywhere else,' said Cupido.

'Not now,' said Kaleni, and spread fresh butter on the bread. It melted into the slices. 'Not now. But we will wait. And we will keep looking . . .'

PART III

# 32

Night-time in the workshop. He'd stripped off his shirt, his chest shiny with perspiration as he sanded the table by hand, back and forth, back and forth. He didn't smell the fine sawdust, didn't see how it sifted and billowed, because he was preoccupied with Lonnie May and the conversation they'd had: it had lasted until ten o'clock that night.

Afterwards they'd climbed up the stairs of Au Bistrot, out of the atmosphere of tension, isolation and intensity, to find the restaurant upstairs cheery and bustling. It was like moving from one universe into another.

Before they left, Lonnie went over to compliment François on a magnificent dinner, saying he hoped he could come back some time. Outside, Lonnie embraced Daniel, shedding awkward tears, impatiently wiping them on his sleeve, as if they were shameful.

'Why are you crying, Lonnie?'

'I won't see you again.'

'Of course you will.'

'They'll get me, Tiny. Unless I can disappear here in Europe somewhere. And I can't do that. I love that country too fucking much.'

He suspected Lonnie was trying to manipulate him. 'The judiciary, the courts, Lonnie. It hasn't *all* been captured . . .'

'*Our* judiciary. *Our* courts. You're still a South African. It's the Russians, Tiny. You know them. They don't play games. Not when they've got so much to lose.'

He didn't know what to say.

Then Lonnie shoved the little rucksack into his hands. 'Think about it. Think carefully. You're the only hope we've got. You're our last hope.'

And Lonnie had walked away, towards the basilica. La Flèche

loomed over him dramatically, the tower like a scolding finger from Heaven.

Daniel stood, now alone. And thought about The African. His brother from a forgotten era. That spot Lonnie was passing now, where in the eighteenth century, in the name of progress and development, they had dug up the graveyard beside Bordeaux's Saint-Michel church. And found the bodies, more than seventy of them, remarkably well preserved, after centuries under the ground, mummified due to a mysterious conspiracy of soil quality and climate. The naked dead were displayed for nearly two hundred years in the church basement, propped upright, shoulder to shoulder, as a macabre tourist attraction. They were given names and descriptions: 'The family poisoned by mushrooms'; 'Buried alive'; 'The General, killed in a duel'.

And 'The African'.

A solitary black man, buried there. Ten thousand slaves were sold in that harbour and carried away on ships, but only one black man from that era had been laid to rest there. When Daniel heard the story for the first time, he felt kinship, a deep brotherly bond.

He wondered what The African's story was. He couldn't have been a slave. Not if he'd been buried there. Did he also flee his motherland, evading the law? In the sixteenth century, the seventeenth? Nobody knew exactly when he'd died. Did he also walk these cobbled streets and sometimes experience the physical pain of longing for the plains, mountains and valleys of his homeland, the scents and colours, the sounds and voices?

Daniel stood watching Lonnie until he disappeared around the corner beside the church square. Was it this feeling of utter loneliness that brought The African to mind?

Lonnie had brought him more than just a commission for an assassination. But he had taken the rest away with him again.

Daniel went home. Frustration gnawed at him. And rage. At Lonnie, who had burdened him in this way, who had polluted this beloved place with stories of the degradation of the land of his birth. Who was forcing him to choose. He had done what he could for so many years. He'd fought for justice and right, given the greatest part of his life for the cause and for his country, and he'd got nothing in return. Only loss. Massive, heart-rending loss.

Let them sort out their own problems.

In his sitting room he paced up and down, the turmoil churning inside him.

He opened the rucksack: 250,000 euros. And a letter.

He didn't read it.

He walked to Chartrons to sand his table because he knew he wouldn't sleep that night.

Sanding. Up and down, back and forth. His conversation with Lonnie driving him on.

The details of betrayal. The way the president had systematically stabbed good, loyal, honest Struggle veterans, comrades, friends, brothers, all of them, in the back. Forced them out of important positions and appointed his lackeys. A premeditated bloodless coup with only one goal in mind – plunder. In collaboration with the three Indians. And to get away with it he had contaminated the National Prosecuting Authority, SAPS, the Revenue Service, the State Security Agency and enough members of his party with money, stolen money, and the promise of more. So that he could be protected, even against the test of democracy.

'He stitched me up, Tiny. First he smeared me. He destroyed my reputation. Totally. And then he pushed me out. From sheer greed. Me, who gave my all for the Cause. And now I know you'll think Lonnie is wounded, Lonnie wants to get his revenge. But that's not true. I can get over it.' Lonnie had told him of how the president and his cronies stole. Billions and billions. Thousands of billions. Stripped state enterprises. Laundered it all overseas. With the help of those who turned a blind eye or by bribing well-known respected international auditing firms, software providers, public-relations companies and banks. British, German and American businesses. Just as greedy. Money that should have gone to uplifting the oppressed, money to create jobs and establish community organisations, rebuild the economy. Money that would have brought relief to the poorest of the poor. Africa robbed once again, raped.

Lonnie was trying to manipulate him, he thought, and said: 'The president's term has only a year or so left to run, not so?'

Lonnie flushed and threw his hands into the air. 'Do you think that will save us?' His voice rose. 'Do you really think when he leaves, everything will just return to normal? Do you think he hasn't put things in place? Made plans? They will destabilise, start another civil war in KwaZulu. They'll . . . They're a cancer, Tiny. Cut it out here, it starts up somewhere else. A Hydra – you can never cut off all the snakes' heads. They're a machine with a thousand gears. It's endemic, ineradicable. You can't wage conventional war.'

Lonnie had prepared thoroughly for the conversation.

'What good would it do to take him out?' Daniel asked.

'We make a powerful statement that in this country you won't steal, you won't cheat, you won't stab your comrades in the back. That's all we have. That's the only thing that will scare them. Death. An example, Tiny. We will make an example of him. Our plans are in place. We'll issue a press release saying he is the first. There will be more.'

'Who are the "we"?'

'MK43,' Lonnie whispered.

'You are a group of forty-three Umkhonto veterans?' he guessed, as the suggestion was obvious. Lonnie was part of the former military wing of the ANC, Umkhonto we Sizwe, the Spear of the Nation. Also known as MK.

Lonnie nodded.

'That's terrorism. Shooting the president is a terrorist act. High treason.'

Lonnie looked at him, disappointed, as if he ought to know better. 'It's a freedom fight, Tiny. It's a continuation of the Struggle. He's a tyrant, a kleptocratic tyrant. We're not free. Not until they're stopped in their tracks.'

'They? You want me to take others out too?'

'No. Just him. We have other people we can use later.'

'Why don't you use some of these *other* people to take him out now?'

'We considered it. We considered every angle. Everything. But the president and his clique . . . They're not stupid. Plus they're paranoid. They're protecting him. They've built a shield, impenetrable, back home. You can't get near him. But he's coming to Paris in just over a week's time. The first of September.'

'In a week? He's coming in a week and you're only making preparations now?'

'We wanted . . . The initial date was in three weeks, but they brought it forward. And we . . . There were complications. On our side. Serious complications. In any case, when he's here they can't protect him as completely. There's a protocol – they have to leave security to the French. So, that creates an opportunity. And you're here. You know France, you know Paris, you speak the lingo, you . . . You were the best, the very best. They say at the time you were the best in the world.'

'Flattery will get you nowhere, Lonnie. I'm not going to do it.'

'Why are the Russians after you?'

Lonnie laughed without humour. 'You know about the president's . . .' he searched for the right word ' . . . proclivities?'

Daniel had heard rumours about the man's preference for young women. He just nodded.

'They saw, the president and his Indian friends, how easy it was to steal some of the state enterprises. They hijacked Eskom, and Eskom's coal supply, they milked the construction of the new power stations, but it was never enough. And it wasn't an inexhaustible resource. So they hatched a plan. Build another nuclear power station. With over a trillion on the table, you could see them drooling. And the entire world was soliciting them for the contract – the Chinese, French, Russians. But Putin is no pumpkin. Two years ago, our president went to Moscow. Putin knew all about the old man's proclivities, and he sent four snow-white gorgeous blondes to his hotel room in Moscow's Ritz-Carlton. And the hidden cameras recorded it all. It's not that he was caught with four white women, Thobela. It's what he did to them. Shocking things. Sick. So I ask you, what will that do to his reputation? Who do you think will get the nuclear contract?'

'*Kompromat*,' said Daniel Darret. An old trick of the KGB.

'Precisely. And Putin and his cronies are also going to benefit hugely from the deal. But the country can't afford it, Tiny. It'll be the last straw.'

'And if you take the president out, the *kompromat* is useless.'

'Exactly.'

'How do the Russians know about you?'

'I'm coming to that.'

He watched Lonnie eat. Oysters first. 'Jeez, this is good.'

Then the *cul de poule*. Lonnie wanted to know what that meant, when Daniel recommended it. 'Literally the hen's backside,' he said.

'Chicken arsehole?' He laughed.

'*Cul de poule* is actually a mixing bowl you use in the kitchen. But here it's a play on words. It's chicken salad. François just wants to make his customers smile.'

'I get it,' said Lonnie.

When he tasted it: 'Jeez, this is fantastic.'

'You should come in the winter, when he makes pig's cheeks.'

A shadow crossed Lonnie's face. 'I wish I could.'

He ate with the same gusto and focus as he had decades ago, when Daniel had met him over a pot of porridge in an Angolan training camp. And with the same hearty satisfaction.

# 33

Lonnie in Angola. Busy, dedicated Lonnie. A lifetime ago. The MK training camp was the Wild West. An ants' nest of activity, organised chaos, perpetual movement. Adrenalin, the constant sense of fear and urgency. And testosterone: a thousand young men living together in the African bush with meagre facilities. A sea of black faces, a hum of African languages. And then there was Lonnie. White and English-speaking, a lawyer from Parkhurst, Johannesburg, though not a very good one, rumour had it.

They called him Ubu. After *ububhibhi*. The Meerkat.

Just like a meerkat, Lonnie could never sit still. He was the cheer-leader, the nurse, the are-you-getting-enough-to-eat-you're-far-too-thin mother-hen figure, even though he himself was still only in his mid-thirties. Open, chatty, he talked to everyone. Darting about, he helped everywhere: in the kitchen, the sick bay, with the induction and processing of new recruits. Some of the few whites among them were real arse-lickers, over-obsequious, riddled with white middle-class guilt, but not Lonnie. He supported the Struggle with all his heart. He let it be known far and wide that he didn't follow any religion or ism or ideology, he had only one goal, to which he was dedicated heart and soul: that everyone in his motherland should be equal. He wasn't a leader. But he was a dedicated, enthusiastic and loyal follower.

Lonnie was taken into the intelligence structure because he was clever and sober. And because he had no appetite for warfare. He served with distinction, although he was no star, by no means the brightest bulb in the chandelier. He was just Ubu, the busy one.

Above all, you could trust Lonnie with your life.

They talked in Au Bistrot's cellar for more than nine hours, Lonnie as loquacious as ever.

'Lonnie, you're white. Why send you?' Daniel asked. Lonnie had never been part of the elite cadre, the true inner circle.

Lonnie was clearly expecting that question: he understood the implications because he knew the structures inside out, the way things were done, the long-standing traditions and the unwritten rules. 'Because I was the only one who wasn't closely watched.' He took a sip of wine, looked Daniel in the eye and said: 'You've no idea what things are like at home. Like Stalin, Tiny, without the killing. It's death by a thousand lies, betrayal by a thousand spies. They know the only way to protect their kleptocracy is to buy and bribe more and more people. You can't trust anyone. You have to be so careful. They suspect . . . they expect, they know, that some of us fought a different Struggle, and want a different kind of country. They know that some time or other we're going to stop twiddling our thumbs. So they keep tabs on the dangerous ones. But I was never seen as a danger to anyone.'

It was Lonnie's honesty that touched him.

# 34

Half past midnight. Daniel sat at the table, arms folded, head bowed, dog tired from the struggle – the effort of the sanding and the wrestling with the past. His cheap cell phone rang – the one that Madame Lefèvre had given him, the number that only she had, for the deliveries. And now Lonnie had it too. He'd given him the number in the restaurant, reluctantly. 'I just want to phone you once, tomorrow or the day after,' Lonnie had said. 'Just one last time, Thobela. Just to hear if you won't change your position.'

His *position*.

He'd said nothing and Lonnie had misinterpreted his silence. 'I'll phone you from a burner, Tiny. Untraceable. I don't want to put the whole operation in jeopardy. Trust me. You know you can trust me.'

He used this phone for Madame's calls, nothing else. He had a second-hand tablet at home that he used to read news on the internet. He didn't want to be reachable or traceable. Hence the reluctance.

Now the phone was ringing, and it wasn't Madame's number. It was Lonnie, could only be him. He didn't want to answer. But he did.

'Lonnie.'

'I'm in trouble, Tiny. They found me. They're at every exit.'

'Where are you?'

'The Novotel by the dam.'

It took him a second to decipher the South African vernacular. 'Bordeaux Lac?' The hotel at the lake, opposite the gigantic Expo centre.

'Yes.'

'How many of them?'

'Six. I'm sorry, very sorry, but they're sitting there waiting for me. They want to get me, Tiny.'

He tried to picture the surroundings. He had made deliveries in the area, had walked beside the lake. The Novotel was one of a few hotels serving the big Expo centre. A good place to hide when some major show was on. But now, in August, perhaps not the smartest choice. It stood close to the lake with only a service road between the hotel and the water. He couldn't remember exactly what it looked like. 'Is the hotel on open ground?'

'No.' Lonnie's bravado, all his verbosity, had evaporated. 'There's a big steel fence all around. Bushes beyond it.'

'How many entrances?'

'There's a through road with an entrance, and a separate exit.'

'Where is the entrance?'

'On the side of the dam. West. The exit is north.'

'That's all?'

'Yes.'

'Where are the Russians?'

'Two in a car facing the entrance, two at the exit, across the street, and two in the lobby.'

'What side does your room face?'

'Towards the dam.'

He was quiet for so long that Lonnie asked, voice trembling: 'Are you there?'

'The back of the hotel borders on the tram tracks, if I remember correctly.'

'Yes, but the fence, Tiny, there are trees and a fence. I looked, I cased the joint, as a precaution. I didn't expect them to find me. I stayed in the city the first four nights, every night at another place, then I came here because it's . . . I thought . . .' He ran out of excuses.

Daniel wasn't listening, trying to work out how the hell to get Lonnie out of there. 'Lonnie, listen carefully. How much luggage do you have?'

'Two cases. Sort of medium-large, and small.'

'Can you leave the big one?'

'Yes.'

'I'm going to have to get you out through the fence at the back.'

'I'm not a young man any more, Tiny. I won't be able to climb over it.'

'Lonnie, just listen. Can you get to the fence without the team at Reception seeing you?'

'I can go through the restaurant – there's a door to the garden.'

'Stay in your room. I'm on my way. Pack now. Just take the little case – and be quick. I'll call you in fifteen.' He disconnected, swore out loud, his voice echoing through the silent workshop.

Six of them. Heavy manpower. In a foreign country, in the current international political climate. The Russians were clearly serious about stopping Lonnie. But there wouldn't be just the six. They wouldn't reveal their hand so obviously. He had to work out where the others were hiding.

He had no weapons. He fetched a tablecloth from the shop, grabbed a few tools, shoved a bunch of cable ties into his pocket, then opened the back door of the workshop. He took the Peugeot, because that was all he had at his disposal – the J5 panel van, twenty-five years old with at least three hundred thousand kilometres on the clock. The white had long since aged to a dirty yellow, *Madame Lefèvre – Antiquités, Brocante* still faintly legible on the sides.

He followed the river, north along the quai des Chartrons, then east along rue Lucien Faure. The city was quiet. It worried him – he felt exposed, one of the very few vehicles moving on the police cameras. If there was trouble, if shots were fired, blood spilled, they would track him down. He rehearsed scenarios in his mind, possible outcomes, made plans, discarded them. He had to protect his identity. His very existence, his precious anonymity.

Past Decathlon, past the big Bordeaux Lac shopping centre, over the E5 freeway, then left on the rue du Grand Barail, keeping an eye out for the hidden ones, the crew who hadn't shown themselves to Lonnie. If they were professionals, they would be behind the hotel.

They were. He spotted the Mercedes Sprinter twenty metres from the crossroads, just in front of the gate of the Hôtel le Provençal. Two men in front, the passenger window open, cigarette smoke drifting out.

He drove past, glancing at Lonnie's hotel to his left, beyond the tram tracks. The men in the Sprinter had a perfect view of the rear side, right where he wanted to bring Lonnie out. He would have to neutralise them. Without drawing attention.

He searched for the CCTV cameras. All the hotels would have

them, mostly at the entrances, but he didn't see any from the city police. That helped.

He drove around the block, came back. At the Hôtel Mercure he switched off the Peugeot's lights. He parked in front of the Hippopotamus restaurant, the dancing hippo on the big advertising board blaring: *Laissez vos envies de viande s'exprimer.* Let your craving for meat express itself. He reached behind him, picked up the dark blue tablecloth and wound it around his face, like an Arab headscarf, so that only his eyes showed. He picked up the heavy claw hammer. Took a deep breath, phoned Lonnie.

'Tiny! You said fifteen minutes.'

'Are you ready, Lonnie?'

'Yes. What must I do?'

'Go down to the restaurant, and stand at the door. When I phone, run towards the fence. You'll see me. But you have to wait until I call. Understand?'

'How long is it going to take?'

'Between five and ten minutes. If I haven't phoned you in twenty minutes, phone the police and say you want an escort. Let them take you to safety.'

'No!' Lonnie's voice was shrill, panicky. 'Why would it—'

'Lonnie,' Daniel kept his voice calm and soothing, 'there is another team of them, two in a panel van behind the hotel. I'm going to try to neutralise them, but anything could happen. I'm rusty, fifty-five years old. They're young and professional.'

'Jesus, Tiny . . .'

'Go and wait at the door. And keep your fingers crossed.'

Silence. Then: 'Okay. See you now.'

The Mercedes Sprinter was parked in the open. There was nowhere to hide, no room for any cunning tricks and no margin for error. These were the only possibilities: speed, surprise, overwhelming force. He got out, hammer in hand, scarf around his head, pliers and cable ties in one trouser pocket. He locked the Peugeot, put the key into his other pocket. Took a deep breath. The night was silent, the breeze off the lake cool, the streets deserted. Bordeaux was asleep.

He stood still, thoughts racing through his mind.

Violence begets violence, and there would be violence here now. Forces would be unleashed, dominoes would fall. Hammer in hand, but he felt naked. His shoulders lacked the comforting weight of the short stabbing assegai, the spear he had carried to war on his back in days gone by.

This was the end of an era. It was the end of the life he'd built here, with so much trouble and pain and loneliness. He felt the loss like a physical agony. What are you doing, Daniel Darret? he thought. What are you doing?

He felt the tingling.

He took off, at full speed.

# 35

He ran towards the back of the Sprinter, his trainers light on the tarmac. He prayed that the pair wouldn't look in their rear- or side-view mirrors, that their gaze would be fixed on the hotel, that they would be bored, drowsy, inattentive.

Adrenalin pumped, the distance narrowed.

He had to reach the left-hand door, the driver, the one with the keys, the lights, the hooter, the one with less room to manoeuvre behind the steering wheel and, most likely, the senior member of the two-man team.

He was at the Sprinter, running down the side. The window was closed. He raised the hammer, smashed the glass. The driver ducked instinctively and Daniel struck again, hard, fast, with the hammer head. The metal struck the man on the forehead, bone cracked, blood spurted. The man's head dropped forward.

His partner recovered from the shock, reached for his gun, tucked under his arm. Daniel saw the driver's pistol lying on the dashboard, an MP-443 Grach with a silencer, beside a small two-way radio. They were planning to shoot Lonnie.

He let go of the hammer, grabbed the firearm with his left hand, and hooked his right arm around the injured driver's neck, dragging him closer. He held the man between him and his mate, pressed the safety catch off, and rammed the pistol barrel hard against the driver's temple. '*Polozhite pistolet*,' he said, in the little Russian he could remember. Put down your weapon.

The passenger stared at him, took out his pistol, swung it round at Daniel. He was young, in his early twenties, with the face of a predator, but still stunned by the unexpected violence.

Daniel jammed the Grach even harder against the driver's head. '*Polozhite!*' But his hand was shaking from adrenalin, and the dread that he could lose everything here, that he was past it, too old for this deadly game.

The driver made a sharp, bewildered noise, his eyes blank.

Number Two's pistol had stopped moving, but as he sat there, the shock dissipated and his training started to kick in. He looked at Daniel's hand; Daniel knew he would notice it trembling.

Daniel swung the Grach a few millimetres and fired off a shot into the dashboard, just to the right of the passenger's knee, a muffled bang. The man moved his hand between his legs, slowly to the floor, put the pistol down. He looked back at Daniel.

Daniel let go of the driver's neck, took a handful of cable ties out of his pocket. 'Tie him to the steering wheel,' he said in English. He tossed the ties onto the passenger's lap, moved to get hold of the driver's neck again.

The passenger's eyes measured him now, gears revolving, risks weighed.

'I hear the prospects for SVR agents with shot-up knees are not that great,' said Daniel, and swung the Grach towards the man's leg.

There was no response to confirm that he worked for Sluzhba Vneshney Razvedki, the Russian Foreign Intelligence Service, but he picked up the cable ties and leaned over to grab his comrade's right wrist. Slowly, calmly, he tied it to the steering wheel. The driver pulled his arm back. Daniel tightened his grip around the man's neck, choking him. The reaction weakened. 'Tighter.'

The passenger pulled the cable tie tight, took the other hand and secured that too. He looked at Daniel. 'Now, your right hand.'

The passenger hesitated, looking in the direction of the hotel, to the radio on the dashboard, and back at him. There was intelligence behind the wary eyes. Daniel knew the man was asking himself: Why doesn't he simply shoot us? That was what the SVR would have done. He would work it out – the attacker had a scarf around his head to hide his identity, so that he couldn't be recognised in future. That meant he was reluctant to kill them. To avoid the scandal of an international incident, maybe, and the consequent intensive search for the gunman. The man would persuade himself he stood a chance.

'Fuck you,' the passenger said.

Then the radio crackled, a voice spoke in Russian, a query.

Daniel pulled the trigger. The radio shattered in pieces with a clapping sound, the passenger jumped.

'You have ten seconds to tie your right hand to the steering wheel or I will finish your career.'

Later he would wonder if it was the ambition and ego of a young man. The fear of a blot on his record so early in his career?

The passenger reached for his pistol.

Daniel fired, shooting him in his right elbow, the nine-millimetre round wreaking havoc. Blood and bone splinters sprayed across the door. The man screamed in pain and shock. Daniel shoved the pistol into his belt, pulled open the door and heaved his upper body over the driver's bound arms. He grabbed the passenger's sound arm and took a cable tie from the man's lap.

The agent reached with his barely usable right hand for the pistol on the floor, bellowing from the effort.

Daniel swore in Xhosa, instinctively. He dropped the healthy arm, grabbed the man's right hand – he had to get the pistol.

The driver's face was against his; the man bit him through the material, in the neck. Daniel concentrated on the pistol, twisted it out of the passenger's hand, hit the driver with his elbow. He threw the passenger's pistol out of the Sprinter. It clattered onto the ground. He punched the man with all his strength, with his clenched fist, full in the face. He wrenched the sound arm closer, struggling to fix the cable tie around it. The man twisted and kicked. Daniel hit him again and again, as he tried to fend him off with his right forearm. The driver moaned. Daniel grasped the accomplice's arm and pulled it to the steering wheel, keeping his elbow ready to strike again as he wrestled with the wrist and the cable tie, his hands slippery with his opponent's blood. He pulled the cable tie tight, aware that the radio voice had been expecting an answer. He knew he didn't have much time.

The passenger tugged against his bonds. Daniel, half inside the Sprinter cabin, jerked the injured arm and the man screamed in agony. He found another cable tie that had dropped between the two men, and fastened the last arm.

He rifled through the men's pockets, found two cell phones and shoved them into his back pockets.

He went to pick up the pistol that was lying in the road, then ran across the tram tracks, taking out his cell phone. He phoned Lonnie.

'Come on, Lonnie, run.' He shoved the cell phone back into his pocket, took out the pliers.

At the fence. He began cutting, from the top down. He heard Lonnie's hurried footsteps.

'Thobela!' Lonnie was panic-stricken.

'Here.' He snipped, snipped, pushed the wire aside, wormed through the hedge. Lonnie was standing there, suitcase in hand, fear written on his face. 'Come on!'

Lonnie obeyed. Daniel helped him through the foliage, and through the gap in the wire fence. Lonnie looked at his hands and arms in horror. 'You're bleeding.'

Daniel laughed. 'It's not my blood. Come, Lonnie.'

They began to run towards the Peugeot that was parked around the corner. In passing Lonnie spotted the pair inside the Sprinter. He looked the other way.

They drove away. Daniel unrolled the cloth from his head, looked in the rear-view mirror.

'Lonnie, do you have a British visa?' He had to raise his voice above the rattle of the Peugeot.

Lonnie was still catching his breath. 'Why do you ask?'

'They will be watching Méringnac airport. And Bordeaux train station. You'll have to fly from Bergerac. It's a small airport. Most of the flights are to Southampton, Stansted or Amsterdam.'

Lonnie thought. 'Amsterdam,' he said. And then: 'Thank you, Tiny.'

'Those are their pistols,' he said, and pointed in the direction of the firearms. Lonnie had seen him put them in the toolbox. 'They were going to shoot you.'

Lonnie's eyes widened. 'I told you they wanted to get me.'

'And they're not afraid to cause an international incident.'

'No.'

'Is this just about the nuclear-reactor money, Lonnie?'

He shook his head slowly. 'You have to understand, there are major forces at work. The rise of China, America on the wane. And in the middle there's a vacuum waiting to be filled. It's a new world coming. And Putin . . . You can say what you like about him, but he's smart.

Cunning. He's playing the long game, positioning himself and his country. Do you know what he's doing in Central Africa?'

'No.'

'Congo, a whole bunch of countries ... Their presidents don't have democratic mandate, and Putin has given them two thousand five hundred highly trained forces to serve as personal bodyguards. To keep them in power. Why, do you think? Out of the goodness of his heart? No, Tiny, it's about influence, about power, getting his hands on the minerals and the diamonds. China's approach is different. China buys up countries' debts and gains possession that way. Look at Venezuela, the most oil-rich country on the planet ... But Putin is playing another game. Russia is the biggest kleptocracy in the history of the world. Their government is in a semi-official coalition with organised crime. What's good for one is good for the other. Politically South Africa presents a foothold on the continent. A port of entry. For Putin's ambitions to become a superpower again. For his New Russia. We're still the jewel in the crown, the biggest, sweetest, juiciest fruit in Africa, even if things are going badly for us. He wants to own us before the Chinese can. He has our president in his pocket, the best leverage. He doesn't want to lose that. He would do anything. And then there's the Mafia that comes with the nuclear contract ...'

They drove in silence over the Garonne at the pont d'Aquitaine, then south on the N230.

'Why did you laugh when I thought you were bleeding?' Lonnie asked.

Daniel laughed again. 'They showed *Predator*, just a couple of weeks ago,' he said. He could see Lonnie didn't understand. '*Predator*. The Schwarzenegger film where he has to kill the alien in the jungle.'

'Oh. Yes ...'

'There's a scene with the one soldier who is with Schwarzenegger at the beginning – he's big and strong, you think he's invincible. They have this skirmish with rebels, and the tough soldier is wounded. His comrade says to him: "You're bleeding." And he answers: "I ain't got time to bleed." I was laughing at myself, because I felt like saying: "I ain't got time to bleed." Like a

Hollywood-soldier cliché. It made me laugh because . . . It's the euphoria after adrenalin – it makes you think you're invincible. But I'm not.'

Lonnie didn't laugh. He just stared ahead.

Eventually the Meerkat said: 'Here's one chicken you saved.'

# 36

In the long hours in Au Bistrot, Lonnie had kept trying to persuade him to act as an assassin for hire, and he had kept refusing. Lonnie, the former lawyer at work, had many counter-arguments and pleas.

Daniel had reached his wit's end. So he said he wanted to tell Lonnie about the chickens.

This made Lonnie frown, as they were discussing very serious matters.

Daniel told him anyway, about the first job he had found in France. It was on a giant poultry farm in Bretagne, near picturesque Morlaix. He was paid a pittance, since he was there illegally, still on his South African passport. His responsibility was to rescue the last of the chicks. It was the least popular job on the farm, hence it was given to him. The conveyor-belt came from the brood boxes. Other hands took the thousands of chicks off as they hatched, for sorting and transfer.

He was at the end of the line, where the last of the chicks – the weakest – struggled out of the shells, the conveyor-belt thick with the yolk of unviable eggs, congealed like glue. The frail chicks stuck fast in it.

When the belt began to move, he could keep up, as only a few chicks reached his station. But as the pace picked up, the numbers increased, with more and more of the struggling little birds for him to pick out of the mess and put aside.

He worked as fast as he could. The little chicks, so feeble and fragile and pretty . . . There inevitably came a time when he simply wasn't fast enough. Then he had to choose which chicks would live and which would die. Those that went past him, went down to the rolling mill, were crushed for bone meal, fertiliser and pet food. It gnawed at him, that job. Horribly.

It reminded him of his last year in South Africa, Daniel said. His voice became hoarse, because he didn't want to remember it. He sat and looked at the yellow-white sandstone wall, his eyes running over the joins of the large cut stones, but his mind was back in the Eastern Cape. That was the time after he lost his stepson, he said. Pakamile, eight years old, shot by that scum during an armed robbery at a filling station in Cathcart. His second great loss. Miriam, the love of his life, dead two years before. And he'd gone crazy back then. He'd wanted to save all the children. He'd wanted to protect them. He'd wanted revenge. He hunted people down and killed them, people who raped, abused and harmed children. He'd wanted to save them all.

Lonnie laid a hand on his arm. 'I know.'

That was when Daniel had realised his eyes were wet. He pulled himself together. The chicks, he said, had taught him this: You can't save everyone. No matter how hard you try and how pure your motives are, you can't save everyone.

He'd lost the desire to be prosecutor, judge and, most of all, executioner. He didn't want to be the one trying to save everyone. They would have to get someone else to take out the president.

# 37

It was just a hundred and twenty kilometres from Bordeaux to Bergerac's small airport, but in the rattletrap Peugeot on the narrow back roads that Daniel chose it was a two-hour trip.

Near Castillon-la-Bataille Lonnie was on his phone searching for a flight.

Daniel asked the question that had been haunting him: 'How did they find you at the Novotel? Your cell phone?'

'No. I made a mistake, Tiny. Novotel wouldn't take cash. And I couldn't remember which credit card . . . When I booked in I was in too much of a hurry. I didn't want to seem like a . . . refugee. It was a long day, I may have had one glass too many of François's wine. I might have used the same card for the flight from Dublin to Bordeaux. That's all I can think of. I'm so sorry . . .'

Lonnie. Not the brightest bulb in the chandelier. But he said nothing.

'The first flight to Amsterdam is at nine twenty-five,' said Lonnie.

'What time is it now?' The Peugeot's flickering digital clock had stopped working ages ago.

'Just past four.'

'They know which identity you're travelling on?'

'I have four passports. They know about three now. I'll have to use the last one.'

'How did you get all those passports?' But he already knew. Lonnie had been a deputy director general at the Secret Service, and he had held a senior position with the new State Security Agency, the SSA, before the president had stabbed him in the back. 'You took precautions?'

'We all took precautions. We could see what was on the horizon.'

'I take it you have other credit cards?'

'Yes. And I know now which one I haven't used yet. I won't make the same mistake again.'

'Lonnie, the money in the rucksack. Where does it come from?'

Lonnie grinned in the dark. 'We stole twenty-five million back. The director general of the SSA and his cronies had so many slush funds, had embezzled so much money and hidden it in so many ways that nobody could keep track. The writing was already on the wall and we channelled it out only just in time.'

'I'm going to send the money back to you. Just tell me how.'

'Later,' said Lonnie, and waved a hand as if to say it wasn't important. 'I take it you haven't read the letter in the rucksack yet?'

'No.'

Lonnie nodded.

'Are you going home from Amsterdam?' Daniel asked.

He nodded. 'We have a safe house in McGregor. I'll go and wait there . . .' then he looked at Daniel, and added, in a hopeful voice ' . . . until you're finished.'

He sighed. Lonnie never gave up. 'Lonnie, I'm not going to do it.'

'You're . . . I'm sorry I dragged you in tonight. And I'm extremely grateful that you saved me. Tiny, I know you feel I've used you, but you're in it now. You're part of it.'

Daniel laughed quietly. 'Nice try, Lonnie.'

'You are. Think about it. You're one of us.'

'No. I was in it to get you out of the hotel because you're my friend. They don't know who I am. I'm carrying on with my life, Lonnie. I've worked hard to build it.' He felt weary, not wanting to argue over this now – the afternoon and evening in Au Bistrot had been draining enough.

Lonnie sighed deeply. He tapped on his phone, looked carefully through his credit cards. He picked one, booked his flight.

They drank coffee and ate day-old croissants at a filling station near Bergerac, the conversation uneasy, chit-chat over the wellbeing of old comrades. The sun rose, put colour back into the landscape, a neat patchwork of grain, fruit and vegetables.

Just before six Daniel dropped Lonnie May and his suitcase at the small airport.

Lonnie embraced him outside, beside the panel van, with barely contained desperation.

'I'm sorry, Lonnie,' he said.

'I am, too. But it's your right. We make our choices, and we have to live with the consequences.'

Lonnie let him go. He looked at Daniel with the eyes of a kicked dog. Eyes that said Daniel would never see him again: he was a marked man.

'Send me an SMS when you're home. From a safe phone.'

'Can I just say one thing, Umzingeli?'

Daniel knew that Lonnie's use of his old code name was his friend's last plea.

'I understand about the chicks you couldn't save,' Lonnie said. 'It's true. It's impossible to save them all. Even trying seems like a lost cause from the start. But there's one thing you've forgotten: all those thousands of chickens you *have* saved. What about them? Don't they matter? Weren't they worth all the effort?'

Lonnie turned and began walking to the airport entrance, his shoulders squared as if steeling himself to face what lay ahead, a man alone.

He drove back to Bordeaux with the sun behind him, all the fierce battle chemistry spent, tired to the very marrow of his bones. The previous day and night were fragments in his mind, fractured images and experiences, emotions and conversations that came and went, swirled and lingered. And a discontent, an unease, a dissatisfaction that he struggled to formulate and get a grip on.

They had sent Lonnie. The conspirators, the so-called MK43. The best they could do was to send Lonnie May. White Lonnie, the Meerkat.

*You're in it now.* As if what he'd inflicted, the hammer blow of concussion and the shattered elbow had irrevocably bound him to the group and their plot. It was a cheap trick, an insult, manipulation. He was worth more than that. But that was what you got when you sent Lonnie May.

What was it about the gods, Fate? First Madame Lecompte in the night, and now this. Only two weeks apart. Hadn't he paid a heavy enough price for this life, here and now? Didn't he deserve this peace after everything? After Miriam and Pakamile and all the death, destruction, betrayal and chaos?

Frustrated, uneasy, discontented because Lonnie had come and unleashed it all. The memories. Of more than thirty years ago. When he'd run away to join the Struggle, only seventeen years old. Swaziland and Mozambique, Angola and Tanzania. His youth, his adult life, his best years sacrificed.

Memories of Saraktash, memories of Moscow and East Berlin and the Wall. Of the war years, victims in his sniper's scope in Munich and Barcelona, Hamburg and Maastricht. He had pulled the trigger with deep ideological conviction, barely aware of the slow harm he was doing to himself. In service of MK, deployed in Europe; a lease agreement with the KGB and Stasi, their comrades-in-arms. An exercise in public relations, his code name Umzingeli, the Hunter. Lord, he'd loved it so much back then. What a boost to a young man's ego.

But now that world order was almost forgotten. Today's children considered it ancient history, were unable to comprehend, to understand it.

All the sacrifices he'd made. And so little to show for it.

Above all the memories of Miriam and Pakamile were let loose, so that the physical pain blossomed again deep inside, revived after nearly a decade of the daily struggle to dull it a little.

*All those thousands of chickens you have saved. What about them? Don't they matter? Weren't they worth all the effort?*

No, Lonnie, he thought, they don't count. Because they're sentenced to be battery hens or go to the abattoir regardless. Ultimately he'd made no difference. It was the story of his life. He'd fought for democracy, and gained a kleptocracy. He'd fought for justice for children, and he'd had to flee his motherland, branded a vigilante, a murderer. He'd saved Lonnie from his hotel, but he couldn't protect him any further. It wasn't his conspiracy; it wasn't his doing. He could save the Lonnie chicken tonight, but the roller mill would just keep on grinding.

Not again. Never again. This wasn't his fight, not any more. He wanted to live in peace. Make beautiful things. Forget.

Daniel Darret drove back to the hotel at the lake. There were no police barriers or a crime scene. There was no sign of the fight with the Russians. Just the gap in the fence, undiscovered.

He considered the irony. Thirty years ago the Russians had been his brothers-in-arms.

He was vigilant, keeping an eye on the rear-view mirror, eventually parking the Peugeot two blocks from his flat. He saw nothing suspicious.

Wackett was standing at the front door, her deep miaow plaintive and resentful. She rubbed herself up against the frame and begged for food, as if she'd last been fed a week ago. He put out food, which she ate, but she kept casting him dirty looks.

He took a long shower, scrubbing off the blood, sweat and memories with soap.

The rucksack of cash was still in his sitting room. And the letter.

He left it there. He would deal with it later.

He walked to La Boulangerie in the rue des Faures. Pretty Marla was at the counter. She greeted him with her big smile, saying, while she packed his usual order into the brown-paper bag: 'Daniel! *Tu as du retard ce matin.*' You're late this morning.

'*Oui, oui, un peu,*' he said. Just a little. He breathed in the aromas of baking, and bought his fresh croissants and his favourite *chocolatines*, and when he walked to the Peugeot, he thought, yes, this was where he wanted to be. At the place where they knew him, the humble labourer, and what his order would be. The usual. Where they greeted him by his French name, with a smile.

He would do nothing to place that in jeopardy.

# 38

In the cellar of Au Bistrot, dinner over, Lonnie, cheeks rosy with contentment, had held a glass of François's red wine from Burgundy.

'How did you find me, Lonnie?' Daniel asked.

Lonnie smiled. 'We're not stupid.'

'I know.'

'First rule of intelligence. Follow the money . . .'

Daniel had always known that was the one way they could trace him. If they really wanted to.

'I found you,' Lonnie said, with a measure of pride. 'The money for your farm.'

The farm on the banks of the Cata River in the Eastern Cape. *Cata* meant 'add a bit', because the river was the confluence of a hundred little streams that added to the river one by one. He'd bought the place two years before Pakamile's death. It was dilapidated, run down, but they had fixed it up in the same way the river had been formed, little by little.

They had cattle, a milk cow for the house, a few hens. Vegetables grew at the back door, a patch of lucerne on the riverbank. Every morning he drove Pakamile to school, and every afternoon he fetched him. And between the schoolwork they farmed. And swam and walked and hunted small game and shot with catapults and lay and watched the stars at night. The child enjoyed it so intensely. And so did he. Two years of peace. Two years without loss.

Pakamile wasn't his own blood. He was the son of the woman he loved, the woman they'd lost, and so the child became his blood. And later his legal son. But Pakamile had died, and he had become a fugitive because of the people he'd hunted down and punished, and he'd had to sell the farm from Europe, using an attorney in King William's Town. He'd had to pay the man a lot of money for his silence and to handle the estate because, it seemed, Thobela Mpayipheli was dead.

The attorney had sent the money to him. Like the Cata River, little by little. Small businesses and trusts, the amounts low enough to send out of the country, to five separate French bank accounts. Which he later consolidated under the name of Daniel Darret.

'It was difficult. That attorney of yours was no fool,' Lonnie said. 'But he wasn't clever enough.'

'How did you know I was alive?'

'You are Umzingeli.'

'How, Lonnie?'

'Your body was never found. There were rumours, Tiny, always the rumours. And when we had to plan to get rid of the president, your name was at the top of the wish list. At the very least, they said, we should make sure that you weren't somewhere . . . I said, "Leave it to me." I'd been an attorney. I knew the tracks people leave. That was always my strong point. And you and I know it was actually my only strong point . . .'

# 39

He drove to Chartrons. He had to leave the panel van at work, and he knew he wouldn't be able to sleep. He swept the entire workshop. His weary body protested, but he did it slowly, deliberately and systematically. Then he made sure the table top was clean. He'd learned from Monsieur Lefèvre never to varnish wood if there was any trace of dust, sawdust or shavings nearby.

He thinned the varnish with tung oil until he was satisfied with the mixture, found the right brush. He painted slowly and carefully, first against the grain, always the first layer against the grain. He concentrated on the job, the rhythmic back-and-forth motion of the brush, the scents of varnish, turpentine and wood.

Thoughts penetrated: Lonnie must be in Amsterdam.

He didn't like to admit it but part of his discontent, unease and dissatisfaction was because he would miss Lonnie now. Lonnie, South Africa and everything that was precious to him. All over again. He had a connection to Lonnie. Yesterday in the restaurant, despite the long arguments and manipulation, he had bonded with an old comrade. A man he knew well. Family. From his world. And now he missed that world. He ached for it.

And he didn't want to.

He slept for ten hours. In the morning he woke feeling relieved, cheerful, as if he had survived something, an accident or great hardship. He fed the cat, picked up the rucksack holding the money and the letter, and put it away in a kitchen cupboard, behind the rubbish bin.

He went to work. There was a great deal to do because it was the Friday before the Lefèvres returned from Arcachon. From Monday on it would be back to him and *le génie* and the familiar routine that made him feel so comfortable. After Monday everything would be back to normal: this summer of violence and upheaval would be behind him.

He dusted the entire front shop, all the furniture. He vacuumed the carpets, polished the silver- and copperware, cleaned the glass of the display cabinets.

Now and then he went to check his cell phone. No message from Lonnie yet.

He thought about the weekend. Tomorrow morning he would go and have tapas at the Capucins market, at Madame Dupuy's La Maison du Pata Negra. He didn't do that often, saving it for special occasions. Monsieur Dupuy's *foie-gras* dish was beyond description, the most delicious mouthful of food in the world.

On Sunday he would take a ride on the motorbike. The Dutch and Germans who camped in the Périgord in summer should have gone home by then. Quiet roads, beautiful scenery. He would clear his head, get his mind off all the disturbing things Lonnie had stirred up.

At four he was finished. He walked to Carrefour on cours Victor-Hugo to buy milk and cat food. He went home. Took another shower, sat down in the kitchen wearing only shorts, opened a tin of tuna, and ate while reading the news on his tablet.

The article on Lonnie's death was lower down on the News24 cover page. *Former intelligence boss dead at airport.* He saw Lonnie's name, but didn't want to read on, didn't want to believe it. Mr May had flown in from Amsterdam; a suspected heart attack. Attempts by onlookers and paramedics to revive him at the exit of Cape Town International had been in vain.

He read it again and again. It felt unreal, surreal, like a dream.

And then he had to get out. He dressed, walked out of the door.

What could he have done? Nothing. It wasn't his fault.

Heart attack? No. They had lain in wait for Lonnie at the airport. They must have known what flight he was on. They had eyes and ears in the world's computer systems, informants everywhere. MK43 was just not careful enough. Maybe there was a mole.

He felt a consuming rage for the people who had murdered Lonnie, administered a pharmaceutical or chemical weapon, or poison – the Russians had their sly, dishonourable methods, too cowardly to stand in front of you, look you in the eye and fight like a man.

In the late-afternoon light he walked down to the Sainte-Croix church. The interior was dusky, silent. He sat down on a chair and grieved for Lonnie, the emotion like a pain in his chest. He remembered Lonnie walking away at Bergerac airport, shoulders squared. Brave little Lonnie. He felt the guilt, the heaviness. There was nothing he could have done, he thought. This guilt was unreasonable. *We make our choices, and we have to live with the consequences.* Lonnie had known what he was dealing with; he'd understood the risks. He had saved Lonnie, helped him, but he couldn't have kept him here. Or gone with him. They should have protected Lonnie. *They* should.

He sat there for over an hour, his arms folded and head bowed, filled with pain, anger and self-reproach. Then he stood up, took a few coins from his pocket and dropped them solemnly into the church donations box.

He lit a big candle for Lonnie.


He rang Madame Élodie Lecompte's doorbell. It was an instinctive decision. Later he would realise it stemmed from a need to experience and touch something pure, beautiful, undefiled and *human*.

She opened the door for him, barefoot as usual. She looked at him with those soft eyes.

'I haven't come to see my painting,' he said. 'I want to look at the others again.'

She felt his distress. He saw it in the way she lifted a hand to comfort him, and dropped it again, doubtfully. '*Bien sûr*,' she said, very gently, and led him to the large room. He stopped there, gazing at the people on the walls. Good souls. Good, ordinary people. In each one she had captured their humanity. As if she was trying to express something: we are broken; we are breakable, but we are good.

He realised she had left the room.

He stood there alone for a long time, staring, searching for a connection, absolution.

Then he went out to thank her, to head back out into the city and the darkness.

'I'll make tea for you,' she said.

He nodded. '*Oui. Merci.*'

They sat in her salon, sipping tea, without speaking. Until he said: 'A friend of mine is dead.'

'I'm so sorry.'

He knew she understood. It was more than just the death of a friend.

A little later she rose, crossed to him, just stood there, held his hand. He cried. His big shoulders heaved just a few times. Then he was still.

Past midnight he took the rucksack out of the kitchen cupboard. He unclipped the catches, found the letter, put it on the small sofa in his living room. Wackett jumped onto his lap as if she could sense his mood.

He tore open the letter. It was in blue ink, with spidery, shaky handwriting.

He unfolded it. A photo slid out. The cat watched curiously as it dropped onto the sofa. He picked it up and examined it. The head-and-shoulders photo of a young woman. She laughed at the camera, her skin smooth and shiny, exuding zest for life.

He turned it over. The name Gugu was written on the back. He didn't know her. He picked up the letter, began to read.

*My old friend*

*I thought for a very long time before I wrote this letter. Because I know how difficult this will be for you. But it is my duty, and you will know I have always done my duty.*

Daniel turned to the last of the three pages to see who had written it. Above the postscript it was signed by Mandla Masondo.

It shocked him to read it, hear it, this voice from the past. Because he knew that Mandla would be able to persuade him. Of all the people they could have chosen, Mandla would be able to talk him round.

The memories flowed back. Thirty-five years ago. Mandla, the one who smuggled food and medicine to him, into Saraktash, that godforsaken training camp in the south of Russia. When Daniel was still Thobela Mpayipheli, in detention for fighting with an Uzbekistani. A bloody fight with a Red Army sergeant. The man had had shoulders like a bull and a neck like a tree trunk and treated Thobela and his black comrades like scum. Until Thobela couldn't take any more, and fought the man in the non-comissioned officers' bar. They'd locked him up as punishment for his victory and the awful damage he had done to the man in his rage.

Mandla had sneaked in every night to bring him food, soup and bread, ointment for his wounds and pills for the pain. Skinny Mandla, the humble one with so much patience, earthy wisdom, the quiet smile and a little cough, always a little cough in the Russian cold. He was ten years older than the other Umkhonto recruits: they called him 'uBaba', tongue-in-cheek at first, but later they meant it. Father. For that was what he was to many of them.

Mandla Masondo. A simple man, the herdsman of Babanango, the harbour worker and trade-union activist from Richards Bay. Never reaching great heights, he was a follower, like Lonnie May, rather than a leader. After 1994 he was an officer at an army base in Bloemfontein, a colonel. Never wanted more than *isithunzi*.

Mandla who brought him the salve and the soup, and the cheap Russian army bread that tasted like baked sawdust. Then he would sit outside the cell and talk to Thobela, who was only twenty years old, full of fire and rage, hate and impulsiveness. He would say to Mandla: 'If they catch you here, they'll lock you up too, uBaba. And that will make your cough very bad, because it's cold and wet in this jail. It would make you very sick.'

Mandla just smiled quietly and carried on talking in his soft, gentle way.

'Why are you here, uBaba, in this terrible place?' Thobela wanted to know. 'Why aren't you with your cows in the KwaZulu hills?'

'I'm looking for *isithunzi*. For my children.'

Thobela knew Mandla meant 'dignity', because *isithunzi* could also mean 'status' in Zulu, or 'prestige'. 'That's all, uBaba?'

'That all that anyone needs, Thobela. *Isithunzi*. The rest comes by itself.'

Daniel Darret came back to the present, rearranged the thin sheets of the letter, so that he could start at the beginning again.

# 40

*My old friend*

*I thought for a very long time before I wrote this letter. Because I know how difficult this will be for you. But it is my duty, and you will know I have always done my duty.*

*I want to tell you a story. It is a story I know you will understand, because I know about your loss. I was so very sorry to hear of it. The story is about my daughter. Her name is Gugu. She is very beautiful. She is now thirty-two years old. She was born in London, when I was in exile. She is my only child.*

*She was eight years old when I brought her back to South Africa for the great liberation in 1994. I was so happy, Thobela, and so proud, because I could tell her that I was part of the Struggle. In 1997 I took her with me to my office when our beloved Nelson Mandela paid a visit to 1 SA Infantry Battalion. Madiba held Gugu's hand and he told her that I, her father, was a great hero of this country. I will never forget that day and how Gugu looked at me with great pride. That was the day I got my isithunzi back, Thobela. Do you remember when we talked through the night about isithunzi?*

*I told Gugu so many stories about all we endured and about the people who fought with us. I told her about you and Rudewaan Moosa and our fearless leader Moses Morape and the great rugby match we played against the Russian Army. And we won! Do you remember?*

*That was a wonderful day. I wanted to tell that one to my grandchildren, but now I may never get the chance.*

*I also told Gugu about the man who is now our president. I told her how brave our president was in the Struggle, how many people he helped to get out of the country, to join Umkhonto. Did I ever tell you he recruited me? Our president. He came to Babanango. He spoke to my father. He spoke to me. He escorted me to Swaziland and to Mozambique. I respected him very much. I was also very proud when he became president. I did not know everything that happened because I was working very hard in Bloemfontein.*

*Gugu studied to become a teacher. She went to the University of the Free State and got her degree. I only wish her umkhulu was still alive to see that, his granddaughter getting a degree. He had no schooling, my father, he could not read or write. And his granddaughter earned a degree, with distinction! That is the moment when you realise how much we have achieved through our sacrifices.*

*Thobela, I find it hard to tell you this story, so I write other things that are not important. Let me say what I have to say.*

*Two years ago, Gugu was teaching in Brandfort when our president came for the Winnie Mandela celebrations. The choir that sang for the president were Gugu's pupils. The president came to thank her and the children after the ceremony, and then she told him that she was my daughter. She told him about all the stories she heard when she was a child. She told him he was one of her great heroes. He said he remembered me.*

*The president then invited her to visit him, Thobela. He got his people to take her name and number, to organise a visit to him in Mahlamba Ndlopfu, that big white house on the hill in Pretoria where he now lives in his official residence.*

*She was very excited when they called. They said she must come for the weekend, as the guest of our president. She told all the school children she was going to have dinner with the president and his wives, because she was the daughter of a Struggle hero. But that is not what happened.*

*That Friday, she drove to Pretoria. They gave her a room in his house, told her the president was very busy, but he would come later to eat with her. There were no wives. Only bodyguards and servants. He came alone, after eight o'clock. He was very charming. Do you remember how charming he could be?*

*They gave her wine and food, and then all the servants and the bodyguards left. And then he changed. He was not charming any more. He made advances and she did not know what to do. She tried to be respectful, to let him understand that she did not want to do such a thing. But then he forced her, Thobela. He raped my daughter.*

*Why did she not run away? Why did she not fight back? Why did she not scream or shout or hide in a bathroom? Those are the questions I have asked myself these past two years, so many times. When she told me about it, she said she was paralysed. She wishes, every day, she could go back to that night and change everything. But she cannot. She is different now. She is sad all the time. She is ashamed of herself. I am sending you a photograph of how Gugu was. Look at her, Thobela. That beautiful smile you see, that is gone now. She has lost her job. She has lost her self-respect. She lives with me. She does not want to go outside.*

*I am not asking you to take revenge for my daughter. I am not asking you to kill this man because he took away Gugu's life. I am asking you, is this isithunzi? If this man is our president, do we have isithunzi? As South Africans, as soldiers, as fathers, as daughters? Is this what we gave the best years of our lives for?*

*I am asking you to join the Struggle again. Please.*

*Your comrade, your friend, your uBaba,*

*Mandla Masondo*

There was a postscript below Mandla's name, instructions that Daniel didn't wish to read now. He put the letter down beside him and picked up the photo again. He stared at it for a long time, then put it down, too. He stroked the cat's neck.

Later he got up, went to lie on his bed with his hands behind his head. He stared at the patterns on the old ceiling. Fatigue overcame him, emotional exhaustion. He fell asleep, although it was fitful. When the sun rose, he was already awake. He went to wash, then fed the cat, ate breakfast.

Before he went out, he saw the letter and the photo on the sofa. He hesitated a moment, feeling a faint unease. He picked them up, folded them, put them inside the envelope and pushed it back into the rucksack. Now, after Lonnie, after everything, he didn't want just to leave it there. He walked out, slinging the rucksack over his shoulder. Which reminded him – the pistols. He was suddenly angry with himself. How could he have forgotten about the pistols in the toolbox? He was pathetic, a mere shadow of what he'd once been.

He walked to the garage at the rue Permentade. He pulled on his riding gear, put on the helmet, climbed onto the motorbike. He set off. First to Chartrons. He unlocked the workshop, walked to the Peugeot panel van, took out the pistols, wrapped them in cheesecloth and packed them into the rucksack too. He would throw them away somewhere.

He took to the road. First southwards. Along the Garonne, Langon and Marmande. At Aiguillon he turned north-east without thinking. He focused on controlling the bike on the road, clutch, gears, accelerator, brakes, through the twists and turns, following the signboards without a destination in mind.

On a straight section of the D676 before Villeréal he suddenly realised he was going too fast, close to 180 k.p.h., that it was dangerous on this road. And that what he was doing was familiar. He had experienced it before.

He stopped at the T-junction where the road sign indicated *Envals 3.3*. His heart beat rapidly. He took a deep breath, tried to regain control, calm. He got off, put the bike on the stand, removed the crash helmet. He felt anxiety, claustrophobia. He remembered what it had been like in the Sudan, ten years ago, when he had last had this feeling, this insight. He had ridden this motorbike from Johannesburg, through Africa. From sunrise to sunset. Day after day. His mind in another world. He talked to others only when it was necessary, to procure food, bed, fuel, repairs to a tyre, getting the motorbike welded. Zimbabwe, Zambia, Tanzania, Kenya, Ethiopia. And in the north of Sudan, on a desert road between Khartoum and Merowe, at nearly 200 k.p.h., on a straight road stretching to the horizon, he had understood what he was trying to achieve. He wanted to get away from all his memories, the pain and trauma, just race away from them. He wanted to leave them all behind, the ghosts who pursued him. He stopped in the sweltering heat beside the road, and knew he would have to confront his demons at some time or other.

He tried. From Alexandria to Sicily to Marseille. Through Europe. Each day he faced a scrap of his history, and a piece of himself. Until he experienced some measure of peace, just enough to stop him running away.

It was back. This time he was running from what Mandla Masondo and Lonnie May had placed in front of him. Running from responsibility, from going back to who he had been and what he used to do.

In Cadouin, a small medieval village, he made his decision. He sat alone outside the street café, in the cool of Le Triskel's veranda, drinking coffee and staring at the church and the monastery, established nearly a thousand years before. He looked at the village around him, the serenity, order, the lifestyle, the simplicity of existence, the *égalité*, the absence of poverty. That was all he had wished for his country. That dignity, that prosperity, this pride, the knowledge that all the blood that had been spilled through history, all the sacrifices, all these had made this possible, produced this, brought this into serene being. With the conviction that it was right and good.

He wanted to approach everything rationally. He tried to work through the emotions stirred up by Masondo's letter and Lonnie's death, systematically, little by little, rivulets of thought flowing together, like the Cata River. He was only partially successful: it remained in the pit of his mind, like lead.

He weighed up each thing against the other. His existence here. He knew his Bordeaux life was a refuge, an escape, a balm for all the old hurts. He knew this life wasn't contributing to a community; it made no significant difference to the world, had no great meaning or purpose. But it was his life. It was the little bit of happiness he had, and surely the most he would ever have.

He would have to give it up. To assassinate another country's head of state in France would make him the most hunted man in Europe. They would not rest until they had him. And they would find out who he was, sooner or later. If he survived, if he got away, he would remain a fugitive. To the very end.

He had to weigh that up against the likely impact of eliminating the president. A symbolic deed at best, showing that it was possible to fight back against corruption and betrayal. *They're a cancer,* were Lonnie's words. *Cut it out here, it starts up somewhere else. A Hydra – you can never cut off all the snakes' heads. They're a machine with a thousand gears.*

Could he believe what Lonnie had said? *We'll issue a press release saying he is the first. There will be more.* Would there really be more? Was the group of forty-three ready for that? Did they have other plans?

He would have to trust them, his old comrades. Lonnie had given his life for this cause, for this strategy. Mandla was ready to put his name to a letter, a letter that could have been intercepted, that could have cost him his life.

His decision was not a sudden moment of clarity, an overwhelming wave of emotion. It was an intellectual decision, slow and reluctant, bearing full knowledge of the consequences.

He sat there, beside the square opposite the ancient church, and reached into his jacket for his cell phone. He called Madame Sandrine Lefèvre. She answered instantly, greeting him warmly, the first time in almost a month that they had spoken. She asked him how he was.

He said, 'Well, thank you, Madame. May I come and see you?'

'*Tu nos quittes?*' Much disappointment, sure that, like his predecessors, he couldn't persevere with Monsieur any longer.

'No,' he said, 'I don't want to resign. I just want three weeks to deal with a personal matter.'

He knew it was only a half-truth. He would never see her again.

# 41

'I knew him, Lonnie,' he'd protested in Au Bistrot, one of his many arguments against doing it. 'I knew the president.'

'In those days we all thought we knew him,' Lonnie said. 'But he was already scheming, I'm telling you. He was planning his coup d'état from *way* back. He's a sly bastard.'

Daniel shook his head. 'He was good to me. He . . . I was still a child . . .'

'You?' Lonnie grinned. '*You* were never a child. I remember you in Angola. You must have been about eighteen, but you were already a man. More of a man than most people twice your age.'

He ignored the flattery. 'I was seventeen when I was smuggled through Swaziland. There was a safe house in Goba, Mozambique, where we slept . . .'

'I remember. That aunty made such delicious food . . .'

'One evening he came and sat next to me. He was travelling, I don't know where to. He was in a hurry, he had a lot to do. But he sat with me at that kitchen table for almost an hour. He told me he was also scared the first time. Because you didn't know what to expect, all that lay ahead of you. And you miss your family, when you're that young. Your mother and father. He said he missed his mother so much. Then he asked me what my father did. I told him he was a missionary. And my father didn't know I was joining the Struggle, though he must have heard about it from my uncle by now. My father was a good man and I felt very guilty. He deserved better. The president said my father would be very proud of me. And that I was a brave young man.'

'He said that to everyone, Tiny.'

'He missed his mother.'

'So what?'

'He told me my father would be proud, when I really needed to hear that. And now you want me to look that man in the eyes and kill him?'

# 42

He went to fetch the rucksack from the motorbike's pannier so that he could read Mandla Masondo's postscript. The pistols were on top, wrapped in cheesecloth. He pushed them down to the bottom of the bag. Better to keep them for now.

He sat down, ordered more coffee and had to remember which district he was in before ordering the *chocolatines*. It was only in the south-west they called them *chocolatines*. The rest of France would ask for *pains au chocolat*.

Then he read Mandla's postscript:

*You were an agent for a long time, so you will know that it would be best if you destroyed this letter once you have read it. I only fear for my own safety because I have to look after Gugu, and the risk of sending it was high enough. But I have to take it.*

*If you decide that this is not your struggle, of course we will understand. You have been through so much. But we need to have your answer, for obvious reasons. These instructions were given to me. I write them exactly as I received them.*

*Please go to an internet café and create an email address at proton-mail.com. It is a Swiss service that provides end-to-end encryption and it is extremely secure. Do not use your own phone or computer or your own internet connection. When you have the Proton email address, log on to Gumtree.co.za. It is a website where people can post advertisements for anything. Place a free advertisement in the Healer Services section, under the name of 'Doctor Inhlanhla, Traditional Healer and Spell Caster' and make your region Pretoria/Tshwane. Only add your new Proton address. If you decide not to join the struggle, that is all you do.*

*We hope with all our hearts that you will accept this one last assignment. If you do, please add the words 'Love potions' to the heading of the advertisement. We will then respond with a message that starts 'Love potions are never enough'. The message will contain a way to contact us.*

*Please make sure that you are not followed to the internet café. If you know how, activate the 'private' setting on the internet browser when you log on to Proton, and delete your browser history before you log off from the computer.*

*Good luck!*

He smiled wryly at 'Dr Inhlanhla', because it meant 'Dr Happiness' in Zulu. It was a good name for a traditional healer. He read the instructions once more, memorising the contents, then burned the letter.

Afterwards he paid for his coffee with money from the rucksack, climbed onto his motorbike, headed for Sarlat-la-Canéda. That was the nearest large town, known for its many British residents. He would find internet cafés there.

He rode the winding, narrow roads of the Périgord Noir, feeling free, right into Sarlat. At twenty to three he stopped at the Resto Cybercafé on the avenue Thiers. He paid for a password, picked a computer right at the back, and followed the letter's instructions.

He created an email address, inhlanhla@protonmail.com, and posted the advertisement on Gumtree. He added the words 'Love potions'. He waited forty minutes to see if there was any response.

No email arrived.

He rode back to Bordeaux slowly, taking three hours.

Daniel didn't want to use an internet café near his flat. He knew there was one near the main railway station, the Gare Saint-Jean. He went in to check if there was any mail. When he saw the message, his heart leaped. He leaned forward to obscure the screen, even though no one was looking in his direction.

*From: vula@protonmail.com*
*Subject: Healer Services*
*To: inhlanhla@protonmail.com*

*Love potions are never enough.*
*Welcome on board!*
*Le Traiteur Marocain, Marché des Enfants Rouges, Paris. Monday. 12.00.*

That was all. Just those few sentences.

He read it again, then deleted the message.

Monday afternoon in Paris. The day after tomorrow.

The easiest and quickest way to reach the capital city was with the new bullet-train service to the Gare Montparnasse, two hours' travel from Bordeaux. There ought to be enough trains tomorrow. He would take one in the late afternoon, and spend the night in Paris in a hotel somewhere. He googled the Marché des Enfants Rouges. He could see that it was the city's oldest covered market, named after the red-uniformed orphans who used to live next door. Up in Le Marais, on the rue de Bretagne. Le Traiteur Marocain was a Moroccan restaurant in the market.

He deleted the history from the web browser before he left.

The shortest route to his garage was past the now-shut Capucins market. In the rue des Douves he saw Mamadou Ali standing with a small group of friends. He looked up when he heard the motorbike, waved his arms wildly to attract Daniel's attention.

He stopped, and opened the crash-helmet visor.

'I've been waiting here for you, Daniel. Are you in trouble?' asked Ali, his voice muted, eyes scanning the streets.

'Why?'

'There are men . . . They're asking everywhere if anyone knows a black man, big and tall, one point nine metres or more, who lives or works around here.'

'What sort of men?'

'White men. There were two. Looked like *les flics*.' He used the street lingo for police. 'But they're not. They talk French with an accent. One is a big block of a man with an ear that's seen better days. And the other has a sore arm . . .'

'How do you know his arm is sore?'

'He has a big bandage,' said Ali and pointed at his right arm. 'The thing is, Sansan Adjoumani, that big guy from Ivory Coast who works at the bicycle shop on the rue Magendie . . .'

'I don't know him.'

'Well, that *crétin* told them it could be you. He was scared they would mess with him, and he doesn't have papers. And Sansan said he thinks you live on the place Camille Pelletan. Are you in trouble? Do you need help?'

'Thank you, Ali. You know me. I avoid trouble like the plague.'

'*D'accord.* If they ask you, just say you know nothing. We have to stand together. They look like trouble.'

Daniel shrugged. 'I don't know any other big black guys around here. Did they say why they were looking for him?'

'Some stupid story about a lot of money he owes them. You could smell the *merde* a mile away. Anyway, I thought I'd tell you. You're the biggest black guy I know.'

'Thanks, Ali.'

He said goodbye, drove on. On his guard now, hyper-aware of every person on the street.

He drove past his garage first, turned at Victoire, doubled back. He didn't see anyone. He stopped in front of the garage door, pulled off his gloves, took the rucksack out of the pannier. He looked up and down the rue Permentade, pushed his hand into the rucksack, struggled to get a pistol out of the cheesecloth. He got hold of the butt of one, pressed the safety off, still holding it in the rucksack, opened the garage door and went inside.

He took off his helmet, pulled the pistol out of the bag, holding it behind his back as he quickly checked, left and right, out of the garage doors. The street was Saturday-afternoon silent.

He tucked the pistol into his belt at the back of his biking trousers, darted out quickly, to push the motorbike inside. Closed the door again, then stood, trying to take stock.

What did they know? They had followed Lonnie May when he was heading in the direction of his flat. They would have learned that the Saint Michel neighbourhood had a high percentage of Africans. They knew he was a black man, as they had seen his hands and a part of his face, on the night he had put them out of action. They knew he was big. Hence that description when they came asking questions. Few people knew where he lived, very few knew where he worked. Sansan would not know.

He kept the biker jacket on to hide the pistol in his belt. He locked the rucksack into the pannier of the motorbike, locked the garage, walked up the rue Marengo, keeping his eyes peeled, on the roofs of the three-storey houses, the windows, doors, street corners.

A scooter approached him from the front. He put his hand on the pistol butt. It went past, just a student in shorts.

There was no one in place Camille Pelletan. He unlocked the front door, jogged up the stairs.

His flat door was open a crack, splinters from a crowbar just beside the lock.

He took out the pistol and went in.

# 43

It was chaos inside. The sofa cushions were ripped open, one chair lay upside down. His tablet was on the floor, screen cracked.

Someone had been through his place, violently.

He stood dead still, listening.

Wackett sat on the windowsill, a bundle of self-pity, and shot Daniel a dirty look, as if this was all his fault.

He could sense the flat was empty, that they had gone, but he kept the pistol ready, feeling the indignation, the rage, because they'd come into his space, his house and his privacy, and destroyed his serenity completely.

To the kitchen. Sugar, flour and oatmeal poured out over the kitchen table, the empty plastic containers and tinned food tossed all over, along with cleaning material and cloths. His fridge door standing open.

His bedroom was a mess, clothes, bedding strewn around. He went straight to where his Daniel Darret proofs of identity were stored, in the space behind the skirting board beside his bed. The piece of wood he had so carefully cut out was undisturbed. He wiggled it loose. The documents were still there, the birth certificate he'd bought from the real Daniel Darret, a man he had met seven years ago at a hairdresser's in the Château d'Eau district of Paris. The real Darret had urgently needed money to return to the Ivory Coast for unexplained personal reasons. Thobela Mpayipheli had money – a farm's worth – and an urgent need to become someone else.

The certificate was safe in the niche, along with his passport. He carried his *carte nationale d'identité* in his wallet, along with his driver's licence. He had obtained the ID card and passport using the purchased birth certificate. His own photo was on it, his fingerprints on record. Official proof of a new life.

He left the documents there, put the block back carefully.

He went to the front door. He would have to repair it, and reinforce his first line of defence. He put the pistol on the kitchen table, took off the jacket, and fetched tools from the cardboard box under the kitchen sink, where it was also overturned and scattered.

He worked on the door – he would only be able to restore it partially. He would have to fit a big bolt, but where could he buy something like that at this time on a Saturday? He wondered what they were looking for. Some form of identity, a photo? Proof that Lonnie had been there, or that Daniel was their attacker? Documentation of a murder conspiracy?

There was nothing here. But he had a niggling doubt, something at the edge of consciousness, a nagging idea. A proof, a clue that eluded him now.

He thought while he worked. The tablet had a South African news app on it, if they had checked. A vague superficial pointer, if they had seen it. But he never used email or social media, so there was no personal content they could use to identify him. He stored his payslips at work. There was nothing in the flat they could connect to him, so why couldn't he shake off this vague worry? The tablecloth he had wrapped around his head was at the shop; the rucksack and pistols had been with him on the motorbike.

His shirt. The bloodied shirt was in the washing basket.

He hurried to the small bathroom. The shirt was lying on top of the pile they had tipped out. The man with the predatory face, the one whose arm he had shot up, would remember it, the colour, design and the bloodstains.

Daniel swore.

They knew it was him. And they knew where he lived.

He jogged back to the front door that he had secured as best he could. He'd buy a bolt tomorrow morning. Two – one outside, one inside. Not that that would stop anyone who was prepared to break in and not care about causing a ruckus. But something. Before he left for Paris.

He'd have to sleep in a hotel in Bordeaux tonight. Because they would come back. Pack a bag now, find a hotel, take the train tomorrow. Early.

Hurry.

With renewed urgency he crossed the sitting room to the kitchen to put away the tools. He thought of what else he should take with him. The rucksack, the money . . . He'd have to leave the pistols as they had a scanner at the station.

He packed away the tools and took out the broom to sweep up the sugar, flour and oatmeal. Then something struck him, and with it a wave of panic. He dropped the broom, went instinctively back to the sitting room, looked through the mess they had left behind.

The bowl. The little green clay bowl he kept on the mantelpiece was empty.

Élodie Lecompte's letter had been in it. With her address. He tried to suppress the panic, picked up cushions and chairs, looked under the couch. It was nowhere to be found.

That was when he ran.

First to the cours Victor-Hugo, then east. The pistol chafed his back. He was desperate – it was Saturday night, there *had* to be a taxi.

He spotted one approaching from the wrong direction. He had to get across the dual carriageway, through dense traffic. The cars hooted. He was just in time to attract the driver's attention. He gave him Élodie Lecompte's address, said, '*Très vite, très vite, s'il vous plaît,*' his voice so urgent that the man made a U-turn with screeching tyres, then zigzagged at high speed across the lanes of the broad street to loud protests from other drivers.

It felt so slow, like an eternity, as the worry ate away at him. And the self-reproach – he should have thrown the letter away the moment he'd spotted Lonnie. By then he'd known it spelled trouble.

The taxi dropped Daniel in the cours Georges Clemenceau, the nearest point to her *appartement* that allowed vehicle traffic. He gave the driver fifty euros. 'Keep the change, thanks.' He ran the last two blocks, his biker boots clattering on the cobblestones.

He turned the corner of rue Montesquieu, saw the ambulance and the police vehicles, the crowd of onlookers, and knew he was too late.

He pushed through the curious to the front. There was a cordon; he tried to pass but a policeman stopped him. 'What's happened?'

The officer didn't answer.

'A break-in,' said a woman behind him.

'Burglary,' said a man beside her. 'Most likely jewellery thieves. Rich people live here.'

'Was anyone hurt?' Daniel asked, still addressing the policeman, who looked up at him now, alert to the urgency in his voice.

And then the ambulance stretcher came out of the front door of Élodie Lecompte's apartment building, and despite the oxygen mask and the paramedics crowding around her, he could see it was her. He could see the blood that had run from her hair across her temple, nearly dry now. He could see her hand dangling from under the blanket, the blackening blood on it.

He cried out to the heavens in Xhosa, feeling a fierce surge of rage at the president, the man he was going to kill. Now, for the first time, the desire was there, clear, overwhelming and final.

He became aware of eyes on him, an instinctive sensation, and looking up he saw Predator Face, the one with the injured arm, facing him on the other side of the barriers. The man was staring at him, his eyes boring into him, seeing his anxiety, his urgency, doubt slowly changing into recognition. Beside him was a massive bear of a man, the one Mamadou Ali had described, his left ear deformed by thick scar tissue, as if a piece had been bitten out of it.

Predator nudged Big Man, pointed a finger at Daniel. Shouted to the left. Another two standing there, lean and wary. Pointed his finger again, shouted to the right. There were *more* of them.

They moved towards him, at least six men.

Daniel turned, crashing against the woman who'd spoken about the break-in. She protested. The policeman called a warning to him. He shoved through the people. They were aware of him now, and stepped back, opening a path for him to race through. He didn't look back, dodged east, towards the old city. It was his best chance, the maze there. The narrow streets. He knew it well – he would have to lose them there, use his advantage, as they had still to get through the crowd.

In the silence of the impasse Fauré he stood in the hollow of a doorway at a kink in the long alley, took out the pistol. He was breathing hard and his lungs burned from running for a quarter of an hour, back and forth through the streets. He couldn't keep up this tempo much longer.

They would be bunched together in this narrow place. He would wait for their footsteps, step out of the shadow and fire. He tried to control his breathing to hear better. Sirens were sounding somewhere. He would be caught on the cameras now, the big black man running away from the scene of the crime.

He didn't hear any footsteps. He stood for one, two, three minutes. Nothing.

Deep breath.

He couldn't go home. They knew where he lived.

He had to get to Paris. They would be watching the station now, and the airport. The motorbike was registered in the name of Daniel Darret. They were sure to establish that sooner or later, within the next twenty-four hours. They would be able to hack into French databases and traffic cameras. He had to think carefully.

He took stock. He had his wallet in his pocket. His driver's licence and ID card. The rucksack with the money was on the motorbike. His helmet was there, but his jacket was at home. A hotel in Bordeaux was no longer a good idea. He had to get out of the city. In a direction that would not betray his plans.

He stayed there for another five minutes, until he was absolutely certain he had shaken them off. Then he walked to the river to toss the cell phone into the water at the quai Richelieu, as they would find that number on the database as well. It was in his name. And if they had it they would be able to track him down.

# 44

In the restaurant that night Lonnie May had asked him: 'Why Bordeaux?'

'What do you mean?'

'It's . . . Why didn't you settle in Paris? I mean it's . . . Paris. Big. Busy. Beautiful. And the women, *ooh, là là!* Or at least the sunshine and blue sea of Nice? Or Provence, lavender fields and sunflowers and old farmhouses . . . That lifestyle. I wouldn't mind disappearing there.'

Daniel said it was something he found hard to explain.

'Oh, come on. Humour me.'

Daniel put his fist over his heart: 'It's here.'

Lonnie raised his eyebrows sceptically.

Daniel said Paris was like a lover. She was beautiful and exotic, exciting and wild. She delighted and tempted you, and in the moments of ecstasy you wanted to possess her with all your heart. But she was not to be owned. Unless you were native-born, her child. He'd lived there decades ago when he was on loan to the Stasi and KGB, young and fearless. Back then he could do the flirtatious dance with her. But when he'd returned, ten years ago, he'd tried it again, sought to reignite the old spark of passion. It was different. No, *he* was different, and what he wanted was different. So he'd moved on, riding his motorbike, without a plan, from place to place. Eventually he arrived in Bordeaux. His first visit. He had no expectations or premonitions. Late in the afternoon he'd found a room in a chain hotel on the rue Martignac, unpacked and wandered through the oldest part of the city looking for a place to eat. At the place Saint-Pierre, at a little table under the gaily lit branches of a giant tree in front of the old church, he had fallen in love. Inexplicable, unexpected, as true love should be. 'I found the bride,' he told Lonnie with a smile, 'who could love me in return, despite my origins.'

Lonnie laughed. 'Never took you for a romantic.'

Daniel shook his head. 'No, I'm an old pragmatist. You're underestimating the charm of this city. There are a lot of incomers here. In Chartrons there are a lot of British expats.' And then: 'Bordeaux has a thing for strangers. Have you heard the Stahlschmidt story?'

'No,' said Lonnie.

Daniel proceeded to tell him the true story of the young German marine. Heinz Stahlschmidt was trained at the start of the Second World War to defuse British underwater mines – a dangerous job: in the first two years all three of the ships he worked on had sunk. He survived each time. In 1941 they posted him to Bordeaux, to do on-shore duty. Perhaps they felt he deserved a less dangerous job, or perhaps it was just the notorious superstition of sailors – by now it was clear that Stahlschmidt didn't have luck on his side. He lived in Bordeaux for three years, walked the streets, breathed the air. Bordeaux won his heart too. When the Nazis had to retreat in August 1944 – it might have been on just such a hot, humid night as this – his superiors ordered Stahlschmidt to blow up the docks. In the war years the harbour stretched seven kilometres downriver, in the city. The explosions would have caused the death of thousands of residents and largely destroyed his beloved Bordeaux – all those beautiful old buildings, the streets and alleys, the little squares, the warm heart of the historic city. Stahlschmidt couldn't do it: his love for Bordeaux was too great. He blew up the German explosives magazine. They said it shook the entire city – you could see the flames and smoke from tens of kilometres away.

'He lived here after the war. Married a Frenchwoman, and even changed his name. To Henri Salmide. He died here in 2010. That's what this city can do to you,' Daniel Darret said.

The Meerkat was silent for a moment.

# 45

He rode the motorbike to Arcachon on the Atlantic coast. He didn't have his jacket, and the night air was initially just cold enough to be uncomfortable, in spite of the BMW's windshield. First he took the eternally busy E5, the main route to Spain, and kept religiously to the speed limit, then the quieter A660, where he was finally sure that no one was following him.

He thought about Élodie Lecompte. They would have rung her bell and said something about him, a shot in the dark. Maybe: 'We have news from Daniel Darret, urgent news.' She would have opened the door.

He didn't want to know what they'd done to her, but he was certain it was Predator and Bear: he could tell from their body language, in those seconds when they'd stood across from him, on opposite sides of the defenceless, gentle, shy woman on the stretcher.

He would get them. When this was all done with, he would get them.

He knew where to find Henry and Sandrine Lefèvre's Arcachon holiday home on the avenue Sainte-Marie, as he had had to go there twice to do small paint-and-repair jobs for Madame. And he knew the code for the house alarm. It was the same as the shop; *le génie* preferred that Madame kept things simple.

The street was luxuriant with trees and it was quiet, most of the inhabitants having left for the city after the holidays. He opened the gate, drove in, parked the motorbike at the back, away from the street. It might be weeks before anyone noticed it. Or the little window in the back door that he would have to break to get in because he was hungry, tired, grimy and cold. The breeze off the Atlantic had been cutting these last few kilometres.

He closed the gate, took the rucksack, broke the window, went in.

He tapped the alarm code in, but didn't switch on the lights. If the neighbours were at home, they would know the Lefèvres had gone back to Bordeaux today.

He waited until his eyes adjusted to the gloom of the kitchen, found *galettes de maïs* and a jar of *confit de canard* in the food cupboard, made coffee, ate. He washed up the dishes carefully before he went to shower. He felt too much of an intruder to sleep on one of the beds and made himself at home on the couch.

He was weary, but he knew sleep wouldn't come quickly: his thoughts were on Élodie Lecompte. How serious were her injuries? How much damage had they done to her? The woman who'd held his hand while he cried over Lonnie's death.

There had been a time, long ago, when he hadn't concerned himself with collateral damage. When he was a warrior, a driven, focused hunter. He could justify it as the price that the world had to pay to balance the scales of justice. The goal sanctified everything. That certainty evaded him now, that ideology, the easy differentiation of right from wrong, black from white. In his anger he wanted to place the damage to Élodie Lecompte on the president's account, and on the Russians, but it wasn't that simple. He had played a part in it. He'd helped to topple the first domino when he'd met Lonnie at the cathedral. He'd known Lonnie would bring trouble, with his tails and secret meetings.

He would have to accept responsibility. He would limit further damage to others. He would just have to. Whatever the cost.

The damage to himself he would accept, as before. The loss. Once again. Of a life. A future. A home. The loss of Bordeaux.

He would like to tell Mandla Masondo that this city was where he had regained his *isithunzi*. And now he was about to lose both.

He thought about the cat. Wackett would have to take care of herself. The animal had been a stray before she had made herself at home in his flat. She would quickly charm children next door for food. Or insinuate herself with someone else. Wackett would survive.

He thought about the task ahead. He'd been gasping for breath in the impasse Fauré. Just fifteen minutes of running and he was knackered. It was the adrenalin, the tension. How was he going to do this? At fifty-five? He was too old to be a hired executioner.

On the brink of sleep, around two in the morning, he wondered who would meet him in Paris. An old comrade? Which one? Who could risk going to Paris if MK43 were being watched, if they knew about Lonnie, and now about him?

Just before nine he awoke with a start. The sun was making long, striped patterns through the shutters. He sat up, listening, heard only the birds singing outside, surprised that he'd slept past daybreak. Exhaustion. The best remedy for insomnia.

Then, as if the revelation came to him in his sleep: the painting of him in Élodie Lecompte's home. Photorealistic. If they'd seen enough of him outside her apartment to make the connection, they would go back and take a photo. So that everyone hunting him would know what he looked like.

That spurred him on, drove him to get washed and dressed. He patched the broken window in the back door, put the alarm on again, took the rucksack and set off on foot. At the gate he was cautious, making sure there was no traffic, and then he walked east, towards the town centre. He only began to unwind as the street began to get busy. He ate breakfast in a café to still his gnawing hunger, while he read the *Sud-Ouest* newspaper. There was a short article on Élodie Lecompte on page two. They called her 'the local artist'. She was admitted to hospital with serious injuries, but her condition was stable. The police suspected it was a burglary gone wrong when she'd fought back. No suspects had been identified yet.

Serious injuries. Her condition was stable.

What sort of people caused serious injury to a defenceless woman?

But she was alive, he was thankful for that.

He went shopping on the cours Lamarque de Plaisance. He bought clothes, durable items: a quality pair of grey trousers, two blue shirts with collars, a smart navy jacket, black shoes, socks, underwear. Then a pair of jeans, two T-shirts, two polo shirts, in dark colours. And two baseball caps, one red, one blue.

He bought a travelling toilet bag, razor and shaving cream, toothbrush, toothpaste, deodorant.

A suitcase of good quality that everything would fit into, including the rucksack with money and firearms. In the toilets of Hôtel La

Perla he packed the items into the case, put on the jacket and walked out.

It took him twenty minutes to walk to the small harbour. There were nearly fifteen hundred yachts, pleasure- and fishing-boats moored to the quays in orderly rows. Rich people's toys bobbing in the hot summer sun. Dotted about, signs offered boat rides in the bay and to Cap Ferret. That wasn't what he was interested in.

He found what he was looking for at the loading area east of the harbour, past the workshops and boat dealers: the older, more weathered boats at the cheap mooring spots. He saw two men hunched over an outboard engine at the second quay. He went over to ask if they knew of anyone who could take him up the coast.

They looked him up and down, cigarettes in their mouths, hands smeared with oil. Father and son, perhaps.

'How far up the coast?' asked the father, and put a screwdriver down.

'Gijón?' He deliberately gave a destination in the opposite direction.

They looked sceptical.

'San Sebastián?'

'Why don't you drive by car?'

'Or take the train?' asked the son.

Daniel said, '*Merci*,' and turned away.

'Wait,' called the father.

He looked back at them.

'Try Olivier.' The man pointed a dirty finger. '*Quai Cinq*.' The fifth quay. 'His boat's called *L'Ange Fou*.'

He thanked them and left, the wheels of his case click-clacking over the concrete joins of the quay. He knew they were staring after him. They would remember him, but he doubted if anyone would ask.

*L'Ange Fou* was the furthermost boat on Quay Five, white fibreglass in need of a lick of paint, two seats on the deck, a torn canvas sunshade on the frame of dirty stainless steel. Not a boat that inspired great confidence.

Daniel stopped beside the boat and called: '*Allô!*'

He heard a cough from the cabin. Then silence. He called again.

'*Qu'est-ce qu'il y a?*' Irritated.

'I want to rent your boat.'

He heard the muffled sounds of someone moving about, another cough, then a head appeared. A man in his fifties, thick dark hair, five days of pepper-and-salt beard, bloodshot eyes. A face that had seen a great deal of trouble and sun.

'Rent?'

'That's right.'

'I come with the boat. I'm the skipper.'

'I understand. I want you to take me to Gijón.'

'Gijón?' The man looked at him dubiously. He heaved himself out of the cabin. He stopped in front of Daniel. 'Gijón? Why don't you take the train?'

Daniel smelt the sourness of stale booze. He didn't react, let the silence lengthen.

'Oh,' said the skipper of *L'Ange Fou*, with a flash of insight, new light in his eyes. He looked at the sun, considered the weather. 'Today?'

'Now.'

'It can be done. But it's expensive.'

'How much?'

'Six hundred euro.'

Daniel smiled and turned, began to walk away.

'Five hundred,' the skipper called.

'Two hundred,' said Daniel.

'Three fifty. Cash.'

Daniel walked back to the man. The skipper put out his hand. 'Olivier Chérain,' he said. 'And I'd rather not know who you are.'

'I don't want to go to Gijón. How much will it cost to take me to Brest?'

# 46

'You're a sly one,' said Chérain, with a crooked, conspiratorial grin.

'Can you take me to Brest today?'

'Brest is far. It's a long trip. That's a lot of wear and tear on the engines. I would have to buy fuel in La Rochelle. And I'd have to sleep over in Brest – that means mooring fees, hotel expenses. If the weather turns I may only come back in two or three days.'

'How much?'

'A thousand. And I'm not going to haggle.'

'Six hundred.'

'I'm not sleeping in a third-rate hotel, forget it. Or get someone else.'

'Seven hundred?'

'Not negotiable. And you pay me up front, before we leave.'

Daniel sighed. 'Half now, half on arrival.'

'Welcome aboard.'

Chérain said the vessel was a Jeanneau Leader 850, which meant the boat was 8.5 metres long. It had 250 horsepower diesel engines, 'and she might need a bit of a face lift, being thirty-two years old, but she doesn't leak and her engines run like clockwork.'

They sailed slowly out of the harbour mouth. Chérain stood behind the wheel and Daniel sat on one of the two mounted seats behind the windshield.

'Is this your job?' Daniel asked.

'Kind of,' said Chérain.

'Oh?'

'I didn't ask *you* why you'd pick the longest, most difficult way to get to Brest.'

'*Touché*. But how far do you go normally?'

'Far enough. Spanish coast. As far as Santander.'

'How far is that?'

'Eighty nautical miles.'

'And Brest?'

'About two hundred and seventy. More or less.'

'You've never gone that far with this boat?'

Chérain reached into his trouser pocket and pulled out a stainless-steel flask, deftly unscrewed it, took a swig and said: 'I've never needed a thousand euros this much.' He offered the flask to Daniel. 'A tot to pacify Poseidon?'

'No, thank you.'

Chérain held the flask up high. '*À votre santé!*' Then he drank deeply of the contents and pulled both throttles open.

The sea was smooth. They sailed north, just a kilometre from the white beach that stretched endlessly on the starboard side, the greenery of pine forests behind. Gulls circled and swooped, a distant rumble of breakers. Chérain pointed out small towns on land – Lacanua Océan ('There's a golf course. I don't get the point of golf. Waste of time, walking after a ball . . .'), Montalivet ('The most boring town in the world, one giant old-age home – not even the nudists can revive the place . . .'). Daniel listened, grinning at the man's gloomy outlook. He felt relaxed for the first time and knew he'd made the right choice to travel this way. He was safe, for the moment.

Just south of the Île d'Oléron Chérain said: 'I hope you don't get seasick.'

'I've never had the chance to find out.'

'Well, you're going to find out now,' said the skipper, and pointed out to sea. 'West wind,' he said. 'It's going to get rough.'

He was right. Barely fifteen minutes later Daniel was leaning over the side of the boat retching.

'Big breakfast,' said Olivier Chérain, impressed. 'Just don't make a mess of my deck.'

He was curled up in misery in the tiny cabin, on sheets that smelt of booze and sweat. Chérain was on deck behind the wheel. Occasionally Daniel heard snatches of song over the never-ending drone of the engines, surprisingly tuneful. He wondered if the man was a smuggler.

There were occasional news reports of refugees being smuggled across the English Channel in small boats, or drugs from Spain. He suspected the latter, Santander being Chérain's furthest journey yet.

Daniel stayed on the bunk until they were in La Rochelle harbour. While they took on fuel, he recovered enough to emerge again. 'How far still to go?' he asked.

Chérain checked his watch. 'Another six hours.'

Another six hours of wretched seasickness. He cursed.

Chérain shrugged his shoulders in the Gallic way that meant 'Not my problem.'

It wasn't just the discomfort of the journey that bothered Daniel. Brest at nine o'clock tonight: there should still be a train or two to Paris, as it was Sunday night, when everyone travelled back to the city from their beach or country house.

Chérain paid for the diesel with a card, then sailed to a mooring place.

'What now?' Daniel asked.

'I'm going to get something to eat. Can I bring you something?'

'No, thank you.'

Chérain grinned as he tied the boat to the quay. 'You'll find your sea legs in due course. Stay in the cabin, out of the sun. I'll be back soon.' The skipper jumped spryly onto the quay, and walked towards the harbour buildings.

If the constant vomiting hadn't left him so limp and drained he might have suspected earlier that 'back soon' was an empty promise. Realisation only dawned half an hour later, when there was still no sign of Chérain. When an hour had passed Daniel was worried enough to begin searching the cabin for anything that could shed light on the skipper and his life.

There was a tiny kitchen on the starboard side, basically a two-plate gas stove and a sink, a built-in cupboard on the port side, and the bunk forward, drawers underneath.

The drawers yielded crumpled clothing, blankets, a few old boat shoes, two soft-porn magazines and three empty booze bottles. The built-in cupboard was where Chérain's safety equipment was stored – lifejackets, flares, engine parts, a two-way radio that seemed to be broken, a few marine map books of the French and Spanish coast.

More reason to suspect that the man was running drugs from Spain, although probably just on a small scale. This was all too disorganised and informal for an important cog in that industry.

In the drawer under the sink he found a brown envelope beneath a random collection of cutlery. After a quick check to see whether the skipper was returning, he shook out the contents onto the bed. The boat's registration documents, Chérain's skipper's licence, passport and ID card. He examined everything, then packed it away carefully.

He got off the boat to stretch his legs, walked up and down the quay, too afraid to leave his bag unattended, with the money and pistols.

When an hour and a half had passed he was certain the man had found more than food. He started to wonder if he should write off his investment of five hundred euros and catch a train from there. He decided to wait a bit longer. Brest had definite strategic advantages.

Just before four a taxi stopped beside the quay. He saw Chérain get out. It was a complicated process, as he was extremely drunk. Chérain paid the driver, talking loudly, took out two plastic bags, pushed the door shut with his hip, staggered on his way. Halfway to *L'Ange Fou* he stumbled and fell. A bottle broke in one of the bags. '*Merde,*' Chérain said.

Daniel sighed, bent down in the cabin and picked up his case. He climbed off the boat and walked to the skipper. He helped him up.

'Where are you going?' Chérain asked, while he held onto Daniel, like a man in a storm.

'Timbuktu.'

'But you said . . .' he struggled to shape the words ' . . . you have to get to Brest today.'

He stood with his suitcase, halfway between the harbour and the station, on the bridge across the Lac de la Sole. The streets were quiet late on Sunday afternoon. He looked out across the lake and swore softly.

La Rochelle wasn't a big city. He felt exposed, visible, and he hadn't entirely recovered from his seasickness. That bloody Chérain. He was annoyed at his own poor judgement – he'd thought it was clever to charter a boat, sail up the coast, throw those looking for him completely off the scent. Brest would have been much safer, a longer, less-predictable leap. To a bigger city. But in his self-congratulatory wisdom over his mode of transport he'd slipped up in his choice of skipper.

Adjust, improvise: that was what they'd drilled into him back then. Things *would* go wrong, but success depended on how you managed the chaos. He had no more stomach for dealing with chaos, especially after tossing up enough breakfast to feed all the fish in the Atlantic Ocean.

He would have to visit the station to find the time of the next train to Paris. There would be cameras. He bent down, opened his case and took out the red baseball cap. He took off his jacket and packed it in the case. He pulled the cap down low over his eyes and started walking. At least there was solid ground under his feet.

He noted the cameras on the pretty sandstone building of the Gare de La Rochelle. He kept his head down, walked in and studied the timetables. There was a six o'clock train to Montparnasse station in Paris. Eighty minutes until he could buy a ticket, just before departure.

He went out again, still uneasy. The station was in a predominantly residential area. He had only one real choice – the 164 Espresso Bar across the street.

He sat down inside so that he could watch the street. There were no newspapers to read, but behind the counter a TV was showing a football match. He didn't feel like coffee yet so he bought a Coke and watched the TV and the street in turn. Neither produced any excitement.

After five his innards had recovered sufficiently for him to order a panini with ham and cheese, and another Coke. At twenty to six he left and went to buy a ticket, *Le Monde* and a couple of motorbike magazines at Relay.

He waited on the platform. Just before six he boarded the train to Paris.

He thought about the workshop in Bordeaux. Tomorrow morning Henry Lefèvre would walk into it and resume work after his holiday. He would inspect Daniel's table, and then he would stoop over a piece of furniture and begin to make it whole again.

Daniel's greatest desire was to be there with *le génie* now.

# 47

He felt an enormous sense of relief when he disembarked at the Gare Montparnasse wearing a new blue collared shirt and his jacket. Even a big black man could disappear in the crush and hurly-burly of this station and city. He hailed a taxi outside, asking the driver if he could recommend a good, affordable hotel near the Luxembourg Gardens. He wanted to stay on the Left Bank tonight, far from the Marché des Enfants Rouges where he had to be the next morning.

The taxi dropped him off in front of the Hôtel Le Sénat. He took a deep breath before he entered: he would have to lie convincingly.

He greeted the woman at reception with what he hoped was a combination of friendliness and indignation. He told her something bad had happened on the Métro: his cell phone and his wallet had been stolen on the way from the Gare du Nord. A pickpocket, so bloody sly. He was left with only the cash he had in his case, a good sum at least, thank God, otherwise he didn't know what he would have done. But he felt bad, embarrassed that he didn't have any form of identification with him. He knew hotels required a passport or something similar. But he had a very important meeting tomorrow: he had to rest, prepare. He was happy to pay in advance, any amount she thought proper, if he could only have a room. He took out some notes from his inner jacket pocket, a bundle he had assembled with care on the train – enough to show he was well-to-do, but not so thick that she might imagine he'd robbed a bank.

All the time he was talking he was sure he didn't sound very convincing or practised. Rusty. And reluctant, he thought, unwilling to fall back completely into the constant deception of the old life.

She looked uncomfortable. 'Just a minute.' She disappeared into the back. He knew she was going to check with the night manager.

She returned with another woman, somewhat older, who assessed him, his smart jacket and quality luggage, while he repeated his story, smoother this time, better.

'Actually,' the night manager said, 'we're not permitted to do that. How long do you intend to stay?'

'Two nights maximum,' he said. 'I understand, it's a dilemma, but I don't know what else to do.'

'You will pay for both nights in advance, and a deposit for the bar fridge?'

'Of course.'

'Very well.'

'You're an angel,' he said.

To his relief her mouth twitched into a faint smile as she began to tap the computer keyboard. 'What is your name?'

'Olivier,' he said. 'Olivier Chérain. And I know my ID number off by heart at least.'

Later, in the shower, rinsing off his sweat, salt and the whiff of seasickness from his pores, he smiled for the first time since Lonnie had made him laugh in Au Bistrot. He stood still, thinking about the day, about Chérain, the alcoholic smuggler skipper. If he had stayed aboard *L'Ange Fou*, they could be halfway to South America by now.

Perhaps he would come to regret not staying on the boat.

But at least he'd got half a journey, a temporary name and an identity number for his five hundred euros.

*Monday, 28 August*

He switched on the TV while he washed and dressed. The sixth news clip reported on the South African president who would be arriving on Thursday for a short visit to France. On Friday he might be meeting the young, newly elected French president.

He ate breakfast, and after that decided to walk. It was the best way to move around the city if you wanted to make absolutely sure you weren't followed. The Russians would need a great deal of luck to pinpoint where he was now. But the Marché des Enfants Rouges was only a clever public meeting place if both parties fulfilled the responsibility to arrive undetected.

He wanted to stretch his legs and spend time in his favourite spots, try to relax. Like the place Saint-Michel, where Paris-the-Lover had overwhelmed him that first time, more than thirty years ago, his eventual deployment after an eternity of military and intelligence training. He, who till then knew only the hills of the Eastern Cape, the remote bush of Angola and Tanzania, the plains of southern Russia and the grey concrete of East Berlin. He had come by train from Munich, then on the Métro from Gare du Nord, his first sight of Paris. He walked up the steps of Saint-Michel station, and emerged onto the street. The atmosphere of pure electricity: dancers and students, musicians and tourists, mime artists, cars and bicycles. The energy, sound and colour of the square overwhelmed, shocked and enchanted him. Swept him into its vibrant heart. He had stood there, glued to the spot, for hours, drinking it all in. The boy from Kat River. Astounded by *la ville lumière*.

Now here he was again, sitting for a while, remembering. Lord, what a country bumpkin he'd been. So naïve. And so unaware of it.

The only aspects that had changed in the three decades at Saint-Michel were the student fashions and the shapes of the cars. And himself.

He kept an eye on the time, walked on, over the Seine, up to the Fontaine Stravinsky, where he had coffee. Tension was gradually building inside him. He strolled through the Anne Frank Gardens, and eventually through Le Marais. He used all his skills, all the nearly-forgotten techniques, to make sure nobody was on his trail.

At a minute to twelve he sat down at a table in the Marché des Enfants Rouges, close to Le Traiteur Marocain. His heart beat faster. He was aware of everything, his senses sharpened. He wondered who would be there.

The covered market was a happy place, full of seductive aromas: stalls for vegetables, fruit, flowers and cheese, a bakery, kitchens selling Italian, Oriental and Moroccan food. Tables and chairs to sit at and eat. Very busy this time of day.

Suddenly a man was beside him, right up against him, and he stiffened.

'I'm sorry, sir, but these tables are reserved for customers.'

One of the restaurant employees.

'Of course,' he said. 'How do I order?'

'Over there at the counter.' The man pointed at Le Traiteur Marocain.

Daniel thanked him, stood up, joined the line. He looked at photos of the various dishes, shuffling forward as the queue progressed. A quiet voice behind him, feminine, speaking French, but with the accent and rhythm of South Africa: 'I can recommend the tagine kefta. It's delicious.'

Slowly he turned and looked at her. '*Merci*,' he said.

She was young, early thirties perhaps, pretty and elegant, wearing a bright yellow strapless dress and a black beret. There was a fine sheen of perspiration on her forehead. In her right hand she held a large shopping bag from Galeries Lafayette. She smiled at him, but he could see she was tense.

'Can I buy one for you too?' he asked.

'Oh, thank you so much, that would be delightful.'

'I am Olivier,' he said, his eyes still scanning the market.

'I had hoped you were Dr Inhlanhla,' she said in Zulu, her voice strained by tension.

She's an amateur, he thought. They sent an amateur. How would she know she wasn't being watched? He tried to take in the entire market, get a feeling if someone was taking an interest in them. 'I am,' he said in the same language. 'But only on weekends.'

She laughed, a forced bark. In French she said: 'It's better that you don't know my name.'

'Of course.'

She gestured with her eyes that it was their turn to order. He turned back to the counter, asked for two tagine keftas, paid. The man who had chased him off beckoned him to a table.

'Shall we eat together?' he asked the woman in the beret.

'Please,' she said.

They walked to the designated table and sat down. She pushed the shopping bag under the table, visibly tenser now. She reverted to Zulu. 'You must take it with you, when you go. Please be very careful. There are incriminating articles in it. If you think it will land in the wrong hands, try your best to destroy it.' Mechanical words, as though she was reciting them by heart.

He slid his hand across the table, took hers and held it. His voice was relaxed and soothing: 'You're Sesotho,' he said, because he could tell from her accent and the careful Zulu word choices.

'Yes.'

'You're not used to this sort of thing.'

'Is it *that* obvious?'

He squeezed her hand gently. 'Take a deep breath.'

She nodded, sighed slowly. He could feel from her hand that she was starting to relax a little.

'Do you think anyone followed you?' he asked.

'No. I really don't think so. Nobody knows about me!' she said anxiously. And then, more quietly: 'And I spent half an hour in the Galeries Lafayette, the department store, the really big one . . .'

'On the boulevard Haussmann?'

'Yes. I was up and down, and in the fitting rooms and out and in again . . . I'm sure there was nobody.'

'That was a good place to slip away. But it doesn't matter. When we leave here, I'll make sure neither of us is being watched. You don't have to worry.'

The waiter brought two plates of food, with little containers of chilli sauce on the side.

'It smells delicious,' he said, picking up the plastic knife and fork.

She smiled bravely. '*Bon appétit*,' she said, and began to eat.

'How long have you been here in France?' he asked, but then realised she might not want to talk much about herself. 'You don't have to answer.'

'I think it'll be okay. Seven months. On a culture-exchange project.'

'Are you with the Department of Arts and Culture?'

'Oh, no. I'm a writer, a playwright,' she said, as if it was a relief to talk of things she knew. Then a self-critical frown. 'I'm talking too much.'

'You're safe, don't worry.'

They ate in a moment of silence. He asked: 'Why are you doing this? This dangerous game?'

She looked at him with a sudden passion. 'Gugu. She is like a sister to me. I'm doing it for Gugu.'

# 48

Her plate of food was half eaten and she was more relaxed. 'There is information I must give you,' she said.

'Whenever you're ready,' Daniel answered.

She put her hands on the table and shut her eyes, as if trying to be sure to remember everything, get it all right. Her eyes opened. 'In the bag there are four cell phones. They are all secure, but don't use any of them for more than two days. Then you must break and discard it.'

'All right.'

'They have already installed the application that you use for email on each of the phones. You must just register with your own details. Keep a regular watch on your email, because the programme of the man you must meet here in Paris is not yet finalised. They will send information.'

'Okay.'

'I can tell you now that he'll arrive in Paris on Thursday. On the thirty-first of August. On Friday he will be at Versailles. On no account should you meet him there.'

'I understand.' That was most likely the meeting with the French president, where security would be very strict and the possibility of a diplomatic storm that much greater.

'He'll be in the South African embassy for meetings all of Saturday. His movements on Saturday night and Sunday are still unknown. He flies back Sunday night or early Monday morning. You'll receive more information by email as soon as it is available.'

He nodded.

'I have to ask – is your financial position still bearable?'

He smiled. 'Bearable? Is that the word they told you to use?'

'Yes.' She surprised them both by giggling. He thought she also sounded relieved, because she had done everything required thus far.

'Yes, thank you, my financial position is still most bearable.'

'The final item. There are five passports in the bag from various countries. You can use them in any sequence if you need a passport. They are all genuine, the Schengen visas too.'

'Right.'

'When you suspect a passport or identity is no longer usable, please ensure that the document is burned.'

'Right.'

'That's all.'

He could see she was lighter, a burden lifted. 'You did very well. Eat your food. It's too good to waste.'

'Yes, Daddy,' she said, with a smile.

When she was ready to go, he told her just to keep walking, not to look like somebody worrying about being followed. He would make sure she was safe.

They stood up. She gave him a hug, looked deep into his eyes. 'I'm praying for you,' she said.

He picked up the big white Galeries Lafayette shopping bag she had left under the table. He kept his distance from her. At the place des Vosges he was satisfied that no one was tailing either of them.

She kept walking, towards Bastille. He watched her go, feeling a surge of compassion for her, and a heavy responsibility to make sure she didn't become collateral damage. When he could no longer see her, he turned west. He wanted to go to the Île Saint-Louis and eat ice-cream, for old times' sake, and prolong the pleasure of her company, enjoy the calm before the imminent storm.

'Yes, Daddy,' she'd said.

He'd smiled with her. 'You're a brave woman. If I were your father, I would be very proud of you.'

'Thank you.' She'd looked at him in a peculiar way. 'This whole thing has been surreal, meeting you here. I – I was *so* nervous, they gave me so many dos and don'ts, I was scared I would . . . ruin everything. But then they sent your passports, and I looked at the photo, and it was like . . . I just knew everything would be okay.'

'Oh?'

She laughed, embarrassed. 'The play I'm writing is about

Christophle le More.' Her voice rose at the end, querying whether he
knew of Le More.

He shook his head.

Her face lit up with enthusiasm. 'Few people do. His portrait's
hanging in the Rijksmuseum. It's the earliest known stand-alone
portrait of a black man in Western painting history. It was made somewhere between 1520 and 1530. They think the artist was the Dutchman
Jan Mostaert. In any case, when the passports arrived, and I looked at
your photo, I thought you looked like him. Like Christophle le More.
Without the beard, of course – he had a beard. And I thought it was a
good sign, an omen. That everything would be all right.'

'Who was he, Le More?'

'A bodyguard and archer in the court of Emperor Charles the Fifth.
He started as a stable lad so he must have been an impressive man to
advance that far.' She expressed a great deal of admiration.

'What is your play about?'

'Le More's pilgrimage from Brussels to Brabant. To see the Black
Madonna. It's . . . They think he was there, because in the painting he
had the pilgrim's badge in his hat. My play is fiction – we know nothing
about his journey. I just thought he must have been lonely. As a black
man in white Europe. There were no other Africans in the emperor's
service so he must have missed the company of his people. Imagine
him hearing about the Black Madonna of Brabant and thinking she
must have come from Africa, and then he goes to – to connect with
something . . . The play isn't finished.'

'I hope I shall see it one day. The play. *And* the portrait.'

'I hope so.'

'Do I look like him in real life?'

'Yes, quite. But . . . you're different from what I imagined.'

'Oh?'

'You're gentler. I . . .' She waved a hand shyly. 'I don't know if
you're the one who is going to do it. I don't want to know. I expected
a harder man . . . You know, someone who . . . Maybe I should just
shut up.'

Daniel Darret didn't want her to shut up. He was enjoying listening
to her speak Zulu, even if it was not quite correct. In it he could feel
the rhythm, hear the music of his fatherland. He liked looking at her,

at her youth and beauty, her courage, knowing she was part of this operation, that she believed in it too. It made him feel better about what lay ahead.

In his room in the Hôtel le Sénat that afternoon he read the email he'd downloaded on the first of the four LG smartphones in the shopping bag. The TV was tuned to the dedicated news channel, volume turned low. He was lying on the bed.

*From: vula@protonmail.com*
*Subject: Medical apparatus*
*To: inhlanhla@protonmail.com*

*Dear Dr Inhlanhla*
*We are relieved and overjoyed that you have taken the package into your possession and remain in good financial standing.*

That meant his anonymous young contact in the yellow dress had informed them that the meeting had been a success. He hoped it was the last task she was asked to perform. He suspected they had used her because she had no connection with them, would be under no suspicion. He could understand that. But she was an amateur: she shouldn't be exposed to further risk.

The other phones were lying on the small desk beside the five passports, arranged in a tidy row. The travel documents each had an identical photo of him inside, one from ten years ago, the last one he'd had taken in South Africa for his driver's licence, before Pakamile's death. There were two South African passports, with Xhosa names. The others were from Swaziland, Botswana and Namibia respectively. When he saw the countries of origin, he suspected they were each procured by an old Struggle contact, well placed in the various neighbouring country governments. Clever.

*You should now be in an excellent position to travel and to stay in contact.*
*The next step of the treatment: you will be in need of medical apparatus for the procedure that awaits.*
*We would like to suggest Ditmir's Trading, 82D Oudezijds*

*Achterburgwal in Amsterdam, an Albanian import/export company. He has a wide range of surgical instruments at reasonable prices. Please make sure you ask for Ditmir personally at this address as he is known to provide significant discount. (We haven't had the opportunity to purchase supplies from him ourselves and a credit rating for his company is unavailable at this stage.)*

*We hope to have the patient's detailed medical records soon, and will inform you the moment we receive them.*

*You are most welcome to share your progress with us via email.*

*Very best wishes,*

*Vula*

# 49

He wondered who the people behind the message were. Did he know them? Were they former members of the South African Intelligence Service, like Lonnie? The cell phones, the passports, the Amsterdam recommendation showed they were informed, still had contacts in that netherworld.

The emails said a lot. Ditmir was a black-market arms dealer; *import/export* suggested Albanian Mafia. The address would house another business; he would have to ask for Ditmir specifically and most likely be escorted to another site to view and buy the weapons. Implicit in their suggestion of a specialist arms dealer was that MK43 thought he would need a long-distance sniper rifle, because it would be impossible to get close to the president. And that had always been his modus operandi when he was in the service of the KGB and Stasi.

But it left him with a huge dilemma: it would be a considerable challenge to move anything larger than a pistol through Europe. Law enforcement across the continent was on a permanent alert, prepared for the risk of terrorist attacks by Muslim extremists. There was a network of informants, roadblocks and CCTV cameras. Soldiers and the police patrolled everywhere in cities, airports and large tourist attractions. Good military-grade rifles were large, usually a metre or more. Not the sort of thing you could pack in a small suitcase. He would need to move a weapon like that from Amsterdam to Paris.

There was only one solution: he had to acquire a vehicle.

He tapped a reply on the cell phone:

*Dear Vula*
*Thank you for the info. Will have to do research before deciding on final type of medical apparatus and means of transport. Medical records would help a lot, as soon as you receive them. Will keep you posted.*
*Dr Inhlanhla*

He plugged the phone into a charger on the desk. He had to plan: reconnoitre the embassy, the trip to Amsterdam. Purchase a vehicle without registering it. He was deep in thought, but something peripheral was drawing his attention, out of the corner of his eye. He looked at the phones, the passports, the window. What was it?

Then it registered: the newsreader on TV was talking about La Rochelle. He looked at the screen. It was an aerial view of the harbour from a helicopter. A dense, dark plume of smoke was rising from a small boat. Two police cars, a fire engine and an ambulance on the quay. He quickly picked up the remote and increased the volume.

' . . . as soon as the port authority releases information.'

Then it switched back to the newsreader, who said: 'Air France personnel plan to go on strike again in September . . .'

Daniel stood frozen, staring at the image. He'd caught only a glimpse of the harbour scene. Too little to be sure that *L'Ange Fou* was on fire. But he could swear it was more or less where Chérain had moored.

He searched the internet with the phone, but could not find more information. He sat down in front of the TV because he knew they repeated news items. He would have to wait. Was it possible that they had tracked him from Arcachon and found Oliver Chérain's boat? But how?

The Russians were masters of technology, of electronic espionage, that he knew. The media were full of that daily, how the cyber unit of the Kremlin's Federal Security Bureau digitally hacked, spied on, stole data, placed fake news, disrupted systems, wherever and whenever they wished, if it was important enough to devote bandwidth, manpower, time and trouble to it. It would have been possible to obtain his motorbike registration number from a French database. Cameras beside the French highways could be used to determine that he must have turned off in the direction of Arcachon.

It was a relatively easy leap then to assume that he would continue his travels by sea. If they had sent the team from Bordeaux to ask questions, the father and son at Arcachon harbour would have remembered him and would have been able to supply information about *L'Ange Fou.*

Chérain had paid for the diesel in La Rochelle with a bank card, another breadcrumb trail for them to follow.

All possible. If they were prepared to supply technology and manpower on a large scale.

How important was the South African nuclear-energy deal? The president in the pocket of the Kremlin?

Apparently just as important as Lonnie May had said. And therein lay his mistake. He had underestimated Ubu, the Meerkat. He had thought Lonnie had been exaggerating the facts, to be more persuasive.

He waited an hour before the news report ran again on the TV. There was new footage, filmed from closer, the fire was out, the smoke dispersing, *L'Ange Fou* a smouldering wreck. And the figure on the stretcher being carried across the quay was completely covered with a green blanket.

The newsreader's sombre voice: 'The vessel was registered in the name of Monsieur Olivier Chérain, a small-boat operator from Arcachon. The deceased has not yet been identified and Monsieur Chérain or his next of kin are urgently requested to get in touch with the authorities. The fire resulted from a small explosion just after twelve noon, according to witnesses. The cause is not yet known.'

Daniel Darret got up, gathered the cell phones and passports and packed them in his bag.

He booked out of the hotel hurriedly, saying: 'I'm very sorry, I have to get to Marseille urgently.' He wanted to get away fast, and considered telling them to keep the money he had paid up front for an extra night, but that might also attract the wrong kind of attention. He waited patiently while the cash was collected from the safe in the manager's office, thanked them for their hospitality, and left.

The Russians would be able to use the cameras in the Gare de La Rochelle as well. They would know what train he had taken. It would take time to examine taxi records in Paris, but they would be able to trace him to this hotel.

He couldn't risk taking another taxi.

He carried his bag down the boulevard Saint-Germain. He was on high alert, feeling exposed, as if he was being watched, as if they were everywhere, could see everything. He used all his knowledge and skill, did a rapid about-face, lingered in quiet places, but nobody was following him. He forced himself not to act paranoid, to focus on the next step. His new accommodation had to be random, picked without a logical sequence. He followed a meaningless route of twists and turns, until he stopped in the rue Jacob at the Hôtel Millésime reception and proffered the Botswana passport. He hoped the young man wouldn't notice the perspiration on his forehead. He used the my-wallet-has-been-stolen excuse for paying cash.

It would not be easy to reconnoitre the South African embassy. He remembered the building on the quai d'Orsay, number fifty-nine. In diplomatic circles it was known as the ugliest building in Paris, despite having been designed by French architects in the seventies. It crouched like a beast in the magnificent wide boulevard, between the much older, classic, cream sandstone buildings of the neighbourhood. Daniel had sometimes walked past it, three decades ago, staring at it with hatred. It embodied all the stolid apathy and bourgeois lack of taste of the apartheid government.

As he recalled it, it was on a corner, looking out over three streets, the quai d'Orsay north of the front façade, the rue Henri-Moissan to the west side, and the avenue Robert-Schuman to the south at the back. All three aspects were equally unattractive, with concrete blocks, like cheese wedges, protecting the windows on its four storeys.

In those days there had been no cameras. There would be now. And if the Russians and South African Intelligence Service knew about him and his mission, they would be monitoring those cameras. Especially today, if they suspected he was in Paris.

He had no choice: he would have to see whether he could work there. Circle the place once, take in as much as he could.

He took the red baseball cap out of his bag and put it into the bathroom bin. He wouldn't be able to use it again because he'd been wearing it at La Rochelle station. He put on the red T-shirt he'd bought in Arcachon, folded the white T-shirt and put it in one trouser pocket. He put the blue cap into the other. He locked his room, and went in search of a white Panama hat in the boulevard Saint-Germain.

He thought of his former Stasi instructor, who had taught him to look at people's shoes. 'Clothes are easy to change, especially shirts and hats. But those following you never change their shoes.' Perhaps he should get a new pair of trainers.

Daniel Darret walked down towards the Métro station Saint-Michel-Notre-Dame, wearing his white Panama hat. He took the RER-C to the pont de l'Alma, climbed the stairs to ground level. He followed the bank of the Seine east, keeping the trees between him and the embassy building. He turned left three times so he could walk around the embassy's block. He tried to take it all in: the buildings opposite, the streets, the four entrances to the embassy, the many cameras mounted on the walls. He dared not stop: it was quiet there, only a few people on the streets.

He knew that he was being rushed, but he had to get a feeling for every possibility. He had the overwhelming impression that the cameras were recording him, that teams were being mobilised to follow him.

Back at the quai d'Orsay he turned west to the Eiffel Tower. His plan was to disappear into the crowds and the maze of the Parc du Champ-de-Mars. That was what he needed – people around him, lots of people.

Just before the tower he turned left into the park, pulled the white T-shirt out of his pocket and put it on over the red one, discarded the Panama hat in a trash basket, and began to run, dodging through the trees and shrubs.

He stopped suddenly and looked back for the first time. Nobody was hurrying after him.

He put on the blue cap.

He rode the Métro for two hours, back and forth across the city to be sure he wasn't followed. He thought about the embassy, and knew instinctively that the building wasn't an option. The only way to shoot the president on Saturday was when he arrived at the embassy, or when he left. Once he was inside, he was hidden.

There were two entrances for vehicles, and two for pedestrians. If they knew there was any danger, they would probably drive the president through the large steel gates at the rear, off avenue Robert-Schuman. His problem was the high wall: he would have to be seated at a high angle to get a shot when the president exited the vehicle. And the buildings around the embassy were all apartments or offices with locked doors and bells or access codes. In addition, the embassy CCTV cameras would record him if he tried entering any of those doors.

That wouldn't work.

Friday at Versailles was impossible; Saturday at the embassy was off the cards.

Sunday was all that was left, but he still had no idea where the president would be.

# 50

He bought bread and cheese at the supermarket on the rue de Seine and ate it in his room as he took stock.

He had to get to Amsterdam in a way that would allow him to transport a sniper rifle back to Paris. He couldn't use public transport. A rented car would put him on the system, where the Russians could find him. He could use one of the false passports, but he didn't have a credit card. Cash at Avis or Hertz drew attention, out of the ordinary, and he suspected they would be scanning the systems for such deviations from the norm. He wished he knew more about digital espionage.

Maybe he was overly cautious, but the death of Olivier Chérain, and how quickly they could track him in La Rochelle, disturbed him. Very much. And, besides, after Lonnie's death, how much could he trust the passports?

He went to search for a vehicle on autoscout24.fr. He looked at Volvos first: only harmless people drove Volvos – good, safety-conscious, law-abiding people. But the second-hand Volvos were too expensive for his taste. He eventually settled on a Peugeot 3008, a 2010 model, for €7500. Grey, nondescript. A middle-class car, a family car with a hatchback and a large boot, offered by a private seller in Montreuil. Forty minutes from his hotel via the Métro. It had been advertised for sale on the website for over a month: 152,000 kilometres on the clock. The owner would be eager to get something close to his price, grateful to settle the deal.

He thought through his story carefully, called the number from the hotel phone. The owner was a man, and Daniel allowed his African accent to be apparent; he used the name on the Namibian passport when he introduced himself. He asked whether the car was still available.

The man confirmed that it was.

Daniel asked if he could come and have look at it the next day. The owner said only in the evening: he wasn't available during the day.

That meant Daniel would have to spend another night in Paris, and only get away to Amsterdam on Wednesday. 'Ay,' he said. 'That's a pity. I can only come tonight or tomorrow morning.'

'Can you come now?' the man asked.

He dressed neatly, took the cash with him. At half past seven he knocked on the door of the simple house in the rue de Plateau. A black boy opened it, maybe nine years old. He reminded Daniel Darret of Pakamile; he felt the pressure over his heart.

The child invited him in, took him to a kitchen-living room where the family were seated at dinner. Father, mother and three boys. There was warmth. A friendly atmosphere. The man rose, proudly introduced his family, invited Daniel to sit. He was reluctant, feeling emotional, a longing for just such a life. The woman asked if she could dish up a plate of food for him. He said, no, thank you, he'd already eaten.

They asked about him, so that he was forced to use his fabricated story. He was from Namibia, a motorcycle mechanic. He and a few friends wanted to tour Europe for a month, and they needed a car. His friends were arriving tomorrow.

The man said their forefathers were from Dahomey, as it used to be called. 'Benin,' said the boy who'd answered the door.

They wanted to know about Namibia, the way of life, the politics. 'Tell the children what it's like in Africa. They've never been there.' Daniel talked; his homesickness for southern Africa was genuine. Then he asked about their family, what they did, how old the children were. He wished the meal would end so that he could buy the car and get away. Get away from this beautiful family. Away from his lies, and what he had to do, away from what he wished he could be.

*Tuesday, 29 August*

He found an email from Vula when he used his cell phone just after seven a.m.

*From: vula@protonmail.com*
*Subject: Restaurant recommendation*
*To: inhlanhla@protonmail.com*

*Dear Dr Inhlanhla*
*Should you find yourself in Paris on Saturday night and in need of*
*interesting conversation, I can highly recommend the Brasserie Lipp at*
*151 boulevard Saint-Germain. It is a popular gathering place of diplo-*
*mats and their chauffeurs. The latter group are always highly informative*
*with regards to social opportunities in that great city.*
  *Of course, we hope that you won't be in need of such social interaction*
*at that time.*
  *As always, you are most welcome to share your progress with us via*
*email in the days ahead.*
  *Good luck and very best wishes,*
  *Vula*

He wrote back:

*From: inhlanhla@protonmail.com*
*Subject: Re: Restaurant recommendation*
*To: vula@protonmail.com*

*Dear Vula*
*Thank you very much for the kind recommendation. I shall certainly*
*entertain the possibility.*
  *I'll be en route to Amsterdam today, to pursue business opportunities*
*there tomorrow.*
  *Yours,*
  *Dr Inhlanhla*

While he ate breakfast in the hotel, he read the article on the website
of the *Sud-Ouest* newspaper. It was about the death of Olivier
Chérain. The authorities had acknowledged that the explosion on
*L'Ange Fou* was the result of gas-stove leak. No foul play was
suspected.

Could it have been an accident? Chérain leaving a gas hob switched on in his drunken state? Had he been unnecessarily paranoid, too optimistic about the Russians' abilities?

It was quite possible. But Daniel pictured the small two-plate gas stove beside the sink in the boat's kitchenette. The metal bars of the hob's pot-stands were speckled with rust. They looked as if they hadn't been used in months. Chérain preferred his meals in liquid form.

Or had he woken with a terrible hangover and decided to make coffee, leaving the gas stove on?

Daniel finished breakfast, checked out and walked to where he'd left the Peugeot, four blocks from the hotel. It was the only parking spot he could find last night, after half an hour of searching. The car was in good condition, despite a faint smell of cigarette smoke.

He chose small local roads, north-north-east. He avoided Lille, Brussels and Antwerp, on the way to Amsterdam. His eyes kept a close watch on the rear-view mirror. He wondered if ever a day would come when he wouldn't need to keep looking over his shoulder.

# PART IV

# 51

Detective Captain Benny Griessel of the Cape Hawks stood on the stage of the MOTH hall in Woodstock with a bass guitar slung round his neck. '"Cry To Me",' he said.

'"Cry to Me"?' Vince Fortuin, lead guitarist, asked in an incredulous tone that said Griessel couldn't be serious. 'That sad old Staccatos' song?'

'Yes,' said Griessel, patiently. 'It's the same song, but we're going to cover the original. The Solomon Burke recording. Blues. Much better.'

'I don't know it,' said Vince, unconvinced.

'Before your time,' said Griessel. 'Nineteen sixty-two.'

'I know the Rolling Stones cover,' said Vince, who, in Griessel's opinion, was the most talented member of the group. He had a preference for sleeveless T-shirts that showed the anchor tattooed on his sinewy shoulder. His small eyes crinkled to narrow slits with sheer joy when the four-man band really got going. He once impishly said: 'I suffer from syncopation, uneven bar movements.' By day he was a plumber.

They rehearsed in the MOTH hall on Tuesdays and Wednesdays during the week before a performance. They called their band Roes, the name chosen because it took the four middle-aged, middle-class, suburban guys five months to shake off their substantial and communal musician's rustiness. They had slowly built a repertoire of old hits in the hope of performing gigs at weddings and parties.

This coming Friday they were due to play at a wedding anniversary at D'Aria in Durbanville. The couple, in their sixties, had requested 'all the old classics'. They were looking for a few extra songs to supplement their usual playlist. They had considered Creedence Clearwater Revival's 'Bad Moon Rising', but Vince said you didn't sing a bad-omen song like that on an anniversary. So they got Booker T. and the MGs' 'Time Is Tight' under their belts, and rehearsed 'Ma Belle Amie' from the Tee Set. The heavy moustachioed rhythm-guitarist, Jakes Jacobs, who usually did most of the singing, had drawn some lively commentary for the way he pronounced the snippets of French. Jakes owned a welding business in Voortrekker Road, Parow.

'The Stones turned "Cry To Me" into a ballad,' said Griessel, 'just like the Staccatos. I don't like that.'

'What does the nineteen sixty-two version sound like, Grampa Ben?' asked the drummer, Japie Blom. His lank grey hair hung down his back in a neat thick plait, tied back when they performed. A cigarette dangled permanently from his lips. He worked as a fresh produce agent at the Cape Town market from four in the morning. He claimed he smoked so much to stay awake during the day.

'Sixteen-bar rhythm and blues, with a soul groove,' said Griessel. 'The chords are one-four-five.' He turned the volume on his base guitar up a bit, laid the foundation in the key of E, boom, boom, boom, and tapped out the next two beats with a fingertip on the guitar's string saddle, tip, tip, and then he repeated it. Boom, boom, boom, tip, tip. And again.

Japie followed him first on the bass drum, then added a bit of kettle-drum. Jakes's rhythm guitar joined in on the second repeat of the sixteen-beat blues, as he said: 'Benny, I can't remember the lyrics.'

Griessel nodded and stood closer to his own microphone, which was usually just intended for his occasional harmony. He kept time with his right foot, his left shoulder making tiny counterpoint motions. He shut his eyes, waited for the beat, and then he opened up, his voice a bit hoarse, a little reedy:

*When your baby leaves you all alone*
*And nobody calls you on the phone*
*Don't you feel like crying?*
*Don't you feel like crying?*
*Well, here I am, my honey*
*C'mon baby, cry to me*

Vince, who'd been standing listening, gradually stopped frowning, and by the end of the second verse he'd made what Japie later called a 'shit-hot turnaround': his fingers danced, notes darting and flying as an intro to the chorus.

Then something happened. It wasn't the first time. Rust had their moments. Like the day Alexa Barnard sang an impromptu version of Ma Rainey's 'See See Rider' with them, just for the hell of it. Or the night at a wedding reception on a wine farm near Wellington, when Vince played the guitar intro to the Hollies' 'Long Cool Woman In A Black Dress', completely out of the blue and unrehearsed. Pure mischief, and the wedding guests, all a few sheets to the wind, cheered and yelled. And Japie Blom and Griessel, inspired by their response, joined in perfectly. Jakes's voice sounded practically identical to Allan Clarke's, and they were just cooking, and the crowd stood a moment and cheered in amazement at the sudden transformation of the mediocre band, then streamed onto the dance floor, and Rust played that song for nine minutes. Vince did a solo and Benny played a riff and Japie showed off his drumming skills, until the sweat was pouring off them and all four were grinning from ear to ear.

But here in the MOTH hall with 'Cry To Me' it wasn't about the crowd, it was about the musicians, about Vince's-shit-hot-turnaround, and can-you-fucking-believe-Benny-can-sing-a-bit, and about nostalgia, when everything just works and they could open the throttle and let the demons loose, and when Vince's final note died away, Griessel was still standing there in the perfect silence with his eyes shut in bliss, away from all the evil of his job, away from himself.

Then his cell phone rang.

He was reluctant to answer, unwilling to relinquish that magic moment: he just wanted to make more music.

He took the phone out of his pocket.

It was Mbali Kaleni.

'Colonel?' he answered, while the rest of the band stood looking at him. They knew what was coming next.

'Benny,' she said, 'I need you. *Now.*' He heard the seriousness, the urgency in her voice.

'Yes, Colonel.'

'I'm going to text you the address. It's in Observatory. Please hurry.'

★   ★   ★

Vaughn Cupido sat at a table outside on the pavement at De Vrije Burger in Stellenbosch, with the delightful Desiree Coetzee and her son, Donovan. They were eating burgers. Cupido hadn't ordered chips. He didn't want Desiree to know he was on a diet, so he told her he just wasn't that hungry. But his mouth was watering for the crispy fries steaming in front of the child.

'Mommy, you must buy the Audi RS 3,' said Donovan. 'That thing is wild.'

Desiree needed a new car and she couldn't make a final decision. 'I want to drive to work, lovey,' she said, 'not go racing.'

'Those Audi dudes were real crooks with their diesel emissions,' said Cupido. 'Not *ayoba*. Not cool at all.'

The child ignored him. 'Please, Mommy, just not a Nissan.'

'What's wrong with a Nissan?'

'Boring. Very boring. I won't ride with you, Mommy. You'll be on your own.'

'You're only worried about your image when I drop you off at school. I'm worried about my bank balance.'

Cupido wondered how he could participate in the conversation; he was trying hard to create a bond with the boy. He remembered something he had recently read. 'You know the Tesla?' he asked Donovan.

'Of course.' He nodded with the know-it-all attitude of a twelve-year-old. 'Cool car.'

'Damn straight. There's more technology in that car than in most aeroplanes of ten years ago. I was reading the other day, you get a phone app with that car, you can sit in a restaurant and tell the car to warm the inside, or cool it down, before you go to it. If you forget where you parked it, the app will tell you where it is. If you're sitting in the restaurant and you want to visit your pal in Athlone, you type the address in the app, and when you get to the car it will navigate for you. Cool, hey?'

'My teacher says there's an Afrikaans word for "app",' said Donovan.

'No, there isn't. Who cares anyway?'

'She does. She taught us it's a *toep*.'

'A *toep*?'

'Yes, Uncle.'

'*Toep*. I ask you.'

'That's what she says.'

'That's never gonna catch on. Nobody in their right mind is gonna talk about a *toep* in Afrikaans or *any* language. You can tell that to your teacher.'

The boy nodded in agreement. 'So, Uncle, are you going to buy a Tesla, then?'

'Nah, too expensive for a policeman.'

'Brantley says Uncle has lots of money.'

'Me?'

'Yes, he said Uncle is captured. All the Hawks are captured so they've got loads of money.'

'Donnie, don't sit and talk nonsense. Eat your chips before they get cold,' said Desiree.

'It isn't *me*, it's Brantley that says so.'

Cupido gritted his teeth. 'We are not captured,' he said. 'We are the Serious and Violent Crimes Unit. Nobody can capture us.'

'Not even the state president?'

'Not even—'

Cupido's phone rang on the table. He could see the call was from Lieutenant Colonel Mbali Kaleni.

## 52

At half past eight that night Griessel drove down the narrow Nuttall Street in Observatory. In the yellow of the streetlights he saw only Kaleni's white Hawks BMW parked in front of a blue Toyota Yaris on the narrow sidewalk. It was a strange sight, in the absence of other police and emergency vehicles. He stopped in front of the old corrugated-iron flat-roofed house with a little white wall and a big lemon tree in the garden.

Mbali Kaleni got out of the passenger side of the Yaris, and walked towards him. Her face was stern. She was still in her full PPE suit, the official prescribed personal-protection equipment that included booties, coveralls, cap and gloves, all in light blue. Only her face mask was pulled down around her neck. There was another woman behind the steering wheel of the Toyota, unrecognisable in the dark.

'Thanks for coming, Benny,' said Kaleni. Her voice was strange, without its normal tone. 'Please bring your murder bag.'

He nodded, went to fetch it from the boot of his car. She waited for him at the gate, opened it, and they went through. He was still thrown slightly off balance by the absence of local station detectives and uniforms.

'The woman in the car is Thandi Dikela,' said Kaleni. 'She has been my friend for more than fifteen years. The man inside is her father, Menzi. He was a great man, he was—'

She stopped speaking and Griessel looked at her. They were standing in the shadow of the lemon tree that blocked the streetlights and it took a second for him to realise that tears were trickling down her cheeks. He couldn't recall ever seeing her weep. He didn't know what he should do – he wanted to put out a hand to comfort her, but she was his commanding officer.

'I'm sorry, Colonel,' he said.

She shook her head, as if she could rid herself of the feelings. After a while she said: 'Thandi called me. Three hours ago. She came here to check on him because he'd said things that made her very worried about his safety. He's seventy-four. She called him this afternoon and he didn't answer. Five times, he didn't answer.' Her voice broke, her shoulders sagged, and she began to sob. Griessel couldn't bear it any more. He dropped his murder bag and put his arms around her shoulders. She stood meekly as he hugged her.

The sobs racked her. 'I'm so sorry,' he said. Those were the only words he could think of. He'd never had to hug a commander in sympathy before.

It took her a while to come down. Then she stepped back and began to dry her tears with her hand. 'Thank you, Benny,' she said self-consciously, straightening up. 'When he did not answer, she came here. The front door was closed, but not locked. When she went inside . . . It looks like he shot himself, Benny.' She took a deep breath to gain control. 'She says that's all wrong. She says he told her on Saturday that if something happened to him she should call me. Thandi was very upset. She asked him what could happen, what was going on? He said he wasn't serious, just an old man with bad jokes, she shouldn't worry. But she did. She called him a few times on Sunday, yesterday too, and he just laughed, said she should forget what he'd said, he was fine. And then, today . . . She works in Nyanga. She's a town planner with the People's Housing Process, and she was very busy, so she only started calling in the afternoon. He didn't answer . . . And then she came . . . He was a solid, happy man, Benny. He was never depressed. She says this is all wrong. She says someone came and killed him. And they wrote that suicide note. That is not her father's handwriting, because she knows it very well. That was someone trying to make it *look* like her father's writing . . .'

She made a small helpless gesture, as if she wished this wasn't real. She said: 'Vaughn is coming too. I need you both. I need you to be very, very careful with this. I need you to treat this as a crime scene. Just . . . be very thorough, Benny. I can't do it. I'm too close, too subjective and too upset. I'll wait with Thandi in the car. Please don't call anybody yet. Just be very thorough. Tell me if this was suicide, Benny.'

Griessel nodded.

'He's in the kitchen.'

\* \* \*

Griessel was covered from head to toe in the PPE outfit, the Canon
PowerShot camera in his pocket, the small LED torch in his hand. He
switched it on, studied the front door. There were no signs of damage
to the lock or bolt.

He opened the door.

It was dark inside, with a soft beam of light shining through one
front window, between the curtains. He could make out the shapes of
chairs and a couch, a coffee-table, illuminating each with the torch.

Nothing else.

He found a light switch on the wall, switched it on. Turned off the
torch.

Beside the switch was the control box of an alarm system. Griessel
saw the motion sensor in the corner of the room.

The sitting-room furniture was smart but not luxurious. Burgundy
and blue Oriental carpet on the floor. Flatscreen TV on a cabinet against
the wall, DSTV decoder below. He walked forward, to just inside the
front door, closed it behind him. The room – the whole house – became
eerily quiet. He stood still for a moment and considered the situation.
Mbali Kaleni, who never let her feelings show, always did everything by
the book. And the book said you reported everything to the local SAPS
station. Regardless of how suspect a suicide seemed. And especially if
you knew the victim. You called the Station Commander in whose area
it had occurred and you let the uniforms come in, cordon off the area
and control traffic, and his detectives come in to inspect and Forensics
and the pathologist, and an ambulance for the body. That was what the
book said. That was what Kaleni always said.

But not a week ago with the Johnson case, and not tonight either.

Something strange was going on. And the eerie atmosphere in the
house didn't help. Evil seemed to linger, as if a tragedy had played out
there. Or would still.

He tried to shake off the feeling. He trusted Mbali Kaleni completely.
If she was prepared to ignore the book, then he was too.

He fumbled pulling the camera out of his pocket because the PPE
coverall made it awkward. He took a few photos to cover the whole
area.

*The front door was closed, but not locked.*

*Just be very thorough. Tell me if this was suicide, Benny.*

He did what he always did – tried to visualise what had happened, tried to put himself in the criminal event.

If the front door was not locked, if it wasn't suicide, had the potential murderer come in through this door and left by it again? Knocked, waited for Menzi Dikela to answer? Or barged in?

No apparent signs of violence.

His eyes traced the logical route from there to the passage at the back. A metre of dull yellow wooden floor was visible, between the skirting boards and the carpet. He saw a mark, like a faint footprint, something that looked like dark grains of sand. It was lying beside the edge of the carpet, where someone entering by the front door would have stepped. He sat on his haunches, clicked the torch on again, and shone it on the spot. A sprinkling of greyish-blue grains of earth. It was the contrast of texture and colour that made it stand out, unusual and coarser than sand.

He took a photo of it, pulled out his cell phone, and called Kaleni.

She answered instantly. 'What is it, Benny?'

'Colonel, did your friend enter the living room?'

'Yes. She went in through the front door.'

'We need to bag her shoes.'

'Okay.'

'Did she turn off the alarm?'

'She says it was off when she went in.'

'Thank you.' He rang off, stood up.

He walked carefully along the left-hand wall, avoiding the direct route to the passage at the back. He shifted one of the chairs slightly, seeing the hollows the chair feet had made in the carpet from years of standing on the same spot. He shifted it back again. He inspected all the other pieces of furniture and the carpet near the feet. He saw no sign that anything had been moved. There were no signs of a struggle.

In the short passage he found another light switch, clicked it on. Bent down again, shining the white beam of the torch on the floor.

Nothing.

The kitchen was through the first door to the left.

He looked inside.

The old man was seated there, slumped forward, his head touching the kitchen table. The gunshot wound was on the right temple, small and swollen. The exit wound was gaping wide, half of it visible where his left temple rested on the table top, in the relatively small pool of blood. In front of him, to the right, lay a single sheet of paper and a ballpoint pen. The paper looked like it had been torn out of a notepad. There were two short lines of writing.

Menzi Dikela's right hand hung down beside the chair, pistol still clamped in it. He sat behind the table and would have been looking at the passage door before the shot.

That was the moment Griessel hated, his first sight of the victim, the grim observation of death. His own damned mind always wanted to reconstruct it, as if he was the one experiencing that horrible moment. He was lifting the weapon slowly, heart beating wildly, the cool barrel against his temple, then pulling the trigger, slowly and deliberately. The bullet ripping through skin and bone and tissue, the shot, the primal scream dragging him down into the darkness. His psychologist had given him advice, techniques to fight the vortex of images, but still he struggled with the visions his brain conjured instantly. He wished Cupido were there. Vaughn understood. Vaughn would talk to him non-stop, keep his attention this side of his imagination's graphic reconstructions with meaningless babble. But now he was alone in the silence. He lifted the camera, took photos mechanically. A few things troubled him about the scene.

Griessel's phone rang shrilly in his pocket, vibrating, making him jump in alarm. '*Jissis!*' he said, so loudly that he felt he should apologise to the dead man for his lack of respect.

'I'm at the front door,' said Cupido, over the phone.

His partner was there; he felt a wave of relief. 'Okay. I'm in the kitchen with the victim,' he said. 'Kaleni sent me right in. Can you check outside if there are any damaged doors or windows? The front door doesn't show any signs of forced entry.'

'Check.'

'Right inside the front door there's a possible footprint. Keep to the left against the wall. The kitchen is the first door off the passage.'

'Check. See you just now.'

Griessel was still standing just outside the kitchen. He put away the camera, then carefully stepped inside. The tiled floor might have been white once, but was now a colourless beige. The table was pine, as were the four chairs. Three were pushed under the table, the dead man sat on the fourth. He was wearing a long-sleeved white shirt and a thick blue woollen jersey, dark blue jeans, comfortable black shoes. Apart from the blood, Menzi Dikela's shattered grey head, the pen and the sheet of paper, there was nothing else on the table.

Behind the dead man was a kitchen window – thick curtains – and in the corner a back door. Small cup hooks were screwed into it from which hung bunches of keys. Below the window was a double sink with a drying rack beside it. Kitchen cupboards were fixed to three walls, all the doors and drawers neatly shut. Work counters with a kettle, toaster and bread bin. Clean, orderly.

Griessel bent down to study the floor. Under the table he found a small pool of dark, dried blood next to the chair Dikela was sitting on. It was directly under the edge of the table, where it had dripped down from the head wound. Twenty centimetres in front of Dikela's black shoes something was visible on the dull floor. Griessel edged closer, switched the torch back on to illuminate it. A small cluster of greyish blue grains. The same texture and colour as those inside the front door. They could have come from Dikela's shoes, although there was nothing at his feet. He would have to mark it, and get the shoes into an evidence bag as well.

He walked carefully around the table, making sure there was nothing he could step in or on.

The sink was empty, the drying rack as well.

He read the two sentences scrawled in an untidy, hurried hand on the paper: *I am sorry. I have failed my country.*

He judged the trajectory of the shot, his gaze finding the bullet where it had struck a kitchen cupboard to the left of the victim. It was badly misshapen, impossible to say whether it matched the calibre of the pistol in Menzi Dikela's hand.

Then he crouched to study the weapon in the dead man's hand, as well as the fine blood spray on the skin, the sleeve of the shirt and jersey.

He heard the front door close, then Cupido's voice: 'Honey, I'm home.'

# 53

Down the years they had seen so many suicide victims – as young constables first on the scene, as junior detectives sent to investigate those nasty routine cases, when their seniors wanted to avoid the depressing drudgery of it all. Cupido and Griessel knew that in approximately 80 per cent of cases where people shot themselves, the victim was male. Using a handgun. Most of them with a shot to the right temple. Nearly always indoors. The trajectory of the bullet was usually slightly upwards. And in more than three-quarters of those cases there was a clear, star-shaped contact wound.

When a suicide note was left, it was always written by hand.

They saw all of that in Menzi Dikela's kitchen. More than enough to believe that no foul play had been involved. In addition, Cupido could find no sign of forced entry.

But something didn't feel right.

Cupido was the first to put it into words. 'Benna, something is just a little bit off,' he said. 'It's the way he's sitting there.' Usually the body would fall in the direction of the shot. To the floor, not forward.

'Still holding the pistol in his hand like that,' said Griessel. 'I only saw that once before. A guy who was lying on a bed.'

'The suicide note,' said Cupido. 'Even if it is in his handwriting, it's not exactly typical.'

Griessel nodded in agreement. Most suicide notes were addressed to someone specific, written with resentment or hate.

'This . . . It looks just a little bit staged to me, Benna. It looks like someone saw a movie about a suicide scene, and arranged it just like that.'

They stood back from the table, trying to identify exactly what was bothering them.

Cupido rubbed the back of his neck thoughtfully. 'Could we be brainwashed by the daughter insisting it's murder?'

'Maybe,' said Griessel.

'What are we missing?'

They stood side by side, studying everything carefully, aware of the two women outside, waiting in anticipation, anxious and distraught. Griessel and Cupido were both quietly cognisant of their responsibility to reach the correct conclusion, and swiftly.

They walked around the table. Deathly silence reigned in the house, besides the shuffle of cloth shoe covers on the tile floor.

Then Cupido said: 'Wait a minute . . .' He crouched on his haunches, right by the bullet lodged in the cupboard door, following the possible trajectory with his eyes. He went round the back of the body, bent down by the pistol that was clenched in Dikela's hand, hanging halfway between the table top and the floor. He examined it closely. 'This is a Z88, right?'

'Yip,' said Griessel. Just like the one on his belt. The Z88 was standard equipment in the army and the SAPS's official weapon of choice up till 2007. Many of the older members of the police force still used it. Cupido had exchanged his a year or so ago for the Glock 17. Cupido straightened up, rubbed the back of his neck again. 'So where's the shell casing, Benna?'

'Shit,' said Griessel. 'You're right.'

'He held the gun like this, so the shell would have jumped forward. That way. To the floor, maybe the counter top, around here by the kettle. Or, if it bounced weirdly, down the passage . . .'

They searched the whole of the kitchen floor and the counters thoroughly, scanning closely with their torches, to be absolutely sure. Then Griessel said: 'Wait, she might have picked it up.'

He phoned Kaleni again. 'Colonel,' he asked, when she answered anxiously, 'did you remove anything from the scene?'

'No. Absolutely not.'

'Could you ask your friend if *she* did?'

'What is missing, Captain?'

'The shell casing, from the pistol.'

'Hold on.'

He heard her speaking to Thandi in Xhosa. Then Kaleni told him: 'She says she did not touch anything whatsoever, except for the front door handle.'

'Thank you, Colonel.' He rang off.

'They don't know anything about a shell casing,' he told Cupido.

'Maybe she didn't see it and knocked it down the passage.'

'Okay.'

The detectives extended their search to the passage. They didn't find it. Next the two bedrooms, the bathroom, and then a room that apparently served as a study or office. Every door was open, though they were sceptical that the shell could have rolled that far.

They searched for close on fifteen minutes, under the beds, the desk, the two mats in the bathroom. Then they went outside to report to Mbali Kaleni.

They sat in the colonel's car, since Thandi Dikela had taken off her shoes so they could be placed in an evidence bag. It was too cold for her to stand on the concrete pavement in her socks.

Thandi was occupying the front passenger seat, Mbali Kaleni beside her, Griessel and Cupido in the back. She was a sturdy woman, her long, thin African braids rippling like a waterfall in the light of the streetlamps whenever she shook her head, so fiercely. Each time Kaleni would put a hand gently on her knee to comfort her. She turned to her right so that she could at least see Griessel.

'On Saturday my father was upset. I could hear he was . . .' Thandi spoke with a British accent.

'This was when you called him on the phone?' asked Griessel.

'Yes.'

'You called him every day?'

'No, I – I called once a week, maybe . . . I . . . He was living an active life – he had many friends, he was healthy, he was busy. There was no need to call that often.'

'Why did you call him on Saturday?' asked Cupido.

'Just to talk.'

'And prior to Saturday? When was the last time you spoke to him?'

'I think . . . maybe the previous Sunday.'

'So you only called him about once a week?'

Her voice rose. 'Why is it important? Why are you asking me that?'

Kaleni raised her hand to interrupt the interview. 'Thandi,' she said, 'they have to ask you about everything, because we have a very big decision to make. We have to be very sure that this was a murder.'

'It *is* a murder. They killed him. I just know it.'

'I believe you. But there's very little evidence. All we have is the missing shell casing. And my detectives say it might still turn up if it was caught in his clothing somewhere, and they can't see it without moving the body.'

'He did *not* write that letter.'

Kaleni's voice remained calm and gentle. 'I believe you on that as well. But you also said that it does look a little like his handwriting . . .'

'It's fake. I'm absolutely sure. And why did he say to me that if something were to happen to him . . .'

'I need you to understand what our choices are right now. The first is that I do what is expected of me. I call the Mowbray station commander, he sends his people round, and they take up the investigation. They'll listen to you, and they'll maybe ask a handwriting expert to look at the letter, if they believe you. But you're a family member, you're deeply emotional, and you said your father was upset on Saturday. So, they will be very sceptical.'

'How could they be sceptical? I wouldn't lie about— He was not upset in that way.'

Kaleni stilled her, with a hand on her arm. 'Just listen.'

'Okay.'

'If you're right about the enemies of your father, there will be very—'

'What enemies?' asked Cupido.

'Keep quiet,' said Kaleni, 'and let me finish.'

'Right,' said Cupido. 'Sorry.'

'The enemies of your father are very powerful. We know that from experience. They forced us to stop another so-called suicide investigation just a short while ago. It'll be very easy for them to get the Mowbray station to declare this a suicide and close the case. Do you understand?'

'Yes.'

'That is why we don't want to involve them anytime soon. So, the other choice we have is to get the very best people in right now, the rest of my team, Forensics and a videographer, and we hit the case as hard as we can, before anybody can interfere. If we can prove that you're right, if we have a very strong case, then it would be much harder for them to stop us.'

'Then that's what we have to do.'

'Yes, we'd like to do that. But there are implications. I'll put my people and my boss in a very difficult situation. I will put my career, and those of my people, in jeopardy. I can't do that if we're not sure it's the right thing to do. That's why you need to answer our questions as best you can.'

'I don't want to get you into trouble. It's just . . . He's my father, he's . . .' Thandi dropped her head, and wept.

Kaleni comforted her, arm around her shoulders.

Griessel and Cupido waited. Three, four minutes.

Despite the peculiar situation, Griessel had to admit that Thandi was a brave woman. She'd found her father there, absorbing all that terrible shock and grief and anger. She must have waited a long time outside for Kaleni to arrive, then had sat in the car in the dark for a few hours, all the while picturing the scene inside the house. It must have been very hard.

At last Thandi shook her head. Her braids rippled.

'I'm ready,' she said.

# 54

She stared into the darkness as she spoke. Sometimes her voice cracked. Then she would pause and drop her head, hiding her face behind the curtain of braids until she had recovered.

'I called my father when I missed him, when I had the time to miss him, when I had the time to think about something other than my job. It's crazy busy, and I often felt guilty that I didn't call him more often. Now I feel I should have. But it's too late . . . Sometimes I called and he said, no, he couldn't talk, he was busy, working in his garden, or he was with his friends, talking, playing Umlabalaba. So I'd respect his wishes, and leave him alone. But he was happy, this past year. We spoke about once a week. Sometimes a little more often, sometimes less. On Saturday we spoke for the first time in a while. I asked him, "How are you, uBaba?" and he said he was fine. But I could hear it in his voice, he was . . . He sounded like he did two years ago, when he was totally fed up with politics. I knew that tone of voice. So I asked him . . .'

'Thandi,' said Griessel, with as much compassion as he could muster, 'I know it's hard, but we need you to describe the tone as closely as you can. Was he sad? Was he angry? Was he anxious?'

'If I said sad, you'd think he was depressed. And then you'd think he did this to himself . . .'

'We won't think anything until we have all the information, and all the evidence we can get,' said Kaleni. 'Just use the words that feel right.'

Thandi nodded. 'He was sad. The kind of sad that . . . Disappointed, that's a better description. Like when I was a teenager and would stay out too late, he wasn't angry then, just that kind of disappointment, sadness that I did the wrong thing. That was what it sounded like to me. I knew that tone well.'

'Thank you,' said Griessel.

'So I asked him, "Dad, what's wrong?" He said, no, nothing. And I asked him, "What are you doing?" and he said he was working in the vegetable garden. You'll see it behind the house. That was his pride and joy. He said spring was coming, it was time to get the beds ready. He was putting in compost. And the whole time I could hear he wasn't himself. He was trying to sound happy, but there was this undertone of disappointment . . . So he asked me how I was, and did I have a boyfriend yet. He was always on about that, in a teasing sort of way. And I always answered that I didn't have time for men in my life. There was too much important work to do. And he asked, "How are things at work? How many houses have you built for the people?" He was very proud of what I do. He asked all the things he usually asked, and how was my mother. They got divorced twelve years ago, when he was never at home because of his work. And I said she was fine. And right at the end, when we were saying goodbye, he said, "Thandi, if something happens to me, I want you to call Mbali Kaleni. I trust Mbali." So that made me pretty anxious, because he sounded . . . scared. It was just . . . out of the blue. I said, "uBaba, don't say that! What's wrong? What's going on?" I was very upset. I think then he realised he'd spoken without thinking of the consequences. So he started back-pedalling. He laughed, said he was just joking. And I said, "You weren't joking! What's wrong?" And he said, "No, no, nothing's wrong." He was just testing me to see if I still loved him. And he could hear I loved him very much. I scolded him, I said, "You make me worried, uBaba, that's not funny." He said he was sorry, it was a bad joke. So we said goodbye. I sat there, very uncomfortable, replaying our conversation in my head. And I was pretty sure he *did* sound scared, when he referred to Mbali. Just for that moment. And then it really worried me. So I called him again, about fifteen minutes later. I asked him again, "What's wrong?" Again he made jokes, he said there was a lot wrong, the weather was wrong, there was the drought – how was he going to get his vegetables to grow? And did I know you can't find a rain tank in Cape Town? Everybody was buying rain tanks, there were none left to buy. So that's something else that was wrong. Maybe I could help him find a tank, so he could catch the rain one day, when God blessed us with rain again, and water his vegetables a little.'

That was when her voice deserted her entirely. She gave in to sobs, and Colonel Kaleni had to wipe away her own tears before she was able to console Thandi Dikela.

Once she had calmed down, Thandi said she had phoned five times on Sunday and again on Monday because she couldn't stop worrying. Each time he told her not to keep on at him, everything was fine. She wanted to pop round, but he said, no, he was very busy.

And then, this afternoon, she had phoned and got no answer. Eventually she came to check. The front door was unlocked. She went inside, saw him. And the letter on the table. She immediately knew it was fake. Then she was certain they had murdered him, and wanted it to look like suicide. She phoned Mbali Kaleni. It was just past six.

'What time did you make the first call?'

'I . . . I think it was around four.'

'We need you to be absolutely sure. Could you check on your phone, please?' Griessel asked.

'My phone is in my handbag. In the car.'

Griessel said he would fetch it. They sat in silence until he returned, gave the handbag to her. She took out the phone, checked her call register. 'It was eleven minutes to four.'

'That was the first time you called?'

'Yes. The first time today.'

'When you arrived and went inside the house, was the alarm active?'

'No.'

'Thank you. Now please tell us about the enemies,' said Cupido.

Thandi said the enemies had surfaced two years ago, when the public protector's report on state capture was leaked to the media. It incriminated the president of the country, half of the cabinet, and some of the provincial premiers and the heads of state enterprises, exposed as corrupt and criminal, and completely controlled by the three Indian billionaire businessmen. Her father was one of a group of sixteen old fighters, former senior figures in the Struggle, who had called a news conference shortly thereafter. They had publicly called on the president and his lackeys to resign for completely destroying Mandela's legacy. The sixteen's declaration was to the point, no beating about the bush.

That was when the trouble had begun. The smear campaign started. Statements that Menzi Dikela and his co-signers were agents of the old apartheid regime, traitors who served the interests of white monopoly capital. Enemies of the national democratic revolution. There were false news reports on social media, quickly taken up and embellished by the hijacked media houses' TV channels and newspapers – stories that the sixteen were not only corrupt but guilty of criminal activities and tax evasion. There were scores of death threats, telephone calls in the dead of night, whispers that they were going to kill him. And her father said the worst of all was that former colleagues were behind all of it: those were their techniques, their old tactics.

'Which former colleagues?' Cupido asked.

'My father was with the State Security Agency for more than five years before he retired, as the deputy director of Systems and Technology. And before that he had six years with the old National Intelligence Service. In the apartheid days he ran the ANC's computer systems in London. He *created* those systems. He was a pioneer, a hero of the Struggle.'

'Is that why you have a British accent? Because you grew up in London?' asked Cupido.

She nodded. 'South London. I was born there. The first time I saw South Africa was in nineteen ninety-three. We came home in such euphoria. We had such great expectations. And now *this.*'

'Why would they want to kill your father *now,*' asked Griessel, 'two years after they made that statement?'

'They never forget, those people.'

'Was he still receiving death threats, these past few months?'

'I'm sure he was.'

'You're sure? He told you?'

'No. I think maybe he didn't want to upset me.'

'Was he still involved in politics, or political activities?'

'They were all political animals, always political, he and the last few friends he had, after their former comrades had shunned them. I'm sure they discussed politics all the time.'

'Can you think of any reason why they would've wanted to kill him now?'

'Because they never forget. Because that is their way. They destroy your reputation. They isolate you. They let you think they've forgotten about you, until you let down your guard. And then they kill you.'

They were standing at the little garden gate in front of the house in Nuttall Street. Mbali Kaleni put her hands on her hips, like in the old days. She told them in a firm, though muted, voice: 'I think you should go home. I can't involve you in this.'

Cupido crossed his arms. 'I'm not going anywhere, Colonel,' he said.

'You'll be endangering your career, Captain. I can't expect that of you.'

'Colonel, I'm not captured. I'm staying. And that's final.'

'Are you absolutely sure?'

'Yes, Colonel.'

'Benny?' asked Kaleni.

'Colonel, if we can prove that this was murder before you talk to Brigadier Manie, I think we'll be in a very good position. I think we need to call Professor Pagel personally and ask him to take some blood urgently. And Thick and Thin. We need to ask them to bring Gerber with them, the blood-spatter expert. We need the best. And we can trust them.'

'Benny, you don't have to do this.'

'I know. But I'm in.'

Kaleni's hands dropped off her hips. 'I appreciate it very much. But tell me why you want Pagel to take blood.'

'Well, Colonel,' said Griessel, 'there are no signs of forced entry. There's no evidence of a struggle and I saw no marks on the deceased to indicate that he was defending himself. If this was murder, then he allowed someone to enter. Which means he most probably knew the perpetrator. Or perpetrators. Or maybe they were posing as law-enforcement officers. But whoever they were, you don't just sit down and let someone put a gun to your head. You fight. Which he obviously didn't. So they must have drugged him. You remember the Sea Point case last year, the murder of the two girls who took the guy home from the nightclub?'

'Of course. The date-rape drugs,' she said. And then she understood. 'You're right. Get Pagel.' She remembered that the biggest obstacle in the Sea Point case was proving that the women's drinks were doctored. The initial investigators hadn't drawn blood in time. The substance that the suspect had used – gamma-hydroxybutyrate, or GHB, as it was commonly known – could only be traced in the urine within ninety-six hours.

'And why Gerber?' asked Cupido.

'I looked at the victim's hand,' said Griessel, and pointed in the direction of the house behind them. 'There's the fine spatter you typically see from a point-blank shot. But the blood is only on the barrel of the pistol, on his thumb and on the sleeve of his shirt and jersey. There's nothing on the other fingers, which is strange. I think someone's hand was on top of his, pushing the gun to his temple. And pulling the trigger. Maybe someone who knew a little about gunshot residue, but not much about spatter patterns.'

'That's good, Benny. We'll get Gerber too.'

'Colonel,' said Cupido. 'There's one thing I don't like about this.'

'Yes?'

'The reason why they killed him.'

'You don't believe her?'

'I think she honestly believes that was the reason. But she wants this to make sense, so she's grasping at straws. It's just . . . I've never heard of such a thing. The president and his people actually having someone killed for dissent? I mean, they disgrace them, they hit them with trumped-up charges, they make them lose their jobs, like they did with some of our generals, some of our colleagues in Durban, but killing the man two years after he was one of sixteen people who signed a declaration? *That* I don't buy.'

'What are you saying?'

'I'm saying we have to look at the forensic and medical evidence to prove that this was murder. But we'd better also find a very good reason why they did it. Or they will crucify us.'

## 55

Kaleni told Thandi Dikela to go home and try to get some sleep. Then she stood outside her car to make calls to everyone they would need to join them.

Griessel and Cupido went to fetch more equipment from their cars, put on gloves and shoe covers again, and went in. They placed yellow numbered markers at each of the four possible sources of clues they were aware of – the possible footprint in the sitting room, the grains of soil under the kitchen table, the pen and the suicide note.

'Not much,' said Cupido, when he surveyed their handiwork.

'Amen,' said Griessel.

They stood at either side of the body, voices muted, affected by the strange atmosphere in the house. 'Benna, let's take a moment here. That drug theory of yours. Walk me through it.'

'Okay. Let's say Menzi Dikela is busy somewhere in the house, and they knock on the door.'

'What time are you thinking of? Thandi phoned her daddy eleven minutes before four, right?'

'Right.'

'So, we know it must have happened before that time.' Cupido bent down and carefully pushed the arm of the deceased that was hanging down beside the chair. 'We'll hear what the Prof has to say, but this feels like full rigor mortis.'

'And it was a cold day.'

'More or less in the region of eight hours, hey?'

Griessel nodded, examining the blood beneath the table at close range. For decades they had been standing by and listening to pathologists and spatter experts at murder scenes. You learned a lot. Such as how long it took blood to dry, a rough indicator of the time of death – provided you touched it, and inspected it, within the first ten hours after the fatal event. The guidelines were the five stages of blood clotting: coagulation took place first; gelation followed, about ninety minutes after the blood had left the body; next, the clearly visible change in colour from rim desiccation, pool centre desiccation and final desiccation, after four hours, nine hours and nine and a half hours respectively.

Benny noted the pool beside Menzi Dikela's head was still reddish-brown in the centre, but the rim was practically black, and relatively broad. 'The blood also indicates about eight hours.'

'Give or take an hour or two, for our non-expert opinions.' Cupido checked his watch. 'That means it was around one o'clock, two o'clock.'

'More or less.'

'During or just after lunch.'

'Yip.'

'Okay. They knock on the door . . .'

'Yes. And Menzi Dikela knows them, lets them in. Now there are two possibilities. One is, they inject him with the drug, or they say, "Come, let's have a drink," and they slip the drug into the glass when he's not looking. Those are the most likely scenarios.'

'Where do you bet your money?'

'I don't know, Vaughn, it's difficult. A needle is going to leave a mark on his skin, which a pathologist will find if he knows what to look for.'

'Fair enough. But maybe they think these dumb cops from Mowbray will buy the suicide idea, so they're not worried about the mark.'

'Possible. But if they were State Security spooks, they went to a lot of trouble to make it look like suicide. They arrived with a plan. They would have thought about needle marks. Look at this place, Vaughn. It's way too tidy. You said yourself it must have been around lunchtime or just after. There's not a dirty plate, cup or glass. My bet is on "Come, let's have a *dop*," and then they cleaned up thoroughly afterwards.'

'Makes sense . . . What about a cleaner? Did he have a char?'

'We should have asked.' Griessel took his phone out again to call Kaleni. It saved him having to take off his booties and put them on again. 'The professor and Forensics are on the way,' when she answered. He asked her if Menzi Dikela employed a domestic worker. She said she'd call Thandi and find out.

Cupido was busy opening cupboards, searching optimistically for glasses or cups that showed signs of recent use. Griessel went through the drawers, inspecting the cutlery. Without much hope.

Kaleni called back. 'Yes, he had a char, two mornings a week. Wednesdays and Saturdays. She'll get the phone number for us.'

Benny shared the information with Cupido.

'Okay,' said Cupido. 'The char hasn't been here since Saturday. And everything's still spick and span on Tuesday. Pretty amazing . . . So, here's my next question: why suicide, Benna? Why not stage a break-in gone wrong. Jimmy a door or window, shoot the old guy, empty a few cupboards, steal a laptop and a cell phone. Happens all the time. Same result, the old guy is dead and SSA spooks are not under suspicion. But, no, they go to all this trouble to stage a suicide. Why? Doesn't make sense.'

Griessel was thinking. 'Maybe something to do with the note? A message? To the other fifteen?'

'I'm not buying.'

'The big question is still the motive.'

'Then we'd better start looking for one, partner. Come on,' said Cupido, and beckoned Griessel in the direction of the bedrooms. 'Let the games begin.'

They each searched a bedroom, carefully, taking their time. All indications were that Menzi Dikela had been a very organised man. The wardrobes, linen chests and bedside cabinets were all painfully neat, the beds made up with perfect squared-off hospital corners.

In the built-in cupboard of the master bedroom, beneath a pile of pyjamas, they found a canvas bank bag with cash in fifty- and hundred-rand notes, totalling just over five thousand.

Cupido packed it in an evidence bag. 'Interesting,' he said.

Dikela had also been an apparently healthy man. There was no medication in the bathroom cabinet to indicate a chronic disease, just the usual collection of flu, headache and heartburn pills, and vitamin capsules, along with deodorant, toothpaste, shaving cream and razor blades. Everything was precisely arranged and stacked. Like the few items of clothing in the washing basket.

'Looks like he was really tidy,' said Benny.

'*Kwaai*,' said Vaughn. 'Maybe his kitchen looked like that every day. Very anal retentive.' He leaned against the bathroom door. 'Benna, can I ask you a personal question?'

'Go for it.'

'Okay. You and Alexa, are you sort of equally . . . I mean, you're quite organised, your office, your dockets, even your car, everything reasonably squared away. Is she also?'

Griessel laughed. 'No. I tease her that she's like an amoeba. If she's busy somewhere, it grows around her. In the bathroom, at her basin . . . There's a circle of make-up and creams and stuff, and it keeps getting bigger.'

'How do you deal with that?'

'I don't. I just look the other way. What can I do? It's her house. It's the way she is.'

'And that doesn't worry you?'

'Here's my philosophy, Vaughn. I work strange, long hours. I have to see a shrink because I'm fucked up. I snore. I leave the toilet seat up. And all that doesn't worry her. It's give and take. Why do you ask?'

'Donovan,' said Cupido. 'Desiree's *laaitie*. *Jissis*, he's a little slob. PlayStation in the lounge, all the games lying around. There's only one bathroom, and his clothes are always on the floor. I don't even want to talk about his room. It's a war zone. And Desiree doesn't worry. She's the one who picks up after him and cleans. I think it's guilt about the divorce or something. And if we get hitched, I'll have to deal with it, and I'm telling you, it will drive me mad. And then he still goes on at me about the Hawks being captured. I don't know how to handle it. I'm gritting my teeth. It's a time bomb, and sometime or other I'm going to lose it.'

'Talk to her. My shrink says conflict is growth waiting to happen. And talking is the only thing that helps.'

'Right. Shrinks . . . Like that's going to help me. Shall we tackle the study? Last-chance motel . . .'

They went into the study. There was a desk with a PC, a laser printer and a big brown cigar box on top. The computer was on, a screensaver weaving hypnotic patterns. An iPhone 7 was plugged into a USB port.

'You know you're going to shoot yourself,' said Griessel, 'but you charge your phone anyway?'

'And leave the PC on . . .' Cupido moved the mouse. The screen activated. Only the Windows home screen, without visible files or active applications. He pressed the iPhone button with a gloved finger. It asked for the password. 'Why do they always have passwords?' He sighed. 'We'll have to send for Lithpel.'

The left-hand drawer of the desk yielded bank statements and municipal accounts, a divorce decree, a few yellow ballpoint pens similar to the one on the kitchen table. And a black hardcover note-book bearing the logo of Spar Supermarket and the words A4 Counter Book. Griessel took it out and opened it. In what was possibly Menzi Dikela's handwriting, *Maintenance, loans and donations* was written on the first page. Below that were long columns of amounts and dates and an extra column that indicated what sort of payment it was.

'It looks like the handwriting on the letter,' said Griessel.

'*Ja* . . . maybe,' said Cupido. 'But I've always been too stupid to spot forged handwriting. It's a dark art.'

They put the book into an evidence bag.

In the right-hand desk drawer they found an ID book, a passport and a notepad similar to the paper the suicide note was written on. Cupido took it out, held it up to the light to see whether the writing would show through. 'Too faint,' he said, and put it into a clear plastic bag as well.

They looked at the bookshelf against the other wall, filled with Struggle biographies, technology manuals for databases and systems, poetry collections and novels by African writers. Some *Reader's Digest* condensed books.

The curtains of the window to the right of the desk were drawn. Below the window was a two-door cabinet. Griessel opened it. They found paper for the printer, rolled-up computer cables, files of typical administration documents – including car registration, proofs of payment for car licences, the title deed of the house, and old home mortgage bond and short- and long-term insurance contracts. Right at the bottom in the corner on the left of the cupboard was an internet modem, connected to network cables.

Griessel's cell phone rang. It was Kaleni. He answered.

'Professor Pagel has arrived,' she said. 'Did you find anything?'

'Not much, Colonel,' he said. He checked his watch, saw it was after eleven. He knew Lithpel Davids was going to be very unhappy with what he was going to say next: 'We'll need technology support too. There's a computer and a cell phone.'

'I'll call Sergeant Davids.'

'The prof is here,' Griessel told Cupido.

'Cool.' Cupido walked towards the door, then looked at the cigar box. 'Was the old *umadala* a smoker? Did you see any ashtrays?'

Before Griessel could reply, Cupido lifted the lid of the box and looked inside. A moment of stunned silence, then he said: 'Hit me with a snot snoek.'

Inside the box, just as orderly as everything else in the house, there was a small cutting block, with two pieces of biltong on top. Sprinkled with coriander seeds.

And an Okapi knife.

The knife was folded shut: the handle of dark cherrywood looked new, the folding lock and handle inlay of stainless steel still bright.

'What are the odds, Benna? What are the odds?' Cupido asked.

'It's coincidence,' said Griessel. 'Thousands of people own Okapis and eat biltong.'

'Maybe, baby,' Cupido said, 'and maybe the universe schemed that the Big V and his intrepid partner, Benna the Bass, deserve a big fat break.'

He pulled the right-hand drawer open again, took out the passport they had seen there. He opened it. It was in Menzi Dikela's name. 'Okay, so the universe is still pissing on our parade. But a man can dream . . .'

He shut the cigar box again. Then they walked to the front door to open up for Professor Phil Pagel.

## 56

To Griessel's relief the pathologist brightened the heavy atmosphere in the house with his genial personality. 'I understand this is highly secret and confidential, Nikita,' he said, in his mellifluous voice, while he deftly extracted blood from the corpse.

'That's right, Prof,' said Griessel.

'And a Leporello from our notorious State Security Agency is our chief suspect here?'

'A Leporello, Prof?'

'Opera, Nikita. Mozart. A character from *Don Giovanni*. Leporello was the poor fellow who had to do his wicked master's dirty work, urged on by promises of much money, threatened with the sword. It seems to me that there are many Leporellos at the helm of affairs in this country nowadays. Wouldn't you say so, gentlemen?'

'But not at the Hawks' Violent Crimes Unit, Prof,' said Cupido. 'Let's just get that straight.'

'Ah, the lady doth protest too much, methinks . . .' said Pagel with a smile.

'Prof, does it seem odd to you that he's sitting pretty at the table?' Griessel asked. 'Wouldn't he have toppled over?'

'I've seen them in every position under the sun, Nikita. I wouldn't say that was terribly unusual.'

'Oh.' A bit deflated.

'You suspect an anaesthetic was administered?' Pagel asked.

'How else do you get a man's pistol against his head without him fighting back, Prof?'

'Valid point. Indeed there are no provisional signs of defensive wounds.'

'We scheme it must have been in a drink,' said Cupido, ''cause why, they wouldn't want you to find a post-mortem puncture.'

'It's not that simple, Vaughn. If the injection was rectal or sublingual . . . It's practically impossible to spot a wound there.'

'What's that last one again in Cape Flats lingo, Prof?'

'Forgive me, Vaughn. Sublingual is in the mouth. Under the tongue, even *in* the tongue, or in the palate.'

'But, Prof, how would you inject a guy in his . . .' Griessel didn't want to use crude language in front of Pagel: he had too much respect for the man ' . . . in his whatsis . . . or in the mouth without a struggle anyway?'

'*Touché*, Nikita. I will test the blood and urine for as broad a range of anaesthetics as I can. We will see . . .'

'What could they have put in his drink, Prof? Let's say you had this scheme, and you wanted to nail a guy, but you wanted to make it look like suicide. And you didn't want to leave any evidence behind.'

Pagel put away the needle and blood-sample tube in his case and began examining the body of Menzi Dikela. 'Naturally it would depend on the drugs I had available, Vaughn. But we can assume that our SSA Leporello has access to anything?'

'Yes, Prof.'

'Very well. Interesting question . . . Look, the easiest is an overdose of insulin, injected. Rapid coma, eventual death, and difficult to trace in post-mortem analysis if you don't specifically look for signs. You bring three, four men, you grab him quickly before he can resist and you inject him, let us say, rectally. Hypoglycaemic coma, then you can do with him what you want. If you just leave him, in six hours he'll be as dead as a dodo.'

'Shit,' said Cupido. 'I didn't think of that.'

'Prof, if you don't know it's an insulin overdose, let's say a guy lands up on your table, what will you think was the cause of death?' Griessel asked.

'Usually pulmonary or cerebral oedema, depending on the specific pathology that you see. Simply stated that's water on the lungs or on the brain, which can be the result of natural causes. Especially with the aged, like the deceased here. If I didn't suspect foul play, I wouldn't test for insulin overdose.'

'But that's my point, Prof,' said Griessel. 'These guys wanted it to look like suicide. Not house-breaking, not natural causes, but suicide.

'Strange modus operandi,' said Pagel, 'but then we must remember it's the SSA we're dealing with here.'

'Exactly,' said Cupido. 'So, if suicide is on the menu, Prof, what would you have given him in his brandy and Coke?'

Pagel peered at them from behind the body. 'Midazolam maybe? Rohypnol? GHB? There's a whole range of possibilities. But you would have to disguise the taste of all these substances. Something like very sweet liqueur, Nachtmusik, Amarula, something like that. Mix a strong dose in a half-jack . . . In any case I'll get it tested for everything, blood and urine. If they used something, we will find it.'

Griessel's phone rang again. It was Mbali Kaleni. 'Forensics have arrived. Would you please come and brief them?'

Forensics and Gerber, the blood-spatter man, arrived. And the videographer. And the Violent Crimes reinforcements, Vusumuzi Ndabeni, Mooiwillem Liebenberg and Frank Fillander. They also changed the atmosphere in the suicide house in Nuttall Street considerably. It was beginning to feel like a normal crime scene to Griessel and at last he shook off the feeling of doom.

He put up with a barrage of Thick and Thin's latest weak weddingspeech jokes. ('Benny, heard the one about the guy who was so happy after he got married because he had sex almost every day with his wife? Almost on a Monday, almost on a Tuesday, almost on a Wednesday . . .' They went round the house laughing uproariously.) He showed them what he would like investigated. He asked Gerber to examine Dikela's hand in particular, and then he went out to give Ndabeni, Liebenberg and Fillander a full briefing. He asked them to do the necessary footwork in the street. Had anyone seen or heard anything?

An ambulance, red lights revolving, stopped while he was still outside. The narrow street was suddenly packed with vehicles. Now, he knew, the inquisitive would start to gather. He went over to Mbali Kaleni. 'We're going to need traffic and crowd control, Colonel.'

'I'll get on it,' she said.

'I'll bring you some crime-scene tape. It should keep them away.'

'Thank you, Benny. Any news from inside?'

He'd been afraid she would ask, because all their theories had been shot down. 'Nothing so far, Colonel. Prof Pagel will have to test the blood and the urine. That's our only hope.'

She nodded anxiously. 'Find something, Benny. Please.'

'I'm going to do my very best.'

Inside more bad news awaited them.

Griessel was back in the kitchen. He watched Uli Gerber examine Menzi Dikela's hand through a magnifying-glass. Sometimes his colleagues referred to the blood-spatter expert as 'Owl', though never to his face, partly because the thick lenses in a pair of black-rimmed glasses made his eyes look much bigger, but also because it was so close to his Christian name. He was a serious, wiry man, a canoe-marathon enthusiast.

He straightened up, unfolding his skinny body, and said, almost apologetically: 'Captain, the pattern is consistent with a suicide shot.'

'But there aren't any spatters on his fingers. Only on the thumb.'

'True. But that's consistent with a suicide where a pistol is used. The firearm itself, especially the butt, prevents the blood spraying on the fingers, the thumb excepted, of course. If you look through the magnifying-glass, you'll see there is secondary spatter on the first joint of the index and middle fingers. That's normal. I don't see anything to make me believe that forcing by another hand was involved.'

'Are you absolutely sure?'

'I'll have another look in the mortuary, and do the residue tests too. But I would be surprised.'

'Thank you, Uli.'

'Sorry, Captain.'

Sergeant Lithpel Davids arrived, grumbling. 'Is there nobody in this unit who watches UEFA Cup quarter-finals? Is nothing sacred?'

'What are you moaning about now, Lithpel?' asked Cupido.

'The soccer on TV, *cappie*. The beautiful game. Nothing that you rugby barbarians would understand. Where are the computers? I'd like to get to work before my Wednesday is ruined as well.'

'Come and look at the body first,' said Cupido, very deliberately, as it was well known Davids couldn't handle blood or trauma scenes at all. Anything the least bit gruesome made him instantly nauseous, and apparently gave him terrible nightmares for weeks after.

'*Cappie*, I swear I'll resign right here and go work for Dial-a-Nerd. You're an evil, evil man.'

'That you haven't yet been had up for insubordination is one of the greatest miracles in the law-enforcement universe,' said Cupido.

'That's because of my sunny disposition,' said Davids. 'Everybody loves me.'

'In your dreams. Come on, the study is down the passage. Body is in the kitchen.'

Lithpel cupped a hand against the side of his face to shield his eyes from the scene at the kitchen table. He followed Cupido into the study and looked at the computer and the cell phone on the desk. 'So, which of my many and varied skills will you be needing tonight?'

'Right. We have reason to believe that the forces of evil staged the suicide of the *umadala* inside there. We're looking for a motive for murder, Lithpel. We're looking at friends and associates, we're looking at hanky-panky, dark state secrets, world-domination conspiracies. Anything. So, unlock the phone, get us the good stuff. Full hard-drive analysis of the PC, including emails, browser history, social media . . .'

'Unlock the phone? Unlock the phone? Wait, let me quickly get my Garrick-Ollivander-manufactured magic wand, the one with the phoenix-feather core . . .'

'Garrick who?'

'*Jissis*,' said Lithpel Davids. 'No soccer, no Harry Potter. You're heavy *gam, cappie*. You're genuinely the least cultured cop I know. What do you do in your spare time?'

'A thoroughbred Hawk doesn't have spare time, Lithpel. We live for our work.'

'*Ja, ja*, whatever.' Lithpel spotted the technical manual on the bookshelf. He took a step closer, ran his finger over the book spines. 'So who lived here with the *umadala*?'

'Nobody. Those are his things. He was a bigwig in State Security's computer systems.'

'A blood brother,' Davids said. 'A fellow geek, a kindred spirit, an alter ego. Why didn't you say so? For him, I'm bringing my A game.'

## 57

Griessel and Cupido unlocked the swing-up door of the single garage with a key they found in a bunch hanging on the back door.

There was a white Mercedes Benz E200, eight or nine years old. The boot was empty.

Against the rear wall racks of cheap shelving held seven cartons of the same size, all with the upper flaps cut away. They examined the contents. Household items, tools, all carefully and logically ordered.

'Benna, the *umadala* was a tidy man. Across the board.'

'But where are the tools for the veggie garden?'

'That there is exactly why we pay you the big bucks . . .'

They went out, walked around the garage. There was an outside room and toilet behind it. They shone their torches through the window. An old, rickety, dusty couch and the worn grass box of a mower were all they could see inside. Cupido swung his torch over the back garden. Vegetable beds, two with support frames, the soil dug over and raked, but nothing currently growing.

'Look there,' said Cupido and illuminated a structure against the vibracrete back wall. 'Wendy house. There's our garden shed, I scheme.'

They walked towards it down the paved path between the vegetable beds. It was a large Wendy house, with its own tiny porch in front. The door was bolted, with a hefty padlock. Cupido held up his torch while Griessel tried various keys on the bunch. He found the right one, unlocked the padlock and unbolted the door.

Inside were garden tools, fertiliser, wooden stakes for the frames, baling twine in a roll, all organised, neatly arranged. Against the rear wall an old kitchen spice rack held dozens of seed packets. A small table, a single old kitchen chair. On a table lay another notepad and a pen. The notepad was of exactly the same kind as the one they had seen in the study. Griessel flipped through the pages. He saw sketches of the beds, with indications of what Menzi Dikela would have planted – maize, beans, carrots, beet, tomatoes, cucumber, cauliflower.

Further examples of the deceased man's handwriting, so Griessel placed that notebook in a bag too. Then they went out, locked the door again, and returned to the house.

Satisfied that they had seen everything.

Mooiwillem Liebenberg was outstanding at interviewing women. He was exceptionally handsome and known as the George Clooney of the Hawks. And he had a 'million-dollar, high-wattage smile', as his colleague Vaughn Cupido described it with a touch of envy. But he also directed his genuine, warm and charming attention like a search-light on women. As if whatever they said to him was of enormous worth. Mostly they responded positively.

So it was just as well that he was the one who knocked on Mrs Mercia van der Merwe's door. Mercia would provide the first break-through in the Menzi Dikela conundrum.

Initially she was incensed at being disturbed in the middle of the night – just after midnight, in fact. She opened the door with a scowl, lips pursed tightly in disapproval. Pink dressing-gown and beige slippers. Sixty-one years old, brunette-dyed hair ruffled with sleep.

Liebenberg apologised with heartfelt sympathy for bothering her so late at night, then went on to tell her of her neighbour's passing and said how much it would mean to him if he could talk to her. Her expression altered to reflect shock, sorrow and concern; she ushered him in, invited him into the sitting room. She wanted to know what had happened. He said it looked like suicide, but they weren't yet sure.

She said that was too tragic, he was a dear old man. She brushed away a tear. And put up a hand to smooth her hair.

He asked her if she'd known him well.

Reasonably well, she said. Well enough for him to send her vegetables in the summer, and for her to return the favour with a milk tart in thanks. 'You know how it is these days. We pass our neighbours by. We didn't visit back and forth much. Not because he was black, don't misunderstand me. I'm not one of those types. But just because that's how it is, these days. We live our separate lives. He was a dear man. Always so courteous, always greeting when he passed by.'

Mooiwillem said he understood entirely. And had she seen anything over there today, anything out of the ordinary?

'Yes,' she said. 'I did. Now that you mention it. This morning. I've got Barberton daisies out here in the front garden, and this is their time to flower. But what with all the water restrictions, the municipality caught so unawares . . . All these people moving to the Cape, they should have foreseen the water shortage. In any case, I have to water the daisies by hand with the bath water, and the daisies don't like soapy water, but what can a person do? So I was standing out there with the watering can and I saw the van stop at Uncle Menzi's house, and three men getting out.'

'What time this morning?'

'*Jong*, it must have been . . . nine o'clock. Or half past nine? Somewhere around there, just after I had my bath, so there was water for the daisies. A shallow bath, mind you, because the municipal water-meter readers spy on a person, and they're just waiting to cut you off if you're not careful. Anyway, I saw the van, a pitch-black van, and three men got out, in suits and ties, mind you, and went inside there with the old chap.'

'How long did they stay?'

'That I can't say. I went back inside.'

'Can you describe the van?'

'Well, I don't know much about cars, but I think it was a BMW van. You know, with the blue thingy on the front.'

'A BMW van?'

'Yes – you know, looks like a station wagon.'

'Hang on.' Liebenberg took out his phone, googled BMW vehicles, and showed her a picture of an X3. 'Something like this?'

'Yes, only black. And a bit bigger, I'd say.'

He played around with the phone again, brought up a photo of a black X5, and turned the screen to her.

'Yes! I think that's the one,' she said. 'Just like that.'

'Can you describe the men?'

'I didn't pay that much attention. They were black men . . . Collar and tie, dark suits.' She waved apologetically to show that was all she could say.

'Did Mr Dikela often receive visitors?'

'*Jong*, you know, I don't hang around in my front garden all day. So I really can't say. People did visit, every now and then. Old chaps like him. But not dressed up in a suit and tie – that's the first time I saw that. I did wonder who the people were. They looked so . . . official. I suspect it was the municipality.'

'Why did you think that? Did you see the number plate?'

'No, it wasn't that.'

'What was it?'

'*Jong*, I don't want to speak ill of the dead. It's not right, you know.'

Liebenberg gave her his fullest, charming, warm focus and said: 'Ma'am, it would mean the world to me if you would tell me what you know.'

Mercia van der Merwe blushed, touched a hand to her hair and cast her eyes down to the carpet. 'I think he's been pinching water. You just don't get tomatoes and cucumbers *that* big unless you're crooking the water restrictions. I think they were from the municipality, coming to tell him they're cutting off his water.'

Griessel and Liebenberg took the news to Mbali Kaleni, who was now sitting on the front of her Hawks BMW. She looked weary, the long day taking its toll.

'Thandi was right,' she said, with a sigh of relief, as she slid off the bonnet. 'That is very good news. And good work, Captain.'

'Thank you, Colonel,' said Liebenberg.

'What do you suggest we do now, Benny?'

'I think we need to look at the street cameras, Colonel,' said Griessel, 'the N2 and the M5, maybe Voortrekker Road in Salt River. Those are the only real exits from here, whether they came from the city or somewhere else. We have a time frame for their arrival, and we suspect the victim was dead by two o'clock, so we know by what time they were gone. And we're fairly certain it's a black X5. They're not as common as the white ones. That does narrow it down. We'll get a number plate, if we're lucky.'

'We should look at black X3s too,' said Liebenberg. 'I'm not entirely convinced she got it exactly right.'

'It'll have to wait until morning,' said Kaleni. 'The Metro Police . . . We don't want to show our hand with too much urgency.'

'I'll be there at nine,' said Liebenberg.

Two ambulance men passed them carrying a stretcher bearing the body of Menzi Dikela. Professor Phil Pagel walked alongside.

Pagel solemnly handed over to Griessel an evidence bag containing the victim's shoes. 'Lady and gentlemen, I bid thee goodnight,' he said. 'All tests to proceed as speedily as the clandestine nature of the case allows.'

The second, even greater, breakthrough in the case happened quite by chance. As is often the way with criminal investigations.

Sergeant Lithpel Davids carefully sealed Dikela's phone, then applied his gloved hands to the desktop computer mouse and keyboard to get the hard-drive copier going. While that was under way, he checked for the most obvious information – recent websites visited, emails with significant subjects, password-protected files, social media accounts . . .

And found nothing.

Not even the normal signs that Menzi Dikela had a lifetime of computer systems behind him. Such as the use of an offbeat, alternative web browser. This PC had only Microsoft Edge. He knew no self-respecting career techie would tolerate that abomination. Far rather Tor, or Freenet, or I2P, or Yandex. At the very least Firefox, Google Chrome or Waterfox.

But Microsoft Edge? Most peculiar.

He knew techies and the world they lived in, the air they breathed, even the old and retired among them. He often ran into them in digital chatrooms. This grandpa was clearly still online, and Davids knew the war cry of computer nerds worldwide was 'Old geeks never die, they just go offline.' He knew the ways they kept up to date, which ingenious, obscure programs they accessed, and where they went to source and hang out on what he – tongue-in-cheek when talking to uninformed detectives – called the 'interwebs'.

And Dikela's computer showed no sign of any of that. Not a trace.

There was email – in orderly folders – from and to a few friends, of the how's-it-going-with-the-grandchildren sort, correspondence with his daughter, and with his divorce attorney over a request for an increase in maintenance. There were digital bank statements and municipal accounts, a few electronic plane tickets, accounts for his internet access and not much more. Menzi Dikela had visited news websites daily, South African and British, Google and occasionally Google Maps.

Lithpel began to worry that he was overlooking something. He sat with his head bowed, deep in thought, and waited for the hard drive to finish copying. Back at the office he would use all his equipment to find out what the old guy was hiding from him.

And so, head down, his gaze randomly fell on the ADSL modem in the corner of the two-door cabinet, the doors left open by Griessel and Cupido. It was an ordinary Netgear N300, two or three years old, completely in keeping with this sort of household use. He noticed two network cables plugged into the back of the modem. Both disappeared into a neatly bored hole in the back of the cupboard.

A bit strange. Two? There was only a single PC here.

He got up and had a closer look. One cable was visible on the left, glued to the skirting board, leading to the computer on the desk.

But the other just disappeared into the wall.

# 58

Lithpel Davids pulled the lockable cabinet away from the wall. It was weighed down with files and documents and, with his slight frame, he had to brace and strain until he had shifted it far enough to see what was going on behind the cupboard.

One network cable ran along the skirting board to the desk. The other disappeared into the wall.

He wondered what the old grandpa's plan was with that. It wasn't a big house. This Netgear modem created a large enough Wi-Fi signal to cover all the rooms. Was something else connected to it? He pulled back the curtains above the cabinet, trying to see if the network cable reappeared on the other side of the wall. But the burglar bars and the dark outside made that impossible.

Lithpel went out into the passage, towards the kitchen. Carefully at first, as he didn't want to look death in the eyes. Then he remembered that the body had been removed. He asked Arnold if he could borrow a torch.

Arnold gave him a big, powerful one from his aluminium case ('Always knew we were the light in the life of the Hawks'), but Lithpel was on a mission and barely thanked him, before hurrying out of the front door, past Griessel and Cupido, who were standing under the lemon tree talking.

'What's up, Lithpel?' Cupido asked.

The sergeant didn't reply, but walked to the left, along the paved pathway that ran along the side of the house. He stopped outside the study window and aimed the torch at the base of the wall. A white plastic pipe led away from it, connecting with an elbow joint pointing down into the paving. Nothing more could be seen. It had to be housing the network cable.

'Weird,' he said out loud. Why would the old man lay a network cable outside the house?

He played the beam of the torch back and forth across the back-yard. At the rear against the concrete wall was a Wendy house. The paved path that ran along the wall stretched to it, with only one kink where it deviated a few degrees from the corner of the house to match the grid of the vegetable beds.

He walked towards the Wendy house. The door was secured with a big padlock. He shone the torch down to where the little house was mounted on a concrete slab. He couldn't see a white pipe emerging from the paving or the ground at the front or on the left side.

He kept walking. At the back, right in the centre, at an angle of ninety degrees the pipe emerged from the ground and ran into the Wendy house.

'*Cappie*, who's got the key for the Wendy house?' Lithpel asked.

Griessel removed the bunch from his trouser pocket and found the right one. He handed it over. 'What do you want to do there?'

'Something weird.'

'What is it, Lithpel?' Cupido asked.

'Seems like the old man ran a network cable all the way to the Wendy house.'

'Are you serious?' With Lithpel you never knew.

'This time on a Tuesday night? Of course I'm serious, *cappie*. Let's keep it real.'

'*Jirre*, Lithpel, it's late. Don't mess with us.'

'*Cappie*, come on, I'll show you.'

They followed him to the study window. Lithpel pointed out where the cable emerged. 'That's a LAN cable inside the pipe there, coming from the inside. And I think it leads to the Wendy house out the back. Come and see.'

The little procession went on into the darkness. Forensics' bright torch lit their way to the back of the structure. 'Check it out,' the sergeant said.

'That is weird,' said Cupido.

'That's my point. Can we look inside now, please?'

He gave the key back to Griessel, who undid the padlock, pulled back the bolt and opened the door. Lithpel lit up the back wall with its rack of seed packets. There was no sign of a cable. 'Impossible,' he said.

'Now hang on a minute,' said Cupido. He went in, paced out the expanse between the door and the wall.

'I see what you're doing there, *cappie*,' said Lithpel.

Griessel said nothing; he waited for Cupido to go outside and pace out the same distance. 'We lost about a metre and a half inside,' he said. 'That's a false wall.'

They found the edge of the door in the rear wooden wall when they looked closely. It was an expert job, an almost seamless match of the pattern and texture of the Wendy house.

It took them some more head scratching and experimentation before they lifted the spice rack and the door opened.

Inside the narrow hidden room a long counter ran the length of the wall. Under the counter flickered the lights of an emergency battery array. On top were power cords for at least two computers, two keyboards, two mice. An inkjet printer stood at one side. The network cable came up from beneath, plugged directly into what looked like a small LAN splitter. An electricity supply came out of the floor.

Under the counter was a two-door cabinet, similar to the one inside the study. It looked as though the doors had been forced open.

'That's more like it,' said Lithpel Davids.

'What do you mean?' asked Cupido.

'This is a techie geek's den, *cappie*. Check it out. Back-up battery pack for power failures, so you don't lose data. Two Logitech performance laser mice. Two slabs of Das Keyboard – that's serious stuff, real mechanical keyboards. Pro grade, not for amateurs. And that! Do you know what that is?' He pointed at the splitter.

'Network cable splitter,' said Cupido.

'No, *cappie*. That is your state-of-the-art Ubiquiti UniFi Security Gateway. You configure it with a command-line interface. Again, for pro use only, it's a serious firewall, and you can also create your own VLAN.'

Griessel and Cupido just stared at him blankly.

'That means nobody gets to spy on you, *cappie*. Nobody is even going to know you're online, or what you're up to. And nobody is going to get inside your system.'

Griessel pointed at the elongated phantom shapes on the counter where the wood was slightly darker than the rest of the surface. 'Were those two computers?'

'*Yebo*, yes,' said Lithpel. 'Looks like they were here till quite recently. But they've gone now.'

Griessel crouched and pulled open the broken cupboard doors. 'Just like whatever was here,' he said. The cupboard was empty.

Griessel, Cupido, Kaleni and Lithpel Davids stood in the Wendy house, speculating on the possibilities, trying to work out what Menzi Dikela might have been doing in this secret room. And how it might have led to the crime scene in the house.

Lithpel said the range of possibilities was as wide as God's grace. The grandpa could have run a massive server there, with a database of who-knew-what, or he could have been mining digital currency. He could have been utilising the dark web to buy wicked stuff, drugs or credit-card information. Or be involved in cyber-fraud or hacking. 'Or maybe he was just watching child porn.'

'*Hayi!*' said Kaleni.

'Colonel, all I'm saying is that you don't build a secret little room, with a heavy-duty security gateway, and use weapons-grade hardware to watch Netflix.'

'He was a decent man,' said Kaleni, firmly.

Griessel said he thought they could assume that this was what the three men in the black X5 were looking for. That they broke open the cupboard under the counter, that they took the two computers away. They would have to assume that the computers contained information the SSA wanted badly. His best guess, based on what they knew of Dikela, was sensitive data on state capture, on corruption.

Then they murdered Dikela, and made it look like suicide.

'So they just came in here, shot him, and took the stuff? How did they know where to look?'

'Maybe they had a guy as smart as me,' said Lithpel. 'Following the breadcrumbs.'

'Wait,' said Griessel, taking out his cell phone, and calling Professor Pagel.

'I hope there is a breakthrough, Nikita,' the pathologist answered, still jovial, even though it was nearly one in the morning.

'Prof, the stuff they might have injected in our victim, or made him drink, could it make someone talk? Can it make you say things you wouldn't normally say? If they wanted to extract information?'

Pagel thought for a long time before he answered. 'It's possible. I'm not an anaesthetist, I speak under correction. But something like midazolam . . . They refer to Guedel's classification, the four stages of anaesthesia. There is a pharmacokinetic window, Nikita, a certain stage after administration of a narcotic when the patient . . . Let us say inhibitions become less restrictive. Many surgeons have stories to tell of the things patients say when they're under anaesthesia, the questions they answer without scruple. Very personal, painfully private things . . . If your suspects knew what they were about, it's surely possible. My advice would be, talk to an expert.'

## 59

Griessel drove home along Philip Kgosana Road, up around the flank of Table Mountain. It was twenty to three in the morning and he was exhausted. His brain didn't want to be bothered by the case any more.

He looked down at the city. It spread out wide below him, flickering with a magical beauty, like the reflection of an imaginary starry sky on a lake of silver. Such a harmless-looking scene, he thought. Cape Town in the early hours had an innocence like that of a sleeping child. Unaware of the evil, the monsters that lurked.

He thought about that moment on the stage earlier tonight – it felt like a lifetime away – when he and Rust came so close to nirvana. He thought about how he'd felt, inside the music. Transported. Safe. Happy. In complete equilibrium, every note precisely in its place.

He played bass guitar because it had simplicity and regularity to it. Predictability. Structure. Music was order, perfect order. And his job was an impossible, constant and mostly frustrating battle against chaos. Every crime, every murder was a false note that shrieked and screamed and penetrated his grain and marrow and bone, a cacophony, a terrible disruption of order. It made him an obsessive policeman, swept him up in a war that he could never win, but neither could he surrender. Because he ached, always, for harmony.

Tonight bothered him particularly.

Too many false notes, and he couldn't find the right chord or key in any of them.

He took his four-minute shower, then climbed into bed behind the warm, soft body of Alexa. She murmured something, barely audible, but it sounded like 'Glad you're home,' and then she slept on. He was in awe of her ability to switch off so easily, sleep with such deep surrender.

Lord, it was good to be with her.

What if she turned him down when he proposed to her on Sunday?
That would be a mess.
Should he rather let things be?
Only five more days before he had to make his little speech.
No, he thought, it's Wednesday already. Four days.
His gut contracted.

# PART V

# 60

His first morning in Amsterdam. There was no email from Vula. No news about the president's programme due to kick off in two days' time in Paris, no pointers to help him make the best choice of weapon.

It didn't matter.

Those seven hours on the road yesterday were the first chance he'd had to think through the operation properly. To weigh up everything he knew against possibilities, variables, strategies. To ponder his motives, ask himself if he could actually pull the trigger in that instant when the familiar face filled his scope.

And he still didn't know.

But he had to plan for it. In the car he'd had the time to do that. To prepare for the deal. Logic dictated that an arms dealer like Ditmir would be dubious about an unfamiliar new (black!) client arriving without a reference and wanting to buy just one firearm. A member of the Albanian Mafia would not hesitate to try to take advantage of such a situation. Consequently, and in general, he would have to guard his identity, his place of abode and his vehicle's registration number. Against Ditmir, and the people who were still hunting him.

He must prepare for the return journey as well, any potential police roadblocks, and for carrying a large and visible, illegal, unlicensed weapon in his car. He had prepared for that by making a visit to Carl Denig, the outdoor shop in the Weteringschans where he'd bought an assortment of camping gear.

Now, after breakfast at the Ambassade Hotel, his temporary home, he put the remainder of his plan into action. He approached Reception for advice: he was looking for a special type of boat owner who could provide a unique service. He fabricated some details to make sense of his request. It took them about a quarter of an hour to find him a suitable candidate. He smiled when he saw the name the concierge had written down. The suggested boatman was Pelle Baas.

Daniel called the number, explaining to Baas what he required. The man sounded considerably younger and a whole lot more sober than the last skipper he'd hired. They made an appointment and agreed on a fee.

Then he took a walk, just after eight in the morning, to stretch his legs, and get his blood flowing after the long drive in the Peugeot the day before. And to breathe in the city, renew his sense of the rhythm and crowds, the ebb and flow, the mood of it.

He wandered aimlessly, choosing his course impulsively, for close on two hours. It had been ten years since he'd last been there, but it felt like the soul of the place hadn't changed at all. There were more offbeat museums, more cheese shops, more cannabis fumes, more tourists. But everything that had inspired and delighted him before was still there. He tried to dissect and understand it. It was the unique charm of the architecture and the canals, the narrow alleys and broad squares. The eclectic blend of ancient churches, art dealers and sex workers, shoulder to shoulder. The frenetic cyclists, trams, cars, rivers of pedestrians. The weight of centuries of trade, battle and struggle, the libertarian history. Everything played a role. But the essence of it was how it felt to him, the atmosphere. There was an intangible, subtle spirit of festivity, a joyful bonhomie, as if freedom, diversity and toler- ance were still celebrated daily. Or could it be the enduring underlying sense of gratitude the Dutch had that the sea had been tamed and the land drained?

This was what the land of his birth should have been like. Now. Twenty-plus years after the miracle of 1994, after all the sacrifice and pain and hard work. It had all the ingredients to make it a second Amsterdam, a land and a place to stand as a monument to the triumph of good. Oppression and discrimination defeated, like a stormy sea pushed back behind a dyke. Maybe it wasn't too late. He consoled himself with the idea that he could pull the trigger to stem the flood, help tip the balance, so that South Africa might one day celebrate her true liberation.

At ten o'clock he found himself in the hustle and bustle of the Albert Cuyp market. He knew he ought to keep moving, stick to his planned schedule and get the weapons transaction started, but he wanted to postpone the pressure a little – and the tension that a military weapon in his car boot would bring him.

He turned and began his approach in the direction of the Oudezijds Achterburgwal, and then he was on the Museum Square and he remembered what the pretty young woman in the yellow dress had told him about Christophle le More, the medieval bodyguard and archer he had reminded her of. *Few people know of him. His portrait's hanging in the Rijksmuseum.*

On the spur of the moment he bought a ticket, and went to find the painting.

It wasn't big, but it was impressive. In a gilded frame, Le More in a blood-red coat, his peculiar hat a lighter shade of red. And the face, his eyes turned to the right as though lost in thought. Self-confident. Proud, as though content with his place, his long journey there. As if he was home.

Daniel thought of the painting that Élodie Lecompte had made of him. How all that he could see in it was his own longing. He turned abruptly and hurried out.

Oudezijds Achterburgwal number 82D was a bell on a door, with a typed strip underneath that read *Ditmir's Trading*. There was a small speaker on the wall. He pressed the button, but didn't hear ringing.

He waited until a woman's voice instructed him: 'Second floor, please.' The door buzzed. He pulled it open, went inside. A flight of wooden stairs, no lift. He climbed the stairs. On the first floor there was a heavy door, no sign, no indication of what went on behind it. On the second floor he found an opaque glass door with *Ditmir's Trading* sandblasted on it and, underneath, *The Best from Albania!*, the giant exclamation mark sealing the good news.

There was a little camera just above the door. He opened it and went in.

The room inside was spacious. There were two women behind an extended desk on the left, their long straight blonde hair styled identically, one half falling down the back, the other draped forward over the shoulder. There were brightly coloured posters on the wall behind them, on each a big logo announcing *Made in Albania*. They featured photos of textile products, tobacco, fruit and vegetables. A lot of vegetables. Three white two-seater couches, stylish and modern, stood against the windows on the right. Two tables with pamphlets and magazines. Two cameras. One in the corner, one behind the women.

They greeted him cheerily. 'Good morning, sir! Welcome to Ditmir's Trading!' More exclamation marks. They could have been sisters. Equally tall, equally blonde, equally painted, their make-up a tad heavy, wearing grass-green blouses and blue jeans that echoed the colours of the *Made in Albania* logo. Rosemary and Thyme. Rosemary's front teeth were slightly more prominent. Thyme had a tiny, shiny gemstone adorning her left nostril.

He walked up to the desk and returned the greeting. 'I'd like to see Ditmir in person, please,' he said. He could see the blonde came out of a bottle.

Still smiling, Rosemary said: 'Do you have an appointment?'

'I'm afraid I don't, but I really don't mind waiting.'

'I'm not sure that he's free today. What is it about?'

'I'm interested in his special range of products.'

'Oh, perhaps *I* can help. Which specific products did you have in mind, or would you like to discuss the whole range of Albanian exports?'

'I'd rather speak to Ditmir in person, if you don't mind.'

'Of course, sir. Won't you please take a seat?'

'Sure.'

He sat on the middle couch, picked up one of the brochures. It said Albania was 131$^{st}$ in the world in exports. He wondered if that was an apology or a boast.

He saw Thyme pick up the receiver of a phone, and speak into it in a language he did not understand. Hopefully she was talking to Ditmir or one of his people, who would be watching him on a TV screen somewhere in the building.

In the brochure he read about Albanian trade. *The top exports of Albania are Leather Footwear ($310M), Crude Petroleum ($277M), Footwear Parts ($187M), Chromium Ore ($134M) and Non-Knit Men's Suits ($129M).* He wondered what 'footwear parts' involved. He had no idea what a non-knit men's suit was. He'd assumed all men's suits were 'non-knit'. Not that he was any sort of connoisseur: he hadn't owned a suit for decades.

Thyme put down the phone. 'Sir?'

He stood up. 'Yes?'

'I'm afraid Mr Ditmir won't be able to see you today.'

'When will I be able to see him?'

'His diary is extremely full. Perhaps you can come back tomorrow?'

'I'm in rather a hurry.'

'I'm really sorry, sir. He is such a busy guy. Maybe tomorrow?'

'Thank you,' he said. 'It will be difficult, but I'll try.'

He said goodbye. They smiled at him amiably and wished him a 'nice day'.

With an exclamation mark.

# 61

When he was back on the street he turned north, along the canal. He couldn't wait till tomorrow, he realised. He really ought to be back in Paris by tomorrow night. But first he must establish whether his hunch was right.

He expected the evasive Ditmir to have a means of evaluating potential clients. He suspected that he would be followed now. Consequently he stopped in front of the Casa Rosso club and pretended to examine the poster advertising a sex show, in order to cover his back. He spotted them. Two men of average height, broad shoulders, emerged from the same door of Ditmir's Trading, about a hundred metres behind him.

He lingered a moment longer, as if he was seriously considering the Casa Rosso show, like a man who suddenly had time on his hands. He pretended to turn away reluctantly, and walked on to the Molensteeg Bridge. He turned right there, and right again, in the direction of the Waag.

They were approaching, about a hundred and fifty metres behind him, making no real attempt to be unobtrusive. Or maybe they just weren't very good. One was a bit bow-legged. They looked as though they might be cousins. There was a hint of the comical about the pair, like something from the silent films of the 1920s. Laurel and Hardy. He wondered if all Albanians came in handy packs of two.

On the Nieuwmarkt Square he sat down at a little table on the pavement of the Café del Mondo, which afforded him a view across the plaza. He took it all in like an entranced tourist. He could see them out of the corner of his eye, as they paused indecisively in front of the Albert Heijn supermarket.

A waiter came to him. He ordered coffee, leaned back, seeming completely at ease.

They sat down next door at the Café Poco Loco. One turned his back; the other man looked towards him, trying to be discreet. He suspected they weren't particularly well trained in the art of tailing.

His coffee arrived. He sipped it slowly, looking at the colourful flower stalls opposite, at the beautiful old Waag building, six hundred years old, once the place where dealers took their goods to have them weighed.

He sat.

They sat.

He ordered another cup of coffee, spent about forty minutes there, placed his money on the table and got up suddenly, walking briskly around the corner and then on, westward. He lengthened his strides. He needed to find out how good these two were, how serious they were about keeping an eye on him.

In the Stoofsteeg he saw them come back into striking distance. On the Dam Square, among hundreds of tourists, street dancers and fire-eaters, he shook them off with remarkable ease, forcing him to stop and wait for them to find him again. No, they were not at all schooled in this art. Or maybe Ditmir wasn't that interested in new customers.

Amused, he calmly walked down the twists and turns of Raadshuis Street, heading for a bite to eat at the Pancake House just this side of the Westerkerk.

The Albanian duo arrived at the restaurant at the precise moment Daniel's food was being served. They walked straight up to his table, pulled out chairs, and sat down.

'I'm really curious,' Daniel said. 'What is a "non-knit suit"?' He looked expectantly from one to the other.

They scowled in complete bewilderment. Both were in their early forties, he estimated. Dark five o'clock shadows, they smelt strongly of expensive aftershave and faintly of garlic. Their muscular shoulders were from heavy lifting, not from working out in a gym. Hair cut short. The bow-legged one had a small sickle-shaped scar under his left eye. They were more like potato farmers than members of the Albanian Mafia.

'What do you want with Mr Ditmir?' the one with the sickle scar asked, in a heavy accent. The waiter brought more menus, but they waved him away with an irritated gesture.

'What everybody wants with Mr Ditmir,' said Daniel, pleasantly. 'His special products.'

'What special products do you want?'

'I'll tell Ditmir when I see him in person.'

'Who do you represent?'

'Myself.'

'Who referred you to Mr Ditmir?'

'An African connection.'

'What is his name?'

'They prefer anonymity.'

'What is your name?'

'Doesn't matter.'

'Where are you from?'

'Africa.'

They stared at him intently. He wondered if they were expecting him to wither under their gaze.

At last Sickle took out his phone and called someone. A long conversation in Albanian ensued. Quite serious. The only word that Daniel could understand was '*Afrikan*'.

At the end of the call Sickle said to Daniel: 'Finish your food. Then we will go to the toilet, you and I.'

'Sounds like fun,' said Daniel. 'I'll show you my footwear parts, and you can show me yours.'

No twinkle in their eyes or even the faintest glimmer of a smile.

It was uncomfortable for both of them, an embarrassment.

Daniel and Sickle were in the toilet. It was a small, narrow room, with barely enough room for Daniel to undress, and for the other man to take and hold each piece of clothing and search it thoroughly for some sort of listening device or weapon. It made sense for a man in Ditmir's business.

Sickle took Daniel's cell phone and wallet out of his trouser pocket, examined them, put them in the washbasin.

Then, when Daniel was naked, the Albanian made an apologetic sound, turned on his cell-phone torch, gestured Daniel to turn around so the man could check for hidden microphones. Daniel swore at him in Xhosa, a short, sharp curse.

Sickle shrugged, gesturing that he was merely doing his job.

Daniel turned around.

Nobody said a word until they were back at the table.

Sickle returned the phone and wallet. He said: 'You can leave your phone here with the waiter. Or you can throw it in the canal.'

'The canal is fine,' said Daniel. He suspected they were afraid the phone could be used to record a conversation. In any case he should start using a new phone, and this would create the correct impression of professionalism with the arms dealers.

They waited for him to pay his bill.

Sickle said: 'Let's go. Back to the office.'

They walked on either side of him. At the bridge over the Herengracht he took his cell phone out of his pocket, let it drop into the canal. Three Chinese tourists gaped at him in disapproval.

Sickle nodded, satisfied, and gestured to him to hurry up. The Albanian walked two steps behind him now, all the way to Oudezijds Achterburgwal, number 82D.

This time the front door swung open automatically, as if someone had seen them coming. They climbed the stairs only to the first floor. Sickle took keys out of his pocket, and unlocked the heavy door. Daniel went in.

There was another world inside. Dark wall panelling, heavy curtains excluding light. A thousand tiny lights on the ceiling and all down the long shelves. Here and there a heavy, old-fashioned lamp with dim yellow light. It looked like an old-world men's club, gleaming, polished wooden surfaces, large easy chairs in dark brown leather, arranged around heavy coffee-tables. The bar occupied the length of the rear wall; bottles of liquor and crystal glasses reflected the lights. A firmament of alcohol. It smelt of cigars and cigarettes, beer, leather polish and carpet shampoo.

Five men were seated on high stools at the bar counter. Four were armed with what looked like Agram 2000 machine pistols from the former Yugoslavia slung over their shoulders. They were younger and leaner than the two potato farmers, their eyes watchful. There were two laptop computers, closed, on the surface in front of them.

In the middle of the small group was a bigger man with a short, styled beard. Unarmed, surrounded by an air of importance.

All five weighed Daniel up, from head to toe.

The door behind him closed.

The bearded one said: 'I am Ditmir. If you waste my time, you will be sorry.'

# 62

Ditmir was a talker. While he sat with his back against the counter and his arms folded, in passable English with an East European accent he said: 'My guys asked you what is your name, who referred you, who do you represent. You give them funny answers. You want to come to me for business, you say who you are and who you represent. You don't give funny answers. I do a lot of business in Africa. I have great respect for Africans. I respect their culture, I respect their ways. But you must come in here and respect *mine*. I give you my name, you give me yours. Maybe we take a drink, or we eat together. You say you represent this general or that president, or whoever you represent. In business everything is about respect. Respect for the client, respect for the product, respect for the relationship. That's why I make good business. So, because I respect you, I'm going to ask you again. What is your name?'

'Barnabas,' said Daniel. The name in his Swazi passport.

'Okay, Barnabas, thank you. Can I offer you something to drink? We have the world's very best whisky. Or gin, perhaps. Would you like the best Dutch gin?'

'No, thank you. I don't drink when I'm doing business. That's my culture.'

'Okay, I can respect that. Now, who do you represent?'

'I represent myself.'

'Yourself? We all represent ourselves, Barnabas. I understand. But where are you from?'

'Swaziland.'

'Swaziland? Is that a place? A real place? A country?'

'Yes. As real as Albania.'

Ditmir seemed to weigh up the statement for a possible insult. But then he nodded. 'Who referred you to me?'

'I'm not going to tell you that. Confidentiality agreement.'

That caused a long silence. Looks were exchanged.

Eventually: 'Are they from Africa?'

'Yes, they are from sub-Saharan Africa. They are revolutionaries. I can't tell you more.'

'Okay, I understand. You want to buy my products for your country? For mighty Swaziland?'

'There seems to be some misunderstanding,' said Daniel. 'I want to buy a rifle. Just one. For myself. For private use. A military-grade sniper rifle, with an effective range of at least one thousand to one thousand five hundred metres. And a hundred rounds of ammunition. And a cleaning kit. I will pay in cash. Full price on delivery. That's all.'

'That is all?'

'Yes.'

Ditmir swung his knees back towards the bar, as if he was losing interest. He exchanged a look with two of the watchful ones. 'I do business with countries, Barnabas. Not one-man shows.'

'Then I have been misinformed.' Daniel turned and began walking towards the door. The two potato farmers stood in front of it, unmoving.

'But I like you,' said Ditmir.

Daniel stopped.

'And I believe markets should be developed,' said Ditmir. 'Grown. I believe in networking, in making contacts. Maybe if you're a satisfied customer, you will go to the president of Swaziland, and you will tell him Ditmir is a good man to do business with.'

'The king,' said Daniel, as he turned back to face the man.

'What?'

'Swaziland has a king, not a president.'

'Okay. But tell me, in Swaziland, do you and your king know about economies of scale?'

'Oh, yes, the clever white *bwana* taught us a lot back in the bad old days. We are forever grateful.'

Either Ditmir wasn't bothered by the sarcasm or he didn't get it.

'Okay, so you will understand, a rifle like that will be very expensive,' he said. 'Because you buy only one. Economy of scale. Supply and demand. Good capitalism.'

Daniel nodded. 'I'm willing to pay a premium price for a premium product.'

Ditmir got up from his chair. 'I like that, Barnabas. Premium price, premium product. I like that. We must talk. Come, sit down. Coffee? How about a good cup of coffee?'

The coffee was excellent. They sat at the bar counter in front of the two laptops. Ditmir used them to run through a display of his products.

He boasted a little. 'Maybe, Barnabas, you were FBI, you were the Dutch General Intelligence and Security Service, or Interpol, and you came in here looking to arrest Ditmir, the great weapons trader. Maybe you come with your whole SWAT team, and what will you find, Barnabas? Nothing. Because there *is* nothing here. My catalogue is just bytes, floating around in the cyberspace. Just bytes. It's like Amazon . . . You know Amazon? Where you buy everything on the internet? You know Jeff Bezos? Big Amazon billionaire?'

'Not personally, but one can dream,' said Daniel.

'Well, my friend, you have now met the Jeff Bezos of the weapons trade,' Ditmir said proudly, still unreceptive to irony or sarcasm. 'That is me. Look. You can search categories on my web shop, you can add quantities, it gives you the price straight away, all deep in the dark web . . .' While one of his machine-pistol cronies demonstrated it all on the computer screen.

They searched 'sniper rifles'. Sixteen matches were listed on the Amazon of Arms. Daniel looked through the choices, pointed at one with his finger and said: 'That one.' It was the Amerikaanse CheyTac M200.

'Four oh eight, or three seven five?' asked the one operating the computer.

'Four oh eight.'

'Very good choice, Barnabas. You know your rifles,' Ditmir said. 'But that one is very expensive.'

'It says right there it's thirteen thousand dollars,' said Daniel.

'No, my friend. Economy of scale. If your king bought a hundred, then the price would come down. For *you* it is twenty-five thousand dollars. Hard cash. Ammo included.'

'Fifteen,' said Daniel. 'And I have euros.'

'Can't do that. Economies of scale. A lot of trouble, a lot of hassle for just one rifle. Not worth my while. And I don't like euros as much as I like dollars. So the price is twenty-five thousand euros, take it or leave it.'

'I'll have to take it,' said Daniel. 'So, what's the next step?'

It was time to get away clean, as per his plan, so that Ditmir wouldn't know where he was staying or where he was keeping his cash. The Albanian was informed now: Daniel was solo, a solitary independent operator. He wanted to pay in cash. A considerable amount of cash. He posed little risk to them, should they decide to take the money without delivering the rifle. Follow him to where he lived, put a gun to his head, take the euros and say: "Leave or you'll be very sorry." No danger of *a lot of trouble, a lot of hassle*.

They would most likely also want to follow him because they didn't trust anyone in their industry. It was just too suspicious when an unknown buyer arrived without an introduction.

That was why he'd hired Pelle Baas to wait for him with his motor-boat on the Geldersekade. His reasoning was that, in Amsterdam's crowds you could follow anyone unnoticed, if you knew what you were doing and your prey was on foot, bicycle or in a car. But if he used the canals, things became complicated.

Therefore he had hatched a plan. Laid the groundwork.

But what he hadn't bargained on was a glimpse of the Russian.

When he walked out onto the street again, the light suddenly bright after the gloom of Ditmir's salesroom, he instinctively looked up at the building, Oudezijds Achterburgwal 82D, because he was certain there would be eyes on him. He looked at the windows on the first floor, where he had just been doing business. A reflex. But it was movement in a window on the second floor, where Rosemary and Thyme worked, that drew his attention.

Just a hint, a glimmer, a second or even less, when he had sight of a man's face before it disappeared again. The big Russian, the bear whose left ear was deformed by thick scar tissue, as if a chunk had been bitten out of it. So quick, so fleeting that Daniel realised he must have imagined it. It was just not possible.

# 63

Lieutenant Colonel Mbali Kaleni's office was different. On the one hand it was because she wanted to create a small oasis for herself in the almost entirely male environment. On the other, she knew she didn't possess the most jovial personality in the Directorate for Priority Crimes Investigations. Consequently she tried to cultivate a touch of welcoming warmth and feminine softness. She did it with a skilful hand, just a touch here and there. Like the subtle scent of air freshener and cut flowers. Today there were three perfect white arum lilies in a slender vase. Like the white teacup with green wings that she had bought at a Pylones shop in the Netherlands, six years ago. There was the colourful, original painting by Lazarus Ramontseng opposite her, beside the door: three happy women in a township carrying big bags of Snowflake flour on their heads, on the way home. The Zulu love letter that was attached to her computer screen, below left: the colour of the beadwork was predominantly white and blue to confirm her virginity and faithfulness; the triangle's point showed that she was an unmarried woman.

And the two small squares of glass she had had made. Not so much for other people, as they were positioned so that only she, not her visitors, could read the words. One with a light green background was a quote from the writer R. H. Sin. It read: *Some women fear the fire. Some women simply become it.* The one next to it, in flamboyant black letters against a light rose background: *There is no force equal to a woman determined to rise,* crediting the sociologist W. E. B. Du Bois with this wisdom.

All of this was on display today, as always, including the neatly stacked files, the practically empty in-tray, and the metal name-plate with her rank and name at the end of the desk.

But when Griessel and Cupido walked in that morning, as the rain sifted drearily down outside, there were various clues to suggest that all was not well. Kaleni's body language hinted at melancholy. Her eyes were bloodshot from lack of sleep and she seemed small and vulnerable behind the large desk.

And there was a gap in the gallery of photos behind her on the wall.

They were accustomed to the perfectly spaced frames that chronicled her life and career: a photograph of her as a young constable, fresh from police college, wearing her blue uniform with a serious expression, full of the zeal to do well; then of her three graduation ceremonies, her parents proudly beside her; of her with Musad 'the Camel' Manie at a special awards ceremony for loyal service; of her with former National Police Commissioner Bheki Cele. But now the *pièce de résistance,* the heart of the arrangement, right in the centre of the wall, was gone: Mbali Kaleni as a plump eighteen-year-old girl, shy and overwhelmed, wearing a dress festooned with too many purple flowers, beside the current president. Twenty-two years ago, when he was still a provincial politician. At an ANC celebration in Pietermaritzburg where her parents were invited as teachers' trade-union members.

She must have removed it that morning. Griessel knew it would have been a painful act. It made him hesitate to deliver bad news to her now. But he had no choice.

'We have determined that the gun in Mr Dikela's hand was licensed to him,' Griessel said.

She nodded.

'We've also spoken to Uli Gerber at Forensics again.'

'Yes?' Resigned, she knew what he was going to say.

'He says the gunshot residue on his hand is consistent with Menzi Dikela pulling the trigger himself. There was no discernible interference from a third party. He says that also corroborates the blood-spatter pattern, and he can give us absolutely no reason to believe it was staged. His conclusion is that it was suicide.'

'I don't understand it,' said Kaleni. 'Then how did they kill him?'

'We're trying to figure that out, Colonel,' said Cupido. 'The drug screening may give us a few hints.'

'I hope you are right,' she said. Then she sighed despondently.

'Those people, they are so very clever. So very sly. They left no evidence.'

She looked at them, realised they had something else on their mind. 'What else? Anything on the X5 yet?'

'Willem is still with the Metro Police,' said Griessel. 'It's going to take time.' Then: 'It is our last real hope.'

'And the neighbours?'

'Nothing, Colonel,' said Cupido. 'The problem is, it was a weekday afternoon. Only the lady across the street was home. Everybody else was at work.'

'There's another issue, Colonel,' said Griessel, apologetically.

'Yes?' Quietly, resigned.

'Professor Pagel says he looked at all the options. There is no way he can get the blood screened and tested without a docket. The system just does not allow it. And even if we gave him a docket number and he called in every possible favour it would take at least three weeks.'

She nodded thoughtfully. Blood tests were in general one of the Hawks' biggest frustrations. Unlike molecular diagnostics, which were handled by the SAPS forensic laboratory, toxicological analysis fell under the Department of Health, which had only three laboratories in the whole country equipped to handle them. Unwieldy bureaucracy, painfully slow and time-consuming at the best of times.

'However, he says under the circumstances we should consider using one of the private laboratories. He has a contact. He spoke to them this morning and they're willing to rush it through, and give a big discount. But we'll have to process the payment through unofficial channels.'

'How much will it cost?'

'Two or three thousand.'

'Ask him to do it right away. I'll pay for it myself.'

'Colonel,' said Griessel, 'the professor is also a little uncomfortable with the . . . uh . . . general situation. He says he can keep the body for another day or so, as a John Doe, but he is a little worried about the ethics . . .'

'We're all worried about the ethics, Captain, none more so than I. Tell the professor . . . Never mind, I'll call him myself.'

\*   \*   \*

They drove to Khayelitsha. Vusi Ndabeni went along, because he knew this part of the Cape Flats, and to help prevent any linguistic misunderstandings when they talked to Menzi Dikela's char.

Her name was Cebisa Jali and she lived in an outside room in Mofale Crescent. She was not yet thirty. Her English was good. She apologised for not being able to invite them in, as the space inside was simply too small for all of them. They stood in a circle, on either side of the wire fence and gate. The rain had stopped; the sky was grey and sombre. Outside in the street three children pushed a scooter without an engine around between the puddles. A dog trotted along with them excitedly.

Cebisa said she worked exclusively for the *umadala*. Wednesdays and Saturdays. For no one else. Her lip trembled while she spoke.

'How did you manage,' Ndabeni asked, 'with only two days' work a week?'

She began to weep quietly. He tried to console her in Xhosa. She just nodded in gratitude and apologised. Then, with her voice still verging on tears: 'He took care of me . . .'

'What do you mean, *sisi*, he took care of you?' Ndabeni asked.

She looked at him reproachfully. 'It's not what you think. I've got my matric. I went looking for a job, but it's hard, there're so many that . . . I got so desperate I went from door to door in Observatory, trying to get a cleaning job even, just so I could eat. He was the only one who said, "Come in, sit down, tell me your story." Then he asked me, "What do you really want to do? What's your dream?" And I said, "My dream is to become a teacher." He said, "Then that is what you must do, and I will help you." And he did. He paid for my studies, my Unisa fees. He gave me pocket money. I asked him a hundred times, "*Umadala*, what do you want, why are you doing this?" Then he said because he can. His child was grown-up, he didn't have a wife any more, he had the money. And he wanted me to have a future. He didn't want me to do housework for him. He said he could do all his own chores. He enjoyed it, it kept him busy. But I said, "No, I will do it." I wanted to give him something in return.'

'When did you start working there, *sisi*?'

'It's a year and a half. You can check. All the money he paid for me and my studies is in that book of his, where he writes everything down. Every cent is listed.'

'And was it always so tidy at his place?' Cupido asked.

'*Ewe,*' she said. 'Always. Very tidy. The whole house. He was like that.'

'What did you do, then, when you went in?'

'Washing,' she said. 'Later he started leaving the washing and ironing for me because he could see I wasn't going to stop coming in. I'm not looking for an *ushukela* daddy.'

They asked her if she knew about a secret room.

They saw her puzzled response, the total ignorance of it. 'No. What secret room?'

They left it at that. They asked about his friends, his activities. She said there were friends sometimes, and sometimes he went to visit them, on the days that she worked. Then he would leave a key for her, under the lemon tree. His friends were all older men. Menzi always introduced her politely, told his friends she was studying, and how proud he was of her.

Had she ever noticed anything strange? Out of the ordinary?

'No. Only on Saturday . . .'

'What, *sisi*?' Ndabeni asked.

Her eyes welled with tears again. She said that when Menzi's daughter Thandi phoned her this morning to tell her the *umadala* was dead, she'd thought maybe he'd felt it coming.

'How so?' Ndabeni asked.

'He was sad, on Saturday,' she said. 'And then he said . . .'

'How could you tell he was sad?'

'He was always full of the joys of living. And about me. If there were no other people he would sit with me while I did the washing, or where I was ironing. On Saturday, I could tell he was working very hard at showing happiness. Trying to talk to me like he always did. So I asked him, "*Umadala*, what is wrong?" And he said I mustn't worry. When you get old, there're some days when you feel the world is not such a nice place.'

'Is that all he said?'

'No. He also said, "Everything will work out for you, *sisi*, no matter what happens, you'll see, everything will work out. You won't have to worry about money." Then I said, "*Umadala*, what are you talking about?" And he said, no, he was just saying. And then he didn't want to talk about it any more.'

# 64

Vusi Ndabeni drove the car back to Bellville. He said: 'Guys, this really is a strange case.'

'Amen, brother,' said Cupido.

'Why, Vusi?' Griessel asked. 'What's your view on this?'

'Well, the colonel really wants it to be a murder. But from everything I've heard, it looks exactly like suicide. I mean, what his char just said. The guy was depressed . . .'

'I've never seen Mbali like this,' said Cupido. 'Bending the rules. *Her.* That's just crazy.'

'Exactly. And why now?' asked Ndabeni. 'Why with this case? Did she know Menzi Dikela that well?'

'I think,' said Griessel, 'for her, the last straw was the Johnson Johnson case. That one broke the camel's back. She's just had enough of all the corruption. It's – it's in the way she sees herself. Those photos on her wall . . . She's worked so hard, for so long, to build a career and a unit on honesty and integrity, and now . . . That must be tough.'

'Maybe you're right,' said Ndabeni.

'I'll tell you what I've been scheming. Maybe there's—' Cupido's phone rang, cutting him off. He could see on the screen it was Arnold.

'*Jis?*' answered Cupido.

'I've got good news for you, and I've got bad news.'

'Shoot.'

'You know the way most guys always start with the bad news?'

'*Ja . . .*'

'I'm not going to do that. I have to give you the good news first.'

'Go, Arnold. Go.'

'Patience, my friend, is bitter. But her fruit is sweet.'

'*Jissis*, Arnold . . .'

'Okay, okay. The good news is, your suicide note is a forgery.

Definitely. Our handwriting expert says without doubt it's not the old man's handwriting. And it's not a very good forgery. He says it looks like they did it in a big hurry. They seem to have had an example of his handwriting, but it wasn't an expert who did it.'

'Okay. Cool. Great.' Because he knew Mbali Kaleni was longing for some good news. 'What's the bad news?'

'I'm not finished with the good news yet.'

'Genuine?'

'Yip, my friend, your PCSI, your elite Provincial Crime Scene Investigative Unit, is a constant source of uplifting news, of glad tidings, guaranteed to put a laugh in your day, lead in your pencil, marrow in your b—'

'*Jissis*, Arnold!'

'The letter, the suicide note on the table. And the pen. That's where things get interesting.'

'Yes?'

'The late uncle's fingerprints are not on them. And, as you know, he wasn't wearing gloves. Now, that's all strange enough. But the thing is, it looks like the pen and paper were wiped clean. Like somebody went to the trouble to remove prints.'

'So there's nothing?' asked Cupido, in disappointment.

'Wait, I'm not nearly done. There is one area of the letter, on the back, that was overlooked when it was wiped. A small corner, near the edge. In this corner we found a partial print. Not enough to make an identification, but that may not be a problem. Because we tested the notepad too, the one that was in the drawer of the desk. Now here comes the big news, Vaughn. First, we're reasonably sure the suicide letter was torn off this pad. The two rip edges match. Second, there are good fingerprints on the notepad. Third, one of the prints matches the partial one on the letter. And fourth, Vaughn, ta-da-da-da, they are not the fingerprints of the deceased.'

'*Bliksem*.'

'Indeed.'

'Whose fingerprints are they?'

'Okay, now we come to the bad news.'

Cupido's heart sank. 'What?'

'We don't know whose fingerprints they are. The database gives no positive results. The guy who tore off the pad and probably forged the letter doesn't have a criminal record.'

'What about the population register, Arnold?'

'That's the Catch-22. If we don't have a docket, we can't get into Home Affairs database. You know they want a number.'

'Okay,' said Cupido.

'Okay, what?' Arnold asked. 'Okay, you'll get us a docket number, or . . .'

'Okay, we have to think about it. I'll get back to you. Anything else?'

'Those soil samples . . .'

'*Jis.*'

'We vacuumed the carpet in the sitting room and we found more. Now, the daughter's shoes test clean, and the old man's shoes test clean. Must have been a third party. Looks like it was part of a series of footprints, someone coming in from outside to the kitchen. He must also have sat down at the kitchen table.'

'Great,' said Cupido.

'We did a preliminary microscopic comparison with the soil on the yard, especially the vegetable garden, and it's definitely not the same.'

'Okay.'

'We will test it more anyway, the garden soil. Density and spectrometer. So far we haven't found any of the unknown soil in the Wendy house. But if they went into the house first, and then went to the Wendy house, it may simply be that it all fell off their shoes. I'll call you if we find something.'

'Thanks, Arnold. Great job. Great job.'

'I know,' he said, and rang off.

Cupido shared the information bit by bit with his colleagues in the car.

'Those SSA spooks won't have their fingerprints in any database,' said Vusi Ndabeni. 'Not even at Home Affairs.'

'I agree,' said Griessel. 'We'll be wasting our time if we put the query through, and we'll be showing our hand.'

The trouble with Cape Town's CCTV cameras was that the SAPS detective couldn't just sit at one central point and tell the Metro Police,

'Come on, guys and gals, show us the image material from Tuesday morning.'

The city had an impressive total of 1544 cameras watching the comings and goings of her inhabitants. But they consisted of three separate systems and were monitored at three different places by three different teams.

Number one: the freeway management system, maintained by the traffic authorities, with a hefty 239 cameras, was erected beside the Peninsula's main routes.

Number two: the so-called Integrated Rapid Transport system (IRT) had an astonishing 711 cameras, all part of the near-bankrupt MyCiti bus service. A team of municipal officers kept an eye on them.

Number three: the Cape Metropolitan Police's pride and joy – their surprisingly effective Strategic Surveillance Unit watched 594 cameras day and night. This network was installed across the city and had made a positive difference to crime statistics since its implementation.

Mooiwillem Liebenberg had started with the latter early that morning, in the hopes of identifying the dark BMW sports utility vehicle that had entered and left the relevant area of the Observatory neighbourhood between 8.30 and 14.00 the previous day. It took him more than three hours to identify sixty-one potential candidates, and almost another ninety minutes to run the registration numbers of all these vehicles through the various databases to obtain the particulars of the owners. And to determine whether the vehicles were legally registered.

The logical next step was to focus initially only on the suspect vehicles, especially those whose registration numbers turned out to be false. His starting point was that the SSA would be conscious of the camera systems and use false number plates to evade identification.

Four of the sixty-one dark-coloured BMWs that were in the right place at the right time in Observatory had false number plates, either because the vehicle registry claimed they did not exist, or the numbers involved were allocated to other vehicles. This relatively low total wasn't hard to understand. BMWs were the eleventh most targeted brand for Cape SUV thieves and hijackers. After Toyota, Land Rover, Nissan, Mahindra, Volkswagen, Jeep, Porsche, Renault, Ford and

Daihatsu. BMW would have ranked far higher, the SAPS vehicle-theft unit liked to say, if cheaper generic parts were available and the newer models didn't boast outstanding tracking technology.

Consequently, most of the BMW X3s and X5s that were stolen in the Peninsula and fitted with false number plates were older models.

Like three of the four that Liebenberg had pinpointed with much patience and thoroughness. He studied images of all three, and saw the signs of only a single occupant, the driver behind the wheel. Not what he was looking for.

The fourth vehicle on his list was less than a year old. An X5. Pitch black, with dusk-tinted windows. When he studied the best camera angles and shots, at the very best resolution, the three occupants seemed to be men. The previous day at 09.19 they had turned off the N2 onto the M75, the Liesbeek Parkway, on the route to Menzi Dikela's house. And again at 13.48 they had beaten a retreat in the opposite direction. The right kind of vehicle, with the right number of male passengers, with the most suspicious combination of year model and false number plate, in the appropriate time slot. Liebenberg decided this was his prime candidate for further investigation.

The trouble was that, when he moved on to the control room of the freeway management system to track the X5 out of the city, he lost it on the N7. He could clearly see the suspects following the N2 east to the Black River interchange, then north on the M5 to the Ysterplaat interchange. From there they took the N1 in the direction of Paarl, and then the N7 north. The last camera to capture them was the one at Dunoon.

They were travelling at 110 k.p.h., demurely within the law, in the direction of Malmesbury.

# 65

His head was buzzing and his focus overloaded by the possibility – the *impossibility* – that the Russian could be there. He had to determine whether Ditmir's men were following him, and he had to concentrate on following the shortest, fastest route to the Geldersekade. The streets were packed and busy.

He stopped in Bloed Street.

One thing at a time.

Let Ditmir's team see he was watchful, because it really didn't matter. They would expect it of him.

He looked back. Men, practically only men, in the red-light district. Nobody who was obviously on his trail.

He lingered. Looking.

Nothing.

He turned away towards the Waag, jogged to the corner. He came back again, carefully noting the rhythm of the pedestrians, or any interest.

Nothing.

He walked back to the Waag, turned left, ran along the Geldersekade canal to the houseboat that lay halfway to Bantammer Bridge. He spotted the small vessel with its powerful engine waiting behind the houseboat, the young man in it. He called: 'Pelle Baas!'

The young man waved at him, switched on the engine, and pulled up against the small quay behind the houseboat, just as they had arranged. Daniel jumped onto the houseboat gangway, ran around the structure, and then into the boat. 'Let's go,' he said, and looked back in the direction he had come.

Nothing.

★   ★   ★

Pelle Baas's boat was a classic open-deck wooden craft, only four metres long, the wood and copper brightly polished. Powering it behind was a Mariner F40 engine, all three cylinders running at full throttle, so that they raced to the right of the Schreierstoren underneath the Prins Hendrikkade freeway, along the Ooster access, into the breadth of the IJ River.

He looked at the young man, fit and sporty, cheeks ruddy with excitement. This morning Daniel had told him over the phone that he wanted a fast boat and an ingenious skipper with in-depth knowledge of Amsterdam's canal network.

'You've got the right guy,' Pelle Baas said. 'As long as we're not doing anything illegal.'

'How about exceeding the canal's speed limit?' Daniel asked.

'That can be arranged,' he answered, with a smile in his voice. 'What do you want to do?'

Daniel said he just wanted to make sure he wasn't being followed. 'I'm not going to tell you who might be following me, but I *can* tell you that I haven't broken any country's laws in the past five years, and that I won't be breaking any laws while you're with me. I want to hire you and the boat for the whole day. I'll pay you whatever you charge, in cash. And I want you to cover up the name of your boat.'

'Three hundred euro, and you tell me the whole story.'

So they made an appointment, with the instruction that Pelle Baas would wait for him in the Geldersekade. For as long as was necessary.

'Thank you!' Daniel called out now, above the roar of the engine.

'You're welcome.'

Daniel looked back, expecting to see someone racing after them.

There was only a long tourist boat slowly cruising past behind them, a few people waving.

'I think you're safe,' said Baas.

'Great job,' Daniel said. 'You can drop me off anywhere in the Prinsengracht. And there's no hurry,' despite the feeling of urgency he actually felt to get clean away.

Baas pulled back the throttle and their speed decreased. Daniel took out his wallet and passed the notes to the young man.

'Thank you. But you still owe me the story.'

'I can tell you that I'm trying to bring a bit more liberty to my country. I'm on the side of the good guys. And the bad guys would like to stop me.'

'Cool! Where are you from?'

He wanted to say he was from a country where the young man's surname could create an uncomfortable situation. He just shook his head. 'Africa. It's better that I don't tell you more than that.'

Daniel walked through the narrow streets of the Jordaan district and pondered the nature of paranoia. He was familiar with it. Thirty years ago he had suffered from paranoia when the KGB and the Stasi had deployed him in Paris for the first time in a lease agreement with the ANC. He had been alone, inexperienced, in a strange city, country and culture. His only contact with them was the complicated communication of chalk marks on post-boxes and tense, clandestine meetings with strangers in cafés, envelopes with coded messages handed over in newspapers. Espionage in the era before cell-phone technology and the internet.

The terrible loneliness of it, all personal connections forbidden. And the fear of capture that had gnawed continually at him, the expectation of a hammering on the door after midnight, a stab of fear at every siren's wail, or the sharp, focused stare of a policeman. You felt invisible eyes on you everywhere, you saw ghosts and danger where there were none, you trusted nobody. Constant anxiety and stress, until you realised you were at breaking point and had to learn to think differently: either get a grip on reality, or lose your mind.

And here it was again. He felt it in the pressure on his chest, the pounding of his heart, the delusion of being hunted.

He kept walking, taking deep breaths, forcing himself to think clearly. He was searching for calm, objectivity, seeking to stick to the facts.

Nobody had followed him after he had done his research at the South African Embassy. Because nobody had known he was in Paris.

Olivier Chérain had left his gas stove burning in his drunken state.

Ditmir was an arms dealer who wanted to make a fat profit out of Barnabas the Swazi. Ditmir had sent two cronies as insurance to follow and search him initially. Standard procedure for a walk-in customer.

After that Ditmir had not followed him as he was satisfied with the degree of risk.

The spectre of the Russian in the window was pure imagination, the overactive mind of a down-at-heel fifty-five-year-old former operative who, after a mere week of high tension and stress, had reverted to the fevered state of many years before. Lonely. Paranoid. The Russians were good, but they weren't *that* good.

And to prove that to himself, he kept walking for another forty minutes, to be certain that nobody was following him.

'I can deliver after five o'clock this afternoon,' Ditmir said, once they had settled on a price in his man cave. 'How do you want to do this?'

Daniel had thought through everything the previous day on the road. He said: 'We'll keep it simple. I want you to buy a four-man tent at one of the big camping stores. One that comes in a strong canvas bag. I want you to take out the tent poles and pegs. Wrap the rifle and ammo in the tent and put it back in the bag. Meet me at the National Monument on Dam Square at a quarter past five. I'll give you the cash. You give me the tent.'

The Albanian thought about that for a long time before he nodded. 'You are clever. But you know we will kill you right there if you try monkey business.'

'You know I will find you and kill you if the rifle is not what I ordered.'

The lackeys laughed. Ditmir too.

'Okay. We'll see you at a quarter past five.'

At half past four he counted out the euros on his hotel bed, wrapped the cash in a T-shirt and packed it in Lonnie May's rucksack. He transferred the remaining cash to his bag, along with the pistols. He booked out of the hotel, rucksack over his shoulder, and dragged his case to where he had found parking the previous night on the Leidsegracht.

In the Peugeot's boot was the rest of the camping gear he'd bought yesterday afternoon. A sleeping bag, inflatable mattress, battery lantern, gas stove, pot and kettle, eating utensils, a pair of Zeiss 20x60 binoculars, camping stool and a folding table. With a tarpaulin over it. Nearly full, leaving just enough room for the tent bag.

He put his case on the passenger seat, locked the car and began walking to Dam Square. It took him sixteen minutes.

The sun was still high; it would only be dark at half past eight. It was hot, the air fresh, just the long white jet trails to and from Schiphol tracing a network in the blue.

Lonnie had flown out from there on his final journey. Daniel breathed slowly, looked at everything, the people, everyone going somewhere, on foot, by bicycle. He wanted to be loose and relaxed, calmly watchful, the antithesis of paranoia.

He reached Dam Square just before five, a middle-aged fossil among the youthful tourists around the National Monument. He listened to the languages they spoke while they took selfies and paraded around for each other in skimpy summer clothing. He looked at the pillar of the monument, a finger pointing at Heaven in memory of the Second World War fallen. He wondered how many of these youngsters knew what sacrifices had been made, what a dreadful toll was taken.

He thought back to his own battles. He had been the age of so many of these young people when he had been ordered to eliminate enemies of the ANC's friends, part of the dark side of the Cold War. No monument would ever be built for those dead.

If only he could be like *that* again, the way he had been once he had conquered his anxiety and paranoia. Relentless.

He saw them coming, at a quarter past five. The two potato farmers, sickle-face Laurel and hairless Hardy, passing the Krasnapolsky Hotel. Sickle, the spokesman and leader of the comedy duo, carried the tent bag on his shoulder. With ease. The two expendables, he thought. Ditmir had sent them.

They saw him. He remained standing with his back to the monument wall until they reached him. Then he took off the rucksack, opened it and took out the T-shirt with the money. He gave it to the other one, Hardy. The man lifted the cloth of the T-shirt just enough to be sure the money was inside. Boldly. He didn't count it. Just nodded at Sickle.

Sickle passed him the tent bag. Daniel hefted the weight of it. It was heavy enough. He loosened the neck of the bag. The barrel of the CheyTac was visible.

They nodded to each other.

The potato farmers turned and left.

Daniel lifted the tent bag to his shoulder, set a course through the crowds, on the way to his Peugeot.

Too easy, nagged a voice in the back of his mind. It was too easy.

# 66

A huge insight came to Benny Griessel on the way home. The ultimate truth. It was the lust for alcohol that brought it on. He knew the three hours of sleep had unleashed his desire, that, the long day and the struggle with the confusing jigsaw of the Menzi Dikela case. Exhaustion demanded stimulation, sedation, escape, and booze had always given him that. He could already taste it; his nerve endings were begging for that tingle of intoxication.

It scared him, as it always did, because he could foresee the consequences, one after the other, of drinking that first Jack Daniel's. And the urge to drink and the terror of it gave him the big truth, made him realise why Sunday loomed like a mountain ahead.

On Sunday he had to ask Alexa for her hand in marriage.

And if she said no, he would want to resort to the bottle. For solace. To escape the humiliation.

It really didn't matter how she was going to try to explain it to him, how she would attempt to soften the blow, a 'no' would mean that he wasn't good enough. He wasn't marriage material and she didn't want to walk that road with a worn-out, rehabilitating and often relapsing alcoholic, general fuck-up and minor police captain. In addition it would damage their relationship irreparably. It would fracture the fragile trust they'd built.

And it would drive him back to drink. It would be his Day Zero, his booze Armageddon.

Sunday. No question.

He drove faster. He just wanted to get home.

She'd made a curry. The aroma in the kitchen was full of delicious promise. He kissed her, hugged her tight for a moment. Then she was clucking over him. 'You must be so tired. You haven't slept at all. Come on, Benny, I've made the most delicious butter chicken. Can I pour you a Coke Zero?'

They sat down to eat.

There was something wrong with the curry. It was faintly bitter. Perhaps she'd been a bit heavy-handed with the turmeric.

'Does it taste okay? It tastes funny to me now,' she said.

'It's delicious.' He looked at her, at her caring face, at her worn beauty. He felt a sea of emotions – the love he felt inside, and the safety he experienced here with her. Here.

Four days before he was due to pop the question.

Four days to Armageddon.

## 67

*Thursday, 31 August*

Three days before he was set to shoot the president of his home country, birdsong woke Daniel at dawn in the wooden chalet of Camping Le Grillon in the Belgian Ardennes forest, on the banks of the narrow Ourthe River. He picked up the cell phone first, activated the Proton application and checked for emails from Vula.

There were none.

He sent one of his own:

*From: inhlanhla@protonmail.com*
*Subject: Supplies bought*
*To: vula@protonmail.com*

*Dear Vula*
*Your recommended medical supplies dealer was interesting, and the transaction ultimately successful.*
*I'm on my way back.*
*Best wishes,*
*Dr Inhlanhla*

He got up, pulled the curtains wide. His little house was on the river and the view was beautiful. It was already dark when he'd arrived last night. The resort was quiet, because high season had ended eleven days before. He'd made the reservation with the cell phone when he'd filled up with fuel in Maastricht. He had deliberately chosen an overnight spot in this area where the trees were dense, to muffle the rifle shots.

He looked at the forest across the river. It was still as he remembered it from when he'd come through here on the motorbike. You could disappear in a place like this.

He badly wanted coffee. He hadn't realised the kitchen in the Camping Le Grillon restaurant only opened at midday. He would just have to wait.

His first priority was a place to stay in Paris. He didn't want to walk into a hotel carrying the big tent bag, and it was just too dangerous to leave it in a car, parked in the open on a Paris street. He didn't want his name on a hotel register again, didn't want to endure the scrutiny, uncertainty and discomfort of the my-credit-card's-been-stolen approach. He wanted a flat on a short-term rental, from tonight till Sunday, that he could pay for with cash. He found it on the Paris Attitude website, a one-bedroom place on the fifth floor of a building on the boulevard Morland. It took him forty minutes to make the reservation and answer the emails. He would have to deposit the cash for the rent into a bank on the way to Paris.

He washed, got dressed, closed the curtains, double-checked that the door was locked. Then he unzipped the tent bag, took out the tent and unrolled it on the floor of the small living room. The CheyTac's stock was folded in, the telescope unattached, ammunition in packets, the cleaning set in a canvas bag. He stroked his finger over the rifle's sleek craftsmanship, the varying textures of the dark grey metal. It was a work of art, he thought. Like all the weapons he'd worked with. He put the rifle on the table and began the ritual preparation.

It was the smell of gun oil that unleashed his rusty memories. Of his training all those decades ago, of the expansive shooting-range plains and intense sniper training, of mathematical distance tables and bleak, frigid hours hiding in the East German woods. He allowed the recollections to flow while he cleaned the rifle, familiarising himself with each part.

He wrapped the rifle in the tent bag again, and packed it into his car. He left the chalet's key at Reception, and drove away. He had used Google Earth to choose an area. He drove down the N89 in the direction of Samrée, chose a forest road high in the mountains, turned off to the right, and parked the Peugeot deep among the trees.

He checked the dirt road that wound into the forest. No fresh tracks.

It was quiet, deserted. Only a light breeze rustled the leaves and unseen animal life called.

He pulled out the tent bag, put it on his shoulder and began to walk into the thicket.

Lithpel Davids's email was waiting for Griessel and Cupido when they arrived – rested and reset for action – at the office just before seven.

*Cappies!*
*Find attached the uncle's call register, WhatsApps and SMSes.*
*PS – It's not like we hit the jackpot. But, hey, I'm not the detective.*
*PPS – Don't just thank me, thank Cellebrite too. Amazing technology!*

Philip van Wyk and his IMC had recently purchased the Israeli Cellebrite software to unlock phones. They were delighted with it and not shy to admit it.

The two detectives looked at the attached files in spreadsheet format. The call register had three columns for incoming calls: the number, the time of the call and the duration. There was also a spreadsheet for called numbers under the same three headings. Dikela didn't use the phone intensively. There were only a few calls, most of them from his daughter over the past week.

The messages were also chicken feed. A couple to friends texting to make or confirm dates for meals or drinks, bank transaction confirmations, the odd short exchange with his daughter, mostly to say he was missing her.

'No smoking gun,' Cupido said.

Griessel stood up. 'And it's too . . . I don't know, too little, Vaughn. Just too little, so few messages . . . Here's a guy with a secret room in his Wendy house, and his SMSes are . . .'

'So innocent?'

'And so . . . I don't know, it doesn't feel right. Let's go talk to Lithpel.'

They found him in his workspace, eating his breakfast of sugary cereal.

'Not exactly the breakfast of champions,' said Cupido.

'But it's yummy. And I'm thin, *cappie*. I can eat what I want.'

Cupido processed the reaction with suspicion. Who knew he was on a diet? Who was gossiping?

Griessel told Lithpel about their problem with the files he'd sent.

'*Ja*, I feel your pain. My best guess is that the uncle had another phone,' said Lithpel.

'What makes you think that?' Griessel asked.

'*Cappie*, computer geeks prefer Android, 'cause why? They can fool around with it, in all different ways. But this uncle had an iPhone? Makes me uncomfortable to start with. Reason number two, he was in that secret den of his, busy with all sorts of shenanigans – I mean, what's the use of a secret den if you can't get up to shenanigans? And where there are shenanigans, the odds are good that you're gonna find burner phones.'

'Not always,' said Griessel.

'Fair enough. There's a lot of very stupid criminals out there. But we're talking about a geek, a very smart man, a guy who used to work for Intelligence. And one more thing. Behind that workbench in his secret den there was a plug adapter with six two-prong slots. And when we arrived only the Ubiquiti Security Gateway was plugged in. I find that a little strange. You don't waste a good adapter like that when they're always in short supply.'

'Circumstantial,' said Cupido.

'If they took the computers, they would have taken the other phones too,' said Griessel.

'It's possible,' said Lithpel, before munching another spoonful of cereal.

'The problem is,' Griessel said, 'we can't just call up the people on his call register, because nobody knows he's dead yet.'

'And we can't get a two-oh-five because we don't have a docket,' said Cupido.

'Mexican stand-off,' said Lithpel.

'Rock and a hard place,' said Cupido.

'Fuck-up,' said Griessel.

They walked back to the office. In the corridor they ran into Vusi Ndabeni. 'Have you heard?' he asked.

'What?'

'The colonel has been with the Camel since seven o'clock. Morning parade is cancelled.'

\*   \*   \*

Three months earlier Daniel Darret had read the article in the *Sud-Ouest* newspaper with a great deal of interest. It was about the British SAS sniper who shot dead an Isis terrorist in Mosul, Iraq, over a distance of 2.4 kilometres using the American-manufactured CheyTac M200. The bullet took three whole seconds to cover the distance before ripping through the throat of the enemy.

The rifle was accurate to 3.2 kilometres. Seven long rounds, 408-calibre, fitted into the detachable magazine.

He shook his head at the incredible progress in weapons technology. In the eighties he'd used the Russian Dragunov, 7.62, accurate to a distance of 800 metres. You had to be an exceptional shot to obtain good groupings over longer distances.

Now he was lying on a carpet of rotting oak and beech leaves on the forest floor, with the CheyTac in front of him. He set it for 1000 metres; he fired only thirteen shots and was satisfied, spotting through his Zeiss binoculars that the grouping was within ten centimetres at that distance. So much easier than in the old days. Even after all these years it gave him a deep satisfaction, the feeling that this was his natural state of being, the weapon merely an extension of his body. This was one thing he *could* do.

He remembered how they had discovered him, on the dust-blown shooting range in Kazakhstan, the Russian shooting instructor who couldn't believe the evidence of his telescope, and walked the 400 metres up to Thobela's target to make sure it was true. Then he'd hung up a fresh target and said: 'Do it again.'

Thobela had. He'd repeated it over longer and longer distances, wholly unconscious of how he was able to do it, to express this talent.

They'd pulled him out of the Umkhonto training and sent him to East Germany.

He remembered the hand of Yevgeny Fyodorovich Dragunov on his shoulder, the legendary yet humble Russian weapons designer. He'd met him in East Germany when he and the other students at the Stasi sniper school had had to help test an experimental SVDS weapon.

Comrade Dragunov was fascinated by the black trainee with impossibly good groupings even with a cross-wind of 17 k.p.h. and the poor light of a heavily overcast winter's day. The sturdy, ageing Russian had made a remark in his mother tongue, pushed up his thick black-rimmed spectacles with his calloused workman's hand, then gripped the Xhosa's shoulder as if to check he was real.

His thoughts were on all those things as he carefully rolled the rifle in the tent, put it into the bag, hefted it onto his shoulder and began walking back to the Peugeot.

# 68

Twenty to ten on Thursday. Colonel Mbali Kaleni came to fetch them, Griessel and Cupido, Vusi Ndabeni, Mooiwillem Liebenberg and Frank Fillander, asked them to come to her office.

The Flower was completely wilted this morning, Cupido thought. A dried floral arrangement. He had never seen her like that. For the first time since he'd known her he felt genuine deep sympathy for her. She was muted, beaten, defeated.

She asked them to sit down, went over to shut the door, took up her place behind her desk. 'Just past eleven o'clock last night, Professor Phil Pagel called me,' she said, in a funereal tone. 'He said he had received the results of the blood tests from the private laboratory. There is absolutely no indication of any anaesthetic agent in Menzi's blood. There is no trace of any substance in his stomach contents that might have been used to camouflage such agents in a drink or food. The professor also did a comprehensive autopsy late yesterday afternoon, spent a lot of time trying to find evidence of defensive wounds, or the symptoms of an insulin overdose. There were none. He told me he has absolutely no reason to believe that Menzi's death was anything but suicide. This corroborates the evidence gathered by Gerber, about the blood spatter and gunshot residue. So, I have made a big mistake. I have allowed a personal relationship to interfere with my good judgement, and I have involved all of you in this foolishness, for which I apologise unconditionally. My behaviour was absolutely unacceptable.'

'Colonel,' said Griessel, 'I don't think—'

'No, Benny, please. Let me speak. I have spent the morning with the brigadier. I have told him everything, and I have tendered my resignation. He refuses to accept it, but I have asked him to think it over. I have assured him that your involvement in the matter has been on my orders, and that none of you should be held accountable for the serious breaches in procedure and protocol. He agreed that this was indeed the case. I will open the appropriate docket, indicating that this was suicide, and I will take it to the Mowbray station commander right after this. I'll tell him that I will fully understand if he wishes to proceed with a formal complaint against me. I have already telephonically apologised to Professor Pagel for involving him. I will also personally apologise to Forensics. That is all, thank you. Please proceed with your other cases.'

'Colonel, may I speak now?' asked Griessel.

'Benny, there is nothing more to be said. Please.'

He wanted to say that she had involved them – and herself – in the case in good faith. She needn't feel bad. He would have done the same. But her tone was pleading. He said nothing.

She rose to her feet. 'I have a lot to do.'

Cupido walked with Griessel down the passage. They watched as Mbali Kaleni walked towards the stairs. When she had disappeared, Cupido said: 'Benna, we can't drop this thing.'

Griessel just nodded, preoccupied.

'It's these state-capture *mofos*, Benna. I don't know how they did it, but it's them. I mean, the missing bullet casing, the secret room, the forged suicide note, the mystery fingerprints, the X5 with fake number plates, three official-looking men paying him a visit. It's them. It's SSA monkey business. That Okapi and the biltong – it haunts me, say what you want. I'm not going to let those people get away with "suicide" again.'

Griessel stopped. 'Mbali isn't going to allow it.'

'Mbali doesn't need to know. Until we have something. If we don't get anything, no harm, no foul . . .'

'There's nothing left to find, Vaughn.'

'We have to find a way to process those prints, Benna. We have to go back to the *umadala*'s house. We must take our time. You must go and stand there, and then you do that thing you do. And I'll put it all together. I have the feeling we missed something. And you know my intuition . . . Just one more go at this. Please.'

'Vaughn, I—'

'Come on, partner. At least we have to try.'

'Vaughn, they will fire our butts. I can't propose to Alexa on Sunday if I'm unemployed. It's just not . . . right.'

Cupido sighed. 'Fair enough. I forgot about that one.'

'If we had more . . .'

'It's okay, Benna. I'll go it alone on this one.'

'You're not going to drop it?'

'How can I, Benna? How can I when that Donovan *laaitie* looks at me with his doubting eyes? I couldn't look him in those eyes and say, "No, we're not captured."You know that saying "The only thing necessary for the triumph of evil is for good men to do nothing"? If I did nothing, then I'm as good as captured. Maybe not on the payroll of the three fat Indians, but captured nonetheless. One day I'm going to ask Donovan's mommy to marry me. Not today, not this year, but somewhere down the line, inspired by your senseless marital bravery. And I want to be able to tell Donovan that his stepdad didn't stand back and do nothing. He stood up for what is right. He risked his career. He did the spirit of the Hawks proud. Even if by then I'm working as a mall cop in Brackenfell.'

'Fuck,' said Griessel.

'Fuck what?'

Griessel walked a few steps down the corridor, and stopped.

'Fuck what, Benna?'

Griessel wrestled with his thoughts, came back shaking his head. 'Fuck, Vaughn, you'd better get me a mall-cop job too if they fire us.'

'You're in?'

'I'm in.'

'I love you, man.'

Daniel Darret deposited the rent for the Paris flat at a bank in Rheims. When he sent on the proof of payment by email, he saw there was a message from Vula.

*From: vula@protonmail.com*
*Subject: Re: Supplies bought*
*To: inhlanhla@protonmail.com*

*Dear Dr Inhlanhla*
*We are happy that you have the supplies. Let us know when you are safely in Paris.*
*Vula*

Was that all? No news of the president's activities on Sunday? It was in two days' time, as today was useless, too far gone. He needed at least two days from when he received a schedule to recce the area, to find a place to lie in wait with the rifle, scope out entry and exit routes.

He wondered who was on the other side of the email, which of Lonnie May's aged veteran comrades. Did they know what they were doing?

Daniel wrote back:

*Dear Vula*
*I am concerned about the time available to prepare for the operation. It is an intricate procedure and needs careful planning. Please supply all available information at your earliest convenience.*
*Yours,*
*Dr Inhlanhla*

He waited for half an hour. There was no answer.

Then he set off, travelling on regional roads and through small towns to avoid the A4 and any possible police presence.

There was a possibility that Mbali Kaleni had already been to Forensics and frozen the case. It was Griessel who had to call fat Arnold of PCSI and ask him to be part of the new conspiracy. Cupido explained: 'They think I'm too full of myself. They like you more, Benna.'

And they think I'm a drunk, Griessel suspected, but he phoned and asked, 'Arnold, has Mbali been there?'

'Not yet. Why would she want to come here?'

Griessel said their commander wanted to apologise and stop the whole case.

'What for? We were just starting to have fun. That soil sample of yours . . .'

'Yes?'

'Interesting. It's not your normal result.'

'What do you mean?'

'We've never seen anything like it. It's . . . Okay, I must remember I'm talking to a Hawk, so I'd better simplify.'

'*Ja, ja* . . .'

'So here's the story. The soil samples we usually get come from footprints and tyres, that sort of thing.'

'Yes.'

'And footprints and tyres run on tar roads and dirt roads or topsoil, or maybe on ploughed land or a bed that's been dug over. Then the tests show you you've got your soil, and your seeds and pollen, maybe fertiliser, bird shit, motor oil, all the usually above-ground possibilities.'

'Yes?'

'And our tests are usually comparative by nature, two separate samples. To prove a suspect was in a specific location, or that the sample corresponds with soil that was on a victim's shoes. You know ...'

'Yes.' He would have to be patient. Arnold wanted to impress him, blind him with science first, as always.

'In this case we don't have anything to compare it to. We have to analyse and try to say where it originated. We have to guess on the grounds of three things: sediment, colour and structure. Are you still with me?'

'Yes.' Griessel had heard them testifying in court, so he was aware of most of what Arnold was saying. But it was best to let him talk, because Griessel had a big favour to ask.

'The colour seemed odd to us from the start. Unusual. We put the sample under the microscope, and then we did a density test, in what we call a density-gradient tube. Your density-gradient test separates the different layers and gives you a base profile. And then we went to the spectrometer to find the minerals. To make a long story short, we haven't seen this combination of colour, texture and mineral composition in our regular tests. We think it comes from a mine. Or something.'

# 69

'A mine?'

'That's right.'

'There're no mines around here, are there?'

'We checked. There's a whole bunch of open-cast mines. Granite, sandstone, building stone . . . You have your clay mines for brickmaking, your building-sand mines, your limestone mines. There are guys who take heavy metals out of the dunes near Saldanha, and towards Dwarskersbos. But this sample doesn't match open cast. The texture and origin is definitely deeper underground. I can give you the scientific basis for our argument—'

'No, I believe you. So that doesn't help us at all?'

'Look, your PCSI, your elite Provincial Crime Scene Investigation Unit's members are generally a notch or two above your average genius. It's common knowledge. We know it, you know it.'

'Of course.'

'But even we, Benny, don't know everything. Hard to believe, strange but true. If you say Mbali wants to shut this thing down, you'll have to take the data yourself and talk to a geologist. There's a chap at the university in Stellenbosch. A Professor Ian Ford. If anyone can figure out what's going on here, he can.'

'Thanks, Arnold. Send the data when you can. And, please, don't say a word to anyone. Especially Mbali. She doesn't know Vaughn and I are going on with the case . . .'

'It'll cost you, Benny, no such thing as a free lunch . . .'

'I know we owe you big-time. And, by the way, I've got another favour to ask.'

'Aha. Wondered why you were being so nice to me.'

'The fingerprints,' said Griessel. 'The notepad fingerprints. Now, I hope you understand what I'm going to say. We have reason to believe it's connected to the case that was thrown out. You know – that docket we were working on about a month ago?'

Arnold was silent for a long time as he processed that information. Griessel waited patiently.

'I think I understand what you're saying, Benny.' His tone was cautious now, sombre.

'There could be consequences, Arnold. If there are any results. And if the results are what we think they're going to be. If they're monitoring access to the population register. You must think carefully. We'll understand if you don't want to do it.'

'I don't think they have the capability to monitor that system. In any case, Home Affairs is chaos, Benny. That database is in such a mess, like all Home Affairs systems, that a single request from us will just disappear into a deep dark hole.'

'Are you sure? You can always say it was our request. Our mistake, getting mixed up with all the dockets.'

'No, it's fine. But we won't be able to do it today. If I ask for priority now, the other guys here are going to smell a rat.'

'Whenever you can, Arnold. We really appreciate it.'

'Enough for us to look forward to an invitation to the Big Wedding?'

'I still have to ask her, Arnold.'

'But who could say no to a sweet Hawk like you?'

Within half an hour everything changed for Daniel Darret.

He had been relaxed, with Paris little more than forty kilometres away. He knew he would have to tackle the afternoon rush hour, but he was nearly there, the journey with his incriminating load nearly complete. And then, on the D934 just before Disneyland Paris, there was a roadblock. National Police and soldiers, a long queue of cars ahead: everyone had to stop at the control point.

At first he swore out loud over his choice of route. He should have known. He should have taken the A1. Then he considered his options. A U-turn would attract a lot of attention – the kind of attention he could ill afford. Staying calm was his only choice, to play his role and hope for the best. He took the car's paperwork out of the glove compartment, got his Namibian passport ready, lined up his story of where he'd been and what he was doing. He concentrated on his approach – be friendly, a touch subservient, a little bit of the lost-African-in-Europe.

He thought about the luggage. The tent with the rifle in it.

Would they make him unpack everything? Unroll it?

When he drew close enough, he saw the soldiers searching some of the vehicles.

He breathed. Slowly in, slowly out.

Until it was his turn. He tried to let an African accent creep into his speech when he greeted them and offered his documents.

'Your French is good,' the policeman examining his passport said. There was a soldier, armed, standing alongside him. Another four nearby, watchful.

'*Merci.* That's why they sent me here,' said Daniel.

'To do what, sir?' the policeman asked, and peered in, first at the front, then at the back, in the luggage space.

'I market Namibia's nature and game reserves – best in the world – to French tour operators.'

'I see. And what is in the back?'

'Camping gear. You're welcome to look.' He held out the key.

'Why camping gear?'

'I was in the Ardennes. I need to be able to compare our facilities to the best in Europe.'

The policeman took the key, handed it to the soldier to unlock.

Daniel forced himself not to watch the rear-view mirror. Just to sit patiently, staring into the distance, now that the policeman had moved on to the next car.

'Sir, could you get out of the vehicle, please?' the soldier asked.

'Of course,' he said, while his gut contracted. Was it going to end here, at Disney World? He, the Mickey Mouse of assassins? He got out and walked to the back.

The soldier was standing at the open boot and pointing his firearm at the contents. 'Can you open that for us?' The weapon was pointed at the rolled-up sleeping bag.

Daniel picked it up, loosened the string that held the cover closed, pulled out the sleeping bag and threw it open on the ground.

The soldier nodded. 'And that?'

He felt the tension, how his heart pounded. He pulled another canvas bag out. It was the camping stool. He opened it, slid out the folded chair, and leaned it against the Peugeot.

'And that?'

It was the box with cooking and eating utensils. He lifted it onto the ground, opened the flaps, began unpacking.

'Never mind. You can put it back, thank you, sir.'

He put the box away with a huge sense of relief and began rolling up the sleeping bag.

'No, sir, you can do that at home. You're holding us up.'

'Sorry,' he said, and shoved everything hastily back.

'Can I close it?'

'Yes, yes, sir, you may go.'

He said thank you, said goodbye, got back in, started the engine and drove away. Only after a kilometre did he look back, reassured to see no military vehicles following. He sighed deep and long. He looked at his hands. No tremors.

Not bad for a middle-aged spy. He had done well.

He had to fill up with fuel, buy a Coke for the sugar and sudden thirst, take a breather, and regroup. He stopped at the Total Access just east of Lagny-sur-Marne midtown.

That was where he discovered the microchip.

It was sheer providence, he thought later, that it had happened there. While he was getting out, Fate intervened. Lady Luck smiled for the second time in half an hour.

He opened the door, swung his legs out, and it was in that movement that the bottom hem of his jeans scratched his ankle. He realised it wasn't the first time that day he'd felt an irritation against his skin. It was just rougher and sharper now. He reached down the leg of his jeans expecting to find a label or staple he'd overlooked when he'd hastily dumped all his things into his case in Arcachon. His fingers felt . . . and found it, the foreign object, a flat block, a small flat tab. He fiddled with it, couldn't see down there, and eventually he turned the hem up.

It was stuck there, matt black, just two centimetres long. He pulled it off, saw the little barbs that made it cling to the material, the gold of four electronic contact points. In that moment he knew how it had got there.

The potato farmer. Sickle. The Pancake House toilet, where he'd been searched for recording devices, when every piece of clothing had been thoroughly felt. While Daniel had had his back turned in embarrassment over his nakedness. Laurel and Hardy. Perhaps they were not quite as stupid and expendable as he'd thought. Now he knew why they hadn't bothered following him. He had a strong suspicion that this little bit of technology was a GPS tracker.

He activated his cell phone, googled 'small GPS tracking device'. He quickly found something that looked a lot like the chip in his hands – a CATS-I, the smallest of its kind. *The combination of GPS, RF and GSM technologies in the one device is designed to provide the best possible chance of recovering your 'tracked' asset, regardless of its current location,* according to the website. *The inclusion of an RF beacon allows for accurate locating when hidden inside buildings, and a new GSM location technology provides almost GPS-like accuracy in mapped areas. The GSM technology relies on a GSM sim chip instead of a GSM sim card ...*

This one looked different, slightly more homemade and rough, but it was definitely the same thing.

They knew exactly where he'd been. And where he was *now*.

# 70

Daniel's first reaction was to get rid of the chip, to throw it into the street. He suppressed the impulse, turned the chip over slowly in his fingers. Eventually he got back into the car and pushed the chip into his pocket.

He filled the Peugeot's tank, his mind racing, searching for answers. Why did Ditmir and his people want to know where he was? Did they still suspect that Daniel represented some law-enforcement agency? Did they want to take precautions, be prepared in case they needed to act? Disappear?

It was still the strongest, simplest explanation. Ditmir was an international black-market arms dealer, part of an extended organised-crime network, with a great deal to lose. Distrustful. Wary. Sly.

Or was it connected to the Russian he'd seen in the window? Or not seen.

He paid for the fuel, went to buy a cold drink, came back to the car and got in.

He sat there for a moment. Be careful of the paranoia. Especially now, after the tension of the roadblock, the shock of the chip.

He sat a while longer weighing his options. He got out again, walked to the cashier, and asked whether there was a good hotel nearby.

Cupido and Griessel looked at the soil-sample microscope photos and analysis tables that had been sent on by Forensics. They didn't understand any of it.

Cupido called the number, provided by Arnold, for Professor Ian Ford at the Department of Earth Sciences, University of Stellenbosch. It rang for a long time. 'No answer,' he said.

Griessel checked his watch. It was after five. 'They've gone home already. We should try again tomorrow.'

'You've still got the keys to the *umadala*'s house, partner?'

'Yes.'

'Benna, I scheme we go to Menzi Dikela's house now. Before Mbali asks for the keys back. And we apply for leave. For tomorrow and the weekend. Give this thing our best shot. Mbali won't be able to say no in the circumstances.'

He was committed: he couldn't pull out now. 'Okay.'

They filled in leave application forms, put them on the colonel's desk, then left, driving separate cars so that Griessel wouldn't have to go back to Bellville.

On the way he analysed why he didn't have much enthusiasm for Cupido's last great effort. It wasn't that he didn't want to contribute to exposing the hijacked SSA for what they were. It wasn't the pathological and forensic proofs that it was suicide. It *was* partly because he was scared of the consequences, to his career and job security.

But most of all it was the feeling he'd had. There in the house. A feeling of . . . tragedy.

He shook it off. Premonitions took you only so far. He had to examine the facts, as Cupido would say. The questions, the things that didn't fit.

He phoned Alexa to tell her he wouldn't be able to go to Alcoholics Anonymous with her tonight. He had to work.

Daniel Darret drove to the Hôtel Restaurant Le Quincangrogne on the bank of the Marne River, forty kilometres from Paris. He parked and walked to the reception desk, the microchip in his pocket. He told the young man on duty that he was meeting someone for dinner. 'I'll wait there,' he said, and pointed outside to the seating area, which was visible through the large glass doors. Beside the water. Tables and chairs, a few couches.

The young man smiled in agreement and Daniel went out. He sat down on a three-seater couch, leaned back comfortably, looked at the tidy lawns, the cool river. He reached into his pocket, took out the chip, stuffed it under the cushion of the couch, with the spikes facing up, so that it would stick to the material.

He sat for another ten minutes. Then he got up, walked to Reception to say that it didn't look like his date was going to turn up. He would find somewhere just outside town to stop and unroll the tent. So he could be sure there wasn't a tracking chip fixed to that too.

\* \* \*

Cupido and Griessel went through Menzi Dikela's house from one end to the other. Slowly and thoroughly. They began in the garage, moved to the sitting room, kitchen, bedrooms, and ended up in the study.

Just before seven Kaleni phoned Griessel. She said she had signed the leave applications. She understood that they needed a break. He thanked her. Right after that she phoned Cupido with the same message.

'Now I feel guilty,' said Griessel.

'We'll have to suck it up,' said Cupido.

It was only when they were in the kitchen that Cupido asked: 'Benna, why did you say yes to me? To join in the investigation. Why take the risk? At this time?'

Cupido waited patiently for the answer to come. Griessel was considering his words. Eventually he said: 'Do you remember last year, December, when I was lying drunk in Caledon Square police cells? When we did the Ernst Richter case?'

'*Yebo*, yes. Alibi dot co dot za boss. We nailed that sucker.'

'That's right. You put your career on the line. You protected me. You lied to save my ass.'

'No, Benna. I did cover for you, but Mbali likes you too much. She would have ranted, but she wouldn't have fired you.'

'Maybe. But that's not all . . .'

'Shoot. But not with your gun.'

'When I . . . In the old days, the previous dispensation . . . It was rough too. There were many things that . . . Back then I was too chicken to say anything, do anything. And my best excuse was that I was newly married, Anna was pregnant, she wasn't working. I was scared, Vaughn, in those days, of losing my job. And you know how the system worked. Once you were marked . . . It still bothers me that I didn't have the guts . . .'

'Partner, you can't—'

'No, wait, Vaughn, there's another thing. You. You come from Mitchells Plain. You worked your butt off to make captain. In difficult circumstances. First you weren't white enough, now you're not black enough. You had the opportunity to take bribes, more than once. But you didn't, because you were . . . You're too proud of the Hawks, of what we do. I know what it means to you. So, if you're prepared to risk all the years and all the pride, then the least I can do is to stand by you.'

Cupido, for all his bravado, was never comfortable with too much emotion. So he said: 'You're getting soppy in your later years, partner. Age is a bitch.'

But Griessel could tell that his colleague had liked what he'd said.

At the side of the road Daniel had searched all the clothing he'd worn the day of the potato farmers' inspection. There were no other sensors in it. Or in the tent, the packs of ammunition or the cleaning materials.

He drove on to Paris. With an eye on the rear-view mirror.

He took the rifle to the flat first, after he had collected the keys at Reception and listened to the woman's explanation of how the stove, washing-machine and Wi-Fi worked. He took his suitcase up too, but the rest of the camping gear he left in the car. He showered, dressed in fresh clothes, walked to the rue des Rosiers to eat at L'As du Fallafel, one of his favourite spots in the city.

Doubt still gnawed at him. Over the Russian in Ditmir's window. Over the Albanian's motives for planting the tracking device on him. If the Russian really was there, how had he known that Daniel would go to Ditmir? That was the thing that bothered him most.

It could only mean that one of Lonnie's cronies had sold them out.

So could he trust the emails?

They had reached the study before the detectives found anything of importance – once they had taken all the books out of the bookshelves, shaken them out, put them back and finally moved on to examine the documents in the two-door cabinet below the window, the cupboard in which Lithpel Davids had spotted the network cables.

They sorted the paperwork: car registration, the proofs of payment for licences, the title deed of the house, the old home mortgage and short- and long-term insurance contracts. Read everything carefully.

When they'd finished and had packed almost everything back again, they were left with four documents on the desk that told a story.

And Griessel and Cupido did not like that story.

# 71

Daniel woke just after seven to the rumble of traffic in the voie Georges-Pompidou, realising he had slept reasonably well for the first time since Lonnie May had appeared in Bordeaux, like the angel of death.

He had grown so weary of the constant wrestling with doubt that, finally, he had decided to ignore all his misgivings and just get on with the job. It was the only way forward.

First he checked for any emails using a new cell phone. Yesterday on the way to the flat he'd crushed the previous one underfoot and tossed it into a bin.

There'd been no news from Vula last night. Nor was there any now.

He brewed some coffee with the machine provided, drank it on the balcony overlooking the building's small back garden. It was cool and overcast, as if autumn was recognising this official date for change. He read the news from his motherland. There was a report on the president arriving in France. He was here, in this very city, today. Their orbits were on course to intersect.

Daniel felt his guts contract. Tension. Doubt.

He read the reports on the back-stabbing and suspected fraud at the Revenue Service, new allegations about the Indian businessmen's tentacles in the National Railways Agency. He tried to draw some impetus, inspiration from this news.

The hotels had spoiled him with breakfasts the past week, so he prepared one for himself from the groceries he'd bought yesterday evening at the Franprix on rue Jules-Cousin: bacon and eggs, a toasted baguette, melting with butter and cheese, and orange juice. More coffee to finish.

Only once the dishes were washed, did he check the phone again. He saw the message with a spasm of anxiety and, at the same time, relief.

*From: vula@protonmail.com*
*Subject: We have news*
*To: inhlanhla@protonmail.com*

*Dear Dr Inhlanhla*
*We can confirm that your target will be at the South African ambassa-*
*dor's residence on rue Cimarosa on Sunday afternoon, from 16.00 to*
*18.00. From there he will travel to the Hôtel Raphael, 17 avenue Kléber.*
*We have firm intelligence that this will happen between 18.00 and 18.30.*
*He will stay at the hotel until it is time to leave for the airport.*
*Good luck,*
*Vula*

On Friday Griessel took his bicycle ride after eight to enjoy the 'day off', at least in some small way. Up the steep incline of Kloof Nek the rush-hour traffic was heavy, but he turned off left as was his habit, across the flank of Table Mountain. He thought through all the possibilities of what they had discovered yesterday.

There was nothing concrete. Potentially a new theory. Insubstantial, but there. Cupido had whistled softly through his teeth as he stared at the documents, displayed side by side on Menzi Dikela's desk, like the chapters in a book. Griessel had been silent: he wasn't ready to speak about it yet. Cupido limited his commentary to the mournful tune. They both understood the implications, and the advantage of just leaving it there: if you didn't talk about it, it didn't really exist.

Eventually Griessel stacked the pile of evidence and stored it in his murder case.

'We'll wait for the fingerprints,' was Cupido's subdued goodbye before they left for home. The fingerprints on the notepad – the one the suicide note had been torn from – would confirm their new suspicion. Or disprove their theory.

He was hoping for the latter.

His phone rang when he was beyond the cable-car station. He stopped cycling, and answered. It was Cupido. He said they had a date with the geology professor in Stellenbosch at eleven. The forensic soil-sample reports and photos had already been sent on.

Griessel said he would be there.

'Benna, you will phone me when you hear from Forensics?' said Cupido, still in the muted tones of last night.

'Straight away.'

He pedalled hard through the final bends of the contour path around Devil's Peak, then stopped, gasping for air at the King's Blockhouse, more than two hundred years old. Months before, he'd looked up the history of the structure, as it was frequently his rest stop and turning point. The British had built it as a lookout to cover Table Bay and False Bay after their invasion of the Cape in 1795 so that no other force could achieve as easy a victory as they had.

Griessel looked out over the crystal-clear day, the cold front long since dissipated, the Cape stretching out to the Helderberg as the morning sun climbed the wide skies. This beautiful place, he thought. Such a long history of conflict and treachery and greed.

When would it end?


Daniel bought a black hoody jacket at one of the many sports shops in Les Halles, grateful that the cooler weather made wearing it more appropriate. A hoody remained one of the best methods to hide your face from the cameras.

He took the RER A-train to the station at Charles de Gaulle-Étoile, emerging just beside the Arc de Triomphe in the Champs-Élysées, then crossed the boulevards into avenue Kléber. He flipped the hood over his head and pulled it down low. He had used his phone map application to prepare, so he knew where the Raphael was, the beautiful, near-century-old art-deco hotel where people like Katharine Hepburn and Marlon Brando had frequently stayed overnight.

And now his homeland's scoundrel president.

He walked past on the west side of the broad street across from the building. He noted the dedicated vehicle-access lane for the hotel. If the president was to be dropped off with a vehicle, Daniel would have twenty to thirty seconds to aim the scope's crosshairs on him and pull the trigger. A moving target, most likely. But if he could find a good hiding place, he would have enough time to calculate the distance tables and wind before that moment.

The technical details would be easy. He had been operational in more difficult situations, in the old days. With success.

The emotional side was the big stumbling block.

He still didn't know whether he would be able to bring himself to pull the trigger when those familiar features filled his scope, the head of a man he had once so admired.

Time to take a look at the ambassador's residence, the alternative ambush location, where the president would be getting into the vehicle.

Professor Ian Ford's office was full of rocks, as were the corridors of the geology building on the Stellenbosch campus.

He was a tall, ascetic-looking man with a wild grey beard and a strong Australian accent. He told Griessel and Cupido that it was a first for him. 'Never had the honour to speak to Soggies before,' he said, and smiled. 'That's what we Aussies call our own Police Special Operations Group. Which is more or less the equivalent of the Hawks, I suppose.'

'But not nearly as good,' said Cupido.

'I'm sure,' said the professor.

He invited them to sit down, told them he had looked at everything and it was a very intriguing case. But could he ask a few questions first?

'Sure,' said Cupido.

'Where did this sample come from?'

'Presumably from a footprint, on the floor of a crime scene.'

'Interior? Exterior?'

'From inside a house.'

'Okay. Was there any drilling done outside the house, or nearby?'

'What sort of drilling?' Griessel asked.

'Drilling for water. You know, a borehole.'

'Not that we're aware of.'

'And when do you think the footprint was made? What day?'

'Tuesday. Why, Prof?'

'One moment, please.' Ford turned to his computer, manipulated the mouse and keyboard, studied something they couldn't see. Then he propped his elbows on the desk. 'Right. If you'll indulge me, I'd like to explain this like . . . What's that wonderful expression you have, about how to eat an elephant?'

'Bite by bite,' said Cupido.

'That's the one, mate. First of all, there's the texture of the sample.'

He reached for one of the microscope photos he'd printed out earlier. 'Look here. These are chips of a very distinct shape. Not granules, not normal flaking. That's very typical of the form created by drilling. Your forensic report identifies it correctly as limestone, a common layer beneath this part of the Western Cape. And then look at the colour. Bluish-grey, typical of the unexposed De Hoek limestone unit, which is so distinctive in appearance. Especially subterranean. Moreover, they regularly target this layer for drilling because, when fractured, it often holds water. The other interesting aspect is that the limestone chips are mixed with lesser quantities of various other commonly found rocks, which is another pointer to a borehole going through the various layers. There's also the complete absence of the sand granules you'll find closer to the coast. And, last, this stuff will only stick to your shoes when it's fairly wet. Now, I won't say this in a court of law, but if you'll allow me a Jack Irish moment, I'd venture to say—'

'Jack who, Prof?' Cupido asked.

'Jack Irish? The character from the late great Aussie crime-fiction author Peter Temple's books?'

They just shook their heads. 'We don't read crime fiction, Prof,' said Cupido. 'It's just too . . . airy-fairy.'

'Right,' said the professor, mildly deflated.

'What were you going to say, Prof?' asked Griessel.

'Well, it's just a deduction, based on the sample analysis, and what you told me now. And I might be wrong, but I think this guy walked in the effluent of a borehole being drilled, or just after it was drilled, less than two hours before he left that footprint.'

'Why?' asked Cupido.

'The effluent needed to be wet to stick to the sole of a shoe. And I don't think it would take much longer than an hour to dry, maybe ninety minutes. I asked you on what day it happened, so that I could check if it rained. Rain would obviously make a difference in terms of the moisture and stickiness of the sample. But it only rained on Wednesday, after almost a week of no precipitation. So . . .'

'That Johnnie Irish would have been proud of you,' said Cupido.

'Jack,' said Ford, with a broad smile. 'Jack Irish. I rather think so too.'

## 72

Daniel could instantly identify the ambassador's residence in the rue Cimarosa as the South African flag was flapping lazily in the light, cool breeze. The camera prominently installed at the front door was the only sign of security. Daniel had expected more than that while the president was in the country; a small police presence, even. But there was nothing. Just the metal barriers that marked reserved parking in front of the residence and the Argentinian embassy directly opposite, probably permanent, and for official vehicles.

He remembered the information provided by the young playwright in the yellow dress that the president was in Versailles today. And tomorrow all day in meetings at the embassy, a few kilometres away. Was that why there were no eyes or security here?

It didn't really matter. This street offered no opportunities. It was too narrow, the neighbouring buildings too low to offer good vantage points and firing angles, unless he was prepared to expose himself on one of the rooftops. There would be intelligence operators in the Argentinian embassy too, and a system that monitored the rue Cimarosa.

He pulled his hood a little lower and walked on. For a moment he wondered what it looked like inside, in the ambassador's residence. Was it a friendly place where countrymen could converse, where the indigenous languages could sometimes be heard, and politics hotly debated? Were there paintings and photos of South Africa to soothe the homesickness?

Griessel asked Professor Ian Ford if it was possible to tell from the soil-sample analysis where the borehole had been sunk.

'I thought you'd ask that. The answer is probably not what you want to hear,' he said, picking up a large cylinder from the top of a cupboard behind him, unrolling it and spreading it flat on the desk. It was a map showing the Peninsula and neighbouring areas. Ford ran his hand over an area stretching from the west coast to near Malmesbury. 'Your De Hoek lime-stone unit covers a lot of subterranean territory, and emerges above ground about here.' His finger prodded near Riebeek-Kasteel. 'So, my best bet would be that the drilling took place west and south of this point. Perhaps this area *here*.' He pointed at an area between Moorreesburg and Durbanville. 'But I understand that it doesn't help you a lot. It's a big area to cover.'

'Yes,' said Griessel. It was just him and Cupido; they had no other help. And they had only today, Saturday and Sunday before they had to return to work. It was a very big area.

'And your problem doesn't end there. The WWF estimates that in the Western Cape somewhere between fifty and a hundred boreholes are being drilled every day because of the drought. That's a potential of some seventy-two thousand boreholes in the last eighteen months, which scares me a lot as a geologist when I think about the water table. This morning I also had a quick look at the various drilling companies offering their services now, and I identified twenty-nine. There might be more, mom-and-pop operations . . . But you'll need to find out who was drilling in this area on Tuesday, and you'll probably only have to investigate about a hundred different drilling sites. But that shouldn't be a problem, right? I'm sure you guys have the manpower to cover them all.'

The only place for an assassin to hide, should he plan to shoot the president while he was leaving the car at the Hôtel Raphael, was just one block from the Arc de Triomphe. Right at the end of the wide boulevard, diagonally on the opposite, furthest corner, there was a building in the process of being restored: number six avenue Kléber.

There was scaffolding, tarpaulins covering windows, ladders leading upwards. There was a mixture of metal-sheeting and steel-mesh fencing, a metre and a half of it, barricading the building site from the sidewalk. The only access was through a steel gate. On Sunday it would certainly be securely locked. But if Daniel could get through the gate or over the fence – not an insurmountable problem – it would be easy to find a vantage point high up.

As long as he wasn't seen.

On Sunday the site would be deserted. With a watchman, perhaps. Who could be persuaded with a few thousand euros to look the other way, if all else failed.

It would be a shot of about 120 metres. A very short distance for the CheyTac. An easy task should the trajectory be clear and uncluttered.

But it wasn't. As with all boulevards in Paris, there were trees on either side of the street. Mostly planes. At this time of year they were in full leaf. And they were tall enough to interfere with his sight, and influence the flight of the bullet.

Daniel had reached the Hôtel Raphael. He went up to the steps of the entrance, stopped a moment and looked at the roof of the building at number six. He gauged it with his eye. Too many leaves and branches.

He walked up the steps, stopped just before the door. At least he would have a clear line from there.

It meant he would have two or three seconds to aim, and fire. While the president was taking the two steps between the last step and the door.

Little time. Very little time.

He walked down again, walked on, crossed the street.

He needed to see how he could get into the building site.

In the parking lot of the University of Stellenbosch, under large bare oaks, the two detectives sat in Cupido's car. Their discussion was serious and they were barely conscious of the students streaming past in the late winter sun, on their way to lunch.

They had used the list of the twenty-nine drilling companies the professor had given them to divide the task between them. Now they were discussing the challenges of the search. Each of the businesses might have four or more drilling rigs and teams, and each had to be asked: did you drill a borehole at a house or a smallholding or a farm between last Saturday and Tuesday, where a black BMW X5 was present?

It was possible that the people might never have seen the vehicle, but that was all the information they had to go on. It wouldn't help to ask if they had worked on a government property because the State Security Agency was known to use front companies, trusts and false personal details, all in the name of state security to make deals and buy or rent property.

It would help to focus first on boreholes that had been sunk north of Dunoon, as that was where the X5 had last been seen, on the road to Malmesbury. It was still a great deal of work for two people to get through in only two and a half days.

'I've got a gig tonight,' said Griessel. 'With the band.'

'That won't matter. Most of these companies won't answer the phone outside office hours. I'm worried about tomorrow too. You know the Cape. People don't like to work on Saturday.'

They agreed that each would work from his home, and let the other know if there were any developments. By six o'clock that evening they would confer telephonically again. Cupido would ask Mavis, the Hawks' reception and switchboard operator, to transfer all possible incoming calls to their phones or refer them to their numbers.

'It's a shot in the dark, Benna,' said Cupido. 'But we gotta try.' Then, with a crooked smile, when Griessel got out: 'Who would have thought, partner, that our docket was gonna depend on rocky science.'

Daniel went into the EXKi Kléber, a health-food take-away shop beside the building site, because he could see some of the workmen in their neon orange work jackets ordering drinks there. He pushed his hood back, asked one if there was a job vacancy on the site.

The man looked him up and down, smiled in sympathy. 'General manual labour? There's a waiting list, my friend.'

'Will it help if I go and see the foreman?' He badly wanted to get through the gate to look at the configuration and layout.

'He'll just refer you to the website. That's where they advertise jobs. But I'm telling you now, if you're not some or other artisan, you can forget about it.'

Daniel studied the work jacket. It bore the logo of Dumez Île-de-France, the contracted construction company. But apart from that it was the usual sort you could buy at the right workwear shops. He looked at the man's trousers, shoes and the yellow hard hat. He thanked him and left.

He walked slowly around the edge of the site, studying the vehicle gate, the steel-mesh fence, the sheet-metal section. He saw the blue-and-white sign on the fence, with the icon of a camera and the words *Site sous vidéo surveillance*. He searched for the cameras. He could see only one in front at the gate, on the boulevard – a turnstile with a small intercom box and a card reader.

Only once he was past, on the side of the Arc de Triomphe, did he see the best place to get over the fence. He would have to be blatant – and agile. And hope for the best.

The biggest problem was that the only entrance would also be the only exit.

By four p.m. Benny Griessel suspected that the fingerprints were not going to produce any results, as Arnold still hadn't called. That would mean they belonged to an SSA spook. Their worries about last night's discovery would be in vain.

By five he was sick and tired of parroting the same two lines over and over.

The first: 'Hello, I'm Captain Benny Griessel of the South African Police Service Directorate for Priority Crimes Investigation, the Hawks. I need to talk to your operators who were drilling between Sunday and Tuesday in the Western Cape. No, unfortunately I can't say what the investigation is about, but it's a priority crime. Yes, they can phone me back anytime. I can give you the number, or you can look it up in the book or on the internet if you want to check I am who I say I am.'

The second, when the drill operator called back: 'We have forensic evidence that means we suspect a crime scene can be linked to a bore-hole that was drilled on Sunday, Monday, or Tuesday. We believe that there was a black BMW X5 on the scene as well. Can you help?'

By six he was finished with his list of drilling companies. Now he could only wait, hope that a drill operator had seen something and would ring him back. He called Cupido to hear if his colleague had any news.

'Nearly done with my allocation, but no news, partner.'

By seven o'clock Griessel was on the stage with the other members of Rust; he got lost for a while in the pleasure of the music. The audience, too, were happily swept up in it.

By eight, when they took a breather, he saw he'd missed a call from Arnold. He called back immediately.

Arnold said: 'Yip, we had a hit in the population register.'

He gave Griessel the name.

Griessel phoned Cupido and said: 'It's what we were afraid of.'

# 73

*Saturday, 2 September*

Griessel didn't sleep well. He'd tossed and turned over the news of the fingerprints, the uncomfortable implications. He and Cupido had agreed last night. Benny must call Mbali Kaleni and tell her they wanted to talk. And Griessel must also confess that they'd continued the investigation against her orders. According to Cupido, she wouldn't come down on Griessel 'like a ton of bricks – she likes you more than me, partner.' He knew flattery was sometimes his colleague's manipulative weapon of preference.

Kaleni was going to blow her top. He knew it. She was going to totally explode over all this.

He phoned her at just after eight to avoid incurring added wrath for waking her up. 'Can we come see you, Colonel?'

She was silent for a few seconds. 'I thought you were taking a break, Benny.' Her voice was sharp, as though she knew something was brewing.

'Colonel, something has come up.'

Another silence. 'Meet me at the office. In an hour.'

The previous night Daniel Darret had sent an email to Vula. He said their recommended operating theatre wasn't perfect, but he could make it work.

This morning they replied:

*That is very good news. Go ahead. You are in our thoughts.*

When he left the flat with Lonnie's rucksack – a large wad of the remaining cash and one pistol in it – he took two hours ensuring that he wasn't being watched. He drew on all his stores of knowledge, acquired here so long ago, using it as he wound through the streets and alleys of Le Marais, then on the Métro system, and eventually in the Château Rouge district in the shadow of the Sacré-Coeur, where a potential Russian agent's pale face would be much easier to spot.

There was no hint of anyone following him. For the first time he felt relaxed, the insecurity and paranoia firmly under control.

At the Gare du Nord he put the rucksack into a locker. Then, when the city's shop doors opened he went into an internet café near the station and downloaded the logo of the construction company Dumez Île-de-France. He asked the manager to print it out for him in full colour.

He hailed a taxi, and went to visit an office-supply store near the Quartier de l'Horloge, where he had the logo mounted in a plastic badge.

Just east of Bastille Métro station, in the eleventh *arrondissement*, he located a shop that sold construction workers' gear. He bought an orange jacket, sturdy boots, blue work trousers, worker's gloves and a hard hat.

He went back to the flat on foot, and packed away everything that was in the big shopping bag. Next he drove the Peugeot to the avenue Kléber. Yesterday he'd seen that the only possible parking spot from which he could survey the building site was in front of or near the EXKi take-out restaurant. He had to drive round the block seven times before he found a suitable place to park, where he could watch the site from the side- and rear-view mirrors.

He sat there for three hours, until his body ached and his neck was stiff.

He had seen enough to know that what he was planning was going to be difficult. But not impossible.

He felt the faint tension of expectation – of the final phase – settle in his body.

Tomorrow it would be worse.

He was getting old.


Mbali Kaleni did not explode.

Griessel told her about the fingerprints. But not about the borehole possibility. He and Cupido thought it was redundant now. The colonel heard them out, listened to their reasons for disregarding her orders, then what they had done, illegally, to have the prints tested against the population register. And the visit to the house the day before yesterday.

She didn't bat an eyelid. No protest, no indignation, no rebuke. She didn't even look at the documents Cupido unpacked on her desk while Gliessel was talking. She just seemed to shrink more into the big desk chair under the photo-montage, with its fresh gap in the middle.

The detectives felt even more guilty and uneasy.

When Griessel had finished, she said: 'I will go with you.' She slid open her desk drawer, took something out and put it into her pocket.

The drive to Parklands, beyond Table View, took over half an hour. Kaleni sat at the back. She spoke only once, when they turned off the N7. 'I would like to do the talking,' she said to Cupido.

'Yes, Colonel.'

At the Olive Park townhouse complex in Folkestone Street Kaleni had to make a call to have the gate opened. It was a very short conversation; the colonel spoke brusquely in Xhosa.

Thandi Dikela opened her front door. They could tell from the fear in her eyes that she knew why they were there, although she still said, with spirit: 'Tell me you caught them.'

Griessel had brought the documents in his murder case. When they were seated around the coffee-table in her open-plan living area, he snapped open the lid and took them out. He kept them on his knee for now.

She looked at the documents, shook her head nervously. The bush of long, thin African braids shivered.

'Thandi,' Cupido said, 'it must have been terrible for you to find your father like that, Tuesday afternoon. We can just imagine, you must have been in shock, and there would have been the grief and everything. In that condition, anyone will do things they later regret. So we want to say that we understand. We absolutely understand. But today we need you to be very honest with us.'

Griessel could hear his colleague trying hard to speak compassionately, probably for Kaleni's sake.

'I *have* been totally honest,' she said, and sat dead still, as though the suspense was paralysing her.

She didn't look at Cupido, only at Kaleni.

'We think you made a mistake on Tuesday. You forgot to wipe the notepad. The one in his desk drawer, the one from which you tore the page for the suicide note.'

'I never did that,' she said, without conviction, just an instinctual reflex denial.

'We have your fingerprints on the pad,' said Cupido.

'No, no,' said Thandi. 'I must have touched it some other time.'

'We don't think so. We also have a partial print that matches yours on the suicide note itself. You missed that when you wiped the note and the pen, after forging your father's handwriting.'

'It wasn't me,' she said, her voice rising. 'Mbali, you know me. Tell them it wasn't me. Why would I do that?'

Kaleni looked at her silently, a great weariness in her eyes.

'We will get to that,' said Cupido, then nodded to Griessel.

Griessel put the first document on the coffee-table. 'That is your father's will. It was drawn up in April of last year. It indicates that your mother will inherit the house in Nuttall Street, as well as the investments he had at the Allan Gray company.'

She stared at it.

Griessel put the next three documents on the table one by one.

'But he did make provision for you,' said Cupido. 'He had taken out three life policies. One for Cebisa Jali, who cleaned for him and whose studies he paid for. And these two for you, as the sole beneficiary. You would have received a total of four and a half million rand . . .'

Thandi began to cry. 'I never knew that. I swear I never knew that. Mbali, please, you have to believe me. I never knew that . . .'

Kaleni pulled a few tissues out of her pocket – she had taken them from her desk drawer just before they left. She stood up and held them out to Thandi. The woman looked at her with pleading eyes. Kaleni stood patiently and waited until Thandi took the tissues, then turned and sat down again.

'The problem,' said Cupido, 'is that all three of these policies were taken out just after your father drew up his will. That means they are only sixteen months old, and all three have a twenty-four-month suicide clause, as well as a contestability clause. So they won't be paid out. We think you knew that.'

'No, no, no! You have it all wrong – you're making a very big mistake.'

'Thandi,' said Cupido, 'we've seen this before. There are a lot of people who have a terminal illness, and want to make provision before taking their own life, but they don't read the fine—'

'No!' It was a cry of despair and grief, loud and shrill in the room, as if it broke her. She jerked, then collapsed into her seat, sobbing into her hands, the braids covering her face. 'You know me, Mbali . . .' she said, between shudders. 'You, of all people, know me . . .'

They let her cry. Minutes ticked by. Eventually she calmed down a bit.

'We think,' Cupido continued, 'you hoped that we would quickly spot the bad forgery of his handwriting. And that we would believe you when you said someone killed him and staged the suicide. The problem is, there is absolutely no evidence that it was staged. None at all.'

'They killed him.'

'Every bit of evidence shows that he killed himself. I'm sorry, but those are the facts. Did you pick up the shell casing, Thandi?'

She emerged from behind the hair. Her voice was stronger, as if she could convince them by force of will. 'No! They killed him. I *know* they did.'

'Thandi, he killed himself,' said Kaleni, speaking for the first time, with a lot of emotion.

'No,' said Thandi. She waved her hands in frustration and despair. 'He didn't!'

'We understand—'

'You don't. You don't know anything. You—' To everyone's surprise, she jumped up, rushed to the window, fists balled, like someone who was about to explode. She turned around. 'I did it,' she said. 'I forged the note. I did it. It was horrible – it was so horrible. You will never know how difficult it was. But I did it.'

'*Hayi*, Thandi,' said Kaleni.

'No, you don't understand . . .'

'Then help us.'

'Yes. I'll tell you the truth.'

'I would really appreciate that,' said Kaleni.

Thandi came closer, stood in front of them. 'The truth is, I never picked up anything – I never saw a shell casing. Yes, I forged that letter. I wrote it. I put it on the table, right there, next to my dead father. I'll never forget that moment. *Never*. I wiped the paper and the pen. I was shaking. But I did it, because I needed you to investigate it as a murder. That is what it was. They killed him. I walked into that house, into that kitchen, and I saw him. Sitting like that. That's not normal. People fall when they shoot themselves. They propped him up like that. They killed him, and then they did that. They are disgusting, evil people.'

'Who?' asked Griessel.

'And why?' asked Cupido, much more sceptical.

'I'll tell you,' said Thandi. 'I will tell you everything.'

# 74

Thandi said she'd phoned her father last Saturday, just as she'd told them the first time. She could hear he was depressed. Sad. Like he'd been when his old comrades had attacked him and tried to cast doubt on his reputation because of the declaration against corruption and state capture that he'd signed. She'd asked him what was wrong. He said nothing, nothing was wrong. She asked him what he was doing, and he said he was keeping himself busy with his vegetable garden. He was digging in compost. Then he changed the subject, asked if she had a boyfriend yet. And how her mother was. But she could tell he wasn't himself.

And then, out of the blue, he told her that if anything happened to him, she should phone Mbali Kaleni. He trusted Mbali.

It shook her, disturbed her deeply. She asked him why he was saying that. What was going on? He could hear how anxious she was. He tried to brush it off, said it was just a joke. Time and again she protested that he was not being truthful with her. He said he was sorry, it was a poor joke, he just wanted to see if she still loved him. She scolded him, told him he couldn't do that to her.

After the call she kept thinking about it. She put the depressed tone of voice and the reference to Mbali together and convinced herself that something really was wrong. So she phoned again. They could check her call register: they would see that it was so.

He'd sounded a bit better during that call, said it was the water restrictions that were getting him down. How could he grow his vege-tables, when he couldn't even get hold of a rainwater tank? If she wanted to do something for him, she could do that. Find a tank somewhere.

'I wasn't convinced,' she said. 'It just kept bothering me. So I got into my car and I drove to his house.'

'This was Saturday afternoon?' asked Cupido.

'Yes.'

'Please proceed,' he said.

When her father opened the door, he seemed broken, and she knew it was a good thing that she'd come. But when he hugged her, he clung to her like a drowning man, and she realised that something very serious had happened.

Menzi Dikela had started weeping, there in the doorway.

'Do you know what it is like to see your father, this wonderful, strong man, this hero, break down and cry? Do you know what it is like? It kills you a little bit, *right here.*' Thandi pressed a finger to her heart, then began to weep. 'And it kills you even more when he tells you horrible, horrible things.'

She fought to control her emotions, then told them how she and her father had sat down together on the sofa, where she held his hands. He'd said: 'They are coming to kill me, Thandi. They killed Lonnie, and they will be coming for me. Very soon.' She could see they wanted to ask who Lonnie was, but she didn't want to be interrupted. She said Lonnie May was one of her father's old comrades, one of his best friends. They'd worked together in the new order, first in the Secret Service, later in the SSA, until they retired. She knew Lonnie well. He was a dear man, always mischievous, always busy with something, his nickname was Ubu, short for *ububhibhi.* The Meerkat.

'How did Lonnie May die?' asked Griessel.

'He died at the airport, last Friday. The official version was that he died of a heart attack. But my father said they killed him. They had the Russians kill him.'

'The Russians?' asked Cupido, very sceptical of that. 'You must be kidding me.'

She just stared at him. A tear trickled down her cheek and her voice was at breaking point. She walked slowly back to the chair, sat down again.

'My father said it was a sort of blind justice. Because Lonnie probably deserved it, and he, my father, deserved it even more. Because they were murderers. They had killed a man. A good man. A family man. On a train, in August. My father killed a man.'

'On the Rovos Rail?' Cupido asked in amazement.

'Yes. And they killed him to protect something even more terrible.'

Tears flowed and her body shook uncontrollably.

Mbali Kaleni got up from her chair and put her hand on Thandi Dikela's shoulder. 'I'm so sorry,' she said.

Thandi nodded through her sobs.

'Perhaps,' said Kaleni, 'I should make us some tea.'

They drank the tea in silence, the two detectives purely out of politeness, because they would have preferred to carry on without a break. They waited patiently until Thandi was ready to resume her story.

After the public protector's report on state capture two years ago had been leaked to the media, she said, her father had joined a group of sixteen prominent veterans who held a news conference and called on the president and his cronies to resign.

The response was rapid and severe. The corrupt network of cabinet members, party members, security agencies and even the police harassed, isolated, accused, threatened, excluded and smeared them. For Menzi and the fifteen others it was a bitter time. But there was one positive result. More old comrades who were similarly disillusioned and deeply concerned over the flourishing kleptocracy – and the devastating effect of that on the Mandela vision – reached out to them. Gradually, over a period of close to a year, a secret organisation was born: MK43. Forty-three former senior members of Umkhonto we Sizwe. Some were former ministers in President Thabo Mbeki's cabinet, a few were still members of Parliament. Most were just wise elders, now retired after a lifetime of service.

They looked at every possible solution to stem the destruction of their land and their struggle. Eventually they recognised there was only one answer.

Menzi Dikela and Lonnie May were both involved in the plan now. The forty-three prepared months in advance. They had secret meetings and gatherings, sometimes in strange places: obscure private game reserves, a small holiday resort on the Cedarberg, a remote third-rate hotel on the Wild Coast. Never all forty-three together, always in smaller organising committees. Menzi Dikela managed and controlled their secret communications digitally. Among other things they created false identities, with the accompanying documents, to evade the watchful eyes of the SSA particularly. The risk was enormous that they would be discovered. And it would certainly lead to their demise.

It was the strain of secrecy, of the mortal danger should they be betrayed, that made Menzi and Lonnie decide to combine a crucial planning meeting with a short luxury holiday. A small treat after all the stress, their plans so close to fruition. They had to go to Pretoria in any case, and the Rovos train was quite out of the ordinary, something the SSA wouldn't be watching. Above all, it would be easy to discuss the final preparations in the privacy of their compartments.

And then they made a mistake.

'My dad saw a man in the train's restaurant who looked familiar, but he couldn't place him. Because the man was young, and he was with this little old lady, Dad didn't consider him a risk. He said he and Lonnie had a few glasses of wine, and for the first time in months they were relaxed, not as vigilant as they should have been. They walked back to their compartments together, my father went into his, and Lonnie stood in the doorway. They were talking – they were sure there was no one else because they had been alone in the passage. They got careless, just for a moment. They were talking about their big solution to the state-capture problem, and then my dad moved, and saw the man from the restaurant carriage standing behind Lonnie, listening. And he could see the man had heard them, because of the look on his face. The man introduced himself, pretending he hadn't heard anything. He said he was Johnson, and that he'd met both of them a few years ago when he was still with the police VIP Protection Unit, when he was the minister of security's bodyguard. He just wanted to come pay his respects. And he asked how they were. But it was an uncomfortable conversation, my father said. Despite his best efforts to seem nonchalant, it was obvious that Johnson had overheard them.

'Johnson left, and my father and Lonnie had to make a decision fast. It wasn't just the operation that was at stake, it was the lives of all forty-three comrades. Their *lives*. Their *everything*. So, Dad took his knife, his biltong knife – it was the only weapon they had between them. And they followed Johnson, saw him enter his compartment and shut the door. They didn't know if he had locked it. So they stood outside. Other passengers were coming from the dining car, so they pretended to walk away. And then they returned, tried the door, and it was open. Johnson was standing with his back to the door, talking on the phone, very intense, reporting what he'd heard. They realised they had to act very fast, and my father stabbed him with the knife. He said he panicked, he was desperate, he just . . . he just . . .' She sobbed again, hid her face.

'Do you want to take a moment?' asked Kaleni.

She shook her head. 'He stabbed him with all his might. The blade broke off. Lonnie shut the door and jumped on Johnson, too.'

Thandi said Johnson fell across the bed, with Menzi and Lonnie on top of him. They didn't think the single stab to the back of the head was fatal and they wanted to make sure. They were ready for a fight, to strangle him if necessary. But it wasn't. Johnson just lay there, dead still. Menzi had come to his senses first, made sure Johnson's call had ended.

They stood up. The two old men were shaking, in shock, overcome by the sudden violence and deadly outcome. Johnson's phone began to ring. Menzi feverishly ripped out the battery. He put the phone and the battery in Johnson's jacket pocket. Lonnie locked the door. Then they sat on the bed beside the body. Slowly they pulled themselves together, discussed their situation in whispers. Made a plan. Later, when the railway line veered away from the N1 and the chances of the body being found decreased, they would throw Johnson off the train. In the meantime Lonnie would stay in the compartment, as they had to be sure the door was locked from the inside.

Menzi tossed the handle of his Okapi out of the window. He saw a laptop on the bedside table. He took it with him, so he could check whether Johnson was involved in any way with the SSA. You never knew, he might have been a plant.

In the early hours, with a great deal of struggle they manhandled the body out of the window. Johnson wasn't a small man.

Then they made up the bed, and pushed his suitcase deep underneath.

'For the rest of the journey they were scared, because they didn't know how much information Johnson had given the people he called. They were filled with trepidation when they arrived because by then the Rovos people knew that Johnson had disappeared. But nothing happened. And my father thought they'd got away with it . . . until Lonnie was killed.'

She took a deep breath, as if she had offloaded a heavy burden.

'Thandi, how could your father be so sure that Lonnie May was killed?' asked Griessel. 'That it wasn't just a heart attack, from all the stress?'

'Because they told him.'

'Who?'

'A man by the name of Zungu. A big man, my father said. Very big. A very dangerous man. He was at my father's house on Friday night. And two other men. All from the State Security Agency. They told him they'd had Lonnie killed. With a Russian drug. And that they would do something unimaginably terrible to him unless he told them everything.'

# 75

Menzi Dikela told them nothing. He denied everything. They said, think it over, think it over very carefully, because they would be back.

Kaleni asked her about the plot that her father had been involved in. She said she couldn't tell them.

Because she didn't know?

No, because her father told her that if she ever told anyone, she would certainly be killed too.

'But he told you that you can trust me,' said Mbali Kaleni.

'He told me I couldn't trust anybody with *that* information. I swore to him. I promised him. I will not betray him now.'

'So, you faked the suicide note because you wanted us to believe it was murder?' asked Cupido. 'So that we'll catch these guys?'

'Yes. Because I *know* it was murder. I think when they came back my father told them what they wanted to know. And then they killed him. With another Russian drug. My father told me the Russians have drugs that leave no trace in the body. That's why Lonnie's death was seen as a heart attack.'

'But you never picked up a shell casing?'

'I swear to you I did not.'

'And you never knew about the life policies?'

'I knew about the policies because my father told me when he drew up his will. But I did not know that they won't pay out if it was suicide. I never knew that.'

They drove back to the office. Mbali Kaleni sat in the back again. When they turned onto the N7 she said: 'I don't know what to do.'

They didn't know what to say to her.

'I'm subjective. I cannot trust my own judgement on this,' she said.

Griessel and Cupido still didn't respond.

'She interfered with a crime scene. And she obstructed justice,' said Kaleni. 'Whether we believe her about her motive, or not.'

'Colonel,' said Cupido, 'a good advocate would plead that she was under huge stress. These state-capture people have stolen so much money, I don't think we should waste any more on a case where a woman wrote a suicide note for a father who probably committed suicide.'

'You don't believe the Russian drug theory?' asked Kaleni.

'No, Colonel.'

'Me neither,' said Griessel. 'Because Prof Pagel would have found something. He's a very smart guy.'

'So we do nothing?'

'There is nothing we can do. For now,' said Cupido, the last words spoken with emphasis. And he looked at Griessel.

Griessel understood. His colleague didn't want him to say anything about the borehole.

'I think there is something else you are not telling me,' said Kaleni.

'If we find anything else, Colonel, we will tell you,' said Griessel.

In the rear-view mirror Cupido watched the colonel cross her arms over her chest. Which meant she wasn't happy.

But she didn't say a word.

Griessel took the ring out of the desk drawer that he always kept locked. He opened the little box, stared at the contents. Tomorrow evening he had to propose to Alexa. And show this ring to her. It looked so small, so cheap. It was all he could afford. He pushed it into his pocket, then walked out.

Cupido heard him in the passage. 'Wait, Benna, I'll come with you,' he said. Then he asked: 'How was the gig last night?'

Griessel said it was good, until he'd phoned Arnold back. After that he'd battled to concentrate.

In the basement parking area Cupido said quietly: 'Partner, let's just see if the borehole thing produces anything. Let the universe show the way.'

'Okay.'

When he got into his car, Griessel wondered what they were going to do if it produced something. What could they do?

All the way back to his and Alexa's house on the slope of Lion's Head, he wondered where he was going to keep the ring tonight. The last thing he wanted was for her to discover it tomorrow. He still wasn't sure he would find the courage to ask her. He felt the fear deep inside. It was like an ultimatum for everything in his life. The enforcement of a final deadline. Make or break.

But shouldn't he rather just drop it?

Daniel stood on the pont de la Tournelle as the sun set over Notre-Dame Cathedral, the western horizon red as blood.

Somewhere in the city was his prey, perhaps enjoying a pleasant cocktail, chortling and chatting to French-government people, countrymen and embassy staff. The president's last sundowner, his last sunset, his final night. Tomorrow he would be killed by an old comrade.

In the name of the Struggle.

His preparations were now almost complete. He studied the weather forecast, so he knew how strongly and in which direction the wind would blow tomorrow. He had measured the distance as well as he could. This afternoon he'd bought a light aluminium ladder and an array of cleaning materials.

Tonight he would eat in the BigLove Caffè, up in the rue Debelleyme. It had looked good to him this morning when he'd walked past, the ham and sausage hanging in the window. Hospitable, friendly and intimate. That was what he needed tonight. To be among people who were laughing and talking and carefree.

It might be his last supper.

And after that he would go and clean the rifle one more time.

He waited on the bridge till the sun disappeared.

# 76

Day Zero.

For Benny Griessel.

And for Daniel Darret.

Daniel was awake before four in the morning. The prospect of the task that lay ahead fuelled his insomnia. He had to suppress the impulse to get up and go for a walk along the Seine. That was what he used to do, back then, in the hours before a hit. Walk to calm down, clear his head, to focus. Head down, kilometre after kilometre. To see the killing in the context of war, part of the Struggle. To build up a kind of rage, but above all, to visualise his plan, each step, every possible risk. And, finally, his escape routes.

But this time he didn't get up, because he knew there was a long day ahead and he wasn't the young man of three decades before. He had to conserve his strength.

So he exercised his imagination: the preparation, walking with the ladder and the rifle, over the wall, up the stairs beside the scaffolding, the selection of the best vantage point. Waiting. Aiming, following the president when he exited the vehicle: through the leaves, wait, wait . . . patiently waiting, until that instant, the two metres of clear sight between the last step and the hotel door, two seconds, maybe three, as the old man wasn't as nimble as he'd once been. Then pulling the trigger. And escape. The same route: there was only one route in, one route out.

Time and again he replayed it in his mind, until he heard the rumble of traffic, Paris awakening, and he finally got up to make coffee.

Donovan came to wake them up.

It still felt awkward to Cupido, in bed beside Desiree Coetzee on a Sunday morning and the kid walking into the room. It was the same every weekend, the boy up and about early as if he was still jealous of his mother's attention. Or he might be wishing his biological father was there. Or maybe he just didn't want *him* there.

Now he said: 'Mommy, can we make crumpets?' And Desiree groaned, she wanted more sleep, and Cupido said nothing, just lay there looking at Donovan. Wondering what else he could do to normalise the situation.

'Yes, lovey.'

'But you have to get up then, Mommy.'

'Mommy will, just now. Get the ingredients ready.'

Donovan was reluctant to leave the room, though he did so eventually.

Desiree shifted her beautiful warm body under the winter blanket, snuggling right up against Cupido, and kissed the curve of his neck. 'Just a little bit more of a cuddle with my boyfriend . . .'

He moved his arm so it wrapped around her back, squeezed her tight.

'Mmm, that's good, hey?' she said.

'Very good.'

'You're good.'

'You're gooder.'

'You're the goodest.'

'True, that.'

She giggled, kissed him again, behind his ear.

'You stay here. I'll go make the crumpets,' he said. 'Bond with Donovan a bit.'

'You couldn't make crumpets to save your life.'

'How hard can it be?'

He got up, went to the bathroom to relieve himself – and to weigh himself secretly on Desiree's bathroom scales.

He was one kilogram down. He pumped his fist in the air. A small victory.


On Sundays they listened to music, Alexa Barnard and Benny Griessel. First he went to buy the newspapers and a fresh loaf of bread for her. When he came back, she would be playing Aretha Franklin, Shirley Bassey, Joan Baez or Janis Joplin on the hi-fi.

Now, in the chill of early spring, he would rekindle the fire in the hearth and make sure it was burning strongly. In the kitchen they would make toast, coffee for him and rooibos chai for her, grate the cheese, put out the butter and jam, set the table with knives and plates.

As they ate she would take each newspaper in turn, sometimes she would read snippets out loud – especially when his name or something about the Hawks was mentioned – but he didn't really want to hear about all the death and murder, politicking and state capture. He just wanted to bask in this warmth.

She might sing along to the music in the sitting room, with that velvet voice of hers, her favourite choruses ringing out with passion. He would grin with delight, because she was so damn good.

'I'm *so* looking forward to tonight,' she said, when she closed the last newspaper.

'Me too,' Griessel lied.

He had left the ring in his jacket. First thing this morning he had felt the pockets to make sure it was still there.

Jeez.

Day Zero.

*From: vula@protonmail.com*
*Subject: Ready?*
*To: inhlanhla@protonmail.com*

*Dear Inhlanhla*
*Please confirm you are good to go.*
*Vula*

The email came in just before nine.

He wrote back: *Yes. Good to go.*

Their communication was much less playful now. The tension on their side must be just as unbearable. That made him feel better.

He tried to relax in the flat until after ten. But he couldn't stand it any longer. He walked to the river, walked along the right bank, slowly, deliberately slowly. He looked at all the people, the walkers and runners and cyclists, the sitters, the smokers, the anglers, the shipping traffic. But his mind kept returning to those two or three seconds between the steps and the hotel door.

*   *   *

The call came at 16.09.

Griessel was at the Waterfront Pick 'n' Pay with Alexa. She was walking down the aisle with her list. He was pushing the trolley. She bought everything she needed to cook supper for him in the coming week: chicken-and-broccoli soup, spaghetti Bolognese, fish cakes, peas, mashed potato and Friday night's curry. Nothing for Thursday, when they went to Alcoholics Anonymous, and had a ready-made Woollies microwave dinner to heat up afterwards.

In the pasta aisle his cell phone rang. He didn't recognise the number. 'Benny,' he answered.

'I'm looking for the captain of the Hawks,' said a man's voice, rough, with a Namaqualand accent.

'That's me. Benny Griessel.'

'This is Herman. From Swartland Drilling. You're looking for the place with the black X5.' It was a statement.

'That's right.'

'*Ja*, look, this week we were drilling other side of Clanwilliam – there's no cell phone reception. I only got the message now.'

'I understand.'

Alexa was walking back with a packet of spaghetti. Griessel stood in the middle of the aisle, all his attention fixed on the call.

'Now, we finished Tuesday late the other side of Philadelphia, on the old Malmesbury road. A small farm, or a big plot, it's hard to say. I smelt a rat, you understand me, it's not racist, but I smelt a rat. I mean, if there was only *one* man among them who looked like he knew anything about farming, but there were these three, three unfriendly okes, didn't want to really talk, you know?'

'I understand.'

'Black okes.'

'I see.'

'And the BMW. Black BMW. Now don't tell me you wouldn't smell a rat too. The place was so-so, not very well looked after, there was actually nothing going on there, but the fancy car, and the three unfriendly okes, wouldn't even let us boil a kettle in their kitchen. They were in that house all day long, then drove off. Then they were back in the house, curtains closed. Tell me you wouldn't smell a rat too. Probably these cash-in-transit robbers, am I right, hey, am I right?'

# 77

When Griessel called, Cupido asked him: 'Are you coming along, partner?'

'Yes.'

A brief silence registered Cupido's surprise. But then: 'Let's go nail some state-capture *mofos*,' he said, louder than was strictly necessary, and Griessel realised that the boy, Donovan, must be within earshot. That was Cupido's motivation for all of this.

They arranged to meet in front of the church in Philadelphia, and drive together from there. As close to five o'clock as possible.

*We can confirm that your target will be at the South African ambassador's residence on the rue Cimarosa on Sunday afternoon, from 16.00 to 18.00. From there he will travel to the Hôtel Raphael, 17 avenue Kléber. We have firm intelligence that this will happen between 18.00 and 18.30. He will stay at the hotel until it is time to leave for the airport.*

Daniel had memorised the contents of the email: timing was going to be one of the most important factors in his success. If he was too early, there was the danger that a watchman would discover him on his rounds. If he went too late, he would be hurried, make errors of judgement. Or he could miss his target completely.

So, he'd packed and tidied, prepared everything, and at four o'clock he showered. Then he dressed in the workman's gear. Carried his bag down to the Peugeot. Came up to collect the tent with the rifle.

Just before half past four he drove to the Éléphant Bleu in the avenue de la Porte de Clichy, a filling station and car wash under the freeway that encircled Paris.

He would unpack everything in the car, and vacuum the seat covers and carpets thoroughly. He would sterilise the interior carefully with his cleaning products. He wanted to limit DNA evidence as far as possible and remove all fingerprints. Then he would pack the camping gear, the ladder and the tent bag with the rifle back in. He would pull on the workman's gloves, so as not to leave more fingerprints. And drive.

To the avenue Kléber.

When Griessel arrived at the church, Cupido was leaning against the front of his car, arms folded across his chest. He was wearing his winter coat, the long one that hung down to his knees, the one that made him look a bit like Batman when it flapped as he walked. He knew it made him cut a pretty impressive figure. 'The Hawk in Winter', he called this outfit.

Griessel got out and walked over to his colleague. He asked the question that he had been struggling to answer in the past hours: 'Why are we here, Vaughn?'

'Well, Benna,' he said, as he straightened up from the car bonnet, 'we are captains of the Hawks. Elite law-enforcement officers. So, we are going to enforce the law. In a very elite manner. There's the stolen property. We have reason to believe that they took Menzi Dikela's computer equipment from a crime-scene *nogal*. And they will say they are government officials, and we will say cool, cats, but where's your search warrant? That's interference with a crime scene. There's obstruction of justice. There's operating a vehicle on national and provincial roads with forged number plates. And, *pappie*, there's the very strong evidence that collectively and individually you're a bunch of cunts. Shall I go on?'

'And our strategy?'

'Partner, I know and you know we're not going to make anything stick with what we have. But I've seen enough of these fucktards to know they feel entitled, they're arrogant and they're a law unto themselves. So, I scheme we're going to piss them off. I'm going to show you the Big V that you always wanted to see. I'm going to taunt them. I'm going to tease and provoke. I'm going to out-arsehole these arseholes. And then, when they react – and they will react, I guarantee you – then I'm going arrest their butts for attempted assault of a member of the Hawks. And let's see where it goes. Maybe we'll involve the media, make a stir, a dent in the armour of the state-capture brigade because we are good men. We didn't stand by and do nothing. That is all I have, and if you tell me now, "Vaughnie, you're soft in the head, let's go home," then this court will seriously consider your motion.'

'Vaughnie?'

Cupido smiled. 'Use it, don't use it. Just a thought. To show the world I can be self-deprecating and humble too.'

'The media, so Desiree's Donovan can read how his future stepfather struck a blow against state capture.'

'Something like that.'

Griessel stared at the wheat fields in the distance. He shook his head as if he couldn't believe what he was about to say: 'Come on, Vaughnie. Let's go and piss our collective and individual careers away.'

'That's my boy,' said Cupido. And then, wagging a finger in Griessel's direction, he said: 'Don't think I don't know why you're ready to commit career suicide. You want an excuse. *Banggat* Benny, the reluctant bridegroom.'


At 17.23 they drove in at the farm entrance. There was a weathered signboard, nearly illegible, showing the property's name. *Kleingeluk.*

A rutted dirt road headed past deserted livestock camps, drooping wire fences, some completely down in places, a windmill with four missing vanes, and then the farmhouse, an uninspiring tin-roof building from the sixties. The X5 was parked under a lean-to. Still sporting its false number plates. The borehole's tied-off pipe, with the mud of De Hoek limestone and other rock drillings, lay in a dried-up stream between the house and the BMW.

'I'll take the front door, you take the rear?' Cupido asked, when they stopped a few metres from the building.

'Okay,' said Griessel. He pulled his Z88 service pistol out of the leather holster on his belt. He got out and began jogging, keeping his eyes on the house windows. If the black X5 was parked there, they were inside.

Cupido held his Glock and walked to the front door.

Griessel disappeared around the corner.


At 17.26 Daniel Darret was lucky enough to find parking in the rue Lauriston. He was ten minutes too early, but he could use the time to check emails again. He pulled off the gloves to tap the screen.

There was nothing from Vula, which meant there was no change in the president's schedule.

He turned off the phone, took out the sim card. He wiped both with a cloth and cleaning fluid. Then he pulled the gloves back on, got out, walked to a rubbish bin and dropped it all in. He went back to the Peugeot, switched on the last of the phones, put it into the pocket of his workman's jacket.

Then he sat and waited for the clock on the instrument panel to move on to 17.40.

Cupido had to hammer loudly, four times, on the front door.

'Go away,' a voice eventually growled from inside, deep and authoritative.

'I am Captain Vaughn Cupido of the Hawks. I am investigating a murder case and I am ordering you to open this door.' He stood beside the door, his pistol in front of him.

'Fuck off.'

'Then I'll have to kick it in, sir.'

A curse from inside, and the door opened. Cupido stepped in front of the door, pointing his pistol at the man's head. He was massive, just under two metres, and obese, his belly hanging over his trousers, the expensive light blue button-down shirt gaping and exposing his navel. The face was sneering and contemptuous.

*A man by the name of Zungu. A big man, my father said. Very big. A very dangerous man.*

'Hallo, Zungu, you sexy thing, you,' said Cupido.

'Fuck off,' said Zungu, but his face registered surprise that Cupido knew his name.

Cupido shoved his pistol into the considerable belly and pushed his way in through the door. 'Not going to happen, butterball.'

Zungu retreated a step. Then came the furious saliva-spraying scream: 'Who the fuck do you think you are?'

'Are you stupid or are you deaf? I said I am Captain Vaughn Cupido of the Hawks.'

Zungu stood with his back against the front hallway wall. 'I am a deputy director of the State Security Agency,' he shouted. 'I order you to put down the weapon *now*. You are interfering with official state business!'

'I don't care if you are the deputy fairy godmother, you fat fuck. Where are your two friends? Tell them to come in here, with their hands on their heads.'

A voice spoke to Cupido's left. 'Put down the gun, you idiot, or I'll blow your head off.'

Cupido looked. Another agent stood there, pointing a pistol at him. Unlike his fat colleague, he was an athletic man.

Daniel shoved the pistol into his belt, under the workman's jacket. Then, leaving his keys in the ignition, he got out, walked around to the boot, opened it. He put on his yellow hard hat. He had tied the tent bag to the ladder, so he could carry them as a unit. He pulled the bundle out now, pushed the door shut, and began walking. He deliberately left the Peugeot unlocked. Perhaps he would get lucky and someone would steal it. He walked in the direction of the Arc de Triomphe.

On the corner of the rue de Presbourg he turned right.

His heart rate quickened. The greatest risk was now, here, when he had to turn right again, into the avenue Kléber. It was only ten metres till he reached the sheet-metal fence, where it joined the wall of the restored building. The only place where the security cameras would not be looking down on him. The only place he could prop up the ladder and climb over.

If he was seen then, if someone raised the alarm, it would all be over.

He turned the corner.

A bunch of teenagers were loitering right there, leaning unsuspectingly against the fence.

## 78

Cupido lowered the Glock, and Zungu hit him against the ear, a tremendous blow that made his head ring, made him stagger, made him completely lose his temper, all the frustration and rage and loathing let loose inside him, so that he bounced back off the wall, swinging his pistol like a truncheon, with fierce intent. He hit Zungu below the eye, splitting the skin. Blood sprayed. But the massive man barely moved. He grabbed at Cupido with both enormous hands, eyes wild. He was clumsy and slow. Cupido sidestepped the attack and kicked Zungu as hard as he could between the legs. The big man uttered a surprisingly shrill sound and crashed to the floor, an impressively swift collapse for someone of his size.

The lean, athletic one shouted a warning, his pistol following Cupido, who dived down on Zungu, hooking his left arm around the big man's neck.

A shot thundered in the small space. The bullet smacked into the wall. Cupido rolled under Zungu to use him as a shield. He throttled him with his left arm, pointed his right hand with the Glock at Lean Man. He saw that the man was younger, focused, full of fire.

'You motherfuckers are soft and slow,' said Cupido. 'Now, put down the gun, or I'll shoot this cunt in his stupid little head.'

'I'm going to kill you,' said Lean Man, deadly serious. He stepped closer, to get a better shot.

'You've got no business here,' said Daniel. 'Go play somewhere else.' He hoped his workman's clothes, the logo on his chest and the authority in his voice would make the teenagers obey.

They stared at him with a challenge in their eyes. But they were conscious of his size.

One flicked a cigarette over the fence. 'Come on,' he told the rest.

They wandered off, looking back at him.

One said quietly: '*Va te faire enculer.*'

He let it go, couldn't afford to waste time. He watched them until they disappeared around the corner.

He untied the tent from the ladder, scanned the area around him once. Now or never. He propped the ladder against the fence, climbed up, lowered the tent on the other side. Gently. He didn't want to bump the scope inside the bundle. He climbed up, jumped over. Reached for the ladder, pulled it over the fence. Laid it flat on the concrete floor.

He crouched low and tried to get his breathing and pulse back under control, all the while keeping his ears pricked, waiting for someone to sound the alarm.

Griessel had seen the paraphernalia beside the back door – the satellite dish and the cables running through a window into a room in the house.

The back door wasn't locked. He found the third SSA agent, the one with the finely styled goatee beard, in the kitchen making three mugs of coffee, his back turned to the outside door. He tried to open the door silently, his Z88 at the ready, but the door scraped and creaked and Goatee turned in surprise.

In that instant, the bellow from somewhere inside the house: 'Who the fuck do you think you are?'

Griessel pointed the pistol at Goatee, put his finger over his lips. The man slowly raised his hands in the air. Griessel pulled the handcuffs out of his jacket pocket. The little box with the ring fell out. Both men stared at it.

'I am a deputy director of the State Security Agency,' they heard another outburst from the front of the house. 'I order you to put down the weapon *now*. You are interfering with official state business.'

Griessel pushed the pistol against the back of the man's head. 'Put your hands behind your back. You are under arrest.'

Goatee obeyed, brought his hands around. To keep his balance he stepped forward. Onto the ring box.

'Fuck!' said Griessel. He stood close to the man, kept him off balance with his shoulder, cuffed his left wrist first, then the right. He bent down to pick up the box. It was damaged but the ring inside was unharmed.

It was a sign, he thought.

Then he jerked the man roughly and angrily, so they could walk forward.

Inside a shot boomed.

Daniel waited. Two minutes. Three.

No shouts, no alarms.

He stood up, picked up the tent and swung it onto his shoulder.

The caretaker was on the other side of the scaffolding, at the turnstile gate to the building site. The traffic around the Arc de Triomphe was humming, but Daniel wanted to be sure that his heavy boots didn't make a noise on the metal stairs. And he had to be quick. He was behind schedule now. He took the steps two by two. Up and up. Each time when he completed a flight, he looked towards the building office. He studied each new level for a camera.

He kept climbing until he was at the top, on the roof. He looked instinctively in the direction of the Hôtel Raphael.

He would have to use the northern corner, hide behind the parapet, a brick wall only thirty centimetres high. Anywhere else, and he would be too exposed, too visible. But the trajectory from there to the hotel entrance might not be perfect.

Griessel shoved the man along in front of him, and ran into the others in the narrow space of the hallway. A wiry man had his pistol trained on Cupido, who was pinned under the frame of a very big man. That must be the big, dangerous Zungu.

He didn't have to say a word, just aimed at the lean one. The man sighed and lowered his pistol.

Lean Man said: 'You are interfering with a very, very important operation of the State Security Agency. You will die in jail.'

'No,' said the fat man lying on Cupido. 'I'm going to kill them. Slowly.'

'You're going to kill me slowly with your fucking weight,' said Cupido, and wriggled out from under Zungu.

'Put the gun on the floor,' Griessel said to Lean Man.

He obeyed, then said: 'I'm telling you for the last time. We are senior SSA agents. We are involved in an operation of vital national security.

This is a crucial junction in that operation. If you don't release us *right now*, you will sabotage it completely. That is high treason, for which you will go to jail. My jacket is in the bedroom. My ID card is in the inside pocket. Before you proceed, I implore you to take a look. *Now*.' His voice was urgent, pleading almost.

Cupido put cuffs on Zungu's wrists, then stood up. He kept his Glock trained on the fat man. 'You're under arrest for assaulting a police officer and for operating a motor vehicle with a false registration number. That provides us with probable cause to search these premises.'

'For what?' demanded Lean Man.

'Stolen goods,' said Cupido. 'Menzi Dikela's computers, for instance. And if we find them, we'll have evidence of murder. So, don't try to bullshit me with this high-treason stuff.'

That shut all three SSA agents up.

Until Lean Man said: 'We're running out of time.'

And Zungu: 'There was no murder. Menzi shot himself. The fucking traitor.'


Six o'clock.

Daniel lay on the roof, behind the parapet, binoculars to his eyes.

The CheyTac lay beside him, out of sight. It was too dangerous to set it up on the parapet, because there were buildings opposite the street that were one storey higher. They were offices and it was Sunday, but he couldn't take the risk of being spotted with the rifle.

He would have to wait until he saw the presidential vehicle, when it drove up from the south in the avenue Kléber.

He visualised his movements – putting down the binoculars, grabbing the CheyTac, placing the two stabilising legs. Aiming, waiting for the shot. The soft squeezing of the trigger. With hands that were delicately trembling. Then getting up, abandoning the rifle there, walking to the stairs, running down, picking up the ladder, climbing over the wall. Getting rid of the jacket, the hard hat and the cell phone. Down into the Métro system.

Seconds lagged, time stood still.

# 79

Zungu's face looked bad. Blood kept trickling down his cheek and chin. It dripped onto the expensive pale blue shirt. He sat upright in the front hallway, his hands cuffed behind him. 'Menzi sat right in front of us, and he shot himself,' he said.

'Why?' Griessel wanted to know.

'What time is it?' asked Lean Man.

'Why did Menzi kill himself?'

'What is the fucking time? Tell me now!'

'Seven minutes past six.'

'Jesus. Listen to me. You're going to ruin months of work. You're going to wilfully sabotage an operation to prevent an assassination attempt on—'

'Don't tell them,' said Zungu.

'We have no choice. We have no time.'

'Why did Menzi kill himself?' Griessel asked again.

'Because he has a daughter,' said Zungu.

'You threatened him with his daughter?'

'Something like that.'

'What did you tell him?' asked Cupido. 'What do you tell a man about his daughter that will make him shoot himself? You pervert. You piece of shit.'

Zungu just sniffed blood up his nose.

'We had to get him to divulge his conspiracy secrets,' said Lean Man, defensively. 'Now, please, we have to resolve this very quickly.'

'The secrets that Johnson Johnson overheard on the train?' asked Cupido.

The three agents exchanged looks, but hid their surprise well.

'Yes,' said Lean Man.

'What was it about? We're not going to release you unless you tell us.'

'Time is running out,' Lean Man told Zungu, the big man clearly the leader of the trio. 'Tell them. They know half of it anyway. You have to tell them *right now*. We can't waste a second.'

The pressure, the urgency, the struggle between frustration and inevitability rippled across Zungu's face. He seemed swollen with conflicting emotions.

'Jesus, Chief, please!' shouted Lean Man. 'Tell them. *Now*.'

Zungu spoke in short, barking sentences: cryptic, abbreviated, blood and saliva spraying, heated and hurried and, above all, with contempt for them and the conspirators, while the Lean Agent kept urging him to hurry, hurry.

Zungu said Johnson Johnson overheard the traitor Lonnie May and someone else on the train conspiring to murder, in cold blood, the honourable and noble president of the country, the hero of the Struggle and the darling of the nation. And Johnson had enough time to share part of the information with his colleague at the VIP Protection Unit, before he was murdered in such a shocking way. The problem was, Johnson hadn't mentioned the second man's name before he died. The VIP Protection Unit contacted the SSA, and the SSA began to look for Lonnie May. They found him easily. In his home in Rondebosch, only a day later, when Lonnie returned from his train trip. And then they began tracking him, tapping him. They broke into his house, searched it thoroughly. Eavesdropping equipment was planted. He never used his registered cell phone or his laptop computer in an incriminating way.

They could have arrested him, interrogated him, but then the others – and the SSA knew there had to be others – could have taken steps to hide or destroy their treachery.

But on 22 August Lonnie May made his first mistake.

A call to a travel agent to book a flight to London. With a false passport. Lonnie had been standing outside on his back veranda. He used a burner phone, but he was just within hearing distance of an SSA microphone.

They obtained the credit-card details from the airline, and asked their good comrades the Russian SVR for help because the Russians had British and European presence, the ability, the manpower, the technology and the will to begin following Lonnie in London and, in so doing, protect a friend of Putin.

The SVR had tracked Lonnie to Bordeaux, France, and identified a black African named Daniel Darret as the person he went to see. Darret was a shadowy figure with a false name, a man without friends or a past. Without doubt an assassin, a trained agent, judging by the way he was able temporarily to overcome the SVR agents. They followed Darret's tracks to a boat captain in a French harbour town, but he disappeared. Lonnie, too. By then, however, the SSA and the SVR were reasonably certain: the president would be targeted during his visit to France. To cancel the visit, or to ask the French for additional security, would be humiliating for a head of state of his stature.

The Russians picked Lonnie up again on video material at Schiphol, and they were able to establish that he took a KLM flight. When Lonnie landed in Cape Town, the plan was to inject him with a drug. A drug they had obtained from their 'good friends', a drug that was meant to make Lonnie collapse. The SSA had an ambulance standing by. Agents pretending to be paramedics. They were planning to take him away for questioning because time was running out; matters were increasingly urgent. But Lonnie's heart failed. It might have been a blood clot after the long flight, or the drug dosage was too much for the old man.

The phone in Lonnie's jacket pocket was the saving of the SSA. He'd made a single call from it only minutes after his plane landed.

That number led them to an address. Nuttall Street in Observatory. Home of the traitorous Menzi Dikela.

They went to see Menzi on Friday. Told him they knew everything. They searched his house for the cell phone, for proof. They found nothing. And Menzi continued to deny everything.

Zungu was there in person. He saw that Menzi Dikela was in a state of extreme distress. Close to breaking point. Just a question of time. They ran the risk of another inconvenient heart attack. So they withdrew. Temporarily. To confer directly with the director-general of the SSA. A team was left to watch Menzi's house. The director-general cautioned them to proceed slowly. We've got Menzi. We've got a starting point, leverage. We've got a few days to manoeuvre. We want to strike a decisive blow, break open this whole ants' nest. Menzi is a marked man, and he will make mistakes. Come, let's watch him closely for a day or two. Let's consider how we can use these things to our best advantage.

That afternoon Menzi's daughter came to visit. That had sparked the idea. They had found Menzi's Achilles heel. On Tuesday morning they struck. Bringing photos of Thandi, at work, at home. Inside her home. It shook Menzi. And then they told him what they were going to do to her.

Menzi talked. He told them everything: about Daniel Darret, the assassin, the email communication, the cell phones that Darret would use. And they found everything in the Wendy house. Once they were sure that Menzi had told them all, they said to him: 'You can shoot yourself, or you can watch us punish Thandi here in front of you.'

Menzi did the honourable thing. There in front of them. It was something to behold.

'Why did you pick up the shell casing, you dimwit?' Cupido asked.

'We didn't pick it up. I discovered it in the pocket of my jacket. It was just coincidence. It must have shot in there.'

'And then?'

The SVR, Zungu said, had good connections with Ditmir, an Amsterdam-based arms dealer where Darret had to buy a rifle. They sent a team of agents, and planted a sensor on Darret. He discovered it, but they still had the cell-phone numbers that Menzi had provided. They could follow every move he made. That was how they knew *that* man, that murderer, that threat to the South African president and the democracy, was lying on a roof in Paris, right now, ready to shoot our president. The Russians had a man stationed on a building right opposite, who could see him at this very moment. It was all visible from the ops room, back here in the house.

And that was the operation they had been running when the Hawks intruded, the operation the detectives were putting in jeopardy. They had set an ambush; they were going to get Darret. The Russians were ready. The president's bodyguards were ready. Everyone was waiting for Zungu to give the word, so that the president could drive from the ambassador's residence to the hotel. Timing was critical. The Russians had to shoot Darret just before the president arrived at the hotel. So that there would be clear evidence of the conspiracy and the evil plan. So that all the world and the people of South Africa would see it.

Cupido frowned. 'What must the people of South Africa see?' he asked. 'That this corrupt, captured president was almost shot? What the fuck, dude?'

'Oh, no,' said Zungu. 'Our president is not corrupt or captured. That is fake news, blatant lies spread by White Monopoly Capital. The South African people will see that the vice-president was part of the conspiracy. The vice-president is the captured one, in cahoots with White Monopoly Capital. The vice-president is the leader of this conspiracy.'

'Bullshit,' said Cupido. 'The vice-president is just about the only honest man left in government.'

'No, we will expose him. He is the man behind Menzi Dikela and his cronies. He is behind the assassination. Because he knows he can't win the leadership election in December.'

'Fuck,' said Cupido, 'you're going to frame the vice-president.'

'No, my friend. He's guilty. The people will realise our president must serve another term, at all costs. To stabilise this country, to root out the enemies of the Struggle. That's why you have to release us *right now*. To help us save South Africa.'

The tension in Daniel Darret reached breaking point at 18.30 when there was still no sign of the presidential vehicle.

He reluctantly pulled off his gloves, took the phone out of his pocket and checked for emails. Nothing.

He feverishly tapped a message to Vula. *Any news? Is he late?*

Every thirty seconds he checked for an answer. He knew he'd been there far too long. Someone was going to find the ladder down below or spot him on the roof.

But this president was notorious for being late.

He would have to wait. He would just have to wait.

# 80

'Look, we'd love to save South Africa as much as the next guy, but I don't believe you. Can you prove all this?' Cupido asked, in a voice full of sincerity and sympathy.

'Yes. Take me to the ops room,' said Lean Man, starting to push down the passage.

'Benna, I'll be back now,' said Cupido. He followed Lean Man.

Griessel kept his weapon trained on Zungu and Goatee. They waited.

Griessel's phone rang. He took it out of his inside pocket with his left hand.

Alexa. He knew why she was calling. It was already half past six.

'Alexa, I'll call you back just now,' he answered, without taking his eyes off the two agents.

'Benny, I'm so sorry, I know you're working. But I just want to know, are you going to be on time? I'm so looking forward . . .'

She sounded so full of hope. Did she suspect anything? Had she discovered the ring in his coat pocket? She never interfered with his clothes.

'I . . . I hope I will be on time.'

'Thank you, my darling, see you soon.'

The 'ops room' was one of the homestead's bedrooms, fitted out with two long tables against the wall that supported four computers, another two monitors, documents and a few cell phones. Cables twisted like fat snakes out of the window.

'There, see, *there* he is.' Lean Man pointed at a monitor. It showed the grainy image of the roof of a European-looking building, the tiny shape of someone lying there.

'That could be anybody, dude. Where's the proof?'

'There, look at that screen. He's just sent an email. It says, "Any news? Is he late?" That's him. He's worried. You have to let us go now!'

'Not enough proof.'

'What do you want from me?'

'Where are those cellular numbers? The ones this guy was using.'

'There, that list. The ones with a line through them are the phones he's already used.'

'So this is the one he's using now?'

'Why?'

Cupido took his cell phone out of his pocket. 'Let's give him a call.'

'No! Are you crazy?'

'Hang on. Let's just see if the guy on that monitor answers the phone. Then I can be sure I'll be saving our honourable president, and the whole country, and that you're not bullshitting me.'

'You can't do that – you can't!' Lean Man saw Cupido dialling the number. He rushed forward, to one of the keyboards. He contorted and twisted his body to get his cuffed hands from behind his back to beside his hip and with feverish haste he pressed a key, then another one.

The international call in Cupido's ear took an eternity to connect.

'I've activated the Russians, you fucking idiot, you moron,' said Lean Man. 'They're going to kill him *right now*.'

The phone rang in Daniel Darret's hand. He could see it was a South African number and his heart leaped. It was news. The president was late, or he wasn't coming. 'Vula?' he answered.

'You won't know me, my brother. My name is Vaughn Cupido. I'm on your side. It's a trap, get out of there. Now!'

He heard another voice screaming in the background: 'Moron! Moron!'

He looked up, scanning for danger, spotted a tiny figure appearing on the office building opposite. He saw the movements, the action, recognised them, a sniper taking aim with a rifle.

Time stood still.

He dropped the phone, grabbed the CheyTac, lifted it. He realised it would be too late: the marksman opposite had a start on him. He rolled in against the parapet. The shot smacked into the clay tiles behind him.

He rolled and rolled to his right, jumped up, ran to the back towards the stairs, dodged left, right. Another shot. The bullet plucked at his coat sleeve, clanged into the metal stairs. Then he was on the steps, jumping – he had to get out of view. He flew down an entire flight of stairs, hit the rail, winding himself, feeling a stabbing pain in his ribs as his yellow hard hat clattered down.

He heard footsteps on the rungs, from below. He sat up, pulled the gloves off his hands, grabbed the pistol from his belt, stood. He looked at the narrow gap between the steps that spiralled downward. He hunkered down, ready.

The first one appeared, saw Daniel, lifted a machine pistol.

Daniel shot him in the chest. The man fell back, slid, lay still.

The second ducked away. Then a hand holding a pistol appeared around the corner of the stairs. A wild shot, hitting the scaffolding behind.

Daniel waited, lifted his own firearm, waited, his breath racing, his ribs throbbing. The urgency in him to get away was almost overwhelming.

He waited. The hand appeared again. Daniel aimed, shot. Red blood mist, the pistol clattered on the stairs. Daniel rushed down, found the man lying there holding pieces of his hand, cursing.

Daniel kicked him in the neck, ran down the steps, boots clattering. Another flight, another flight, and then he was nearly at the bottom and he grabbed the support pole with his left hand to use his momentum to swing himself around in the direction of the fence and the ladder. And the block of a man was there, in full flight towards the stairs. They ran into each other, two big bodies colliding. Daniel fell to the concrete, tried to break the fall, the pistol spinning out of his hand. He scrambled upright.

It was the big Russian bear who had talked to Mamadou Ali, the one whose left ear was misshapen by scar tissue as if a piece had been bitten out of it. The one he had seen in front of Élodie Lecompte's apartment, and again in Ditmir's window in Amsterdam. Bear also stood up, lifting a short, chunky weapon from below. Daniel recognised it: the RMB-93, a pump-action shotgun, beloved of Russian special forces, six twelve-bore rounds in the magazine. Usually loaded with double-zero shot: one shot at this distance would rip out Daniel's heart.

Daniel dived at Bear's midriff, hit him with his shoulder. Hard. The shot resounded in the small space between the scaffolding and the metal fence, the ricochets clanging and banging above them. They fell together. Daniel's hands were on the weapon, he turned and pulled with all his might to force it from the man's hands.

Bear was strong, he gripped it, kicked with his knee, hit Daniel against his sore ribs. His grip loosened, then regained. Bear kicked again, the pain sharp. Daniel jerked his head up, hit the Russian on the nose, cartilage cracking. Both men bellowed now, growled, wrestled for possession of the weapon. He tried another whiplash with his head. The Russian was ready for it, and he missed.

Bear wrestled, pushed and rolled, back and forth, to get Daniel off him. Each time with more success.

Daniel knew the Russian was younger. Bigger, stronger. Sooner or later he would wrest the weapon away. And shoot.

He fought back fiercely, trying to neutralise the man's actions with all his strength and focus. The shotgun was between them now, the barrel pointing upward. Daniel's finger sought the trigger guard, found it, his finger over the Russian's: he squeezed. The shots cracked, one after the other, the lead shot tore into Daniel's left shoulder, the Russian's right shoulder. Daniel knew it was his only chance, he kept pulling the trigger, counting the shots until the last fell on his now deafened ears. Then he let go of the man, pushed him away violently, aware of his shoulder bleeding, using the momentum to stand up. He saw the pistol on the ground, just out of reach. The ladder was closer, the aluminium ladder he'd left there. He picked it up. Bear stood up. Blood on his face, blood on his shoulder, he dropped the shotgun. He charged. Daniel crashed the top of the ladder into the man's face. The Russian tried to block and parry, grabbing the ladder with his massive hands. Daniel kicked him with incredible violence, his workboot's steel cap cracking into the man's knee.

Bear bellowed, his leg buckled. Daniel rammed the ladder forward again. The Russian lost his balance and fell backwards.

Daniel dropped the ladder, ran the five steps to the pistol, picked it up and turned around. The Russian had thrown the ladder off him and was trying to get up, but his knee was unstable.

'This is for Élodie Lecompte,' said Daniel, and shot him between the eyes. He pushed the pistol into his belt, picked up the ladder.

He heard sirens. He put the ladder against the wall, climbed up.

On the other side were people, civilians, wide-eyed, terrified, at the battle raging on the other side of the wall.

Daniel jumped down. And he ran.

The sirens were coming closer. He sped across the street, preparing himself for the bullet from the sniper above – it would hit his back now, in the ten metres that he was running exposed. He dodged between the onlookers: if he could just reach the entrance to the Métro station, if he could just get down there . . . He wriggled out of the jacket, threw it down. He was nearly there, nearly there.

# EPILOGUE

## 81

Griessel wanted to wait until after the main course.

They sat inside, next to the cosy fireplace. They sipped sparkling water, ate a starter of braised wildebeest with orecchiette pasta, wild mushrooms, capers and Parmesan.

'Benny, this is divine,' said Alexa. 'It's such a wonderful evening.'

'I'm so glad,' he said.

'Tough day, my master detective?' she asked. 'I can see you're not too happy.'

Then he knew he couldn't wait any more. He couldn't spoil the evening with his anxiety and nerves, and he couldn't lie to her here, now.

He took a deep breath. 'Alexa,' he said, 'you are the love of my life . . .'

'Benny . . .'

He could see her eyes growing moist already. 'Please, just let me say what I want to say.' He reached across the table for her hand.

She looked worried. She gripped his hand tightly.

'Today Vaughn and I took on the State Security Agency. We ruined an operation of theirs, because we believed it was the right thing to do. Because they are a bunch of corrupt bastards. We left three of their agents in front of a farmhouse, handcuffed to the door handles of a BMW X5. We hope it's very cold out there tonight. When I get to work tomorrow morning I'm going to get fired. I'm absolutely certain of that. Because Vaughn took a photo of the three of them chained to the BMW. He sent it to the newspapers, so that he could tell his girl-friend's little boy that he is not captured. And so that Mbali Kaleni can have a new photo for the gap on her wall. I told him I supported him in all of it. Alexa, I will get another job. There are opportunities in the private sector. I promise you now, I will get another job.'

'Benny,' she said and squeezed his hand. 'You know—'

'Wait, Alexa, I'm not finished yet. I promise you I will get work. The thing is . . .' Now he just had to get Vaughn Cupido's recommended speech straight in his mind. 'You are the love of my life, and I want to be with you for ever . . .' He put his hand into his pocket, produced the little box. He had tried to fix it with a bit of Sellotape from his murder case.

He let go of Alexa's hand, opened the box. The little ring sparkled in the soft light of the Overture restaurant. 'I would be so very honoured if you would be my wife, Alexa.' And then, because the box was crooked and the ring small, and her face slowly began to melt, and he knew what she was going to say, because it was like his dream, just as he had dreamed it, he added: 'Please.'

The tears rolled down her cheeks. She took his hand again and, with all-embracing tenderness, she said: 'I will, Benny. I will . . .'

Daniel Darret walked into the workshop. *Le génie* was sitting at his workbench, bent and focused on a beautiful old chair.

'*Bonjour, Monsieur,*' said Daniel.

The old man didn't greet him, just looked at the bandage on his shoulder, showing from under the sleeve of his T-shirt.

Then he pointed with the chisel to where planks and shavings and sawdust were heaped up. And he said: '*Vite, vite.*'

Lefèvre's head dropped down again, as he gave himself over to his work.

Daniel smiled, went to fetch the broom.

Then he spotted the farmhouse table. Monsieur had done the final finish for him. And it was beautiful.

# ACKNOWLEDGMENTS

*The Last Hunt* would never have been written without the advice, support, generosity, knowledge, time, insight, imagination, friendship and love of a large number of wonderful people. The mistakes and deficiencies (and poetic freedom!) in this book are mine alone. The rest are thanks to their unselfishness. Many, many thanks to:

My agent Isobel Dixon, Afrikaans editor Etienne Bloemhof, British editor Nick Sayers, and my brilliant English translator Laura Seegers. I am enormously privileged to be able to work with you.

Commissaire Divisionnaire Jean Paul Faivre and Commandant Brigitte Volle of the French National Police in Bordeaux. Jean Paul, thanks for allowing us to attend your retirement celebration. It proved once again that crime fighters are an international brother– and sister–hood. Benny and Vaughn would have been completely at home there.

My dear friends Henry Lefèvre, Stephanie and Stephane Doublait of Bordeaux. Thank you, Henry, for lending me your and Sandrine's names, and for your incredible help, support and enthusiasm, and for 'our' house in Bordeaux. Stephanie, thank you for filling in my many French deficiencies, and for sharing the history of Bordeaux. Stephane Doublait, thank you for the comfortable office chair so that I could keep writing there.

Outstanding crime-fiction colleague and journalist Olivier Truc, and *Le Monde* journalist Jacques Follorou, for deep insight into the French intelligence world.

Kerneels Breytenbach, who introduced me to the legendary diplomat the late Leo Conradie, and his wife, Renée. Renée, thank you for your and Leo's hospitality and great help. It was a privilege to get to know him, even if it was for a short time. You remain in our thoughts.

Joy Strydom, Brenda Vos and all the delightful people of Rovos Rail, for the unforgettable journey between Cape Town and Pretoria, and the never-ending questions you answered. You (and the world's most luxurious train) are incredible.

Catherine du Toit who corrected my French so precisely, Schalk Joubert (my *and* Benny's bass-guitar idol), my neighbour and anaesthetist Dr Johann Steytler, geology prof Ian Buick, and His Excellency Monsieur Christophe Farnaud, French ambassador, for the chicken story.

The formidable and brilliant Monsieur Dominique de Villepin for his insight into international politics. Thank you, French Consul Monsieur Laurent Amar, for arranging the meeting, and the wonderful support. Also the staff of the South African embassy in Paris, especially Marion Caill. Thank you, Ronnie Kasrils, for your friendship and insight. You remain an inspiration.

The Hawks unit for Serious and Violent Crimes in Bellville, and Captain Elmarie Myburgh of the SAPS Investigative Psychology Unit, and pathologist Dr Hestelle Nel.

All my other translators, overseas editors and publishers, who each in their own way make a contribution to my books, as well as all the proofreaders, for their eagle eyes.

Many thanks, too, for your unending love, patience and support, Marianne Vorster, Lida Meyer, Johan Meyer, Mart-Marié Serfontein, Marette Vorster, Hannes Vorster and Bekker Vorster.

Thank you also to all the people whose names were lost between the notes, digital notes and cut-off phone calls.